HAGGARD

HOUSE

HAGGARD

HOUSE

ELISABETH RHOADS

Copyright © 2025 by Elisabeth Rhoads

First Bodger Books edition: 2025

Library of Congress Control Number: 2025941117

ISBN 979-8-9928027-2-6 (hardcover)
ISBN 979-8-9928027-0-2 (paperback)
ISBN 979-8-9928027-1-9 (ebook)

Library of Congress Control Number: 2025941117

Cover design by Allison Michele Horwath
Cover art: Lover's Eyes, ca. 1840. The Metropolitan Museum of Art, New York

Bodger Books
Irvine, CA
www.bodgerbooks.com

Printed in the United States of America

10 9 8 7 6 5 4 3 2 1

For Ken, my solid rock

Chapter 1

The Narrative of Adam Bolton
1859

I, Adam, was formed in the dust of an attic, and from thence, I emerged into the world. On this day, eleven years after that inauspicious nativity, a sharp wind gnashed at the hardened crust of snow upon the ground and grated against the edges of my bleak house. I waved at Mother, waiting in the gaping doorway. She stood at the threshold, as if to step beyond it would cause the pillar of her body to crumble into grains of salt, whipping in the wind. The intensity of her sharp, black eyes forced mine to the path ahead.

"Keep to the straight and narrow," called she.

The door suddenly shut upon her white house-cap and stiff, black gown, and I was left in the swirling snow. Gathered under my arm were my blue-backed speller, Murray's *English Reader*, and Daboll's *Arithmetick*. Pulling my goatskin coat tighter about me and tucking both hands, together with my cambric lunch rag, behind my back, I pressed forward down the long wagon track for my two-mile trek. As I entered the safety of the forest surrounding the little clearing, the wind died away; and the snow, which had been boot deep, thinned to a fine, sugary powder.

The trees too began to thin, opening onto a vast, white

meadow, Whittemore's Prairie. Having left the protection of the trees, the grating wind returned, its force gaining in fury as I followed the faint tracks made by Pa's Belgian and heavy cart. The snow whirled upward, and tiny grains mercilessly scraped my face, making my cheeks burn red. I pulled my muskrat cap further down my forehead and bowed into the wind.

The first building I reached was McNeil School, so named for Farmer McNeil, who had donated a corner of his field for the purpose. This was the first year the village of Nomaton had a proper schoolhouse, and now that there was a male teacher who would spend time in religious instruction, I was, for the first time, at eleven years, allowed to attend.

As I neared, my belly churned when I realized other children had already arrived. Certainly, I knew of the other village children. I had seen them on my way to Pa's shop at the far edge of town and at church, sitting behind me in the pews. However, I had little experience with them up close, and I was, at once, anxious to be taken notice of and anxious to be disregarded. It was quarter of an hour before school, yet Farmer McNeil's children already romped in the snow, and a pair of older boys loafed near the woodshed. In order to avoid an encounter with either, I kept my eyes trained on the building ahead.

I had spent considerable time at the schoolhouse in the summer months, assisting Pa in building the place. It was a sturdy frame structure, simple, yet well-made, only wanting a coat of paint; but that perhaps would come the following year. In a square tower above the roof hung the bell. A small portion of the building extended forward as an entrance and cloakroom. Beyond that was a simple rectangle with three windows on either side. A placard near the door informed me of its name and the year in which it was built, eighteen hundred and fifty-nine.

The nearer I drew, the more rigid my body became. The absence of other children, as I ventured inside, stilled the churning in my belly. I stamped the snow off my boots and hung my goatskin coat on a peg. I removed my outer horse-hair mittens, then the inner wool ones. I placed these, along with my cap and the knotted rag containing my lunch, on the shelf above.

Mr. Caskell, with his large, scrawling hand, was lettering the day's lessons upon the blackened pine boards on the rear wall. The sight of a grown person, the company I was used to keeping, put me more at ease. I made my manners, bowing as I entered the room. Mr. Caskell turned from his work and laid down his bit of chalk.

"Adam, I presume?"

"Yes, sir," said I.

The schoolmaster stepped upon the platform and took a seat at his desk, motioning me to the front. I skirted round the stove in the center aisle, just beginning to emit an orange glow, and took a seat at the recitation bench. Mr. Caskell was a well-built man capable of dispensing discipline and keeping order; it was only a week past the start of school, and already he had earned a reputation for delivering swift justice in the form of sound thrashings to the Fowler twins after they had broken two of the school windows in hope of keeping the term from commencing. He was dressed smartly in a black frock coat. For the first time in my remembrance, I became conscious of my own clothing—tweed jacket and brown wool trousers, both tight and ill-fitting, neither as clean as they ought to have been.

"We haven't much time before class begins," Mr. Caskell said, icy blue eyes narrowing. "I must tell you that the other students have had a week's advantage. I suppose you can catch up?"

"Yes, sir."

Pa had required my assistance in his carpentry shop—at least, that was the story Mother had given the schoolmaster. The real reason was that she wished to see what kind of school Mr. Caskell would run, and seeing that he offered both physical and spiritual discipline, I now found myself here.

"Let's begin the assessment then."

I quickly answered each question put to me, voice low but firm and clearly audible. With inward satisfaction, I observed Mr. Caskell's cold, impartial gaze changing to one of approval. Consulting the clock at the back of the room, he hastened the completion of the assessment. My heart quickened as he stepped forward and vigorously pulled at the rope, bell clanging in its wake.

The girls filed in followed by the boys. There was a great deal of stamping of boots and hanging of coats. Then the girls and boys made their manners, curtseying and bowing respectively. The room quieted, and the students took their seats.

"Master Bolton will be joining our class this term," Mr. Caskell announced as he directed me toward the back of the schoolroom with the higher grades.

I strode to my place amidst whispers.

"She's allowed him to come."

"Never thought I'd see him here."

"There's a trap-door she keeps him locked behind."

"Keeps 'im dressed in rags."

As I took my seat, the boy sharing the double wooden desk scooted to the far edge. I was accustomed to my notoriety, and I did not allow it to trouble me.

Classes commenced with a recitation of the Lord's Prayer, after which Mr. Caskell read a selection from the Bible. The reading was Malachi 1. I knew the entirety of Malachi by heart, so as I listened, I took my leisure in examining the occupants of the seats before me. Most were familiar. However, I had spoken to few, and none had ever dared to venture to the place where I lived. I was the old blood of Nomaton, a village situated up the Menominee River in the Upper Peninsula of the State of Michigan, Mother having been one of the very first inhabitants. All the other children here now were offspring of newer settlers, most of whom had come from New York and Ohio—some as far as Sweden.

By and large, composing perhaps two-thirds of the class was farmers' children, including Farmer McNeil's rambunctious bunch of five. In addition, there were Victoria, Florence, and Priscilla, the three daughters of Mr. Tenney of Tenney's General Store, each of whom wore a single braid down the back of her neck. It was joked that the first thing you saw coming whenever any of the sisters appeared was her upturned nose. There were also Henry and Rebecca, the miller, Mr. Riblet's children. The blacksmith, who had just moved to Nomaton, had a son, William, in class. Mr. Fisk, the stonemason whose wife took in laundry, had three children present. Too, there was a Swedish girl, Ingrid, and her young brother, Jakob, whose father worked in the logging camp farther north.

Thomas and Gunther Fowler I knew by sight but had never been closer than a stone's throw away. Their father owned Fowler's Saloon. In their teens, they had matching string-bean limbs and greasy brown hair. When Gunther turned round to gape at me, I saw a heavily freckled face and squinting gray eyes with either natural or acquired viciousness. Thomas shared his brother's freckles, but his eyes were softer and his face, broader.

The final personage was a girl, sitting ahead of me on the opposite side of the room. I had seen her once or twice while accompanying Pa to his shop, and I knew of the tragedy that had befallen her six months prior. She might have been a year or two younger than me. It would have been impossible not to notice her, for her hair was the bright color of copper, and from the calling of the roll, I knew she had a name to match—Penny. Her clothing, unlike the simple calico of Mr. Tenney's girls, was made of fine brown broadcloth, over which she wore a starched, white pinafore and bright red, coral necklace that made her hair shine all the brighter. Penny made no pretense and openly turned to stare at me.

Mr. Caskell began the day's lesson, and my attention shifted. The other children seemed to have temporarily forgotten about me, except for Penny. Whenever she had opportunity, she looked back. I kept to my work, only once glancing up to meet Penny's bright, laughing eyes. Her smile was infectious; I felt my features relaxing for a moment, a warm, joyful sensation flooding me, and discovered that I was actually smiling. I looked away.

When nooning finally came, I took my rag and settled myself on an old stump, away from the other children, with my back to the schoolhouse. Here, I had an excellent view of the schoolyard: the east backed against Farmer McNeil's wheat field; the west, Whittemore's Prairie, which I'd passed through earlier. It was empty, excepting a young, solitary white pine.

My lunch rag contained bread, an under-baked potato, and a meager supply of questionable goat meat. As I broke the bread, a putrid scent issued forth and slender, worm-like filaments appeared. It was nothing unusual, and I took it down without giving it a second thought. One could become accustomed to anything.

After eating, most of the children tramped down snow in the shape of a spoked wheel to play Fox and Goose. I kept to my place against the wall, and no one came to invite me. It was a relief, for I couldn't have joined. Mother had prepared me to face them—to reject their play should they offer it—to repulse them should they attempt to claim my time. We had practiced, Mother playing the part of a schoolmate. I was happy not to be forced to play my part now, at least for the time being.

Victoria, presumably too refined for such play, hung back as well. William, three years older than myself, went and whispered in her ear. Victoria's eyes lit up, and she suddenly joined. It seemed she was not afraid to drop her airs and graces when a handsome boy was about. Once the game began, William, the self-appointed Fox, chased Victoria and her sisters, screaming, down first one spoke, then the other, until Victoria leapt out of the path and, disqualified, became the Fox herself.

Whilst the students were thus engaged, Thomas and Gunther Fowler slunk through the snowy wheat field into the thin line of trees on its southern edge. As I observed them, a corpulent man clad all in black appeared from the same direction and strode toward the school. Thomas and Gunther, also seeing the man, suddenly broke into a run and disappeared.

Minister Judd had been old in Mother's time. He appeared now doubly so, with deep wrinkles and fat, heavy jowls. His hair, in no way diminished over the years, was parted severely to one side and hung in gray and white curls over his ears. The glitter of a gold chain sparkled from beneath his open greatcoat. Belly bobbing up and down, he neared.

I stood and, along with the other children in the schoolyard, who had paused their game at sight of the holy man, made my manners. Minister Judd surveyed them and waved an imperious hand, allowing them to continue. I straightened my posture and tucked my hands behind my back.

"And how is the first of God's creation on his first day of formal education?" Minister Judd asked.

"I am well, sir."

I could not bear to look directly into his watery, bluish-gray eyes, so I stared instead at his large nose. He laid a hand on my shoulder. I stiffened like ice.

"I am glad to see you keep yourself separated," he said, lowering his voice. "Your mother will be happy to hear it. You know, she has requested that I keep an eye upon you. I told her I would keep two." Minister Judd gave a self-satisfied laugh, then he glanced pointedly at the other children dashing back and forth. "Devote yourself to study, Adam. Spend your time with those older and wiser than yourself. Do not engage in the foolish play of children."

He parted his coat and pulled the gold watch from his velvet waist pocket, glancing at me as he did so. "A gift from a parishioner," he said. "It's fitting for a man of God to keep the time, since time has been entrusted to me. Don't you agree?"

"Yes, sir."

Minister Judd slipped the watch back into his pocket. "Keep

to the straight and narrow, my boy." With that, he bobbed across the schoolyard and down the lane into the village proper.

My posture relaxed as he disappeared.

Penny, for one reason or another, had not joined Fox and Goose but was engaged instead with the Swedish girl, Ingrid, in footraces near the lone white pine. She had captured my interest, and I watched her with growing curiosity. Penny, clearly the stronger of the two, would dash forward at full speed; each time, she would make it to the pine first. When she did so, she looked triumphantly at me. I averted my eyes. On one of these occasions, Penny looked back prematurely, causing her to swerve. Ingrid, close behind, stumbled against her, and slipping on the snow, they both tumbled into a heap. Ingrid laughed, but when Penny stood up, I saw that her cheeks were very red, and she would not look at me. I had to turn to hide my smile. *"Pride goes before a fall."*

When nooning was nearly at an end, Penny parted from her friend and dashed in my direction. The nearer she grew, the more alarmed I became. It pained me to think of having to repulse her. I strode toward the empty wheat field. As my boots snapped the hardened stubble, I caught the sharp, bitter scent of pine. I whirled round.

"Here," she said, thrusting a sprig of green needles into my hand. "It's for you."

I ought to have hurried away, but something made me stay. She was like the sun, glowing; and looking at her, I, who had never felt bright in my short life, began to feel like the moon, absorbing and reflecting some of her radiance.

"I...thank you."

"Penny!" Ingrid waved from near the tree. "Bell almost ring."

"We have to get back," she said.

As suddenly as she had come, Penny disappeared. The pine needles were long and green and hardened with cold. I could not keep the sprig. It was a gift from a heathen, and so I must dash it to the ground. I held out my arm intending to do just that.

Yet something about her thoughtfulness touched me. I looked from the retreating girl to the gift. Things were not as I had imagined. A gift was not what I had planned for. Kindness from this girl was not what I had practiced for. I drew my arm back, tormented in mind.

The bell rang. A half second's indecision altered my intention, and I hurriedly tucked the sprig into my trouser pocket.

At the close of the school day, I was the first to leave. I hastened away, full of the secret knowledge of the bit of pine in my pocket, hands tucked firmly behind my back, and solemn face turned toward Haggard House. What I did not know then, was that the course of one's life may be altered by the smallest of events—even one as small as accepting a forbidden gift.

Chapter 2

The Narrative of Adam Bolton

Unlike the fresh-lumbered frame houses in the village, ours was not evidence of Pa's carpentry. It was of plain, rectangular build like the old colonial homes. Some invisible force seemed to have compressed it inward like a tightly cinched corset. The wide planks had shrunken and shriveled in the elements, and time had weathered the wood to a mossy gray. There were four windows, one in front and one in back of the sleeping attic, and two in the front lower story. All were covered in a thick layer of grime, blackening the view of the inside and giving the house an insidious presence.

Beyond was a poultry yard with its hen-house, and the kitchen garden, now hidden by thick snow. A lean-to, jutting out from the eaves, contained our meager supply of firewood. Farther on, a small footpath led through the trees, and opposite the house sagged the enormous barn toward which I now made my way, followed closely by goats. They rounded themselves into the large corner stall, and I separated the bleating kid from its mother, placing it in the smaller stall. The dam would be left enough milk for Mother to collect in the morning. Whilst Pa fetched water from the well through the path in the trees, I went aloft and pitched down fodder for the horse and goats respectively, happy to have a few moments alone with my thoughts of the day. The goats bleated and scrambled over each other to get to their grain.

As I thrust my hands into my trouser pockets preparatory to returning to the first floor, my breath caught: there was the gift. I had entirely forgotten its existence. I retrieved and examined it again, catching the pungent scent.

"Adam?" Pa's voice called.

I replaced the gift and went below. Pa had already finished watering the gelding and goats. He turned expressive brown eyes to me and crossed his arms, leaning his tall frame and slumped shoulders against the closed door of one of the empty stalls.

"How were the school day, son?"

"As well as could be expected, sir." I feinted for the door in hope that he would leave off.

"Naught more than that?" he asked.

I turned back. His face was pale and drawn, and his eyes pleaded with mine. *Tell me more.*

"A girl stared at me all day," said I.

Pa chuckled and visibly relaxed. "Well, that weren't so bad. Who were it?"

I wished I hadn't spoken. "Penny."

"Well, well," he said.

"I didn't like her staring." A lump crept into my throat, as if to silence me from revealing anything further, and I turned away again. "We ought to get on with the chickens."

I hurried from the barn, Pa's footsteps close behind. He would not press me, and I was grateful, for I had already said too much. Soon enough, the chickens were fed and roosting in their coop, and Pa began to make his way toward the house.

"I've forgotten something," said I. "I'll join you inside shortly." It was strictly truthful, if not misleading.

The barn was divided into two, the southern section with room for carriages on one side and horse stalls on the other. This was also where we kept the goats. However, I made my way to the smaller northern section, which was never used. I pulled back the iron latch of the huge double doors, jerking one of them open over the snow. Once inside, I peered at my surroundings. The cold winter light of early evening trickled through the windows. There were enough stalls for sixteen cows. These were all empty, laden only with cobwebs, dust, and dirt.

I hurried to the opposite end of the passage and entered one of the stalls there. Inside was a plain, dome-topped travel trunk. The ancient hinges groaned as I lifted the iron latch, then the lid. It was empty of contents. I tenderly stowed the sprig inside and latched it shut again. Some of the pine sap had stuck. Fearful of being discovered, I rubbed it between my fingers until it turned into a dirty brown ball and flicked it to the floor.

Hiding the gift was the lesser of my dilemmas. I knew Pa would not repeat what I had told him, but Mother was bound to ask me about school; I could not lie to her, for lie or omission was always discovered. It was best to push the occurrence from my mind.

However, after I stood, preparatory to leave, the image of the pine sprig immediately danced before my eyes. My heart quickened as I thought of my impending encounter with Mother. I opened the trunk again, intending to dash the sprig into the dirt. It was bent from its cramped hiding spot, and as I took it up, I fancied I saw Penny's smile. She had given it to me, and the thought of tossing it away as I ought to cut me. Again, I replaced it.

What was I to do?

I closed my eyes, searching for some answer to my difficulty. Almost as soon as I had done so, I saw within my mind the image of a vast, empty expanse. At some distance was a solitary building —two stories, plain, rectangular, and shriveled. It was the very image of Haggard House. I suddenly found myself inside. The first floor was utterly empty. I climbed the stairs into the attic. Pa's mahogany tool chest was there, as well as a pile of lumber. I took up a piece of wood and at once understood what I must do. There, slat by slat, I constructed a small room and set within it a door. Gripping the trunk within my mind by one of its handles, I dragged it behind. At each step, I heard the scrape of wood on wood, then a loud thud as it slammed against the top of the next stair. Once above, I pulled it into the room I had constructed. A key appeared in my hand, and it fit perfectly in the lock. I turned it.

I was suddenly brought back to the present by a sharp wind which struck the barn, rattling all the loose boards. I stood once more, averting my eyes from the trunk, and made my way toward the house, hands tucked behind my back.

What had I been thinking of? I searched my mind but could recall nothing.

Chapter 3

The Narrative of Adam Bolton

I saw Mother through the first story window. I had inherited her dark eyes, although hers were sharper. Her appearance was Quakerish, with her severe, almost mourning-costume, a black crepe gown from a decade prior. She was slender—nearly gaunt with deep, purplish pockets under her eyes. In the dim light, her hair appeared black, though in actuality it was deep brown with streaks of silver.

As I entered the house, there was an immediate, overpowering odor, the distinct scent of cheese. Neither cheese, nor butter, for that matter, had ever been made within these walls. Instead, the scent came from an earthenware bowl near the fire, filled with a mixture of goat's milk, cornmeal, sugar, and salt. This was Mother's leavening. She called it milk-emptyings bread and had learnt of it from a young Virginian woman who had moved to Nomaton and subsequently died in the cholera outbreak. I rarely took notice, for it was simply the familiar scent belonging to my house.

Pa was descending the steps, having just washed for dinner. He moved to the head of the table and eased himself into the chair. His workman's frame filled and exceeded it, making him appear giant-like. Mother ladled stew into a bowl and placed it directly before me, resting her bony fingers upon my shoulder for a moment before returning to her seat.

A massive hearth filled nearly the entirety of the back wall of the first floor. Despite its enormity, only a flicker played above the spindly sticks. At one end of the room was a mahogany grandfather clock, mournfully out of place amongst the sparse surroundings. Near the clock was the set of stairs leading to a door which opened into the attic.

Plain, unvarnished wood composed three chairs, a table, and shelves stacked with an assortment of chipped pewter cups, plates, and bowls. The walls and ceiling, whitewashed long before my time, were black with soot. The wooden floor planks were without variation, with one notable exception. At one corner were streaks of dark brown stain.

We bowed our heads, and Pa murmured the Lord's Prayer in the low, sluggish hum of one accustomed to repeating the same words again and again. The hum ended, and I ate my stew, consisting chiefly of water with scanty lumps of goat, potato, and even fewer bits of carrot. The potato had dissolved into a starchy mass, and the meat was toughened to such a considerable degree that it was impossible to chew. From long practice, I gave three gentle bites, then swallowed it whole.

Pa lifted his bowl to his lips and drained the liquid off first. Mother's beady eyes followed him like a crow. He ate the single piece of watery carrot. Next went the mass of potatoes. Mother continued her own measured bites, watching and waiting. He scraped all the unforgiving lumps of meat into his mouth at once, closed his eyes, and forced them down. He saved the bread for last. The crust was hard, almost black. As he broke it, I observed the same slender strings that were its trademark. He ate it in two bites, not bothering to chew. Then he took a swig from his cup and leaned back in his seat, color draining from his face.

"I've had a favorable report from Minister Judd regarding you," said Mother, shifting her attention to me.

Pa glanced at me, but I kept my gaze upon my dinner, tilting it and watching the clear clusters of goat fat slide across the surface of the thick, gray soup—color compliments of the iron pot.

"Was the reading from Malachi profitable to you?" asked she.

How did she know the schoolmaster's reading for the day? That I had not anticipated. I squirmed in my chair, draining the contents of my bowl before answering. "I'm sorry, Mother. I...I was watching the other students."

"I see," said she. "You will recite it to me during this evening's reading."

"Yes, Mother." I had gotten off easily, I knew.

"Is there anything else you ought to tell me?" asked she.

Without intending it, I looked up and caught her eye. I could not look away. Was there something else? An immense pressure started at the back of my neck and worked its way into my head. It was so great, I almost thought it became visible.

"There's naught more," said I.

For a long time, Mother gazed at me. Then she said, "Very well." She believed it.

Chapter 4

The Narrative of Silas Whittemore
1828

I threw back the whiskey resting on the small table between Walter and I. "Company damn near burned out my holdings. But I found them out beforehand. Came right back after I'd set out and laid wait for them—right there in my cabin. Scared them off, I can tell you. Wounded one in the shoulder. They'll think twice about coming after my furs again."

Across from me, Walter Douglas, clad in a black, single-breasted jacket, over which a starched, white collar poked, kicked his feet onto the ottoman at the end of his leather armchair and threw his arms back behind his head. He sat in stark contrast to myself. I wore moccasins, a plain linen shirt with no vest, and my tangled brown locks came to my shoulders. Where his face was smooth and beardless, mine was leathery from the sun, and my beard fell to my chest. Yet despite his gentlemanly appearance, he was the shrewdest businessman I knew, running our trade under the very nose of the largest and most powerful of its kind—the American Fur Company—shipping off my furs in broad daylight, and laughing about it too.

"You're a pork-eater no more, Silas," said Walter. "I must tell you that the islanders placed bets when you first arrived. Said you'd be run out of business before a month's time. A scrawny English-man, known only to life cooped up in a small office. I'll have you know, my bet was for you, not against. And I made my money back and then some, I can tell you." He laughed, leaning across the table to slap my shoulder.

I doubted his story very much. He was a man who knew how to spin a good tale to sell his wares, and this was flattery at best. Who could have known that I, a lanky law clerk fresh from the shores of England, could have established my own fur trade, and become so accomplished in that life that, within eighteen months, I was able to send to England for my wife and child.

Walter's laughter trailed off. He saw I was not to be fooled. "When does your wife arrive?"

"If all goes well, I expect her within seven days. I've instructed her to wait in Port Sarnia until my men arrive."

"I don't mind telling you she mustn't get in the way, and if she does, you'll have to find a new merchant to move your wares. This isn't a place for women and children, and if you'd listened to my advice, they never would have come to interfere."

This was irksome to hear, especially as I knew he was right.

"Trust yourself for your own business and trust me to mine. I've done what was necessary."

There was a knock upon the door, and Walter grunted out an acceptance to enter. It was his wife, Mrs. Douglas. She was a short, plump woman, and her plain white gown and cornette cap set off the redness of her face and neck; she was out of breath, apparently having hurried down the hall to our study.

"What is it?" barked Walter.

"Visitors," said Mrs. Douglas, glancing curiously behind her. "I think you'll want to see them."

"Very well then. Show them in."

A Frenchman, a man I recognized as one of the Company men, appeared at the door, red worsted voyageur cap in hand. His head was none the better for it, for it exposed matted, greasy hair.

Behind him was a woman dressed in a fine, geranium silk gown and feather-festooned hat.

"Escuse, Meester Douglas," said the man.

Before he had the opportunity of explaining himself, the woman pushed ahead of him, yanking a child forward. The bottom of the child's white frock, too long for her short legs, was coated in dirt.

The woman tightened her lips and drew up her shoulders, looking directly at me.

"Eve!" exclaimed I. "What are you doing here? How did you manage to...My men set out only this morning—"

"I waited in Port Sarnia for three days," said she. "I would wait no longer."

Fool of a woman. It was sheer madness traveling half the length of the state by water with a stranger. "My apologies, Walter," said I. "This is...my wife, Eve, and my child, Sarai."

Mr. Douglas stood from his chair and proffered a hand. She neither took it nor looked at the giver.

"Take the man's hand, Eve," said I.

Eve complied and offered a false smile and curtsey.

"How in Heaven's name did you get here?" asked I.

The Frenchman, who had remained hidden just inside the door, stepped forward. "Escuse, but se woman said er usband would pay for er passage."

"This is the man that gave you passage?" I knew him by name, Mr. Gauthier.

My wife merely nodded assent. Walter glanced at me in surprise but said nothing. I counted out a small stack of silver coin.

"This should more than cover my wife's passage," said I, handing the stack begrudgingly to Mr. Gauthier.

The Frenchman looked disinterestedly at the silver. "But sere were two passengers, not one."

"Confound it," said I. "What I've given you there more than covers two."

"Never se less," said Mr. Gauthier, smiling placidly.

I counted yet another stack of silver coin and handed it to him. "Take it and let me not see your face near my wife again."

He smiled once more. "And somesing for se luggage wheech we weel breeng to se...tavern?"

"Nothing for the luggage," said I, striding towards the man. "Leave it at the harbor."

"As you weesh," said Mr. Gauthier and sauntered from the room.

Walter turned to me. "The Company men will never let you alone, you see." Although he laughed, his expression told something different; there was a warning look there.

"Quite," said I.

Chapter 5

The Narrative of Adam Bolton

My second day at the village school was very much like the first. Penny again stared. Minister Judd appeared, observed me from a distance, then disappeared. The children played Fox and Goose in the tracks from the previous day. The Fowler twins, along with two of the larger boys, slunk through the field into the woods, one with a dirty, canvas flour sack slung over his shoulder. However, after these events, the day began to diverge.

Settled on the stump outside the schoolhouse, I had just eaten the last crumb of foul bread when a commotion in the woods caught my attention. There were half-intelligible shouts, one of which was, "Don't let 'im go, Gunther!" A few of the more adventurous souls hurried after the noise. More excitement and consternation ensued as nearly the entire schoolyard emptied in pursuit.

I observed Penny beckoning Ingrid to follow her into the field. After careful consideration, I too followed, though at a distance.

The children were gathered in a tight ring in an opening just inside the line of trees. Most of the girls were stuck on the outside, their shouts mingling with the boys' as they attempted to get a glimpse. My short stature made it impossible for me to see what the commotion was, and in their excited state, none of the other students noticed me. In the confusion, I could easily have pushed the others aside to let myself through. Instead, not wishing to draw attention to my presence, I chose a tall boy with a wide stance and hurriedly crawled underneath. I nearly got a mouthful of snow in the process. Almost as soon as I stood, a copper-haired girl, half covered in white, popped up beside me—Penny. She grinned as she used her mittened hand to brush off her mantle. Myself and Penny were now the persons closest to the action.

Gunther, Thomas, and their two bulky companions had stretched a rope betwixt two trees at some height. In the center of this, hanging upside down by a cord wrapped round its hind legs, was a large hare. It wriggled savagely as it attempted to kick itself free. Thomas, Gunther, and their companions were taking turns running underneath the rope, gripping the hare's head with their bare hands and attempting to yank it off. Gunther, the current sportsman, if such he could be called, had fitted his hand with a leather glove and had stopped running in order to yank harder.

Penny's sparkling eyes turned livid. "Stop it!" she shouted, but her words were lost in the chorus of shouts.

"You're cheating, Gunther," Thomas yelled. "You can't stop running. Those are the rules."

Thomas' words were wasted: with a final tug, Gunther succeeded in twisting and tearing the hare's head from its body. Bright red drops spilt onto the snow and froze. Penny covered her eyes. Gunther, seeing her distress, approached and shoved the mangled hare head before her face, its black eyes wide and mournful.

"Aww, leave her alone, Gunther," Thomas called.

Gunther, heedless of his brother's words, gripped Penny's mittened hand and pulled it away from her eyes. "It's just a li'l ol' hare."

I had waited, until this time, hoping that Gunther would relinquish his taunt, but his violence now left me no alternative but to act.

"Let her go," said I.

The shouts, hallooing, and pleadings suddenly stilled. All eyes turned to Gunther and me.

"Why?" Gunther asked.

"Let her go," repeated I, drawing myself up to my full height and crossing my arms.

Gunther laughed uncertainly but gripped Penny's arm still tighter. I widened my stance. There was no going back from the step I had taken. Still, he did not move.

Without further warning, I sunk my fist into Gunther's stomach. Immediately, the boy dropped his grip and stumbled back. I turned and, wide berth given me, withdrew from the circle. As I did so, he regained his footing and charged. Sensing the motion and guessing its intention, I stepped aside. A bit of root caught Gunther's foot and sent him sprawling forward into the snow. There was laughter behind me, but I did not stay to enjoy my success. I retraced my steps to the schoolhouse where I resumed my position on the stump. I had acted from impulse rather than design. I wondered if my actions were pleasing to God, but I was too heated to commune with Him. There I remained until the bell rang.

As I took my seat inside, there was a shift in the murmurs and stares directed my way. The consensus seemed to have changed from one of notoriety to one of admiration.

Mr. Caskell's voice and my schoolfellow's recitations from the front of the room made it impossible to think clearly. I felt ill, both in body and spirit. When Mr. Caskell finally released the class for the day, I sprinted from my seat, collected my things from the cloakroom, and sped outside. I wished for nothing but solitude.

As I put distance between myself and the schoolhouse, I settled into a steady march. Presently, I heard the light tread of hurried feet. Turning slightly, I saw from the corner of my eye that it was Penny, copper hair streaming behind as she attempted to catch up. I did not alter my pace but continued my march, expecting at any moment for the sound to recede. It did not. Shortly thereafter, I heard the tread of more feet crushing the snow, and the voices of Thomas and Gunther Fowler singing a none-too-clever chant.

"Penny. Penny. You haven't got any
Brains. Penny. Penny. All you've got
Is a lot
Of red hair.
Better have a care
Or all that red
'Ul knock you dead."

As the words ended, I whirled round. Penny had already stopped. She seemed to have heard the chant before because she rolled her eyes. The twins, standing several feet behind her, snickered. Gunther hooted and bowled over in the snow, holding his stomach as if he had said something extremely amusing.

I planted my legs firmly apart and surveyed the twins, knowing that I would again back my claim if necessary. Gunther continued rolling in the snow, laughing, but Thomas grabbed his arm and yanked him to his feet.

"What?" Gunther said.

Thomas nodded toward me, and Gunther stopped chortling. For a moment, all three parties waited. To my great relief, the twins decided not to press my limits and slunk away as quickly as they had come. Before resuming my course, I allowed myself one quick glance into Penny's eyes. I was surprised to see neither fear nor gratitude there, but her usual bright expression. I turned on my heel and continued toward Haggard House. Penny's light tread again followed. I marched for a few more rods and stopped. Penny halted behind me. I repeated the experiment with the same result. She was like a kitten play-stalking its mother, stopping every time the mother looked round. *I* looked round.

"Why are you following me?"

She stood fixed, small head held high. Her expression, beneath her thick hood, secured by a thick bow, was earnest. "I wished to thank you," she said.

I summoned my most dignified tone. "There is nothing to thank me for."

"I think there is," she said, her mouth tightening stubbornly.

"Then you're most welcome," said I.

I resumed my march, but so did Penny, only this time she hurried next to me and pushed her hand through the crook in my arm to keep pace with me. Every muscle in my body became taut at the unexpected touch.

"Where are you going?" she demanded.

Momentarily, all words were lost. I stared at the hand tucked against my arm until she, looking up and seeing my expression, dropped it.

"To the house," I managed to say in a strained tone.

She gave me an odd look. "You mean you're going home?"

"Yes," said I.

My breath came easier now that her hand had returned to her own side. I started off, fully expecting Penny would now leave me on my solitary way. She raced up again.

"I want to come," she said.

"Isn't your mother expecting you?" asked I.

"Yes." Despite her words, she did not arrest her movement and continued to keep pace.

"Listen," said I, halting for what felt like the hundredth time. "You must return home. You mustn't accompany me to mine."

"Why?" she asked, crossing her arms.

"Because your mother is expecting you," said I. "And because mine is not."

She suddenly stopped. "I'll come tomorrow then."

"No."

Her head cocked to the side, and her large eyes searched mine. "Then how can we be friends?"

"At school," said I. Frightened that she would not take no for an answer, I darted away. "We can be friends at school," I shouted back to her.

I hadn't really meant to say it. We certainly could not be friends. A pang of guilt told me that I had spoken falsely. However, I had needed to get away from those searching eyes, and I could think of nothing better to say.

Chapter 6

The Narrative of Penny Haworth

I ran my hand over the Shorthorn's creamy belly, pulled up the tri-legged stool, and commenced milking, my fingers closing one after another round the udders like waves. Steam rose from the milk as it collected in the cold bucket. Everything was cold, but with my head pressed against the milch cow's warm flank, I didn't feel it quite as much.

Father had followed the lumbering camps with his saloon. Every spring thaw, he had amassed large sums of money as lumbermen flooded into town. He had heard of a vast supply of pine farther north and west, still untapped. As the lumber supply in the eastern states dwindled, he had moved us to Michigan, to a village called Nomaton, named so for the Menominee word *noma*, for beaver. This portion of wilderness had been opened by fur traders, most of whom had long since abandoned the growing village. A few, however, had stayed, and now a steady trickle of settlers moved in from the east, seeking escape from growing towns and cities in search of rich farmland.

A few small lumber operations had begun near the river north of the village, and Father's saloon, the first in Nomaton, was an immediate success. Though, he was left no time to enjoy the fruits of his labor. He met his death in a carriage accident shortly after, and his saloon was sold to Mr. Fowler.

Father had left us well-provided for. Still, we lived modestly, doing most of the work on our own until hired help was needed for planting and harvesting.

Thinking of him always saddened me, so I changed the course of my thoughts.

I smiled, recalling Adam and the pine sprig. He had appeared so surprised; one would have thought he'd never in his life received a gift. Certainly, I knew the rumors about the place in which he lived. My mother, Mrs. Haworth, never believed the stories. There were plenty of tales about the two of us, a saloon keeper's widow and her daughter, and that alone was enough to give her pause.

There was an obstacle, something unknown and unspoken, between Adam and the other children. He stood apart, as did I. That was why I gave him the gift. It was a mark of fellowship. Possibly too, it had originated from my impetuosity, for I was impetuous.

The last of the warm milk trickled into the pail, and I left the barn, following the rope, level with my shoulder. Every winter, Father—and now Mother—strung a rope from the barn to the house, so that when blizzards came, which they surely would, there would be no trouble in finding the way to and from the barn.

My home was a brick structure, the only one in Nomaton, and had been built at some cost. A protrusion from the front center of the house formed a square veranda outside the entrance. Upon entry, a center hall separated a parlor and dining room on one side and a study and drawing room on the other. At the back were the kitchen and larder, and four chambers made up the upper floor. I took the rear entrance into the kitchen where Mother was at the range, her back to me. Her thick, sturdy arms thrust birch logs into the flame, already licking upward from the cedar kindling. Mother was a robust woman with perpetually red cheeks, and even from behind, I could see they were brighter than usual from exertion. I left the milk for her to strain and hurried upstairs to wash and dress for the day.

When I appeared in the dining room, I found a plate on the linen-covered oaken table, stacked with sourdough pancakes for breakfast. I took a seat in one of six perfectly matched oak chairs with cornflower blue upholstery. Mother presented me with my lunch pail—an empty tea tin with a latch—and I peeped inside. She had packed biscuits, turnips, a boiled egg, a baked potato, and, to top it all off, a large apple turnover. I would eat it all.

Mother took a seat at the head of the table. "Perhaps I should take a pie to Adam's house as thanks."

"Please don't," I said, looking up from my plate. I had related the story of the Fowler twins' misdeed, but I would not have done so if I had known it meant she would make the journey to Haggard House. "I don't think he would like us coming."

"Very well," Mother said. "You must thank him, though. And I'll be speaking to the Fowler boys' father. They've never laid a hand on you before, and I swear, they'll not do it again."

I devoured the remaining pancakes and donned my mantle, boots, and mittens. As I opened the front door and stepped onto the veranda, I dropped my lunch pail with a clang. My throat tightened, and I clapped my hand over my eyes, unable to bear the sight.

There, strung up by a cord from the arch of the veranda, was a hare's head.

Behind me, I heard Mother's steps as she hastened to the door. "Damn those Fowler boys," she said, momentarily borrowing my departed father's rough language. "Wait here." She disappeared inside.

I pulled my mittened hand down just enough to peek out. The hare's eyes were clouded and mournful. The neck was no longer jagged, as it had been when Gunther wrenched it from its body, but cut clean. It didn't seem the same creature, yet this must be the same the Fowler boys had tortured.

I pressed my mitten back to my face, again blocking the sight. I was intimately familiar with death, both the human and animal variety. I was even used to dead rabbits as far as that went, Farmer McNeil delivering a brace of them for supper every now and again. Yet, it was the head, cruelly detached from its body, hung and waiting, that chilled me. Rarely had I felt fear, but I felt it now.

Mother, wearing her boots and woolen mantle, returned with a knife. I heard the scrape against hemp as she cut. Only when Mother said, "I'll dispose of it in the back," did I remove my hand from my eyes. I was still on the veranda when she returned.

"Come." She took hold of my hand and hurried me down the steps. "The visit to Mr. Fowler can't wait. I'll not have those boys trying to frighten you."

Though I had tried to block it, the grim aspect of the mournful rabbit hung like a tapestry in my mind. Yet, I summoned my courage; I was not to be put off by Gunther and Thomas. Instead, I distracted myself with a view of the scene round me.

The street on which I lived gently curved round the westernmost outskirts of the village. Directly across the way from my home was a new, frame-built structure, which was occupied by my friend Ingrid's overflowing family, all with their Swedish parents' flaxen hair. Their father worked farther north in the lumber camp, returning every spring thaw. Jakob, a full five years younger than me, had his nose pressed up against the glass window. He stared until his mother pulled him away; he was always getting into mischief. I hoped he had not seen what had just occurred. Before we passed, however, Ingrid's mother, Mrs. Nilsson, appeared at the door.

"Gud morning Misses Havorth," she said. "Ingrid iss sick today. She vill not kome to skul."

"I'm sorry to hear it," Mother called. "I'll stop over on my return. I've some medicine that might bring her round. It always helps Penny."

Mrs. Nilsson's eyes lit up. "Wery kind. Thank yu wery much," she said and retreated into the house.

I scrunched up my nose at the thought of the brown bottle's foul contents, which burned my throat and brought flames to my ears. Poor Ingrid.

We continued down the street, homes haphazardly abutting each other. Some were log cabins, chinked with mud—unsightly windows dashed here and there. Some were newer frame structures of varying styles but all with the same, plain shape. Main Street, which ran perpendicularly to mine, boasted a raised sidewalk of wooden planks and housed nearly all the village's shops, including the saloon Father had owned.

As we neared the whitewashed building, I couldn't bear to look. Whenever I had to directly pass the place, I made a conscious effort to look away. Father had kept the place impeccably, but now, after only six months, it was falling into disrepair. The whitewash was chipping away, and the front door hung loose since a brawl had nearly torn it down. Now, I was dragged through the side entrance to confront both the place and its occupants.

When we entered, no one was present. Mother and I picked our way through the bar-room sawdust, riddled with lumps of chewing tobacco and what appeared to be dried blood, and entered the back kitchen. The cook and former schoolma'am, Mrs. Fernsby, wrinkled face upturned and mouth sagging open, was busy slumbering in a rocker near the cooking range. I was glad I had never been compelled to attend her classes. Mother stamped her foot upon the floor, startling the old woman into wakefulness. Without looking round, Mrs. Fernsby burst into animation, stoking the fire.

"Breakfast'll be ready in but a moment, sir."

"Mrs. Fernsby, it's Mrs. Haworth. Would you be so good as to ask Mr. Fowler to step down for a moment to speak with me?"

Mrs. Fernsby started to her feet in surprise at Mother's voice. She immediately exited the kitchen and climbed the stairs to the apartments above. I noted the familiar room with dismay. The cooking range, which had been my job to keep brushed and polished with blacklead, was crusted in soot and pocked like brick. The air, which once smelled of delicious roast meat and baking bread, was tinged with smoke and the sour odor of Mrs. Fernsby.

Mr. Fowler entered the room, leaving Mrs. Fernsby behind. His scraggly black locks were rendered even scragglier by the ample application of bear grease. He was excessively tall, but his stooped posture made him appear of average height. His shrewd eyes immediately showed that he knew the reason for this visit.

"How dare your boys," Mother said, pushing me before the man. "Do you know what they've done at school? What they've left at my doorstep this very morning, frightening my daughter?"

I shrunk away, but Mother placed a hand on my back.

Mr. Fowler stared, disdain evidenced in every feature. I began to think perhaps he would not answer, when he bellowed at the top of his lungs, "Gunther! Thomas! Come down here!"

He shoved his hands deep in his trouser pockets and whistled quietly to himself while the heavy tramp of the boys' feet neared the door. I wished I was anyplace else.

The twins sidled up to their father. Gunther glared, but Thomas kept his gaze fastened to the embers burning in the cooking range.

Mother looked the boys up and down, contempt clear. "How dare you lay hands on my daughter and leave that head strung up at our door. I know what you've done at school even if your father does not. Touch her, or try to frighten her again, and you'll be sorry you were ever born." She clamped me to her side.

"Hear that boys?" Mr. Fowler coolly followed. "Leave her alone." With that, he left the room and slammed the door shut behind him. Gunther departed close behind, but Thomas lingered for a moment.

"Twasn't me," Thomas said.

"There's no point in lying," Mother said. "If Gunther was party to it, so were you."

"But we didn't leave the head at your door."

Mother folded her arms. "Lies, as usual."

Thomas dropped his head, and Mother whirled about, pulling me after her.

"I'll accompany you to school," she said, taking my hand once we were outside.

"You needn't," I said, attempting to pull away.

Yet, she gripped my hand tighter, and off we went, myself lagging as far behind as my arm would allow. When we reached the schoolhouse, I dropped my head, hoping to go unnoticed. Mother marched with me right through the schoolyard full of children and inside, just as Mr. Caskell rang the bell.

"I'd like to speak to you outside, Mr. Caskell."

"Certainly," he said. He didn't appear surprised. Nothing fazed the man.

The other children streamed into the school, each staring at me as they passed, the three Tenney sisters with their upturned noses especially. As Mother and the schoolmaster stepped out, I was finally released. I took my seat without even removing my cloak, gaze firmly upon my desk. I could hear Mother's heightened voice but could not make out what was being said. Gunther and Thomas strolled in, the former with a puffed-out chest. Farmer McNeil's boys flocked to the window. I felt a set of eyes on me, and I whirled round to glare at the culprit.

It was Adam. Caught, he immediately dropped his eyes, but not before I recognized something familiar in his gaze. It took me the full school day to puzzle out what it was: Adam had the same mournful look I had seen in the eyes of the dead hare.

Chapter 7

The Narrative of Adam Bolton

The other children had steered clear of me, and for that I was glad. Today, all the boys, and a few of the stronger girls, were engaged in a game of Ante-Ante-I-Over at the large woodshed behind the school. Gunther was absent. I was surprised to observe Thomas, so thorny when his brother was present, allowing Farmer McNeil's youngest to join when the boy was clearly too small to do the throwing. It appeared almost kind. Penny was apart from the rest, making snow angels alone. I was uncertain whether she chose to be apart or whether she was excluded. Whatever the case, she appeared happy enough.

Thomas, Henry, and William were clustered together, discussing something in hushed tones. They glanced in my direction. There was further whispering, then Thomas strolled to where I stood.

"Teams are uneven," Thomas said. "Don't s'pose you'd like to even them out?"

This was the first test of my faith, I knew. William was warming up; throwing the pig bladder over the woodshed roof. The team on the opposite side caught it and raced round the building. Thomas stood, arms crossed, looking past me. This temptation was easily fought.

"I can't," said I.

Thomas shrugged. "No matter. No rule the teams have to be even anyway."

He strolled back to William and Henry and whispered to them. They also shrugged and began their game.

I had no sooner begun to feel a great flood of relief for keeping myself apart, than I sensed a presence at my side.

It was Penny. Her fine mantle and hood were coated in snow, frozen chunks hanging from the ends of her copper hair.

"They asked you to join?"

I nodded without looking at her.

"They never ask me," she said. I could feel her beaming. She didn't mind. "They're dolts anyway. It's better you said no." Suddenly, her mittened hand grabbed mine. "Come. I want to show you something."

She tugged me forward. It was different when she asked. To Thomas, I was able to refuse, just as I had practiced with Mother; but Penny's invitation was a different sort; and after a moment's struggle, I found I couldn't resist. I pulled my hand from hers but matched her brisk pace, hoping that Minister Judd was off visiting a parishioner. We came within the line of trees.

"I want to show you something," she repeated, out of breath.

One of the cedar branches above, bowed from its heavy weight, loosed an avalanche upon us. Snow slid down my neck, into the collar of my goatskin coat and down my back, making my linen shirt damp and cold. Penny, head and shoulders covered in white, suddenly trembled with laughter. She looked funny, and I was certain that I did. I too laughed. It was a strange sensation, that laughter; it loosened and lightened me.

"What did you wish to show me?" asked I.

She waved her hand and led me farther into the line of trees, past where Gunther and Thomas had held their cruel contest. I became alarmed that she would press on far enough to reach the swamp ground, but I quickly realized that it mattered not; the water would be frozen hard in all but the deepest of places. Nevertheless, she halted on what I knew to be dry ground.

"Look," she said, pointing.

"What?" asked I. I saw nothing but a thick cedar. She beckoned me to the opposite side of the trunk. I hid my smile by brushing my mittened hand across my mouth. A low, broken branch protruded perpendicularly from the tree. Leaning against the branch vertically were sticks of the thinnest variety, such as a child might easily move. I saw now that what she wished to show me was a sort of fort which she had made. She beamed, and it was all I could do not to smile as I removed my hand.

"I built it myself," she said.

"I see that," said I.

She knelt and struggled with her skirts to crawl inside. The sticks were so thin and so few that I could easily see her from any angle. "Come," she again beckoned, patting the snowy ground before her. "Sit." She was quite demanding for a girl of nine.

Glancing through the surrounding woods and seeing no one, I knelt and scooted under the low structure. There was nothing to sit upon, and not wishing for my thin trousers to become wet, I squatted.

Penny faced me and stared. I glanced through the wide slats of open space between the branches, waiting for her to speak.

"I like your nose," she said at last. "Mine is pointed, but yours is nice and round. I hope it won't get big when you're old. That old drunk about town, he has a big red nose. I hate it."

The blood in my nose pulsed, and I rubbed it at the thought.

"Don't speak like that," said I.

"Why not?"

"It's rude."

"Why?"

"You oughtn't speak about people's features in that way. It's..." I struggled for a reason, "vain."

"Well, I don't believe it's vain. It's nothing to do with me."

"My nose is none of your concern," said I, leaning back on one foot preparatory to leaving.

"Wait," she said. "I'm sorry I offended you." She gripped my arm. "Please stay."

I stared at her small, mittened hand. "Don't do that."

"Very well," she said, removing it. "I won't, but please stay."

I could say no to any of the other children, but I could not say no to Penny. I was like a moth drawn to the brightness of her flaming hair. I settled back into my crouched position, shifting my weight on first one foot, and when I grew tired of that, the other.

"What did you want to do?" asked I. "The bell will ring soon."

She shrugged. "Show you my fort."

I waited for her to continue, but she did not. She was completely at ease. I searched for something, anything to say, but could think of naught. I gave up the struggle and waited.

There was nothing unfamiliar about silence; it was, in fact, a regular feature in my house. Unless it was something to do with the running of the household or the Word of God, Mother rarely spoke. However, there was always meaning in her silence, and I had grown able, over the past eleven years, to read each kind. My unfamiliarity, this discomfort I felt now, stemmed not from the silence, but from Penny's meaninglessness therewithin; she was perfectly content. She had no message to convey, and this was the very thing that made the quiet difficult to bear.

Recalling Mother suddenly brought me to my senses. I oughtn't to be here.

"I must go," said I, jumping up and nearly knocking down half the sticks in the process.

"What's the matter?"

"Nothing," said I. "But I...I must get back. And you mustn't go farther than this spot in the woods," warned I, as I made my retreat. "It's all swamp in spring."

As I crossed the field, I again glanced in the direction of the parsonage. I began to run, though it mattered little if I had already been seen. Almost as soon as I left the field and entered the school-yard, heart thumping in quick rhythm, Minister Judd appeared from the direction of town.

He had been out, then, and could not have seen me. There would be no report of my actions. I took a deep breath and slowed the rising and falling of my chest.

Chapter 8

The Narrative of Adam Bolton

S abbath came, a day of rest. There would be no buying or selling or working of any kind. I awoke in the frigid air of the attic, joints stiff from the cold. I felt more rested than usual, and I glanced from my mattress on the floor to the rusted iron bed across from me. Mother was already missing. Pa was nearly finished washing himself at the basin atop the chest of drawers. The grandfather clock below struck five. Mother could not have slept above four hours for, as was her wont, she had paced to and fro, reading the Scriptures from midnight until one o'clock.

Pa finished washing, and I hurried in my stocking feet across the freezing wood to the tiny patch of rug just before the wash basin. I ought to have remained on the bare flooring; Pa, in his haste, had dripped water onto the carpet, and it soaked my stockings, making me colder still.

I cleansed myself quickly and thoroughly and dressed in my Sabbath best—starched, white collar and black frock coat, much better fitting than my school clothes, though still tight. I combed and parted my hair, pushing it nearly all to one side. This was really the only similarity I had to Pa, for his hair was parted and combed in exactly the same manner.

The fire below appeared a little warmer and brighter than usual. I never understood how it was that we could place wood upon the fire on the Sabbath. To me, it seemed to be work. However, Mother allowed it, and I had never had the courage to inquire about the matter. Seated in her rocker with the Bible, she nodded me toward the corner.

I went and, facing northeast behind her, mutely performed my prayers upon my knees. Then, the three of us silently breakfasted. The meal consisted of yesterday's gruel, so thick it might have been used as plaster. The animals would be munching down the double ration of grain and hay I had left for them the evening prior, and the kid would be happily emptying its dam of her milk.

We met no other parishioners on the way to church. It was, in fact, a full hour before service. We could have taken the cart, but it would have been work to harness the Belgian. So, we walked instead, Mother and I side by side, Pa on the outside edge. He was handsome, dressed in his Sunday finest with his tall top hat and trimmed, brown beard and mustache worked through with the occasional white. His expression was the same as it was every Sabbath; pained. Mother wore her only good dress— lavender silk—dull and stiff from weekly wear, oddly paired with a plain, white collar and no jewelry—which she said was vain. It was the same dress she had worn brilliantly, I had been told, upon her marriage to Pa. But now the garment hung wearily on her scant frame, and seeing it always gave me a melancholy feeling.

No one spoke during the long walk.

Minister Judd was outside the church door, ready to receive us. Above his black broadcloth cape, the white points of his collar just touched his sagging jowls. He took Mother's hand warmly.

"Punctual as ever," he said, swinging the church door open.

Pa and I removed our hats as we stepped inside. The church was unexceptional, a tall, whitewashed building with an unassuming spire, bell, and cross. Minister Judd had requested that Pa keep the structure plain so his parishioners' minds remained on God rather than distracted by the earthly building.

He followed us inside and settled himself at the white pulpit on the raised platform at the front of the room. There, he made preparations for the sermon, and we took a seat in our accustomed pew at the front.

It was bitterly cold, and the lack of movement made it even more so. Mother and I knelt on the hard floor. The minister, I knew, stood upon a foot-stove, and I felt an evil pang of jealousy for his warmth as the pain in my knees began in earnest. Next to me, Mother made no outward complaint or sign of discomfiture, and I was certain she made none inwardly either. Her thoughts were only of Heaven. It brought to mind a verse from the Epistle to the Romans: "For they that are after the flesh do mind the things of the flesh; but they that are after the Spirit the things of the Spirit." I forced bodily pain from my thoughts and fixed my attention upon my Heavenly Father.

When, finally, Minister Judd stepped down from the pulpit and rung the church bell, a pang of guilt struck me as I realized that I welcomed the respite from the intensity of my devotions and the pain in my knees. I inwardly begged forgiveness of God for these worldly concerns as I took a seat on the stern, upright pew. It was now but a quarter of an hour before service, and I opened my Bible to the passage from which Minister Judd was to speak. He consulted with Mother on his sermons during his weekly visits to the house, and I felt a sense of pride in being allowed into this knowledge.

The other congregants trickled, then streamed in: Victoria, Florence, and Priscilla, gaudily colored frocks following their noses; the farmers and their children with their starched collars, their best calicos and suits; the tradesmen with their almost imperceptibly neater, nicer, newer clothing. I had a new understanding of the people sitting in the pews behind—at least the children. Before, I had regarded them as I did the people in my Bible, real yet distant. Yet now, for an entire week, I had shared the same school-house and classes; I had been invited to join in their game. The gap of separateness had imperceptibly narrowed.

The minister began his sermon.

"'And Aaron shall cast lots upon the two goats; one lot for the Lord, and the other lot for the scapegoat.'"

Mother sat perfectly upright next to me.

"'And Aaron shall bring the goat upon which the Lord's lot fell, and offer him for a sin offering. But the goat, on which the lot fell to be the scapegoat, shall be presented alive before the Lord, to make an atonement with him, and to let him go for a scapegoat into the wilderness.' A *scapegoat*." Minister Judd's hand thundered against the pulpit, seeming to shake the very church. "But what of the goat offered to the Lord? There is no scapegoat without sacrifice. The flesh must be slain to atone for sin."

Mother's bonnet turned, and she examined me. I swallowed but kept my gaze firmly on the minister.

It was a long sermon, even for him, lasting well over two hours. But at last, it came to an end.

As the parishioners emptied the church, Mother thanked the minister for a *profitable* sermon and unnecessarily informed him that we would return for evening service.

We ate a hasty lunch of cold baked potatoes and bread, both from the day prior. Mother then disappeared to the attic. When she returned, she held something wrapped in a white cambric handkerchief. There was something rare in her expression, something like excitement.

"This is for you," said she, offering the bundle.

I could never recall having received a gift from Mother. From the shape and weight, I immediately knew it to be a book. I turned the gift over and saw that my initials had been stitched into the corner of the handkerchief. This itself was gift enough. Mother rarely had time for sewing or mending because it took from the time she might devote to God.

"Thank you, Mother," said I.

She smiled, and I was surprised by the youth it brought back to her features. Unfolding the material, I found an old volume titled, *A Token for Children*.

"It was gifted to me after my first week at Sunday School," said Mother. "It's a reminder to set an example to the heathens and pagans that surround you." She took her place in the rocker with her Bible. "You will find the hymn in Example Five especially pertinent. It's suitable reading for the Lord's day."

I sat on a small stool beside her and began my new book. Inside the front cover was an inscription, which I immediately recognized as Minister Judd's hand.

For Sarai: "Train up a child in the way he should go: and when he is old, he will not depart from it."

The preface was quite lengthy. I hadn't time to complete the book before the second sermon, so I passed over the beginning chapters and went directly to the hymn Mother had counseled me to read. I read it again and again, instinctively committing it to memory. I was in the midst of this process when my tranquility was suddenly broken by the image, in my mind's eye, of Penny. Immediately, I knew the Lord was using these words to remind me, not to avoid the other children, whom I had very little temptation toward, but Penny, who even the thought of warmed me. It was she this hymn, this warning, was for.

Chapter 9

The Narrative of Penny Haworth

"Today iss too cold to go outside," Ingrid said, removing her steaming potato from the top of the schoolhouse stove and lingering near the heat.

Adam stood and made his way toward the door. I stared, hoping to attract his attention. However, he would not meet my gaze and simply walked past. The Tenney sisters were all huddled in a corner, poring over a drawing lesson in *Godey's Magazine,* which they'd brought from home, certainly too cowardly to step outside in these temperatures. I glanced wistfully out the window. It was abominable to be stuck indoors for the entirety of nooning with only the girls and Mr. Caskell, not that there was any rule about such things, simply that the girls preferred to be as near the stove as possible on such days.

Ingrid drew something from her wooden lunch pail. A stick had been thrust through the holes where the cord should have been, and that was how Ingrid carried it to school. The *something* was a tiny doll. It had, to me at least, a strange blue wrap tied round its hair and an odd style of dress.

"Oh, may I see?" I asked, holding out my hand.

Ingrid looked from the doll to me. "If yu wery careful," she said.

I seized the doll and held it up to the light. Ingrid extended a hand in case I dropped it. It was as detailed a doll as I had ever seen. It had tiny dress cuffs, and very fine lace bordering the bottom of the apron covering the dress. "Did your mother make it?" I asked, turning the doll round and round curiously.

"Ya," Ingrid said, waving her hand insistently. I returned it. "Mama bring it from Sveden. She say I old enough now to take care."

"She *said*," I corrected, turning from Ingrid and gazing back out the window. It really was a shame it was so cold. Ingrid would undoubtedly want to play with me, but I wasn't in the mood for playing inside.

"Ve can share," Ingrid said.

"I want to go out. Will you come with me? You can bring the doll."

Ingrid stared, wide-eyed, at her doll. She wouldn't think of doing such a thing.

"Very well," I said. "I won't be long."

Hurrying to the cloakroom, I bundled into my mantle and mittens. Some days, I still enjoyed dolls, but some days I thought they were for children. Today was the latter. However, lately, it seemed dolls and babies were all Ingrid thought about. Her mother had just come to the conclusion of a confinement, and Ingrid's new baby sister was all she took interest in. I found it all very *un*interesting. I would rather be outside.

Adam was not there with his back against the schoolhouse. I wondered if this was due to the cold. He would have to move to keep warm. Yet, it was the second day in a row he was not there, and yesterday had hardly been cold. He was nowhere within my line of sight, so I rounded the schoolhouse to the woodshed behind. It was a large structure, even larger than the schoolhouse itself. It was open on one side, divided in two, and the only place Adam might be able to hide. I peered in the first section, but there was nothing but towering stacks of split birch. I peered into the next. At first, I saw nothing, but when I glanced up to my right, there he was, sitting atop the pile of wood, tucked away from view by the center beam holding up the roof. His head was bowed, nearly touching his chest; and his lips moved as if he was speaking, yet no sounds came out.

"Adam!" Immediately, I regretted calling. He glanced up, stern, startled.

"What is it?" he asked. "Is something the matter?"

He leaned forward, away from the edge of the woodpile and leapt down, standing just before me.

"No," I said. "I...well, I thought you might want to play."

"Play?" He glanced in the direction of the parsonage. I too turned to look, wondering what in that direction might interest him.

He suddenly stood taller, and his expression became cold.

"I'm sorry. I don't expect you to understand, being a child still, but you must know that I can't play with you." He paused, waiting for my confirmation.

"A child!" I said. "I'm not a child." I stamped my foot.

A twinkle came into his eye as if he were about to smile. "I'm sorry," he said. "Yes, perhaps you're not a child, yet...Listen, Penny, I simply can't."

"Why not?"

He looked at me for a very long time, confusion in his eyes. Then he simply repeated, "I'm sorry," and fled in the direction of the woods.

Turning round, I saw that Minister Judd had stepped out of the parsonage and onto the veranda. I avoided meeting his eyes and hurried back toward the schoolhouse. Whatever it was that had made Adam say he could not play with me must have something to do with Minister Judd.

Tumbled bits of Mother and Father's conversations were

recalled to mind. Perhaps it had something to do with Father donating the money for the school.

When we had first moved to Nomaton, while we were living at the inn waiting for our home to be built, Minister Judd had come round. The whole visit had been tiring and trying, sitting so long in one chair and listening to the minister drone on. Mother had offered tea and biscuits, and after what seemed like ages, Minister Judd at last got to his purpose, an invitation to church. He seemed particularly interested in my attendance at the Sunday School. He had joked with me, jokes I could now not remember, only that they were not at all funny. Finally, he had left, after discovering my parents had no intention of attending, not being religious.

The next time the minister came round had been half a year later, after we had finally settled in our brick house. He came about a special offering, a bell for the church. Father had been irate. How could Minister Judd think of buying a bell when school was held in Widow Fernsby's filthy cabin, the woman a drunk? It had been then that Father had made the decision to fund the building of the schoolhouse, complete with a bell and schoolmaster from the east. If being the daughter of a heathen saloon-keeper hadn't set the minister and his congregants—who composed nearly the entirety of the village—against me, then this certainly had. This must be the reason. The minister hated me for Father's sake, and he must have instructed Adam too to keep away.

I returned to where Ingrid was at her desk, stuffing her mouth. I opened my own lunch tin. The Tenney sisters looked up from their magazine, peering at my food. Undoubtedly, they were envious. I glanced at Ingrid's solitary potato, then took the golden-crusted pasty from my box and carefully broke it in half, revealing a thick filling of turnip, onion, potato, and pork.

"Here." I offered a piece to Ingrid, "I'll trade you. I'd much rather have potato than pasty."

Ingrid glanced from the pasty to me. "Nay, nay," she said,

taking another bite, steam curling up into the cold air. "Yu must eat."

"No," I said, "*You must eat.* Besides, I've had pasties all week, and I'm getting rather tired of them."

Ingrid stared at me dubiously.

"Really," I said.

She passed half her potato to me.

"Tank yu," Ingrid said, a smile working its way into her eyes as she took my pasty.

"Ingrid, I've a question to ask. If someone was upset with you, or avoiding you, how would you make them think well of you again?"

She shrugged and took a bite. "Give food?"

"Give him food? Yes. Yes..." With that, I took up Ingrid's potato and stuffed half of it into my mouth. "Yesh. It a wandahfah idea!"

Mr. Caskell, without looking up said, "Young ladies and gentlemen do not speak with their mouths full."

"Yesh, sah," I said.

He glanced at me sternly, and Ingrid and I had to choke down our laughter.

Chapter 10

The Narrative of Adam Bolton

I t had been a week since I had spoken to Penny when, after the evening meal, whilst Pa was in the privy, I saw a blur of horse and sleigh through the begrimed windows. I hurriedly stowed the towel I had been using to dry the dishes, embarrassed that an outsider might observe me sharing women's work. I assisted Mother with this simply so that we might more speedily begin our evening reading of the Word. Mother made fewer distinctions than most between women's work and men's, for whatever spared her more time for reading and studying and prayer was the course which she adopted.

There was a hardy, friendly knock, and Mother, eyeing me to ascertain if I might know who was calling, moved to the door when she perceived that I did not. I was taken aback to see that it was Penny and Mrs. Haworth. I could think of no reason for their visit, and my heart thundered against my ribs so hard, I feared they might see its beating. I took a deep breath to collect myself, tucked my hands neatly behind my back, and neared Mother.

"We're sorry to drop by unannounced," Mrs. Haworth was saying. "But, well, we've made an extra pie and thought perhaps you might like it."

I heard the words with deep relief, but Mother regarded Mrs. Haworth and her daughter with suspicion. Penny's feet, in their small black boots with small black buttons running up the sides, were tucked straight together like a soldier's at attention. She held up a dish, neatly wrapped in white cloth, and glanced at me hopefully. Mother and daughter looked so neat and tidy in their fur-edged mantles. Penny had pushed her hood aside, and her bright hair stood out in sharp contrast to the snow. Behind them, their bright red sleigh was piled in thick furs and blankets. They seemed to have come from a different world.

Mother's words cut the cold air. "Adam is not allowed rich foods."

"Oh," Mrs. Haworth said uncertainly. "We didn't mean to impose?"

"I helped make it," Penny said, folding back a corner of the cloth to reveal a perfectly mounded pie. It smelled of sweet, unfamiliar spices. She grinned up at me, still more hopefully.

I had never wished for rich foods. I had certainly never tried them. Yet suddenly, I found myself longing to eat it. I could see through slits in the golden crust, rich apples in syrup beneath.

"I'm sorry for your effort," said Mother. "But Adam isn't allowed—"

Her words were cut short by the appearance of Pa returning to the house from the privy.

"Mrs. Haworth," he said, nodding, surprise shining in his eyes.

"Mr. Bolton," she said, "I'm happy to see you. We're sorry to have inconvenienced. We'll be on our way."

She turned to go. My mouth, which had begun to water expectantly, drained.

"What's this?" Pa said, gently extricating the half-uncovered pie from Penny's hands.

"We made it for you," Penny said. She looked up at Pa with renewed hope.

"It were very kind on you," he said. "Thank you both for your thoughtfulness."

Penny beamed, but her mother paused, uncertain of the gift's acceptance.

"Peter," said Mother, "I was just telling Mrs. Haworth that Adam is not allowed rich foods." She gave Pa her familiar look of command.

To my utter astonishment, Pa ignored her glance and said, "Thank you again, Mrs. Haworth. We much appreciate it. Let me help you back to your sleigh."

Pa handed the pie to me and took Mrs. Haworth's arm, leading her and Penny. The crockery, though cool to the touch, burned like red hot coals in my hands. I watched to see what Mother would do. Her lips were pressed tightly together, but she said nothing.

I looked back at the sleigh and saw a flash of copper curls bounce on their way up into the seat and disappear as Mrs. Haworth pulled Penny's hood over her head. The hood turned, and Penny, grinning, waved at me as the sleigh jangled away. I couldn't help but lift my hand and wave her off.

When Pa returned, he took the pie from me—I had not moved so much as an inch during this episode—and banged it upon the table.

"Fetch a knife, Sarai," he said.

Again, I was astonished. I had never known Pa to do anything contrary to Mother's wishes and certainly never to command her. They stood glaring at each other, room fraught with strife.

"Fetch a knife," he repeated.

Suddenly, Mother whirled round and did as he said. She slashed into the pie, hacking it in jagged, uneven pieces.

"Bowls and spoons," Pa said.

I could hardly believe what was happening was real. Mother gathered the dishes and dropped them onto the table with a thud.

I didn't want the pie anymore. I had rather Penny had taken it back home with her.

"Come, eat," Pa said, taking a spoon and scooping a mass into one of the bowls.

Pa's manner was such that I knew it would be useless to say no.

"Eat," Pa said, to Mother this time.

We all sat, and Pa took a huge mouthful. I took a small one and so did Mother. Despite the strain, after the initial bites, I found myself enjoying the food. The crust almost melted in my mouth, and the flakiness of it contrasted sharply with the soft, sweet, spiced apples. A smile formed in spite of myself. Even Mother's tight lips were relaxing. No one spoke, but Mother took a second helping. With her example as permission, I took one too. Mother's posture eased, and after the last bite, she too smiled.

We ate the entire pie.

"Perhaps you were right, Peter," said she, scraping the juices from her bowl.

It was the first and last time Pa ever stood up for anything, and it was the first and last time I ever heard Mother say he was right.

Chapter 11

The Narrative of Adam Bolton

I sought Penny out the following day at school. I must, for courtesy's sake at least, thank her for the pie. I had observed her running into the woods with Ingrid, and when I finished my lunch, I followed the trampled path they had taken. Gunther and Thomas watched me go. They had not taunted Penny since that day with the hare, and this was fully due to my efforts; I watched her, from a distance, in the same manner Minister Judd watched me.

As if summoned by my thoughts, the minister appeared on his veranda. I immediately altered my course so as not to be seen, entering the wood from another point. I was as familiar with these trees as I was with the Word of God, and I had no difficulty finding my way.

Penny and Ingrid were tucked into Penny's little tent, sticks and dead, brown leaves placed in a careful pattern between them. From the lifting and sipping gestures that the girls made, I understood they were having tea. Suddenly, I felt bashful, and instead of stepping forward and making my presence known, I waited behind a snow-laden cedar. From my position, I could not be seen, but I could easily peer through the boughs.

"You ought to have seen Haggard House, Ingrid," Penny said.

Her hood was pulled down, and the flash of her bright hair came through the sparse sticks.

"Did it frighten?" Ingrid asked, small gray eyes widening.

Penny shook her head. "No, but it's filthy, and there was the most awful scent when his mother opened the door. It smelt of rot."

"Yu see trap-door? Vere she keep him?" Ingrid asked.

Penny laughed. "There's no such thing, Ingrid. The Fowler boys made that up. You ought to know better."

"Certain?" Ingrid asked, unconvinced.

"Yes, I'm certain," Penny said, lifting a nicely curved, brown leaf and taking a sip of air. "I pity him. His mother is so hard."

The entirety of my body stiffened hearing these harsh words spoken of Mother. I had a sudden urge to rush forward and shout that Penny must not speak that way. However, I ought not to be here listening, and to announce my presence would be to reveal my own wrong-doing. I crept away from my hidden position behind the tree. Of the reputation I understood I held, pity had never occurred to me to be part of it. Penny's words smarted like Mother's willow rod against my back. I had imagined her eyes opening wide with delight when I told her that even Mother took down three slices of pie. It was not to be. The wound to my pride was too great. I returned to the schoolhouse, leaving Penny un-thanked.

During secret prayer that evening, I unburdened myself to God. As I communed with Him, I discovered it had been His plan that I should hear Penny's words. It served as a reminder to keep myself separate.

Chapter 12

The Narrative of Adam Bolton

Winters were always frigid in my corner of the world, but this winter was especially so. One particularly cold night, I lay down on my corncob mattress on the floor, deeply disappointed. John McDonnell, as thanks for some work Pa had done, had offered to take me ice fishing the following day. I had requested if I might go. Mother had said no. Reading and pacing had commenced. When Mother released me, she herself stayed behind to continue in prayer.

I half drifted off to sleep when I heard Mother returning to the attic. I roused myself upon one elbow. She knelt, cupped my cheek in her hand, and trained her glittering eyes upon mine.

"The Lord has spoken to me," said she in a rasping whisper. "You may go with Mr. McDonnell. He will provide you a useful skill. But beware. Beware his thoughts and words." She removed her calloused fingers from my cheek and went to bed. I was elated beyond words. It was the first time, excepting school, that I was allowed to go off unaccompanied. Whatever the reason, I felt lighter than I had in many months, and I fell into a deep and sound slumber.

It seemed that no time had elapsed before Mother shook me

awake. She returned to the kitchen, face bright red from exertion, steam rising from the wooden wash tub. Her spindly arms alternately pushed and pulled the wooden dolly, violently scudding water and soap suds along the edges of the mound of clothing and linen.

"Finish your chores, and then you may go," said Mother, as I bounded down the attic steps.

When I returned to the house, I found my lunch rag waiting for me. Pa was breakfasting.

"Joining Ol' Mr. McDonnell, eh?" Pa said, playfully knuckling my sides.

"Yes, sir." Only the sparkle in my eyes gave my excitement away as I sat to eat.

Pa rose from his chair and snuck behind me. He lifted me up and held me like a trophy in the air. "My boy, the prize ice fisher!"

Quiet dignity unsettled, I stared at the blackened ceiling. Then, suddenly, I grinned. I couldn't help it. In quick, long strides, Pa paraded his prize ice fisher round the room. I burst into laughter—hearty, natural laughter. I felt light upon his shoulder, as if I were five instead of eleven. Pa laughed too. Mother's hands went to her hips, but I could see that the downward turn of her lips was forced, and there was something like joy hidden behind her eyes. She could not maintain her disapproval as Pa strode directly before her and halted abruptly, sending me jolting forward and nearly toppling off his shoulder.

Mother laughed. I could have counted upon one hand the number of times I had heard Mother laugh, but she laughed now. She laughed and laughed and laughed, face turning even redder with it.

Pa set me back upon my feet with a pat on the shoulder. An uncomfortable silence reigned. Each person stood in their place, not quite certain what to do after our moment of frivolity.

I broke the stillness by collecting my lunch rag. "I ought to go."

"Heed my words," said Mother, turning back to her wash.

Now, I faced Pa, uncertain how best to part. He eased my discomfort by extending a hand. We shook heartily, and I was off.

Though elated at the prospect of fishing with the famed hunter of Nomaton, I was more than a little unnerved at being alone with the great man, whom I had only seen a few times in my life. John McDonnell's place was five miles distant, but I was so eager to arrive that I ran much of the way. This served the dual purpose of keeping me warm and allowing me to reach the place quickly. If possible, the homestead was more remote than my own. A rough circle had been hewn from the middle of the forest, and in this rough circle was a new smokehouse, which Pa had built. It was a wooden structure on a raised stone foundation, nearly as large as the shanty Mr. McDonnell resided in. More care and expense had been put into that smokehouse than his home.

Treading with silent feet, I was nearly to the shanty door, when McDonnell's hunting dog sent up a terrific howl. Not a second passed before McDonnell himself was at the door with his rifle. The beast of a dog appeared to be part wolf. It had one brown eye and one blue, and its gray-and-white coat was ravaged in places with scars. It halted at a word from his master. McDonnell, hair matted on one side as if he had just woken, stroked his grizzled gray-and-black beard while eyeing me.

"Peter's boy?" he said.

"Yes, sir," I managed to say, hardly above a whisper.

"Hmm." McDonnell scratched his head. "One minute." He dodged back inside the shanty and returned, outfitted in a heavy bearskin coat with a thick wool blanket draped over his shoulder. His weathered hands held a quantity of fishing apparatus, including two pails, an axe, and two cedar rods, one of which was lashed with cedar-bark twine to a five-pronged iron spear. As the man neared, I could smell the sickly stench of whisky seeping from his skin and reeking on his breath.

"Nice coat," McDonnell grunted.

I glanced down at the aforementioned article. There was always plenty of goatskin to be had at Haggard House. I had tanned this very hide and helped to sew it into its present state. Mother said that no man was beneath learning to mend his own clothes.

"Here." The hunter proffered the rods and pails, and I took them. "C'mon." McDonnell gathered his own coat closer and beckoned the dog, aptly named Beast, to come. I stood stock still while Beast sniffed me. The dog nosed my lunch rag before quickly losing interest and trotting after his master. It was with some difficulty that I kept pace with McDonnell's stride. I was relieved to find the man had no intention of filling the silence with discourse. He said nothing as we moved through the woods.

A lengthy trek revealed a vast, gourd-shaped field. However, it was no field but a large lake covered with ice and snow. McDonnell and Beast traversed the frozen surface ahead of me and came to a rectangular hole that had been cut through the ice. The frigid temperatures had already crusted a thin layer back over it. He took one of the pails from me and tipped it upside down to form a seat. As he used his axe to clear the hole, he gestured me to seat myself on the other pail.

"Here. Bait the line," he said, nodding to a carved wooden minnow. "That was a gift from the Menominee. She's weighted with lead. Never failed me yet."

He pulled the wool blanket off his shoulder and motioned me to come closer. I scooted my bucket across the ice.

"Closer. Closer!"

It felt strange to sit so near him—hardly more than a stranger —but I did. McDonnell took the blanket from his shoulder, unfurled it in the air above us, and let it land over our heads and fishing apparatus. The close confines intensified the spirituous stench. As my eyes accustomed themselves to the dark, I found I could see under the water to a greater depth. I heard Beast sniff our perimeter, and the blanket pulled taut as he plopped down at his master's back.

"You fished before?" McDonnell asked.

"Once," replied I.

"Once!" McDonnell repeated.

"With all the work at Pa's shop, I haven't much time," said I.

McDonnell must have heard the apology in my words, but I felt it fortunate that the darkness of the blanket covered my embarrassed expression.

He heaved a sigh and said, as if speaking to a child, "Drop the bait and wiggle her about."

I resented the man's tone but did as I was told.

"Time to wait," McDonnell said. From somewhere inside his bearskin coat, he retrieved a tin box, and soon the scent of tobacco added to the already stifling scents mingling under the blanket. "You learning the trade from your pa?" McDonnell said, sucking at the quid.

"Yes, sir. It's why I haven't much time for fishing." It was another apology and truly only part of the reason. My endless hours of Scripture study and prayer were closer to the mark.

"No need to call me sir or mister. Just call me McDonnell." The man spat a brown wad onto the ice and wiped the back of his hand across his mouth. "An excellent carpenter, your pa. Musta seen the smokehouse he built me when you come in." I nodded, certain he would feel my motion across the blanket. "You learning good?"

"I am."

"Helping your ma at home too?"

"*Mother*. Yes."

"Good." McDonnell sucked at his quid for a moment and spat again on the ice.

I was on guard. McDonnell was a heathen, and his questioning made me ill at ease. I would have preferred the conversation be kept to fishing.

"Seen that old toper about town lately?"

This was a topic I was not allowed to discuss, and I resented McDonnell for bringing the subject forward.

"Great trapper, that man." McDonnell shook his head. "Famed throughout the region. Put the Company to shame. They never were able to get a foothold in these parts."

I remained silent, hoping that McDonnell would forget the subject and move on. He did not.

"Too bad he took to drink. S'pose you could say he went from trapper to trapped—by the new trapper in the region—the saloon." Another thoughtful spit. "Speak to him. I b'lieve he could cast some light on—" McDonnell was interrupted by the appearance of a gray-backed fish, and he thrust the spear into my hand. "Spear her, Peter's son."

Usually I cared little what children, or adults for that matter, thought of me, but something about the gruffness and self-assuredness of the hunter beside me made me yearn to make him proud. My hands tightened on the spear. I thrust it into the fish below and jerked it upward.

"Not like that! Not like that!" McDonnell shouted. "Let her wear herself out first. Easy! Give her some space."

It was too late. I had already brought the pike to the surface. The struggling fish made use of its powerful tail, and with one hard slap against the ice, forced itself free of the single barbed prong I had managed to work into it, crashing into the water with a splash. I was thrust backward from the force. My fall brought the blanket down with me, softening the blow to my head. I looked up at a gray sky.

Once the dizzying pain dwindled, I sat, then stood. My outward calm remained, but I felt foolish. It was the first time that I could remember feeling my pride so wounded.

McDonnell gripped the blanket and hurled it back over us, glaring at me in the process. "What'd you do that for? Can't yank on her like that." The man gestured with the spear toward the hole. "Got to give and take. Let her come to you when she's all tired out. Yank on her like that, and she'll wrench her way free." McDonnell shook his head and handed the rod with the carved minnow back to me.

Despite my fumble, we managed to catch half a dozen respectable fish, none the size of the first. McDonnell seemed content to stay out all day, but after peeking outside the wool blanket at mid-afternoon, he tossed it from our heads. I was, by turns, relieved to breathe the fresh air and dismayed to see an oncoming storm.

"Blizzard looks to be on her way," McDonnell said, hastening with the fish and apparatus. "Better hurry home. You'll have to take my mare. Never make it in time on foot."

Inside the small barn, McDonnell bridled his bay and pointed to an empty grain sack.

"Wrap three fish in that. Your share."

I did as I was told.

"No time for saddling." McDonnell lifted me onto the mare's back.

I tucked the fish inside my coat, under my arm.

"Hurry now," he said.

"Thank you, McDonnell. I won't forget what I learned."

With that, I turned the bay out into the rapidly rising wind.

Chapter 13

The Narrative of Adam Bolton

Though used to riding, I had never ridden a creature like this. All my riding had taken place on Pa's massive Belgian, a gentle giant. Unlike the Belgian, this bay was young and excitable; the slightest pressure from the reins sent her left or right. As we navigated through the trees, the growing wind and snow slowed her gait. She lifted her wide nostrils into the air and snorted. Without warning, she turned and bolted homeward.

"Easy, girl," said I, tightening my grip and pulling back on the reins.

The bay whinnied loudly in protest, but my firmness moved her, and soon we were facing back in the direction of Haggard House.

We continued along for what might have been a mile before my resolve, already tested once, was tested again. The snow began to drive down, the flakes changing from soft and feathery to hard and glassy. The path, which I could divine so clearly on any other day, became unreadable. Now, I would have turned back to McDonnell's, but it was impossible to tell in which direction that was, and our previous tracks were all covered in fresh snow. Panic crept in. The mare sensed this and bolted again. I kept my head low to her neck to avoid the onslaught of branches and tightened my grip as she ran, dodging the trees. Doubtless, she was attempting to return to her master, and I decided it was better to trust to her instinct than my own.

The bay stopped suddenly and lifted her nostrils to the air. Snow fell so heavily that I could see nothing but blinding white ahead. I dug my heels into her flanks and shouted, "Gee-yah," but she balked and shook her head, refusing to move. Any courage I had remaining fled. If the horse didn't know her way back home, how would I?

One thing I did know: to remain here, out in the open, meant certain death.

I hesitated, then dismounted, still clutching the fish under my arm. I sank into sponge-like snow, already up to my knees. Taking hold of the bridle, I led the mare, step by step, through the driving precipitation. Cold crept through my leather boots and thin stockings, numbing my feet.

Only one thing kept me from absolute despair, and that was my faith. I knew, or believed rather, that should I die, I would be transported to Heaven. Yet however much I believed in that place, I had no clear image of it to comfort me. I did, however, have a vivid notion of Hell, seared into my mind through Mother and Minister Judd's teachings. Before my eyes rose roaring flames, and into my wind-deafened ears came screams of agonizing pain. Yet, this fire had no power to light the darkness, and the wailing never ceased. All was black and burning terror.

Then, a new vision flashed before me—Penny wrapped in flames. Her bright eyes burned with pain. She reached out for me, gasping, "Water, Adam. Please...a drop of water."

A branch suddenly struck my face and brought me back to my present condition; I found that I was shaking. There, under the tree, I knelt in the snow. Pressing my hands together, I prayed for guidance. Christ had preserved my life once before, coming to my aid in order to make me his disciple. My work was not yet complete. He would rescue me again. Fortified by prayer, I trudged ahead as quickly as I could. It was difficult going though, and my legs tired quickly from constant sinking. I saw only trees and snow.

I stretched out my hands to prevent striking objects in the growing dark. At first, I felt trees every few moments, but as the minutes passed, all such obstacles seemed to disappear. Night, birthing prematurely, began to envelop me, and I became desperate. I had felt such peace and assurance after my prayer, but now I began to doubt. Had Christ not heard? The snow deepened all the time, my joints stiff and fingers numb. The howling wind was worst of all. Even with the flaps of my cap pulled down, the sound deafened my ears and my senses, making it difficult to think. My teeth chattered so hard that I thought they might crack. I took a deep breath of icy air and forced myself onward.

I had lost all track of time when my hand struck something— something manmade—a corner. The bay whinnied loudly as if she too sensed our impending salvation. I kept my body close to the structure. The horse pranced closer until her nose nuzzled my head. Feeling my way along, I came to a wooden shutter—a window. Farther on, I rounded yet another corner. Farther on, there was a door.

I knocked. There was no answer. I pounded. The howling made it impossible to hear any movement inside. At last, the latch lowered, and the hinges creaked, swinging open a crack. A narrow slit of light from inside glittered across the snow, and a woman from within peered at me.

"Heaven's sakes!"

"Who is it?" a voice called from inside.

"Adam," the woman said.

Chapter 14

The Narrative of Silas Whittemore
1828

M usic, laughter, and shouts echoed eerily through the empty alleyways between taverns. A dog, a hideous mongrel, bone with ragged edges of raw meat hanging from his mouth, raced past, nearly barreling into Eve but swerving at just the right moment. After it came another, growling and tearing after him. Dust plumed after them, and Eve put a handkerchief to her nose.

The rocky island shore of Michillimackinac was crusted in French bateaux and birchbark canoes like the one in which my wife had just arrived. A dirt road, extending in either direction, was lined with frame houses and shops: a bakery, a fish merchant, a blacksmith. Beyond, the island rose up steadily, and a long, white limestone fort crested the top of the first ridge. We were nearing this fort when I saw Mr. Gauthier's rowers, attired in long, plain white linen shirts, colorful sashes, and bare lower limbs, hoisting three large trunks from the bowels of their bateaux. They were Eve's. Too many and too heavy to carry by hand, I would return for them later.

Mr. Gauthier waved, an enormous grin on his face.

I led the way farther along the coast where only a few scattered houses remained.

"There will be rain tonight, certain," said I.

Eve remained silent.

As the child struggled to keep pace, a sudden gust of wind nearly bowled her over. Seeing my daughter's difficulty, I chuckled and lifted her. "We'll get you your sea legs in no time."

As soon as the girl was in my arms, tears formed and threatened to burst into a flood. I hurriedly deposited her back upon the ground. I wanted none of that, especially at a time like this. She ran ahead until she was out of reach of both Eve and myself.

"Last I saw her," said I, "she was but a year old. She must be above three now."

"Then it should be no wonder she shrinks from you so," replied my wife.

"I'll not soon forget," said I, "that you disregarded my instructions. How dare you accompany that man. My men were to come for you, if only you'd waited. They'll be none too happy to discover that my wife has forged ahead into the wilderness with Company men and that their journey has been in vain. It's not a convenient time."

"It's never a convenient time," said Eve. "Mr. Gauthier was kind enough to offer me passage when he discovered we were journeying to the same place."

"I've no doubt he was." I shook my head. Best to accept the inevitable.

"It was not my wish to come to this godforsaken place, was it?" continued Eve. "If only you had stayed in New York and continued working as a clerk—"

"That would have made you happy, would it?" said I. "I will make a fortune in fur, Eve. When I do, we may go anywhere you please."

"This is no place for a lady," said Eve. "Surely you knew that before deceiving me into coming."

"I? Deceive you?" I laughed. "I told you this was no place for a woman and a child. It was you who insisted upon joining me."

"I was happy enough to be left alone," said she.

Even knowing my wife as I did, I could hardly believe what she said. Best to speak of it no more. What was done was done.

A footpath led from the road up a steep hill. I followed this and came upon a rude cabin sending smoke from its small chimney into the air. My wife, now ahead, reached it first.

"Hallooo!" shouted I.

A man in a black surtout and a white stock lifted the blanket that hung in place of a door. "You've brought your family at last, I see."

"Come, Eve, this is the man of whom I wrote to you. He's offered to house us for the evening, and he will accompany us to the mainland. He is taking up missionary work with the natives."

He bowed. "You're very welcome."

Eve stood stock still. "I'll not enter that cabin," she said, ferocity exuding from every feature.

The missionary looked quizzically at me. I regarded my wife.

"You journey on your own through the wilderness with men of low character, and you will not spend the night where I make provision for you?"

"No."

"You will," said I.

"I will not." She folded her arms, the immense puffs of silk on her shoulders coming forward like two boulders.

"Our home on the mainland," said I, "will be no better than this cabin. Perhaps worse. You may as well get used to the fact."

"Take me back to your friend, Mr. Douglas. At least his home was decent."

"He's no friend," said I. "He's a man of business. I've no wish to ingratiate myself with him."

"Then I remain here," said Eve, glaring at the bare structure.

"Very well. Stay here if you like, but the child will go indoors.

As will you when you've felt enough cold." Already the sun was falling behind the stone face beyond the cabin, and the breeze coming off the lake made currents of frigid air.

Eve said nothing, but remained with her arms crossed and daintily took a seat upon a low stump; I deposited the child with the missionary.

"I'll return in the evening."

"Very good," said he.

It would be quite the job getting Eve's trunks to the cabin, but it must be done. Before rounding the curve in the path, I gave one last glance behind. My child and the missionary had already disappeared into the cabin, but Eve remained stubbornly on the stump. I heaved a sigh. There was nothing for it.

Chapter 15

The Narrative of Adam Bolton

"Come in," Mrs. Haworth said, taking my arm and leading me into the warm house. The dim light in the hall momentarily blinded me.

"My horse," said I.

As if invited, the bay's muzzle came sniffing and snorting over my shoulder. Mrs. Haworth leapt back and then laughed. She took hold of the bridle and motioned me inside.

"I'll stable your horse," she said, moving to put on her boots.

"I can stable her," said I, stubbornly holding my place. "You oughtn't go out."

"Very well," she said, eyeing me curiously. "Follow the house that way." She pointed toward the back. "You'll find a rope that leads to the barn."

I found and followed it. Once inside, I took a deep breath of air. It smelled familiarly of sweet hay blended with manure. The Shorthorn, being unexpectedly disturbed, lowed loudly, and the Haworth's Morgan, several hands shorter than the bay, shoved her head over the stall door to see who had interrupted her dinner. It was a small barn, easily a quarter of the size of mine, but it was large enough to store the Haworth's buggy and sleigh. I laid my fish, which had been clutched inside my coat, at the door. I led the bay into one of the two empty stalls and gave her an ample supply of oats and hay. A pail of partly frozen water rested against the wall. I broke the ice and gave her a drink, passing a reassuring hand over her neck.

"Well done, girl," said I.

At the door of the barn, I knelt and offered up a prayer of thanks to God for saving me. As I did so, I was overcome by how near I had been to death. In the storm, I had felt so certain of Heaven, but now that the danger was past, I wondered if I had only deceived myself. Had I been too bold in claiming the promises of Heaven? I humbled myself before God and begged forgiveness for my pride.

At last, I took my fish and returned to the house, where I dug out a hole in the snow next to the veranda steps. It was unlikely any animal would come to take the fish in such a storm.

Again knocking, I was allowed inside. Penny was at the door waiting this time, and she nearly tumbled into me in her excitement to let me in. My eyes adjusted to the light as I shuffled off my frozen boots and snow-crusted goatskin.

Mrs. Haworth took my coat. "You must be frozen. What took so long? I was about to come after you," she said, tenderly placing a blanket over my shoulders. "Come." She led me into the dining room off the hall. "Sit by the fire."

Inside that house, I felt I had somehow walked into a new age. I had rarely been in other homes, and the difference was striking. The dining floor was covered by an ingrain rug with repeating patterns of roses. Against one wall was a sideboard exhibiting cut glass and several fine china pieces. Above the deep brown wainscot, the walls were slate blue with a pendulum clock hung upon one and an ornately framed painting of kittens tumbling over a ball of string hung upon another. There were no fewer than three windows, all of which were covered in heavy, navy window dressings. Care had been taken with every detail. Light and life and warmth radiated from every corner.

Mrs. Haworth led me, now bashful, to the chair before the fire. The heat struck my face and benumbed fingers. The dryness, after the harsh, wet air outside, momentarily stifled me. Penny, who had disappeared, returned with a book in her hand and plopped in the chair opposite. She opened the volume only to stare over the top.

"Don't stare," her mother said.

Penny dropped her eyes. I stood and stepped aside from the blaze. "I don't wish to be rude, Mrs. Haworth, but it's too warm for me near the fire."

"I'd have thought you'd be frozen after being out of doors in that snow," she said. "Well then. Take a seat over here." She patted the chair next to Penny and bustled toward the door set in the back wall of the room. "You must be famished. There's some stew left over from dinner. And I'll make you some hot tea..." she called through the closing door.

Penny, despite her mother's instruction, was again staring at me curiously. My face, already bright from the hot fire, grew brighter still. I took a seat next to her, sitting a little taller and pretending not to notice. Instead, I looked about the room and immediately caught our reflection in the mirror above the mantelpiece. I could not help but make comparison between my wet, dirty, homemade clothing, and Penny's perfectly ironed blue frock —her soft, plump complexion and my taut, lean one. What must it be like, to be raised in such a place? Even in my limited experience, I could not help but compare hers to the life I was accustomed to in my bare, frigid house.

A steaming bowl of stew and a slice of delicate white bread were placed before me. Penny watched expectantly as I took up a spoonful. Never had I tasted anything like it. There were bits of venison so tender they seemed to melt in my mouth—turnips, cooked just to firmness, pearl barley, and onions. It was indescribably different from anything I had ever tasted of Mother's. I took up the bread, which Mrs. Haworth had generously slathered in butter; something I never tasted apart from the rare moments at Minister Judd's parsonage with Mother, when he had scraped a thin layer acrost dried toast before handing it to me. Yet, as I took a bite, I first regarded nothing but the bread. It yielded easily to my teeth—soft, yet chewy—dense, yet light. Only after did I note the butter, rich and fatty; somehow it seemed sinful.

The food invigorated me and roused me from my ruminations. Mrs. Haworth, hands on her hips, was in the midst of speaking.

"You'll have to spend the night," she said. "I'll go upstairs and make up a bed. Penny, please bring Adam his tea."

Mrs. Haworth's footsteps receded. I wished Penny would look someplace else.

"Why do you always stare?" asked I.

"I don't know," Penny replied.

"Perhaps you could read your book? It's difficult to eat while being watched."

She laughed, then abruptly disappeared into the kitchen. Relieved to have momentary respite from her bright eyes, I savored another spoonful of the stew. No sooner had Penny disappeared than she reappeared with a silver tea caddy containing white teacups and saucers covered in delicate blue flowered patterns. She placed it and knelt on the chair, tucking her knees up under her so she could face me.

"Do you know our schoolfellows call your place Haggard House?" she asked.

"Yes," replied I, startled at the directness of her question.

"Does it trouble you?"

"No."

"Why not?"

I swallowed slowly so that I could formulate a reply. "People may call it what they will."

"That's not an answer," Penny said.

"If someone called your house Haggard House, would it trouble you?"

"Yes," she said.

"Why?"

"Because it would be unfair. My house is not haggard at all."

"I'm accustomed to it," said I.

"To the name or the place?"

My body warmed, as did my spirit toward Penny. Yet, I could not forget her harsh words in the woods. "I heard you," said I. "Last week, in your fort with Ingrid." I thought at least Penny would blush, perhaps even deny it. She did neither.

"Oh," she said.

She did not avert her gaze. What else was there to say on the matter? She simply didn't know better.

"What are you reading?" asked I.

Penny handed the volume to me. The title was *Frankenstein*, and I perused its contents, stopping now and again to read a paragraph or two. The opening letters in the book indicated it was some sort of adventure novel. However, as I continued my examination, particularly upon the fifth chapter, I discerned that the contents of the story were blasphemous, that the story gave into man's hands the power to create life. I slammed it closed, my mind contaminated by the foul words which I had just read.

"Does your mother know this is what you're reading?" asked I.

"Of course," Penny said, with a look of surprise. "It's from Father's collection. He brought them with us from New York."

I was too appalled to know what to say. I was horrified by the thought of Penny's mother allowing her to read such things. I recalled the last bit of the hymn I had memorized from *A Token for Children*: "Lord, may I hate to walk or dwell, With wicked children here; That I may not be sent to Hell, Where none but sinners are." Surely, Penny did not realize the consequences of reading such evil.

"You oughtn't read such things," said I. "You ought to read your Bible."

"Why?" Her expression was one of complete ignorance of her wrong-doing.

"You don't wish to be sent to Hell, do you?"

Penny laughed, but sensing my seriousness, her expression sobered. The conversation was cut short, however, by her mother bustling back into the room, hair flying in wisps about her face from recent effort.

"Now, are you warming up?" Mrs. Haworth asked. She put a hand on my forehead, and I stiffened at the unexpected touch. "It seems you are. I've laid out one of my husband's old night-shirts upon the bed so you may sleep in something clean and dry."

I was embarrassed to receive so much attention and affection, especially considering my recent discovery of Penny's book, of the depths of heathenism within the Haworth household. Their warmth moved me, yet I loathed myself for the feeling, coming as it did from such sinners.

Mrs. Haworth suggested, as I was finished with my meal, we adjourn to the drawing room. Again, I was struck with the difference between our residences. Our scant collection of books had only one lowly shelf. Here, the entirety of the back wall was covered in bookcases, containing not only books but also fine vases and plates upon stands. There was a pianoforte against one wall, which Mrs. Haworth informed me was rarely played. There were, what seemed to me, a dozen chairs and sofas, and we took our seats upon those closest to the roaring fire.

Mrs. Haworth produced a chessboard and suggested that Penny and I play. She made more tea and insisted I take it with a lump of sugar. It was like nothing I had ever tasted, perhaps apart from the apple pie the Haworths had brought to Haggard House, and so unlike Mother's bitter tea, served on Saturday afternoons during Minister Judd's visits.

Mother believed games to be frivolous and never kept any, so

Mrs. Haworth had to teach me the movements of the pieces and the general strategy; I lost quickly, playing first with her. Then I played with Penny and lost again. I was embarrassed to lose to a girl, and one younger than me, at that. Upon a third game, I began to catch on, and after that even won once. Mrs. Haworth heartily congratulated me, and even Penny was pleased I'd won. I sat a little straighter, cheeks flushed with pride.

The evening was the most pleasant I had ever spent. I was even beginning to forget the evil of having such godless companions.

However, I could not completely forget it. Upon my request, Mrs. Haworth took down the family Bible from its shelf, and I read them a selection from Matthew 7, particularly dwelling upon verses fifteen through nineteen: "...Beware of false prophets...every tree that bringeth not forth good fruit is hewn down, and cast into the fire." Then, further, the parable of the wise man whose house was spared when the floods came because it was built upon a rock. Penny and Mrs. Haworth listened politely as my voice rang out, and I had the distinct impression that God's Word made some impact upon them.

Afterwards, I made my way up the stairs, taking the Bible with me. Mrs. Haworth said I might keep it for the evening for my private study. She had lit a fire in the bedroom, and I was amazed at the warmth. How could such kind people be destined for eternal damnation?

I knelt upon the floor near the bed and prayed. Then I took up the Bible, pacing and reading silently. However, to my great shame, though it was still early, I became fatigued and could not focus upon the words. More than once, I felt my head nodding forward, almost falling asleep even as I moved. At last, after nearly tumbling into the fire, I lay down on the four-post bed upon the feather mattress.

I had never slept upon such a thing. My limbs felt strangely different, and I realized with surprise that it was because I felt not an ache or pain anywhere. I pondered my forthcoming interview with Mother. I knew she would not be anxious, as she had implicit faith in both God and me for my safe return. Nevertheless, nothing good could come of an evening spent at the Haworth home. I should not be in a household of such sinners. I briefly considered spending the night in the barn in order to redeem myself and soften the blow to Mother, but when I heard the howling of the wind, even I could not resist warmth on such a night.

Instead, to put my mind upon Godly things, I recalled the day of my salvation.

Chapter 16

The Narrative of Adam Bolton

5 Years Prior

E ven as a child, I detested Minister Judd's visits. During these weekly interviews, the minister catechized me, and then banished me out of doors to keep from being underfoot. Afterwards, I often played near the kitchen garden, keeping close to the house, and as a result, often heard the conversation occurring inside—Minister Judd's booming voice clearly audible through the thin walls and Mother's, though not as clear, decipherable. I had no fear of punishment for eavesdropping; Mother told me I might listen as much as I liked, for I might receive some edification. On one of these occasions, about a year after I had been breeched, I heard the following conversation as I played near the back door:

"You know, Sarai," Minister Judd's voice lowered, "Farmer McNeil saw him cast out of Bard's Tavern last evening."

Mother's chair scraped the floor, and I heard the rhythmic stamp of her feet as she stood and paced. I knew I ought not to listen to whatever was to follow. I was forbidden to speak or hear of the old village drunkard. I was never certain why, but always presumed it was due to his oft repeated sin. Yet, though I knew Mother would not approve of my hearing this particular conversation, I could not pull myself away. For the first time, I found myself consumed with curiosity regarding the man.

Minister Judd continued. "He saw him again this morning, still asleep, slumped against one of those houses in the alley near Peter's shop. Had it been winter, he would have died."

Mother's chair scraped across the floor again as she resumed her seat. "'Thou shalt be filled with drunkenness and sorrow, with the cup of astonishment and desolation.'"

"Indeed," the minister said.

I knew Minister Judd well enough, even at my tender age, to know that he hung his head at Mother's words, humbling himself preparatory to giving her counsel.

"Perhaps, Sarai," he said. "Perhaps there is yet hope for him. I would like to propose..." There was a pause.

"Go on," said Mother.

"I would like to propose that you offer more—only a small portion more, mind you—to the church. And with this special offering, I shall collect goods for a basket of necessities for the man. I will engage Mrs. Fernsby to take the basket to him once weekly." He paused, and receiving no resistance, went on as if the fact was settled. "In so doing, you shall heap coals of fire upon his head. His bodily needs, at least, will be cared for, and this shall purchase him time. Time in which he may yet be able to redeem his soul."

Mother again stood, and I heard her suddenly near where I listened. Frightened of being caught within hearing, I hurriedly withdrew to the woods. Whatever my confused ideas of the man, I was not to be fully enlightened on this day.

The heat, even under the trees, was stifling, so I followed the footpath to a small lake, about an acre in size, hidden in the woods. The surface of the water was covered in places with bright green algae and lily pads. Reeds and cattails grew in a half-moon at the edge of the lake farthest from me. It was an excellent place for capturing frogs and watching tiny fish. A flat rock rested half a dozen paces into the water, and I removed my shoes and stockings, rolled up my trousers, and walked through the mucky water to it. Leeches clung to my legs, but I didn't mind. I sat upon the rock and removed them one at a time, sliding a fingernail under their mouths until they let loose. Then I broke a bit of reed and twirled it in my hands, scanning the water for frogs.

A soft breeze picked up, cooling the back of my neck. Birds twittered in the surrounding trees, lulling me into reverie. I had rested there for perhaps quarter of an hour when I saw a large green frog clamber onto a lily pad a dozen paces away. The frog filled his neck with air and croaked. I stood stealthily, balancing. The frog's back was to me, so I had a good chance of catching it.

I cautiously slid into the water and muck. Half a dozen steps and the bottom changed to coarse sand. I had never ventured this far. Mother had told me the lake was deep in places and not to wade farther than where I could feel mud. Yet, I was only a few paces from the frog, and the water barely touched the top of my trousers.

The frog tensed, sensing my movement. I leapt forward, hands outstretched. The next moment, the frog was in my hand. Yet where was the firm sand? I kicked and thrashed, still tightly clasping the frog. I couldn't reach the surface: there was nothing but water all round. I opened my hand and struggled to the surface. I gasped, shouting as loud as my lungs were able.

"Help!"

Again, I went under. I opened my eyes but saw nothing but blur. All was terror. My legs and arms pumped wildly, to no avail. I could not near the surface, and I could no longer hold my breath. I opened my mouth and inhaled, flooding my lungs with muddy water. As I looked upward, a glint of sun reached through the murk.

A hand grasped my arm and yanked.

I couldn't breathe the now plentiful air. My rescuer struck me hard on the back. A trickle dribbled from my mouth. I saw the dirt and the sky and the pond where my feet still lay. There was another strike to my back. I coughed, and mud came spluttering out. Then I retched and coughed so much that I could scarcely breathe between. This all seemed to take many hours, but it was all over within moments.

I looked up to see my rescuer. It was Mother, and near her stood Minister Judd.

"My son. My son," said she. "It's all right. I'm here." She clutched me to her and held me with tenderness I had never before felt. "I nearly lost you."

An unspeakable warmth spread through me at Mother's outbreak of love, but I was still too overcome to speak.

"I nearly lost you," repeated she. "And that without God!" She clutched me tighter still. "Oh Lord, thank you for preserving my son so that he might now call you Savior. Thank you, Lord. Thank you. Thank you." She grasped my face so hard it hurt. "Adam, promise me. Promise me you will pledge your life to the Lord. You must. God has saved you so that you may accomplish His purpose here. Do you not see? He has saved you for Himself. You must pledge yourself now. You will do it?"

I felt with absolute certainty that this was my path. Had God not rescued me? Did I not then owe Him my life, my devotion? A kind of ecstasy coursed my veins. I felt a closeness to God that I had never before experienced, despite my many hours of reading and prayer.

"I will, Mother." Coated in muck, I separated from her and clambered to my knees. At first, I was uncertain what to say; but then I recalled Mother's words and applied them to my short prayer. "Lord, I pledge myself to you. I pledge you my life."

Mother again wrapped her arms round me, and I felt her warmth through my cold skin.

"Oh Lord, hear his prayer," called she. She stood and took me by the hand. "Come, chosen of the Lord."

"Well done, my son," Minister Judd said. "Well done."

Chapter 17

The Narrative of Adam Bolton

Just before dawn, I searched and found paper and an inkwell on a desk in the small study, and I wrote a note thanking the Haworth women for their hospitality. After feeding the mare and collecting my fish, now frozen hard from the cold, I set off across the deep snows. I would return for the horse when the paths became passible, as I intimated in the note.

All the way to Haggard House, I was in turmoil. Mother would undoubtedly recognize the necessity of staying at the Haworth home in the midst of a blizzard. However, I had no reason, no necessity for associating with them in conversation, in play. Even reading the Word to them would not be enough to atone for that.

What was I to do? Certainly, I could not lie.

When I arrived, I saw that Pa had cleared a path to the barn and was just returning to the house. His expression was anxious, but upon seeing me, a broad smile crossed his face, and he waved in relief.

I waved back, shouting, "All is well!" I did not wait for him to reach me but, after removing my boots, went directly inside, for I dreaded my interview with Mother, and I wished it over as soon as possible.

She was settled at the table with our copper kettle, scrubbing away at it with a cloth and fine, red powder—sharp scent of vinegar obliterating the usual odors. Her elbow pumped vigorously up and down, but the cloth immediately dropped from her hand when she saw me.

"*He* has seen fit you should live then," said she, so low I could hardly hear it.

She closed her eyes and pressed brick-dust coated hands together in silent prayer. Then she looked back up, and I knew that the next fear to be relieved was for my soul.

"Have you kept to the straight and narrow?" asked she.

"Yes," said I, though, for the first time, I was uncertain whether this was the case.

Her expression was the same as ever, the only hint of anxiety that her lips were more tightly drawn than usual.

"Where have you weathered the storm?"

My innards churned. I could not say I had stayed with McDonnell. It was a falsehood and easily discovered. An image, Penny's hair, her smile as I won the game of chess, flashed before me. It was then that I knew I must keep Penny hidden in the same place as her gift. But how to do it? If I were to close my eyes in order to build a new room in my mind, Mother would note it, and it would be as much as to confess my guilt. Yet, that momentary flash of Penny gave me my way out. There was no need to close my eyes.

Mother's image blurred. I was on the veranda of the house within my mind. Penny was there too, smiling at me. I took her hand and led her up the steps to the sleeping attic. I unlocked the room where the chest with her things was kept and led her forward. She looked at me reproachfully. I avoided her eyes and locked the door, her inside. I was safe.

I suddenly realized that Mother was shaking me by the shoulder.

"Adam, what is it? Are you unwell?" Her expression was terrified.

"Yes. Yes," said I.

She appeared relieved. The door opened behind us—it was Pa returning.

"You have not answered my question," said Mother, but her tone had gentled.

"I spent the night at the Haworths."

Her eyes grew large. "I see. And did you...associate with them? Or have you kept yourself separate?"

"I read to them the Word of God."

"That is well and good," said she, "But you still have not answered."

"I read to them the Word of God, and once I had warmed myself, I spent the night in the barn with McDonnell's mare. I did not even sleep under the same roof." There was a squeezing sensation in my mind. I wished it to stop.

"You've done well," said Mother.

I had once seen a steam engine, a fascinating site. Before starting off, the train had shuddered, steam puffing gently at first, then in solid sheets, sending the train into quick motion. I was like that now. I had been still as stock, but as I inhaled, the breath revived me, sending me back into motion.

"Here," said I, proffering my fish to Pa. "It turns out I am a prize ice fisher after all."

He laughed, examining my catch. "Why don't you cook this up, Sarai," he said. "Some fine fish our son has caught."

Mother continued to gaze at me for a moment, then nodded and took the fish.

Chapter 18

The Narrative of Penny Haworth

I bounded out of bed. It was quite cold in my room, so much so that my breath curled in white mist from my nostrils. Dressed in a thick night-gown, copper hair wild about my face, I lifted the heavy window dressing and cast open the shutter blinds, revealing large bits of fluffy snow falling from the sky. The ground, two days since the blizzard, was still stacked thick with it.

Adam's appearance that day was the most exciting happening in my memory. I had been surprised and saddened to discover that he had left before dawn. Yet, I was certain that whatever it was that had kept him from regarding me as his friend would no longer be an obstacle. And today, the day following Adam's departure, my mind was still full of the unexpected pleasure of his visit.

"The snow is falling again!" I called as I entered the kitchen, now dressed for the day. I was wrapped in my thick wool shawl, and I held the pail of slops, preparatory to emptying out of doors.

Mother was busy stoking the fire in the range.

"Did you collect the slops from my room?" she asked. "I had to take them out myself yesterday because you'd forgotten."

I paused. Mother rested her hands on her hips and shook her

head as I turned and plodded back to the stairs. Presently, I returned.

"I've got it," I said, grinning and holding up the pail, now visibly heavier.

I opened the back kitchen door, revealing more falling snow, and stepped just outside, holding out my tongue to catch the flakes.

"It's freezing, Penny. Close the door," Mother called.

"Isn't it glorious?" I did a little skip in the snow.

"Close the door!"

I laughed but then obeyed. I emptied the slops in the privy, then made my way to the barn. McDonnell's mare, still our guest due to the impassible snow, whinnied and kicked at the stall as I entered. I ran a hand over its neck. The mare quieted, nickering gently and breathing great puffs of air as it ducked its head over my shoulder.

When I returned to the house and washed for the day, I found a thick stack of pancakes waiting for me at the dining table. I lifted the earthenware jug and flooded them with maple syrup.

"Not so much," Mother remonstrated. She placed the jug out of reach and took a seat. "Slow down. Those pancakes will be like lead in your stomach if you eat them like that."

I paused my fork, already in my mouth, and instead of taking a tremendous bite, took only three-quarters of a tremendous bite. I finished only half the stack before springing from my seat and skipping to the kitchen to collect my lunch tin.

"You've not finished your breakfast," Mother called.

I was too excited to see Adam at school to finish. I heard Mother sigh and clear the plates.

"Goodbye," I called from the hall.

Stomping my feet into my leather boots, I hurried the buttons closed with my button-hook, collected my mantle, and swung open the door.

I screamed and clapped a hand over my mouth. A severed

deer head swung before me, hung from the roof of the veranda. The ears were stiff, alert, and the tongue protruded from its mouth. Blood had hardened across the black nose and neck stump.

Mother appeared at the door. "As I live and breathe!"

I stood, frozen to the spot. The falling snow had covered any footprints the culprit might have left.

"Gunther," Mother proclaimed. She slipped the cord off the deer's neck and held the head uncomfortably. "He's always been the worse of the two. Clearly, it's no use speaking to his father." She clasped me with her free arm. "We'll speak nothing of this and let his prank go unnoticed. Are you all right?"

I tried to shake the chill that had filled me and attempted a weak smile. "Yes, I'm fine."

"Go ahead to school then. I'll take care of the head."

Without another word, I hurried off. The brightness of my spirit was dampened by the bodiless deer. It was cruel. Certainly, Gunther was responsible. Not two months ago, Gunther was discovered to have mutilated a deer on an old path in the woods. The animal hadn't been carved for meat but nailed to a thick board, and its eyes had been gouged out and its tongue removed. McDonnell had found the deer before the wolves had. Gunther had denied doing it, of course; and he might have been believed, were it not for the fact that several of the older boys at school had bragged about Gunther doing a similar feat in the summer months to another poor rabbit.

I paused outside Ingrid's house. Jakob, as usual, had his nose pressed up against the window. I wondered if he ever did anything else. Ingrid appeared at the door, flaxen hair parted and braided neatly and tied with blue ribbons which peeped out from her hood.

"Ready?" I asked.

"Ready," Ingrid said.

Jakob bounded out the door.

"Hurry," Ingrid said. "Yakob been mean all day. He vill try to catch us."

We broke into a run, Jakob falling further behind, though he ran as fast as his short legs could carry him. At last, when we looked back, it appeared he had given up, for he walked slumped in disappointment.

I decided not to share the incident of the deer head with Ingrid. Even if I'd felt inclined to, it would have been difficult to explain with her imperfect understanding of English.

However, by nooning, word of the grotesque discovery had spread throughout the school, details of the incident repeated within reach of my own ears whilst starting a game of pickup sticks with Ingrid at my desk.

"I svear! I saw it from te vindow! Tere vas deer head hanging before Penny door." The words came from a boy with curly, flaxen-colored hair—Jakob.

I despised him. He would say anything to gain attention.

As he continued his tale, I searched the room for Adam. He had not gone out of doors as usual but had remained at his desk with his lunch. He looked up, and I was certain he had heard, for his face turned pale with anger.

Ingrid interrupted. "Is true?"

Everyone was listening now, and I was only happy the schoolmaster was in the privy.

"It must be," one of Farmer McNeil's boys interjected.

I remained silent, though I might as well have told the truth, for all the good it did. The whole group concurred that Gunther was the culprit. His lack of presence seemed to confirm the fact, although, in truth, he often missed school.

Presently, as if summoned, Gunther appeared, ambling into the schoolyard. Apparently, he had decided to play truant for only half the day. I leapt to my feet, intending to confront him; but Ingrid's firm hand grasped my shoulder.

"Don't," she whispered.

Everyone in the schoolhouse flocked to the windows and stared at Gunther's slinking figure.

I rushed out the door, breaking Ingrid's hold on me, the others following close behind.

"What?" he snarled, as he drew closer.

No one replied. What exactly I intended to do when I reached him, I wasn't sure. I was an arm's length away when I thought better of it, but it was too late, and I skidded in the slippery snow. Gunther met me with a hard fist to the stomach. I lay on the ground, breath knocked wholly from me.

"Always thinking you're better than us," Gunther said, rubbing his fist.

For a moment, I thought I might die. Then air suddenly rushed back in, and I took a deep gasp. I hardly heard the commotion above me, but I saw Adam's fist. Gunther was down on the ground just next to me, and I turned my head to see Adam kneeling over him, pounding until specks of red spattered the white snow.

All I could think of or see was Adam. Adam was scooping snow to wipe the blood from his fist; Adam was offering his hand; Adam was pulling me up.

"Are you hurt?" he asked.

I shook my head, still catching my breath. He immediately released my hand. The still figure in the snow stirred, then stood, holding a limp arm, nose dripping blood. Gunther slunk away, glaring vehemently.

Adam hurried toward the schoolhouse, and Ingrid rushed to my side.

"All right? Tere iss blood!"

Looking down, I saw bits of melting snow mixed with red from the hand Adam had held. It was from Adam, not me.

"I'm all right. Let's go inside," I said.

Mr. Caskell was none the wiser. Most of the students tended to think Gunther had gotten what was coming to him. And those who thought otherwise were now too frightened of Adam to speak up.

I settled myself in my seat but couldn't slow my heavy breathing or my rapidly pounding heart. I felt Adam's presence. I knew that he too sensed me. The other students, and even Mr. Caskell, grew blurred; as I turned back, I saw Adam's figure clearly.

Whatever was within me that made up my essence, whether it was my soul or something else, rose before me like a white fog. And Adam's figure, whatever made up his essence rose too like black smoke. The two joined, creating a gray mist. Just as suddenly, the vision vanished, and I was left to wonder whether I had seen anything more than fog from the other students' breath.

Chapter 19

The Narrative of Adam Bolton

The first term of my schooling had ended without further event. The evening, now lengthened by the first day of summer, was still warm; and the sun was just beginning to set on the western edge of the horizon. Pa hitched the Belgian to the cart, and I climbed in. Behind us was the beginnings of a house, neatly framed above stonework.

"It was a good day's labor, Adam," Pa said, giya-ing the Belgian into motion. "You'll be an excellent carpenter someday if you continue as you are." He clapped a reassuring hand on my shoulder, then removed it.

"Yes, sir," replied I.

I knew carpentry to be a noble profession, perhaps the noblest. Joseph, Jesus' earthly father, had been a carpenter. The business was a common theme, repeated for as long as I was old enough to join him in his work. Yet somehow, I felt as though it was not the path for me.

The wagon creaked and groaned and rocked its progress across the ground. We jolted along in silence until we reached Whittemore's Prairie. An owl called a lonely *whoo* across the tall grasses. Presently, there was a low, whining noise. I was about to ask what it might be when Pa lifted a finger to his lips. He pulled on the reigns, and the cart came to a halt. Again, there was the noise. He cautiously lifted his rifle and clambered from the wagon. I followed at a short distance.

The grass was trampled down a ways, and along this path were drops of blood. There was a low growling sound as we neared. It must be a wolf, perhaps wounded. Pa poised the rifle, then suddenly lowered it, stooped, and waved me forward. It was a black bull-terrier with a grizzled, gray face. Its throat was badly gashed, with wounds along its legs and body, and its left ear had been completely ripped away.

Pa's placid features became angry. "This is Fowler's work. They've been holding dog fights behind the saloon." The dog whimpered and laid his head down. "We'll take it home. If he recovers, he'll be yours, Adam."

The bull-terrier seemed to understand the speech, for it rolled its eye in my direction, as if to take stock of me.

"But Mother won't allow it," said I, looking down at the wounded creature in the grass.

"He'll make a good watchdog," Pa said, "and even Sarai won't oppose that...so long as he minds his manners." Pa stood from his crouched position. "Bring him along."

I paused reluctantly. Nothing had ever belonged to me before, and I was not so certain as Pa that Mother would allow it. I would rather not bring the beast home at all if she would make us return him to the field.

"Go on," Pa said.

I laid my hand on the unbloodied portion of the dog's black coat and patted. The dog tolerated my touch and even closed his eyes as if he enjoyed it. I gingerly lifted him and returned to the wagon. Pa took the dog, allowing me to scramble into my seat. I held him in my arms like an oversized baby, and we continued on our way. By the time we reached Haggard House, the dog had not moved nor made a sound for many minutes. He appeared on the verge of death.

Mother stood waiting for us on the front veranda.

"Go on to the barn," Pa said. "I'll speak to your mother."

I had followed his instruction thus far, and there was no point in going back. Perhaps he would be successful. I slid down from the cart and made my way to the barn with the dog as Pa went to Mother to offer explanation.

I could not hear what he said, but Mother responded, "Very well."

A sigh of relief escaped. At least she would not turn the beast away immediately. The goats saw me and chased me into the barn, and I hurriedly closed them into their stall. They bleated angrily for their fodder. They would have to wait.

Pa soon returned with pails of water. While I bathed the bull-terrier's wounds with my handkerchief, Pa said, "You may care for the dog tonight. I'll complete your chores."

I looked up at him gratefully, and he smiled.

Mother even appeared with a worn linen night-shirt for me to dress the wounds. She stood for several moments, arms drawn across her chest, monitoring my progress.

"He'll likely die in the night," said she. "Then we'll have a dead dog to bury in addition to our other work."

I knew she was thinking of the time this would take from her devotions.

"But he may live," said I. "We might pray for him?"

Mother's drawn lips relaxed somewhat. "Yes. We'll pray for him tonight." So saying, she turned and left the barn.

Pa finished the chores and returned to the house, leaving me alone. I finished dressing the dog's wounds and gently lifted its head, trying to wake him enough to drink. The bull-terrier's eyes remained closed, so I opened his jaw and poured water onto his tongue. He swallowed feebly. Encouraged, I continued the process until the dog had drunk perhaps a small cupful.

It was late by this time, so I returned to the house and ate a cold supper. After the nightly ritual of pacing and reading, Mother allowed me to return to monitor the dog. I took a small piece of venison which I had saved from dinner. The bull-terrier showed no progress either for better or worse. Again, I lifted his head in an attempt to wake him, but he would not rouse. I placed the venison before his nose, but that also produced no response. When I placed the meat on his tongue, it simply fell to the ground. I ran my hand across the few patches of fur that had not been gnashed and inwardly said a prayer, begging the Lord to allow the beast to live. Then I returned to the house and tried my best to sleep.

When morning dawned, my first thought was of the dog. I leapt from bed, hurried into my clothes, and rushed to the barn. Pa was already there, stooping over the creature.

"How is he?" asked I, breathlessly. I didn't dare to look down in case the dog was dead.

"See for yourself," Pa said, stepping aside.

The bull-terrier's eyes were open, and the bit of venison was gone. His tongue hung on the ground as he panted, and he looked at me, gratefully—or at least, so I fancied. I ran to the dog and wrapped my arms about him. It was perhaps the first time I had ever allowed myself to be so swept away by such warm feelings.

I brought the wooden pail, which had a little water remaining, and tilted it sideways so the dog could easily drink. The bull-terrier lapped it up in mere moments. I laughed and squirmed as he turned from the pail to my arm, covering me with his slobbering tongue.

"It looks like you have a guard dog," Pa said, laughing.

The Lord had answered! I hurriedly sent up a prayer of thanks for preserving the life of the bull-terrier. I brought more venison, which the dog swallowed in great gulps, then I set off with Pa to continue work on the new house.

Chapter 20

The Narrative of Penny Haworth

I dashed to the parlor window and scanned the street.

"Come back," Mother said in exasperation. My sampler remained starkly white against the deep burgundy sofa on which she sat. "You've hardly made progress," she continued, lifting it and glancing at my tangle of stitches on the back of the fabric. So far, the design consisted of a complicated border of flowers, only half completed, perhaps not as even as it ought to have been. Amidst this was to be a poem, but I had not gotten nearly that far.

"I advised you to choose a simpler pattern," she said. "You might have done a plain border and the alphabet. But now you've chosen it, you must finish it."

Mother was correct, of course. I had picked a design that was far above my abilities, and it wasn't the first time. I was always rushing headlong at things.

Adam, for one of his strange, unknown reasons, had finally agreed to play with me but had insisted that it only happen when school was out and summer arrived. I had begged Mother to let me out the previous three days, but she hadn't allowed it. It was now the fourth day of summer, and I was torn by the thought that Adam might have gone to our agreed upon location and missed me. I couldn't bear staying indoors for another hour of work.

"May I go out? Just for an hour or two? I will finish working on my sampler afterward. There will still be enough light." I gave my brightest, most hopeful look.

Mother looked dismally at my tangled stitching. "Very well."

Leaping from the window, I hugged and kissed her. "Thank you. Thank you!"

"An hour only," she said, holding me at arms' length to impress her point. As I bounded from the room, I saw Mother shake her head and smile.

I must hurry if I only had an hour. I took to the woods behind my home. The trees, mostly maple and oak, stretched west to the Menominee River, a good day's journey by foot. I had never ventured that far. During the spring months, I had built a new fort at the site of our intended meeting. It was constructed the same as the first, only I had added more sticks to make the walls thicker.

Now, nearly there, I heard a sudden galloping sound, as of a wolf. Wildly searching about for a tree that I might climb but seeing nothing, I ran to the only place I could think of—my fort. I threw my knees up, covering my face, and waited for vicious teeth to tear into my limbs at any moment. I heard the beast stop before me, panting violently. My body tensed in anticipation of the pain.

"Esau," a familiar voice called.

Trembling, I lifted my head and opened my eyes. There, above the pale pink of my skirts was a great and terrible beast. I screamed.

"Esau! Here, boy," the voice called.

There was Adam; the beast—not a wolf but a dog—trotted back to Adam's side. I half choked as my trembling changed to laughter.

"It's you. You came!" I said, struggling out from under my fort. The rows of ruffles at the base of my skirt were coated in dirt.

"I'm sorry I couldn't come before," he said. "But Pa's allowed me a half day's holiday today, and every future Saturday."

Esau came trotting back over and I, now unafraid, caressed its head.

"Where did you get him?" I asked.

"I found him."

I knelt and scratched the dog's head, carefully avoiding a missing ear crusted with scabs. "He's from the dog fights?" I asked.

There was surprise in Adam's eyes. "How do you know about that?"

"The saloon isn't far," I said. "We hear them sometimes in the night." Esau licked my hand, and I laughed. "Well, he's not much to look at, but I suppose he's a bit handsome in his way," I said. Esau sat and thumped his tail on the ground. I laughed again, and my voice rung through the woods. "He agrees."

Adam's eyes suddenly sparkled. "Would you like to see something? A game I've invented?"

"Yes, please," I said.

He marched farther into the woods, hands tucked behind him. Despite his short stature, his steps were broad and bold, like a man's; and I had to take two quick steps to every one of his. Esau happily trotted ahead. Presently, we reached a portion of the woods where the trees thinned out. Here, the younger saplings had a chance to soak in the sunshine without competition from the older, taller ones. Esau took off, sniffing the perimeter in search of squirrels or chipmunks or any one of a number of treats.

Adam halted at the base of one of the saplings. It was narrow enough to fill the circumference of his thumb and forefinger. He took a high grip on the trunk and leapt, wrapping his limbs round the tree to hold himself in place. He continued to climb in this manner, sliding his hands up the trunk, then hoisting the lower half of his body higher each time, skirting round the small branches jutting out here and there. He did this until he reached the slender, upper limits.

"Careful!" I called up. "You're too heavy."

I gasped. The tree toppled, and Adam, clinging to it, rushed toward the ground. I clapped a hand over my mouth. Just as his feet were about to hit the dirt, he let go. The sapling snapped back upward, leaving him safely behind.

"Are you all right?" I asked, clasping his hand.

He looked down at my fingers, clinging to his. I quickly dropped them, remembering he didn't like to be touched.

"That's the game," he said.

My eyes widened, and I looked up at the top of the tree. "Wasn't it frightening?"

"Yes," Adam said. "That's the fun. Would you like to try?"

My head bobbed up and down in assent, and I stepped to the trunk of the sapling as I had seen Adam do.

"Oh," he said, looking embarrassedly at my skirts. "Perhaps I ought not to have..." He turned away as I lifted the dirty pink ruffles and tucked them between my limbs. "Perhaps you ought not..."

"It's nothing," I said. "You may look now."

With that, I lifted my arms and attempted to hoist myself up the trunk. However, I wasn't strong enough to accomplish the job, and I slid back to my starting position. After several more attempts, Adam shook his head.

"Let me help you." He stood next to me, interlocking his fingers. "Step in," he commanded.

I stepped into his hands and immediately felt myself lifted. But I hadn't straightened my knees, and I tumbled into an awkward sitting position on his shoulder.

"Grab the tree," he said, grunting under my weight.

I gripped the tree with my limbs as I had seen Adam do.

"Go on," he said.

Pushing my hands higher, I attempted to pull my body with me, but my strength was not enough. I had to grip with all my might to keep from sliding down.

"Try smaller motions," Adam said.

This time, I lifted my hands only slightly, scooting myself a little higher. It worked. I tried it again, and it worked again. It took me treble the time it took Adam to surmount the summit, but I made it at last.

My heart lurched at the swaying of the thin upper limits. It felt as if even a slight breeze would send the sapling toppling over.

"Now let your limbs go and let your weight carry you down," Adam called.

It was terribly frightening.

"Let go!" Adam shouted.

Closing my eyes, I released the grip of my limbs on the tree, hanging only by my hands. Immediately, the tree shifted as my weight began to drag it down. Once the motion started, it picked up speed. My innards, safely held in place by stays, seemed to float upward; my head dizzied, frightening but somehow exciting too. I wondered briefly if this was a healthful activity or if I would be damaged for life, but then I didn't care. I was sailing through the air, screaming. Adam's words, as if far away, called.

"Let go now, before it swings back up."

There was a little yank as the sapling reached its lowest point, then began to snap back upward. Panicked, eyes still closed, I released my grip and dropped. The fall was farther than I expected. With my eyes closed, I couldn't be sure if my face was toward the earth or sky. Suddenly, I thudded against something. When I opened my eyes, I found myself cradled in Adam's arms. He immediately put me down. Bits of pink fabric were strewn about the ground, torn from my dress.

"Why didn't you let go when I told you?" he asked.

I crossed my arms. "I did."

There was a growl and then sudden crashing and scampering in the undergrowth. Esau had found a meal.

Adam looked at me. I looked at Adam. We grinned.

"I like your game," I said.

Chapter 21

The Narrative of Adam Bolton

The northerly wind died down, and at first light, the cool night air dissipated, giving way to waves of warmth. It would be a hot day.

I had scarcely moved a muscle in my cramped perch for some two hours now. I shifted my gaze from the mound of salt at the base of the white pine before me to Pa, about a rod south, long limbs slung over a platform such as the one upon which I sat, nailed to two sturdy branches perhaps a quarter of the way up the tree. He was barely visible, but I saw that he stared intently north. He lifted his left hand, just perceptibly, and straightened a finger, pointing. As he did so, I heard timid footfall coming from the same direction.

At some distance, a young buck, with two short antlers, picked his way between the trees, following the deer trail. I tightened my grip on the old flintlock, heart pounding at double its ordinary rhythm. Gunther and Thomas were crack shots. I had never felled a deer before but what a prize this would be—better than any they had killed I was certain. I soundlessly raised my rifle to my shoulder and peered down the barrel, hands quivering like the pine needles which hid me. The buck neared, cautious. A long, streaked scar ran down one side of his body: he had been hunted before, only that time, the bullet had just grazed the length of his side. *Lord, if it is your Will, please direct my shot.*

The buck paused and lifted his black, wet muzzle, sniffing the air. I feared he was about to bolt, but then he continued forward. I held my breath, aimed at his broad chest, and flexed my finger, closing my eyes and wincing at the anticipated impact to my shoulder.

Nothing happened. The deer, calm, still approached. I glanced down at my mutinous weapon and inwardly groaned: the gun was only half-cocked. What a fool. It was just as well, for I had been overeager. The buck was still at some distance. Soon enough, though, I would have a better shot. Steadying my hands, I cocked the weapon fully.

Crack! The young buck staggered as if drunk, stumbled a distance of twenty feet, then collapsed, sending up a cloud of damp leaves, pine needles, and dirt. The whites of his eyes showed as he jerked his head, first one direction, then the other. Below, Pa was already sprinting toward the beast. *Crack!* Pa's gun rang out, and the buck went completely still.

"Come," he called, waving me down.

I glanced at my rifle: it was still cocked. I felt like a bit of wood on Pa's worktable, clamped to the spot. Cold sweat trickled down the dent in my back. I uncocked my gun and deliberately descended the boards, nailed at regular intervals, on the tree trunk. Thoughts galloped through my mind. Surely this was divine intervention. It must be. The Lord had directed my bullet without my pulling the trigger.

As I stood above the deer, my nostrils filled with the sickly-sweet scent of game. The Lord had answered my prayer, had performed a miracle. I imagined Mother's face when I told her. Meanwhile, Pa retraced the deer's steps, pausing at each tree and running his hands up and down their trunks. He stopped and drew something from the crotch of a tree, just off the deer path. He waved again, and I left the buck to see what he had found.

"Just as I thought," Pa said. He lifted a rifle high in the air. A string, attached to the trigger, drew taut across the path. "Lucky we didn't follow the trail any farther up."

I froze in my tracks, unable to comprehend. *Was it not the Lord?*

"I'm sorry you lost your chance," Pa said, "but there'll be plenty others." As we returned to the deer, he pulled off his cap and scratched his head. "Poachers. On our land. Could be Gunther or Thomas, I s'pose." He glanced through the surrounding woods. "Well, whoever it were, no knowing when and if they'll be back. I'd prefer not to encounter them. Here," Pa handed me his hunting knife. "Careful, she's good and sharp. Do it as I've told you, but do it quickly."

This was not at all as I had imagined. The miraculous story I had been building to tell Mother would now only be a lie. The Lord had provided but not in the way I wished. I pushed away my rebellious thoughts. *"Thy will be done."*

Rolling up my shirt sleeves, I punctured the skin between the front legs with the sharp point of the knife, and turning it upside down, sliced a line along the belly to its rear legs. After pulling these apart, I plunged my left hand into the hot innards and worked it up the neck until I found the throat and lung cords. Pinching these closed, I worked the knife up the neck and cut them just above my hand. Tugging, I brought the cords, along with the deer's entrails, out of the body, leaving an empty, steaming cavity.

Pa had disappeared into the pines and now returned with our ancient sledge. I took the buck's head and he the haunches, and we slung it aboard. The sledge was meant to be pulled by two, and Pa stepped behind the handle on one side, preparatory to pull, when a voice rang through the woods.

"Oy! Oooy!" The village drunkard, a stooped old man wearing

a red worsted cap, gray, matted hair sticking out below, came stumbling through the trees. He shook his hand above his head. "That's mine! My trap. My kill."

As he closed the gap between us, his leathery, craggy face became visible. A thick, heavy odor trailed him, filling the air like fog. His nose was bulbous, covered in red, spidery veins. I cringed, putting my hand to my own nose.

"Oooy..." His exclamation fell short. "Adam? Is that you? Sarai's son?" He pulled his red cap from his head and held it between his hands.

I took a backward step and averted my gaze, training it instead on the cracked gray bark of the enormous white pine opposite, four widths of a man.

"Peter," the old man said. "Is there something wrong with him? Doesn't he speak?"

"Now," Pa said. "You know what she's said. I'll not go against her will."

"My own—"

Pa held up his hand. "We want none of your lies here."

"It's devilish unfair," the old man said. My eyes flew up to his. "Oh...ahh...I'm sorry, boy. I know she doesn't like those words. I didn't mean any harm, you understand?"

"Fair or not fair," Pa continued, crossing his arms, "those are her wishes. And you've not helped your case, have you?" He nodded at the bulge in the man's thick, worn overcoat.

The old man patted it. "When you've lived as hard a life as I have, you need a little comfort now and then. She of all people ought to know that."

I stared at the coat, incredulous, understanding there was a flask of spirits hidden there. Mother's words and warnings about the man came back to me. He noted my expression.

"No need to look at me like that," he said. "When you've lived and seen the things I have, you'll see. You won't judge me then."

My fist tightened at my side. How dare he speak to me like that?

"It's time to move along," Pa said to him, voice both gentle and stern.

The old man paused, glancing at the deer.

"Hand me the knife, Adam," Pa said.

The old man was a thief and a liar. He deserved nothing. Yet, I recalled to mind the verse about heaping coals of fire upon our enemies' heads. I handed over the tool. Pa knelt, cut a slice of meat off the deer's back haunches and tossed it.

"That's all you'll get," Pa said, "and be thankful for it. Now, be gone, and don't let me see you on our land again."

The old man glanced over at me, meat in hand, and, to my surprise, a tear rolled down his face. "Someday," he mumbled, turning. "Someday, you'll understand."

He ambled away, stench dissipating with his retreat. Pa uncrossed his arms, pulled the sledge's handle up, indicating that I should do the same, and we yanked it forward across the forest floor. He opened his mouth as if to speak, then closed it again. We trudged on in silence, excepting the methodical swish of the sledge and the occasional scrape of rock and branch under runners. I was to learn no more about the old drunkard today.

Chapter 22

The Narrative of Adam Bolton

E sau bounded ahead through the woods. The trees Penny and I used for our game had become so bent that their tops nearly touched the ground, and they would no longer remain upright. The area had become a sapling cemetery with the arched trees acting as their own gravestones. Now, I thought it was time for us to find new ways of occupying our time. Penny suggested playing in her fort.

"Penny," said I when we reached it, "I don't wish to hurt your feelings, but you've no idea how to build a fort."

"Well, I think it's quite good," she said, eyes blazing.

"Yes, for a girl, I suppose it is," said I.

"For a girl!" she screeched.

"Shhh!" I put my fingers to my lips, glancing round the woods. We weren't so far from her home that we couldn't be heard. "I didn't mean it like that. Only, I should have said you're less experienced in...carpentry."

She glared. Esau hurried to my side and let out a halfhearted growl, uncertain if I was in danger.

"Perhaps," said I, patting Esau's head, "we could build a better one, like a small house—together."

She appeared unconvinced.

"I can bring scraps of lumber from the shop," said I.

"Do you think you could get nails too?" She was still sulky, but underneath it, I saw a bright glint.

I shook my head. "They'll rust out in weather like this. We'll fasten it with pegs."

"We can build a whole castle," she said, speech increasing in speed. "It could have a moat and a drawbridge too! Very well. I accept. Let's begin next Saturday."

There was no trace left of anger. She was all excitement. And so, it was agreed. Esau, seeing the tension had dissipated, barked and ran in a circle from Penny to me, licking our hands.

However, there was too much work to be done upon the new house which I was assisting Pa in building. It was not until the second Saturday that Esau and I returned to the fort. Penny was there, waiting, eyes wide and grinning as if she had a secret.

"Look," she said, placing a small box in my hand.

I glanced at the package she had produced; it was full of nails.

"I found them," she said. "I searched the barn loft and found two boxes. I only brought the one though. Do you think it will be enough?"

"There's no need," said I. "I mean to do it with pegs."

"I thought it was going to be a castle," she said. "And anyways, that sounds like too much time. Nails will be faster."

"Penny, you understand we can't really build a castle? A small house is the best I can do."

"Very well," she said with an exasperated sigh. "But we must use the nails."

"As I've said, they will rust. And in any case, they're plancher nails. They're meant for securing flooring not building." I crossed my arms and stared at her to impress my point.

She shrugged. "A nail is a nail."

"If we use the wrong materials, it won't last."

"Oh, it doesn't matter," she said. "It's not a real house after all, is it?"

So, we commenced building. It might be more accurate to say that *I* commenced building. Penny did try to help, but more often than not, she was only in the way. I would put her on a task, and she would perform it for two minutes before bouncing over to me and offering suggestions such as, "It ought to have a cupola," or, "A cellar might be nice."

It took every Saturday of a month to complete the project. I was proud of the result of our efforts; with only ragged and unwanted pieces of lumber, we produced something quite nice. It looked just like a miniature house, tall enough for both of us to stand without our heads touching the peaked roof. I had covered it with cedar shakes, and there were windows with wooden shutters that opened and closed on leather hinges. The door, like the house, was made of scrap lumber, and I even made for it a sliding wooden latch system. I thought it looked quite homelike. Penny seemed to agree, for the day after it was finished, she met me in the sapling cemetery and, full of excitement, dragged me back to our house.

"Look," she said, pushing me forward toward the door.

I was getting used to her passion: she was always excited about one thing or another. I stepped inside and saw that a store-bought doll with a china face rested upon the floor. Next to it was an allotment of cracked and chipped teacups her mother had given her.

"You oughtn't to keep the doll here," said I. "It will break, and your mother will be angry."

"It won't," she said, putting her hands on her hips. "And Mother wouldn't be angry even if it did. I certainly wouldn't care. I brought it here for a reason. I want to play house. The doll will be our child, and you, the father."

Her expression was so fierce and expectant, I almost laughed. I believe this was one of the things that drew me to her; whether she meant to or not, she always brought out the lightness in me. However, I had no interest in her game. I thought it childish—

even for her age. My only interest had been in the building of the project.

"I'm sorry, Penny," said I, "but you'll have to get Ingrid to play."

Her face dropped. "But that's the whole reason I agreed to the house. It won't be any fun with Ingrid as the father."

I hated her look of disappointment. I could hardly stand it.

"Well," said I. "Perhaps while you and Ingrid play, I could build some furniture to furnish it. Then it would almost be like I was the father."

She appeared unconvinced.

"Your house won't be much fun without furniture."

Penny shrugged. "Very well. If that's the only way you'll play."

"It is," said I.

And so, I was a part of, and apart from, the game. Ingrid came when she was not needed at home. Off to the side of the little house, I built them a small table, or a shelf or a small bench, until the whole place was furnished. I knew it to be wrong, and I knew I oughtn't, but I was beginning to feel a sense of belonging.

Chapter 23

The Narrative of Adam Bolton

I spent the remainder of the summer with Esau. Mother had never spoken against him, and now I saw him as my own. During any spare moment away from working with Pa building the new house, or doing chores or cultivating the garden, we ran through the clearing and woods. The dog indeed made an excellent guard and spent his days and nights prowling the grounds for any unwanted intruders, though, of the human variety, there were never any.

As summer waned, Pa stayed behind at the new house one evening, completing the final touches so I might return to Haggard House earlier than usual. I entered the clearing to find Mr. Fowler's horse in the yard and Esau barking furiously at the front door. He ceased upon seeing me and bounded over, nuzzling my hand. I rubbed his head and entered the house, leaving the dog on the veranda. Mother stood near her rocking chair, arms crossed, facing Mr. Fowler and speaking in low tones. There was a plain look of surprise when she saw me, and for a moment, I fancied, a look of guilt.

Mr. Fowler was still wearing his boots indoors. Mother spoke to him in a low voice, so that I could not hear, then took the man's arm and marched him to the door.

"I expect," said she, louder, "that you'll take better care of it than last time?"

The portent of Mother's words landed heavily.

"Of course," Mr. Fowler said. "He'll get nothing but the best treatment."

Mr. Fowler regarded me with a sly wink. He stepped outside, and I followed in disbelief, hardly able to breathe. Upon seeing his former master, Esau immediately resumed barking furiously.

"Adam," said Mother. "Quiet that dog."

I looked from Mr. Fowler to Mother, then knelt and whispered in Esau's ear. The dog issued a low growl of protest before quieting. I stared at the top of Mr. Fowler's boots. I knew what must come, what was coming. Rage burned me: I could look at neither Mr. Fowler nor Mother.

"Find some cord that Mr. Fowler may use to take his dog home," commanded Mother.

The injustice of it all infuriated me. *Home! His dog!* The dog no more belonged to Mr. Fowler than to the Devil. I caught myself short. It was a wicked thought. Yet, I couldn't help it. I seethed inwardly, allowing my mind to wander down passages I never would have otherwise.

Mother's voice rose. "Did you hear me, Adam?"

"Yes, Mother," was my immediate reply.

I stood and turned my face away to hide the emotion so obvious there. The whole walk to the barn, my stomach churned. Tears were very close, but I swallowed and swallowed and fought them away.

There was the hated cord, twirled neatly on the peg in the wall.

Returning, I knelt and tied it round Esau's neck. The dog whined gently and licked my hand, as if to soothe me. I made the knot wide, hoping Esau might break loose and return, but Mother saw.

"Make Mr. Fowler's dog secure, Adam," said she.

More tears fought their way to my eyes, but I resisted them with great effort. I tightened the knot: Esau would not be capable of breaking loose.

"Now return him to Mr. Fowler," said she.

I rubbed the dog's solitary ear, and he whined. I stood and, turning away my head, held out the cord. Mr. Fowler immediately took it.

"You've done the right thing."

As Mr. Fowler neared his horse, Esau sat his haunches on the ground and refused to budge. "Come!" he shouted. The dog snarled. "Come!" he shouted louder, raising his arm.

"Don't hit him!" cried I.

Mr. Fowler gave me a look that indicated he might like to hit me too.

"Go, boy. Go, Esau," said I, voice half choked by the tears that tried to force themselves out.

Esau looked back at me and whined, then stood and followed Mr. Fowler to his horse. As they made their way down the lane, the dog looked back once more, eyes so mournful, I believed perhaps even dogs could cry. The speed of the horse pulled at the cord on its neck and jerked him forward. I watched them until they disappeared into the trees and, without looking at Mother, entered the house.

Before I had made much progress, I felt myself caught in her arms.

"I know it's difficult, Adam." She guided me to her rocker and sat me on her lap like a child. "But, you see, it wasn't your dog after all."

"Mr. Fowler cast him away," said I. "He left him to die."

Mother brushed the hair from my forehead. I wished to break free, to run from the house and never return. I knew it was evil—wicked to think so—but I could not banish the thought.

"You tried to rid me of Esau while I was out," said I.

"I know it's difficult," repeated Mother, holding me tight, "But you became too attached to an earthly thing. That dog was taking the place of your Lord."

Mother's hold was suffocating, and I squirmed under it. "I never ceased praying or reading. I love both the dog and the Lord." I trembled under my own admission. Never had I meant to use *love* for a creature, and certainly not in the same sentence with *the Lord*.

"There. You see!" said she. "'Ye cannot serve God and mammon.' You'll hate the one and love the other." Her hold loosened, and I climbed down and knelt before her.

"I did it because I love you," said she.

"But he'll kill him. He'll kill Esau. You might have given him to anyone else."

"It is his dog, not ours." She sighed. "I see it in you too much, this love of the world. Escape the snare the Devil has laid for you, Adam."

At this last line, her voice was so full of tenderness that my heart melted. This was nothing but Mother's concern for my immortal soul. No one cared for me as she did. Better that I break on the rock than be crushed beneath it. Her softness and entreaty calmed me somewhat.

"I can let go of earthly things...of Esau," said I, "...only, I can't bear to think of what they'll do to him."

"Yes, yes," said Mother, as if I had finally hit upon something worthy of action. "And that is a matter for the Lord. We may pray for him." She shifted from her rocker, knelt next to me, and took my hand in hers. "Lord," said she, lifting her closed eyes to Heaven, "if it is your will, protect the Fowler's dog." She paused for a moment, as if searching out the right words. "And if it is not, resign us to your other, better will."

I could only whisper, "Yes, Lord."

We remained in silent prayer for many moments more before Pa returned. I heard the door latch behind him. He did not intrude; he knew better than that. However, when we finally stood, he asked, "What's happened?"

"Nothing," said I.

"It's past time for dinner," said Mother, standing and gathering up the green beans from the iron spider and slicing short strips of venison from the carcass roasting on the spit above the flames—meat I had looked forward to sharing with Esau after our meal.

Pa looked at me in his earnest, imploring way. His concern only renewed the pain of my loss, and my throat constricted so tight that I felt I could not eat. I took up the hunk of bread on my plate and regarded it. Taking a bite, it twisted within my stomach like poison.

It was the first time I recalled perceiving that Mother's leavening was tainted.

Chapter 24

The Narrative of Adam Bolton

Pa's labored breathing issued forth in frosty, white circles from the bed. Only yesterday, he had complained of a headache and cold sweats. Now winter, I pulled my trousers on under my night-shirt, to keep warm in the frigid morning air. Closing the door silently so as not to disturb him, I went below. Mother was just rising from her knees.

She finished her breakfast and made her way to the attic. I heard her voice increase in pitch and insistence and Pa's deep-toned replies. I remained at the table, stomach churning so that it made me feel full, despite having only taken a single bite; I forced the gruel down regardless.

Mother stormed down the attic steps, face flushed. "Peter will not join us today," said she, hurriedly donning the bonnet in her hand. "Come."

I glanced down at my night-shirt.

"How preposterous," said she. "Go finish dressing. Quickly."

As I made my preparations, I glanced at the rusted iron bed. "Are you ill, Pa?" asked I, voice low enough that Mother would not hear.

Pa's large frame somehow looked shrunken. His eyes, usually

so kind and expressive, were dull and cloudy. Despite the winter air, sweat beaded profusely about his large temples. He truly did not look well.

"Only a bit," he said with a feeble smile. "I'm sorry to miss service with you."

"Don't worry yourself," said I, laying a hand on Pa's forehead. It sweltered against my cold palm.

"Adam!" called Mother from below.

"I must go," said I.

Pa nodded and closed his eyes.

Mother waited for me with a darkened expression. She pulled a heavy black shawl over her gown, and we stepped out of doors. As soon as we left, I felt something tugging me back.

"I've forgotten something," said I. "Continue on. I'll return shortly." I hastened inside.

"Hurry!" called Mother.

Carefully closing the door behind, I gathered Pa's untouched bowl of oats from the table in one hand and the pail and dipper in the other. Water sloshed on my trouser leg as I struggled up the stairs. I placed the pail upon the floor.

"Sit up, Pa. Hurry," said I.

Pa, surprised, shifted upright, his back wedged between the wide bars.

"Eat this," said I, handing him the bowl of oats. "Oh." My cheeks brightened. "I've forgotten."

I clattered back down the stairs and returned, holding out a spoon.

"Thank you, son," he whispered, voice cracking with emotion.

I made a movement toward the door, but Pa grasped my hand and pulled me into an embrace.

"I must return," said I, again attempting to leave. Yet, he would not let me go. He clung to me like the dying cling to the hands of the living. My throat constricted, and my eyes squeezed shut. What was this sensation?

A choking sound came from Pa. There were tears in his eyes—he was sobbing. It shook not only the bed, but me. He wept like a child, tears wetting my coat. A tear came into my own eye. I desperately wished to allow it to fall, but to allow one would be to allow a flood. I suddenly accepted his embrace, pressing into it instead of holding back. Warmth trickled through me, releasing my tightly drawn muscles and relaxing my entire frame. Now, surely, I would weep.

"Adam!" called Mother's voice from outside.

Pa's sobs died as suddenly as they had begun. I blinked away my own tears and wrenched myself free, hurrying down the stairs.

I did not look up at Mother as we resumed our walk, and she did not question me. Yet, I was certain she had noted the water freezing into my trousers. As we resumed our walk, the sensations that had filled me—warmth, softness—fled as quickly as they had come.

During the sermon, Minister Judd spoke from Mark 3:25, "'And if a house be divided against itself, that house cannot stand.'" He referred, of course, to the recent secession of South Carolina. It was spoken of often in the village but never within my house. There was a strained feeling in the atmosphere, but it was immediately replaced by my own troubled thoughts as we stepped outside the church doors.

When we returned to the house after service, Mother immediately flew up the attic stairs. This time, I heard every word of her squawking at Pa. She berated him for feigning illness to avoid the sermon and railed on him for setting a poor example for me. "Know you not that, 'it shall not be well with the wicked, neither shall he prolong his days because he feareth not before God?'"

My head ached with the shouting.

There was a dull thud, and Mother's voice stilled. Instinctively, I shrunk from the stairs, as if to disappear. There was a moment of silence, then a blood-curdling cry, "My cross. You've desecrated my cross. See what you've done! By forcing me to carry out God's punishments on you, you've broken it!"

Feet shuffled above. The attic door swung open, and in Mother's hands was her wooden cross, broken in two and smeared in red. Behind her was Pa. Blood trickled from a gash on his ear. Still in his night-shirt, he hurried after her down the stairs. I recoiled into the shadow of the grandfather clock as Mother reverently pressed the broken pieces into his hand.

"Repair it," said she.

"I'll take it to the shop with me tomorrow," Pa said, still looking feverish.

"It must be done today," said she, voice rising to a commanding pitch. "And leave the blood. It's fitting that your blood should be where our Lord's was."

"But it's Sabbath," Pa said.

Mother thrust him toward the door. "Now!"

Pa fumbled with his boots. He slipped outside with the pieces clenched tightly in his hands.

When our nightly ritual of pacing and reading came to an end that evening, Mother tucked her Bible into its place on the shelf and left the house. I ascended to the attic. Moonlight flooded the room, and I found Pa resting comfortably. A notch had been split in his ear, but the bleeding had stopped. The cross, stained with blood, was repaired and resting on the chest of drawers. A commotion from the barn woke him, for he stirred and rose on one elbow. We both looked out the window as Mother retreated into the woods with a bit of rope, dragging something behind her.

After this date, I constructed a new room within my mind, and into this room, I placed Pa.

Chapter 25

The Narrative of Peter Bolton

I were a humble man, a carpenter, and some ten years Sarai's senior. My parents, neither of whom were still living, were pioneers, settled in Ohio. Some time after their death, I moved to Nomaton. It were then hardly even a village. Imagine then my surprise upon finding one of the most beautiful women I had ever laid eyes on. She were something to behold, fine dark eyes, fine dark hair, and a way of carrying herself that left no doubt that she were one who could hold her own.

I were a man who enjoyed the simple pleasures of life, but my union with Sarai did not enrich my life in the way I supposed. Our courtship had been a steady flicker without the eruptive flame of passionate love. It were she who had pursued me, asking me to call upon her. Sarai were poor, and her guardian, Minister Judd, were always complaining that he had too little money to raise her. To make ends meet, she baked and sold bread. In matter of fact, no one liked Sarai's bread, but the villagers, myself too, bought it regardless because we felt for her—lone and abandoned by her parents.

Until our marriage, I had been content to live in a small, single-room shack behind my carpentry shop. It were unsuitable to bring a young wife into and unsuitable to house the children I soon hoped to father. So, with the money I had diligently saved, I purchased a property on the outskirts of the village. Most believed the place to be haunted, though none could say why. Nonsense of that sort wouldn't put me off. Though humble, the house were larger than my old shack, and it had a large old barn to boot. Years of solitude had left the house's wooden slats weather-beaten gray, and a smattering of boards had fallen off or rotted. This worried me none. I put my skills to use before our wedding and turned the melancholy house into something brighter.

Now, I ought to mention a strange occurrence before I bought the place. Sarai had warned me off 'bout the old village drunkard. She told me he were not to be trusted. He told all kinds of tales, some in connection to her, all lies. Well, word were spread that I were to buy the old, haunted place, and the drunkard came to the shop before I had the opportunity to go *down below*, to the Lower Peninsula, and get the land patent. He told me he had something, a story about the house I were going to purchase. Of course, I 'bided by Sarai's wishes and made the man leave before he had a chance to say one word of whatever it were he wanted to say about the place.

The day of our marriage were clear and completely silent. Even the crickets didn't chirrup. Sarai praised God for the sunshine, but the villagers said that a wedding with no rain were a bad omen. I didn't care two pennies about the weather or the silence. I were thrilled to have the handsomest and most devout woman in the village.

That evening, I took Sarai's hand, only the second time I had touched her, the first being the kiss I had placed upon her cheek that afternoon. Her face spasmed, but she allowed me to lead her. At the door she halted, rooted to the spot.

"Tisn't haunted," I said. "If that worries you."

Sarai seemed not to have heard me though, for she cast her eyes wildly about.

"Please, come in." I placed my arm round her shoulders. "Come."

She reluctantly stepped inside as I held open the door. Again, she cast her eyes about, searching for something or taking in her new home, I could not tell. Darkness were descending; already it were difficult to see. I took the aged iron betty lamp from its peg on the wall. I fumbled for a moment with the brass tinderbox, then lit the wick.

Without warning, Sarai snatched the lamp and strode to the far corner of the room. She knelt upon her knees and examined the flooring.

"I can easily rub out those stains, if you like," I said.

She returned and handed the lamp back to me without a word. I led the way up the attic stairs, the grandfather clock I'd brought in earlier ticking behind us, marking our steps. When we arrived, the lamp cast dim, orange light on a rusty iron bedframe tucked beneath the slope of the ceiling.

Sarai, my wife, were already inspecting the bed. I thrust my hands into the pockets of my best trousers, uncertain how to proceed. I hesitated. She were engrossed in the faded Job's Trouble piece-quilt upon the bed. I had never been assertive: Sarai had led the whole relationship. It were she who had suddenly asked me to call upon her. She had told me that the Lord put it in her heart to seek me out. From there, it seemed almost no time had elapsed before we were betrothed.

Now, I thought perhaps this were the time for me to take the lead. I stepped gingerly forward. Her whole body become rigid like a board. I paused, a hands-breadth behind her, and let my hands slip round her waist. Innocent enough, I thought. But her body lurched forward, wrenching my hands away. She spun round and let herself fall on the bed, forcing a cloud of dust up from the mattress. I grew hot with embarrassment.

Sarai's face, which had grown taut and tense since our entrance, grew more so. I shifted from one foot to the other, waiting. One stiff movement later, Sarai had pulled up her petticoats and the skirt of her lavender silk dress. She lay across the bed, knees bent over the edge, dress still covering her. She minded me of a dead frog, limbs dried and bent in the sun. I leaned down to kiss her, but she turned her face. How were it that I could work the edges of a bit of wood with my chamfer knife until they were smooth as butter, but I could not soften the edges of a woman? I did not wish to frighten her, so I straightened and stepped away. Sarai gripped my arm and pulled me back.

"Unbutton your trousers," she ordered from the bed.

I were uncomfortable beyond words, but not wishing to offend, I obeyed.

"The drawers too," were the next order. "I suppose you know what to do?" she asked.

"You want me to...?" I asked.

"It's God's will."

She were cold, for it were her first time with a man. I comprehended that. Even so, I were hardly inspired by the stiff and fully clad figure on the bed before me, so I did my best to conjure images of Sarai undressed. What must she look like without the thick petticoats and stockings covering all but the necessary flesh? My imagination, more inspiring than reality, did its work. I knew her, in the Biblical sense. Yet whenever I bent to look into her eyes, Sarai turned her head away. She would not even allow me on the bed, pushing me back if I attempted. Whenever I thrust, still standing, clouds of dust from the mattress buffeted me from between Sarai's limbs.

When, finally, I released, hardly a moment passed before she pushed me away, drawing her petticoats and skirt down. She moved to her trunk, which I had brought to the room earlier that day. It contained her scant supply of worldly possessions, but the only thing she took from it were a wooden cross, which she rested on the chest of drawers. Having done so, she climbed into bed without removing her dress. By now, I were sitting quietly at the edge of the bed, but she turned her back to me.

"Goodnight, love," I whispered into her ear.

I were bewildered beyond words.

Chapter 26

The Narrative of Peter Bolton

The preceding occurrence happened again and again, the details varying little. I attempted to woo her with gentleness, but Sarai remained cold. She were unsusceptible to affection, yet I craved it. Whenever I ventured to discuss the matter, she reprimanded me for my desire for earthly pleasure, or worse, said nothing at all.

When I arrived home one evening, Sarai sat me down on the rusted iron bed. My heart leapt, believing I had finally won my wife over, that she would finally know me tenderly. But her face wore the pinched expression that had become customary since our wedding.

"God has blessed us with child," she said.

Hardly able to contain my excitement, I leapt up and wrapped my arms round her. She remained stiff like a corpse. I pulled back to look at her expression, hoping to see the same joy I felt reflected there. Yet, the eyes I looked into could have been made of marble, and a numbness trickled through me as she stared back unflinchingly. My arms dropped dead at my sides.

"We have no more need to..." Sarai's voice trailed off, as if to say the words would be a mortal offense to God.

The cross on the chest of drawers caught my eyes, and I held them there, too stunned for words. I understood what Sarai meant; she would not know me anymore, at least not until the child were born. Inwardly, I cursed religion for making my wife so cold.

As I attempted to sleep that night, Sarai's weight shifted from the bed as the clock struck twelve. I cracked my eyes a slit to watch as she opened the uppermost drawer of the chest. She lifted and unwrapped a huge book protected by gauze. She closed the attic door, steps creaking as she made her way down the stairs. Then her footsteps moved from one end of the room to the other. Once I were sufficiently certain that my movement would not be detected, I crept across the floorboards and opened the attic door a sliver. From my vantage, I could see Sarai by the dim light of the betty lamp, open book in hand, pacing.

She read, "'For the wages of sin is death,'" voice lingering over the last word. I knew the verse well, but the way Sarai seemed to enjoy it made me shudder. I crept back to bed and slept uneasily.

The sunshine and the sound of the birds chirruping the following morning, Sunday, brightened my mood and, consequently, my feelings toward my wife. I kissed Sarai's cheek as she slept. Her eyes flew open, and I turned from her, strangely guilty. I got out of bed and hurried into my clothes.

"Come," I said, buttoning my trousers. "Farmer McNeil has promised to sell me a trio of chickens. We'll have time before sermon."

Sarai rubbed her eyes and sat up stiffly. "Peter, it's the Lord's Sabbath. We must not do any work or selling or buying."

Not having thought of this protest, I scratched my head. "Perhaps we could go tomorrow then?"

"Yes, tomorrow."

The walk to church were long, but I enjoyed its vigor. The day were bright, and the prairie into the village proper were filled with Queen Anne's lace and milkweed. Tufts of silky seeds drifted past.

Sarai were radiant with her condition, looking more handsome than I had ever known her. As every Sabbath, she wore her best dress, lavender silk, which set off her dark hair and eyes. Even if our relations were somewhat strained, I felt the pride of having a handsome woman by my side. The villagers nodded and tipped their hats in greeting as we entered the church. Minister Judd grasped Sarai's hands. With a pang, I realized that Sarai welcomed the minister's touch more warmly than she had any of my own affection.

She sat perfectly upright and rapt as Minister Judd's voice droned from the pulpit. During our courtship, I had found intense admiration for Sarai's perfect posture and undivided attention throughout his gravelly sermons. But today, her motionless form and devotion irked me.

Monday arrived, and with it, the chickens. Sarai requested I purchase seven—six hens and one rooster. Delighted to have an opportunity to give her something she desired, I eagerly did so. Hoping the purchase had softened her, I attempted to know her that night. She pushed me away with more force than I had thought capable of such a small woman. Her eyes, cold and unreadable since our marriage, burned.

"It's not God's will," she said. "I've told you so before, and I'll not tell you again."

Her tone hurt more than the thrust of her strong hands.

"Very well," I said, jaw tightening.

A well of bitterness sprung up in me and, not knowing where to place it, I stormed from the house and past the chickens fluttering in the yard. Accustomed to sober and simple living, I had looked forward to enriching my life with a beautiful young wife and family. But every day that passed convinced me more and more that this were not to be so.

The long walk to the village gave me no joy. My feet, knowing my purpose better than my mind, carried me to Bard's Tavern. The exterior had a barn-like, domed roof, and the front door had a window just above, making it appear taller than it really were. I entered. It were dimly lit and smelled of tobacco. Immediately, I made my way to the tap-room. The seats of the scattered tables were full, and the proprietor's gray- and white-streaked cat were making its way from one to the next in search of scraps of food. I nodded familiarly to the miller and McDonnell, deep in a game of All Fours. As I neared the bar, a familiar, deep laugh rung out. I met a pair of beady eyes and a grizzled beard.

"Three months and already you're here?" He gave another full-bellied laugh and pressed a reddened eye over the mouth of his empty glass. "Oy, Greene! Another. And another for my—" I gave him a warning look. "For my *friend* Peter here." The old man rumbled again and scooted his chair closer.

The proprietor, Mr. Greene, placed a heavy decanter on the counter and poured the liquor to the top of two tumblers. I had rarely entered the dimly lit saloon, and I stared stupidly at the amber liquid. The raucous voices calmed my overactive mind.

"So," the old man said, "What's she done to drive you here?"

"I much appreciate the drink, sir," I said, draining the glass.

The man laughed even louder. "Whoo-eee. Must have been a hell of one to make you drink like that. Oy! Barkeep! Another."

It were Sarai's express wish that I not speak to the man, and however angry I might be, I would keep my word. Mr. Greene filled our tumblers, and I swirled the contents, determined to drink more slowly.

"Hell of a one, eh?" the old man repeated.

"No, sir. I needed a respite from a full day at the shop, that's all."

"Ha ha!" He grinned, worn, yellow teeth showing. "I see it in your eyes. No *sir* will put me off the scent. She's a damned crow, that's what she is now. Doesn't deserve you, I can see that."

My jaw tightened. I emptied the second glass and placed it back on the counter. "Do not speak ill of my wife, if you please, sir."

The old man changed tack and slapped a reassuring hand on

my back. "No harm meant, son, no harm meant. Here, have another," he said, gesturing to Greene.

I stumbled home and up the attic steps. I felt the desire that comes with drinking and had not drunk enough to temper my ability to appease it. I lay in bed next to Sarai as quietly as I could, careful not to touch her.

As surely as clockwork, at the stroke of midnight, she got up, as if she had never really been asleep, and took her Bible downstairs to pace and read, pace and read. I waited until the footsteps below had attained their steady rhythm, then with thickened pulse and the audacity born of drink, I sat back against the iron bedframe. My head crunched downward against the slope of the attic and my back wedged uncomfortably between the bars of the bed. Settled this way, I knew myself.

The results of my efforts were so satisfactory that I did not hear my wife creaking back up the stairs. The door of the attic opened, and Sarai's eyes, heavily ringed from lack of sleep, loomed in the dark. There were one thing of which I were certain: she had seen the completion of my act.

I watched as she approached. She drew back her hand and struck my face, hard. The palm that had appeared full and soft at the time of our courtship, felt like a bludgeon. I were so shocked that I were uncertain how to respond. My instinct were to hit her back, but how could I hit the mother of my child? That aside, I had no taste for being that sort of husband.

Instead, I found myself meekly saying, "I'm sorry, Sarai. I'm sorry."

"I will pray for your sin," she said as she creaked back down the attic steps.

When I awoke the following morning, I looked outside and saw that the frost had set in.

Chapter 27

The Narrative of Peter Bolton

Crunching across the frosted grass after a long day at the shop, I dreaded my arrival home. My face and pride still smarted from Sarai's stinging slap. My stomach detested the abominable bread I would certainly be fed for dinner. Worst of all, my heart hurt with the thought of my shrew of a wife. However, when I entered the kitchen, instead of seeing putrid crusts piled on a plate, I saw Sarai facing me with a smile. In her hand were a platter of the most delicious-smelling meat.

"Sarai, is this one of the chickens or...You've been to the butcher's today?"

She did not answer. She merely placed the platter before me and handed me a thick napkin.

"Eat."

In addition to roasted meat, there were potatoes smothered in gravy and green beans. I smiled at my wife, feeling that, surely, this must be her way of making amends.

"Will you eat with me?"

"No, I've eaten already," Sarai said. However, she lowered herself into the chair across and watched.

When I had completed the meal, the first hearty one I'd had

since marriage, I took Sarai's hand. "Thank you...dear. That were wonderful."

"Your sins are atoned for," she said.

The words troubled me. Sarai stood and went about her business.

When I took the scraps out to feed the chickens that evening, six hens clucked and pecked at my boots. Where were the rooster? Anxious that a fox might have snatched him, I neared the tree-line and found a trail of feathers leading into the woods. There were drops of blood leading still further. I followed until I discovered a mound of dirt, freshly turned. A compulsion caused me to press my hands into the softened soil and dig. I had not dug long before I uncovered the charred remains of a rooster's head, claws, and entrails.

A strange panic gripped me. I rushed back to the yard and again counted the chickens. Still, there were only six hens. As I made my way to the house, I passed the shed where I kept my tools. My axe rested against the edge of the structure, instead of fixed in the log where I always kept it. I lifted it and found blood beaded across the blade.

Rationally, I knew each of the chickens would eventually make its way to the dinner table. But I had purchased the rooster at Sarai's behest. Without him, there would be no new chickens. My wife had killed the rooster and fed it to me. Why?

Recalling her words on atonement chilled me. I wiped the axe blade clean with the handkerchief from my trouser pocket and entered the house with a sinking heart and a sense of foreboding.

"My dear," Sarai said. "You look tired. You ought to go to bed."

Bloody kerchief in hand, I stared at my wife, but she acknowledged neither the cloth nor the look in my eye. Her sudden warmth cooled my resolve to confront. She took my hand and led me to the rusted iron bed.

"Sleep well," she said. "I'll be in shortly."

In the morning, Sarai were irritable at breakfast. This, combined with the cold seeping indoors, darkened my mood further. I were determined to discuss the rooster. Sarai's icy glances matched the coldness of the house, but I pressed on.

"Dinner were excellent last evening."

She snatched my half-eaten breakfast, gruel thick as plaster, and clattered the dishes into the wash basin. Though I had every right to ask, I suddenly felt as though I were in the wrong. Still, I persisted.

"I think...Well, I'll get to my purpose. Why did you kill the rooster?"

Sarai's spine straightened at the wooden sink, but she didn't turn. "I believe you know why."

"I'm not certain...That is...Perhaps with the little sleep you've had—well, the mind might suggest strange things."

She whirled round. "Do you think that I wish for the sins of the father to be visited on the son?"

Sarai's belly were still flat, but since the news, I had imagined a little girl running about the house. I weren't certain why, but Sarai's belief that the child would be a boy cut me.

"But Sarai, I must...There need be some...relief for me."

"How dare you speak of such things?" Her dark eyes burned.

Again, I felt strangely in the wrong. "I'm sorry, Sarai," I found myself muttering.

As suddenly as she had turned, she knelt to the floor and wrapped her arms about me.

"It's forgiven now," she murmured.

The warmth of Sarai's affection were colder than her coldness. In a single movement, her hand were in my hair, grasping and yanking until I dropped my head back to ease the pain. Tears come to my eyes, but I remained silent.

"Bring no more sin across this threshold," she said. And with that, she let me go.

A windstorm swept the village that night, straining every joint of the house. I were at the tavern throughout most of it, but when I understood that the storm would not blow over, I left and struggled against it all the way home. The wind were bitterly sharp, stinging my face and burning my ears, glowing red. The Queen Anne's lace were dead now, and the milkweed that had given me such delight, had given up the ghost. There were only empty husks now.

When I reached the house, I stopped short. Wind blasted me, but I could not move forward. The house, which had looked so fresh after my recent repairs, suddenly appeared concave. It were as if the very boards of the house had been sucked inward. Inside, I saw the betty lamp through the window. It were past midnight, but Sarai's shadowy form paced to and fro, reading her heavily worn Bible. I got the horrid feeling that, rather than the wind, the house's implosion had been caused by my wife. I felt cursed. And later, no matter how I tried to repair the boards, the house refused to straighten.

In the village, the house, owing to its sunken features and haggard appearance, come to be known as Haggard House.

Chapter 28

The Narrative of Peter Bolton

Although I were disappointed that my wife had not born a girl, I were by no means disappointed in my child. The boy were healthy and strong, if somewhat small. It did sadden me that Adam bore almost no resemblance to me but took strongly after his mother. Even as an infant, he had the same dark hair and eyes, even the same dark half-circles ringing them.

Around that time, Minister Judd become a weekly visitor at Haggard House. I were always at my shop when the minister arrived, but I were aware of the visits. I didn't mind, as they seemed to have a calming effect on Sarai, at least for the day. She would prepare tea and be quite cheerful on the mornings the minister visited.

Midnights, Sarai would take Adam down the attic steps and tuck him into a barrel, one side having been sawed off and lined with wool. This were yet another wound. I had spent many hours in my shop carving a beautiful cradle for the boy, but Sarai repulsed the gift, saying that she didn't wish her child to grow in expectation of earthly comforts. On one occasion, under the guise of fetching a ladle of water, I had come below stairs to see how my child fared. I expected Adam to be fast asleep in his makeshift cradle, but when I reached the end of the steps, I saw him, eyes wide open, as Sarai paced and read aloud.

The next occasion, I attempted to dissuade her from taking Adam down with her, saying it were bad for the child's health. But all I received for my efforts were a resounding slap and sharp words, and so I never mentioned the subject again.

As soon as Adam were old enough, he begun to toddle, in his dress and pantalettes, behind Sarai as she paced and read. All of Sarai's spare moments were spent teaching Adam his letters, big and small. Soon, Adam were reading portions of text from the Word. I observed that what he could not read, he began to know by heart. By the time he reached five years of age, he trod with the same deliberate steps as his mother across the room, reading from Sarai's leather-bound family Bible, which he could hardly hold for its weight and size. Whenever Adam's curious mind found a question on the readings, Sarai were more than delighted to find an answer for him in the Scriptures.

One night, when I'd come down the stairs for a cup of water—which I had made a habit of in order to check on the child's welfare—I saw Adam, wearing his most serious expression, pacing the floor with my wife, heavy Bible in hand. Mother and child looked alike, both with deep, dark circles looming under their eyes. Sarai read from her own, a smaller copy.

"'Look not thou upon the wine when it is red, when it giveth his colour in the cup, when it moveth itself aright. At the last it biteth like a serpent, and stingeth like an adder.'"

When she had finished, Adam asked, "Why does Pa drink spirits?"

His question were no surprise to me. Often, of a night, when I returned from the tavern, I heard Sarai telling the boy that his Pa were full of spirits, and not of the Spirit of God but of spirits one drinks.

Her face kindled. "There you have lit upon the right question. Let that teach you to be not like your Pa, nor to seek his company.

He does not follow the commands of God, even in this small thing."

Adam's little mouth constricted. He appeared to be in deep thought for a moment before he said, "Yes, Mother."

Neither looked at me as I filled the ladle from the pail.

Chapter 29

The Narrative of Adam Bolton

War loomed. It was all anyone in the village spoke of now. Even so, Pa and myself never brought word of it to Haggard House, and whenever I was in that place, I hardly remembered anything of the sort was occurring. Like many other things, I put it from my mind.

The difference between Pa and myself was striking. Pa had grown thin and gaunt as he aged, but the foul bread, watery soup, and occasional chicken or goat worked upon me like Samson's long hair: my strength grew and grew.

During Minister Judd's weekly visit, he remarked on the difference.

"Adam, come here."

Only a month was owing until I turned thirteen. I was practically a grown man by my own estimation, and I held my place. I still held an intense dislike of the minister who, by all rights, should have lain in the churchyard many years since.

"Adam, come when the minister calls you," said Mother.

Her tightly drawn lips were enough to cause me to obey. Yet despite my outward obedience, I inwardly seethed as I came within reach.

Minister Judd laughed. "Closer, my boy. Closer. What have you to fear from a man of God?"

I struggled with the wrath that surged within me. What right had he, to treat a nearly grown man like a child?

"Kneel down here," he said, nodding to the floor before him. "Let me look at you."

Jaw tight, I knelt and looked straight ahead at his thick middle. With great difficulty, I kept my features collected.

Grasping my chin and lifting it, Minister Judd looked at me pensively. "Hmm." He dropped his hand and turned to Mother. "Sarai, this boy has only you in his face. I am happy to see that he has not been tainted by that reprobate husband of yours. You know where he is now?"

I leapt to my feet, eyeing him savagely.

"How dare you speak of my Pa in that way."

The minister glanced mildly at Mother. "You allow him speak to your guests in this manner?"

"Adam!" said she, face turning redder than I had ever seen it. "Apologize immediately."

I glared at the man.

Minister Judd chuckled. "What a look. Is this Peter's expression? Perhaps you do have something of your Pa after all."

I could have torn his head from his body.

"Apologize," repeated Mother.

"You know," Minister Judd said, turning back to me, "I preached on the passage only two days ago, but I believe those words from the Scripture do apply here as well. 'Every kingdom divided against itself is brought to desolation.'"

My face grew hot, and I clenched my fists. I could not make the hated apology. Mother sensed the danger for, for the first time I could ever recall, she did not press me again.

"Go, Adam," said she. "Fetch your Pa. I must speak to the minister privately."

I knew there was punishment in store. I would be made to go

to Minister Judd and apologize later when my anger had cooled, but now, I was only happy for the respite.

A change happened when I left Haggard House. I was not aware of the change in myself in those days, but every time I departed, my face brightened, my back straightened, and the circles under my eyes appeared lighter. Then too it might only have been a trick of the lighting in that place, as sunlight rarely found a home there.

The cold light of the early spring sun cast an orange glow over Whittemore's Prairie as I trudged along, deep in thought. The time spent with Penny during the previous summer, and again this spring, seemed to stretch and expand the room within my mind which I had built for her. This greatly troubled me. However, I could not dwell on my ruminations, for I soon reached Bard's Tavern.

Pa, bleary-eyed, and the old drunkard, the poacher, appeared almost simultaneously at the tavern door. I did not so much as look at the old man as he walked away. We turned silently down the lane and walked through the village. The tavern was at the edge of town, but it was Pa's custom to walk once round the village before returning. He claimed it was to check on his shop before returning home, but I knew better. He simply wished to delay his return as long as possible—and sober himself enough to meet Mother.

"Minister Judd is still at Haggard House?"

"Yes," replied I, unsurprised by Pa's use of the villager's term. He used it whenever he was deep in drink.

"You'll be up later than usual tonight then? Reading?"

"Yes," said I.

He snorted. "I don't see why you must read that damned book—"

I stopped abruptly, horrified. "Please, Pa. Don't speak ill of the Word of God. There is a price—and to call the Word...It's sin... blasphemy of the worst kind. Mother will—"

"Well, she needn't know," Pa said. "You needn't tell her."

I resumed walking. "'The eyes of the Lord run to and fro throughout the whole earth.'"

"Adam?" a voice called. We turned. It was Penny. In her arm was a basket laden with paper-wrapped parcels, neatly tied with string, from the butcher. I tipped my hat and continued on.

"Wait," she called, running towards us.

I tucked my hands and turned back to her. At this moment, she was a hindrance to my thoughts and conversation with Pa; I wished she would leave off.

"Will you—"

"Good day," said I. I could see from her face she wished to ask if we could meet later, and I knew that Pa would never breathe a word to Mother. Yet still, here in the middle of the street, what was she thinking of, in speaking to me? I tipped my hat to her again and returned to the street. I felt Pa's gaze, and my cheeks burned red. Silent, I kept my eyes trained on the path before us. The bitter cold of evening crept across the ground.

Pa suddenly spoke again. "There's a notice up inside." He nodded back toward the tavern. "Lincoln is calling for seventy-five thousand volunteers. One regiment's to come from Michigan. McDonnell is going. Farmer McNeil too..."

"Are you going?"

"I don't know as of yet," he said. "I've only just seen the notice." Seeing that I did not respond, Pa continued. "I've a load of work tomorrow at the shop. Will you come?"

"If I can spare the time," said I. "I've a great deal of prayer."

"Come if you can."

Despite his calm voice, Pa was tense. The whole walk home he seemed to be lost within his mind, turning something over and over, a new idea forming and growing like a ball of yarn.

Minister Judd was gone by the time we returned. Even so, the house was unusually noisy, both in terms of the building's creaking and groaning and later, in its occupants' exchanges. Pa called

Mother into the attic after the evening meal. There was no screaming or shouting, but both voices were heightened, excited. I could hear every word through the floorboards. More steadfast than usual, Pa made his case; he wanted to volunteer for the war. Mother, in no uncertain terms, said that Pa was not to go. "'All they that take the sword shall perish with the sword.'; 'Vengeance is mine, I will repay, saith the Lord.'; 'Whoso sheddeth man's blood, by man shall his blood be shed,'" quoted she, and many other such verses.

I used the time for prayer, and as I prayed, it became certain to me that it was against the Lord's will for Pa to leave. Whilst his pleading—no doubt influenced by the drink—droned on I, finished with my prayer, sat on Mother's rocker, took the family Bible upon my knees, and closed my eyes. I let the book fall open where it would and pointed my finger at the page. This is what I read:

"Blessed be the Lord my strength which teacheth my hands to war, and my fingers to fight." I immediately closed the book. It seemed that the Devil, not God, had guided my hand. Immediately after however, I was swept with a sensation, a yearning. What was it?

The attic door swung open, and Pa came down the steps, face red despite the cold.

"Well, son? What have you to say?"

"Don't go," said I.

He sighed, body sagging in defeat. "I cannot oppose you both. Very well. It's not to be."

Chapter 30

The Narrative of Adam Bolton

"I've taken on Thomas as an apprentice," Pa said.

I looked up from my bowl of gruel. "Thomas?" I glanced at Mother across the table, but her features revealed nothing. They had spoken of this already.

"What if he thieves from you, Pa?"

"Thomas has mended his ways," Pa said. "I've seen it. Can't say as much for his brother, though. I believe Gunther is getting worse. Shame he has no intention of volunteering. Might straighten him out."

"Like as not, he'd run off and enlist with the Rebels," said I. "His pa is a Copperhead, is he not?"

"Perhaps," said Pa. "But Fowler's too shrewd a businessman to make it public. I'd like you to make Thomas welcome. He's keen to do the work, and I think he'll come along quickly with both our help."

I had never thought much about either of the twins, but I suddenly felt a twinge of jealousy. Though I had learnt much of Pa's trade, I could not settle myself to the work. And although I myself did not wish to take the trade on, I couldn't bear the thought of Thomas doing so. To be forced to see Thomas daily in the shop would only make the sensation more acute.

For the first time, I felt restlessness, a desire to leave Haggard House and Nomaton; and it dawned upon me that this was the yearning I had felt after my prayer the previous night.

"Did you hear me, son?" Pa asked.

"Yes, sir," said I.

Chapter 31

The Narrative of Penny Haworth

Now fifteen, I had completed all the schooling that the village school was prepared to offer. Four years had passed, and in what felt to me a faraway world, the war betwixt the states had raged and then ended. Its presence was most felt in Nomaton by absence, the absence of those men who had volunteered, the absence of men to work the farms. Ours was a state that prided itself on never shirking its duty, so much so that President Lincoln himself had said, "Thank God for Michigan." Even so, on the rare occasions that such was necessary, men were conscripted. Ingrid's pa was gone, volunteered. Mr. Riblet's son, Henry, and the black-smith's son, William, had volunteered. Mr. Fowler had been conscripted but, after feigning deafness and being caught out, paid his three-hundred-dollar commutation and returned to his work at the saloon. The twins were of conscription age just as the last year of the war came on. Thomas was never called; Gunther was, joining one of the Sharpshooter Regiments.

William had already returned and, to no one's surprise, had immediately become engaged to Victoria Tenney. Two years past, Mr. McNeil had been killed at the battle at Port Hudson, Louisiana. His wife and children had moved to Ohio to live with

Mrs. McNeil's sister and her husband. Mr. McDonnell was still missing. Ingrid's pa, Mr. Nilsson, died of war wounds in a hospital near Baltimore. Mrs. Nilsson had gone to him, staying at the hospital until his death, returning with child.

As for Adam, I had been happy that he had been too young to go. Though, as far as our friendship was concerned, it hardly mattered. Since he had completed his schooling, two years prior to me, our friendship had waned, and he rarely spoke to me now. There had been very little opportunity to be together, and Adam's time was taken up at the shop with his pa and at home. There seemed to be less linking us now, our sexes and environments pushing us further apart. Too, Adam, for unknown reasons, had withdrawn into himself. He appeared discontent, restless, like an animal in a cage. Yet, I remained vividly aware of his presence, whether he was near or no.

Gunther's conduct, upon his return, was discovered to have become infinitely worse. Small livestock, usually chickens and geese, began to disappear from the villagers' farms, and Gunther was shortly discovered as the culprit. Next came more serious theft; several homes were broken into, their owners reporting missing valuables. Again, the villagers had no doubt who the thief was. However, Gunther was elusive, and all attempts to catch him in the act failed. He had wit enough never to sell the stolen goods within the village and so went unchecked.

We were the victims of the second theft. Mother's wedding ring, which she had not worn since Father's death, was stolen, along with my red coral necklace and several other pieces of jewelry. The silver coin kept in the house, which, most fortunately, was not much, was also gone. The silver plate had been untouched, presumably because Gunther had been frightened off before he had opportunity to snatch it.

Mother had spoken to the marshal but to no avail. Although Gunther's whereabouts could never be confirmed by anyone outside of himself during the thefts, there was no direct evidence against him. At last, Mother decided to warn the villagers herself, and I accompanied her. We went from house to house, speaking with the neighbors. Being at the far reaches of the village, Mother saved Haggard House for last; and summer dusk was quickly approaching when we stepped into its clearing.

The house had not changed in the intervening years, except that, perhaps, it appeared more shriveled. It was only the second time I had ever been there. Adam's mother, Sarai, appeared at the door, her severe black dress blending with the dark interior. Behind, Peter sat on a low step of the attic stairs. His head was drooped in his hands, and the air reeked of recent discord.

Mother spoke to me in a low tone. "It's best you go look in on the animals while I speak with her. Go on."

I was more than happy to oblige, having no wish to near the woman. Before I reached the barn, I turned and saw Mother disappear into Haggard House. I had grown taller, and my checkered dress had lengthened past a child's skirt; it was full and bell-like, having taken up the fashion of the cage crinoline. My hair was less wild, as I was careful now to keep it perfectly curled, and my hands were enveloped in black-lace, fingerless mitts. I was caught somewhere in the middle, neither fully woman nor fully girl.

I passed a trio of goats, ripping up mouthfuls of grass and staring at me through rectangular pupils. I slowed my gait at the northern end of the barn, pulled the door open and stepped inside. I had expected to see Peter's Belgian stalled here for the night, along with a handful of cows. Instead, it was damp and dank and had most certainly been abandoned for many years. A cobweb, strung across the aisle betwixt the empty stalls, clung to my dress, and I hurriedly dashed it away.

Continuing down the empty aisle, I reached the far wall. It was then that I noted the trunk on the floor of the stall nearest me. It was ancient but, despite this, appeared as if it had been opened recently. The rust on the hinges was scraped away in places, and when I lifted the lid, as if freshly oiled, it did not groan. I leaned, careful of my dress, and lifted out a dried sprig of pine needles, yellowed and flattened with time. I did not think much of it until I noted the second object in the trunk. It was a scrap of pink fabric which I immediately recognized as my own, having ripped from my dress the summer we made a game of climbing saplings. Next was a folded scrap of paper on which I had practiced my penmanship and signed *Penny Haworth*, with a flourish, and which I had given to Adam so that he might use the backside. I returned to the bit of pine, suddenly remembering its origin: it was the one I had given to Adam upon our first meeting.

I felt something, a little thrill. I couldn't place what it meant, but there was a kind of tenderness beyond the interest I had held for him when we were children. At that time, my interest was the same kind I took in Ingrid. Both Adam and Ingrid were different from the rest, somehow apart. And that apartness had drawn me to them. Yet, discovering this trunk caused a change. There was something else, something new and indescribable.

I returned the sprig, careful not to press the needles in case they crumbled. Then, fearful lest Adam should come upon me, I hurried from the barn.

Making my way across the yard, I saw movement at the edge of the trees just beyond the house. I paused and, seeing that Mother was still inside, strolled toward the woods. There was Adam, rifle resting on his shoulder. In his hand hung a dead squirrel. He had changed little since school. He had grown slightly taller, now on a level with me. His plain trousers and jacket, as ever, fitted him tightly.

I meant to call out to him but, suddenly, I felt timid and could not speak. He came very close before looking up, and when he did, his face violently drained of color.

"What are you doing here?"

"Gunther's been thieving again," I said. "Mother is spreading the alarm."

"I see." Adam rested the butt of his rifle on the ground, and some of the color returned to his face.

It was then that I noticed a trickle of blood oozing from the hand with which Adam held his rifle.

"What happened?" I asked.

He pushed it sheepishly behind his back. "Nothing. An accident."

"Let me see."

Adam shook his head.

"Let me see it," I demanded, holding out my palm, timidity melting away.

He examined me a moment, then slowly withdrew his hand from behind his back and offered it for inspection.

"Come. Into the light."

Adam obeyed. There was a clean slice across his palm. I produced my handkerchief and used it to gently wipe the blood from his hand. As I did so, I felt that little thrill dart through me yet again.

"How did this happen?" I asked.

"I tripped and caught myself on a sharp bit of wood."

It didn't appear as a cut from a jagged piece of wood would have, but I kept silent and wound and knotted the handkerchief tightly. His hand was still in mine, and I felt foolish. I dropped it and glanced at the squirrel in his other hand.

"There won't be much meat," I said.

Adam laughed. It had been so long since I'd heard his laugh that I beamed.

A sharp voice called from the house.

"Adam!"

His laughter disappeared just as quickly as it had come, and he was serious again. He hurried toward the house. Sarai stood on the front veranda with my mother. When I reached it, a little behind him, Sarai was staring, horrified, at Adam's bound hand.

"What have you done?" She stared at the handkerchief. "And what is that?"

"I fell," Adam answered, meeting his mother's gaze. "Penny bound the wound."

Sarai stiffened. "Remove the binding."

Adam's face drained of color, just as I had seen it do earlier.

"The bleeding will begin again—"

Sarai reached out to grab his hand, but he yanked it away, hiding it behind his back.

"Give me your hand," she said.

"No." His voice quivered as he said it, and I felt a sudden urge to run forward and face his mother with him, so that he would not be alone. Only, just then, my mother grasped me by the shoulders and turned me bodily away from the house.

"We must be going. Goodbye—"

Sarai did not wait to hear.

"Take it off," she said.

I heard, rather than saw, Adam bound down the steps and take to the woods. When I looked back, I saw Sarai running from the house, willow rod in hand. She half leapt off the veranda and took off after him. I wanted to somehow help Adam, but Mother hurried me forward.

After a long silence and after the quick beating of my heart had slowed, I asked, "What did she say?"

"I told her of Gunther's doings. She really seemed grateful. She must have a deal of money hidden in that house somewhere, for Heaven knows she doesn't spend it on her boy and husband." I was surprised at this rebuke, for Mother was perhaps the one person in the village who never spoke ill of Sarai or Haggard House. "It was clear enough," she continued, "that she'd just had an argument with Peter—no doubt bested him.

"I always thought the rumors and whisperings were unfair. I always thought Sarai only a bit eccentric, perhaps a bit controlling.

But after seeing that...the way she treats Adam...I don't wish you to have any association with them."

"It's not Adam's fault. It's all his mother. Why should I not be his friend?"

"Nothing good can come of it," Mother said. "I ask you to keep away for your own sake, Penny. Stay away from that boy." When I didn't respond, she said, "Please, Penny."

There was no point in arguing and, in any case, I never associated with Adam these days.

"Yes," I said.

"Yes what?" Mother asked.

"Yes, I'll keep away from Adam."

I heard her take a deep breath. "Good."

My word was easily spoken. It did not mean I had to keep it.

Chapter 32

The Narrative of Penny Haworth

Much to Mother's chagrin, I began to take to the woods. Every day I, sometimes alongside Ingrid, wandered past the old schoolhouse, the church, and the parsonage, into the woods, rich with the sweet scent of honeysuckle, and covered in thick ferns and mosses. As Adam had warned long ago, there was a cedar swamp. The water was deep in places, but I discovered a path through dry ground and mossy, fallen trees. The swamp led into more forest and finally into the back of Farmer McNeil's field. The farm was owned by a new family now, yet I still thought of it as McNeil's.

One afternoon, Ingrid and I had a particularly long stretch of time with which to explore. As we wandered through the woods, we came upon the beginning of a narrow path.

"Look, Ingrid," I said. "Let's see where this leads."

Ingrid shook her head, gray eyes growing wide. "Nay," she said. "That lead to Haggard House. I know yuu not scared, but I am." Her flaxen hair still fell in two long braids from beneath her wide-brimmed, straw hat, making her appear childlike.

"You *are* not scared," I corrected. "And certainly. Why should I be? Why should you be?"

"It *iss* haunted," Ingrid said, choosing her words carefully so as not to be corrected.

I laughed. "We're not schoolchildren, Ingrid. Surely, you can't believe those tales?"

Ingrid shrugged. "I rather not go."

"Please," I said. "I can't go without you." Ingrid was not convinced. "If there is anything haunted, we may leave immediately."

"Vell," Ingrid said. "All right."

We started down the narrow path. The woods were no different than they had been behind the field. Nevertheless, Ingrid stuck close behind me, alert as a hunted deer. At every cracking branch or hurrying squirrel, both of which were frequent occurrences, she gripped my arm.

The path curved until we realized that we must've been somewhere near the backside of Haggard House. The woods were thicker here, and the sunlight came through the branches less freely, making it darker and gloomier than it had been; Ingrid held me so tightly that it hurt. Despite my friend's fear, I was secretly elated at the thought of being so near Adam.

"Look," I said, halting.

We had come out upon a small lake, about an acre in size, in the midst of the woods. The sun glittered on the murky water as a family of ducks paddled placidly across the surface. A deer on the opposite shore, legs splayed in order to get a drink, leapt straight upward in fright at our appearance, and then bounded away, white tail lifted high. This side of the lake was thick with lily pads and cattails, but the path led round to an open bit of ground leading down into the water. From there, the path split into two, leading left and right.

"Come," I said, grasping Ingrid's hand and pulling her along. "I want to swim." The water appeared inviting in the heat. The boys at school had always bragged about fishing and swimming in such lakes, and I had often wondered what it would be like to do the same.

"Ve can't svim," Ingrid said.

"We don't know *how* to swim," I said, "but that doesn't mean we can't stay in the shallows."

By now, we had skirted the border of trees, and I pulled Ingrid down the slight incline to the shore. I began to yank at the bow on my bonnet.

"Stop. Ve can't." Ingrid said. "Ve're nearly vomen now."

"Stop worrying yourself," I said, unpeeling my clothing. First came my collar, then my checked waist and matching skirt, my petticoat, the hooped crinoline underneath, my corset cover, the corset, my shoes, and finally my stockings and chemise. "If you don't hurry, I'll have to go by myself."

Reluctantly, Ingrid began the same process, slowly peeling off her calico waist and skirt. I had never been naked before, not outside the confines of my own chamber. It was freeing, the sun warming my skin and the slight breeze caressing my body. No wonder the boys loved it so. I pressed a toe into the water.

"It's warm," I called.

Ingrid paused at her chemise. "I leave this on," she said.

"I *will not* leave this on," I said, correcting her sarcastically. "Do you want to have soaked undergarments, freeze all the way home, and get us both in trouble?"

"But I do not vant to be..." she whispered, "naked."

By now, I had stepped out nearly to a large rock protruding from the water, and muck sucked at my feet. I stretched my arms wide. "It's wonderful. Try it!"

Unconvinced, Ingrid slipped from her chemise regardless, folding it and placing it on the fallen log along with mine. She clutched her arms across her chest.

"Come on," I said, waving her in.

When Ingrid's foot touched the warmth of the water, her face broke into a smile. "It vonderful!"

"It *is* wonderful," I said, drawing my hands through my hair and laughing.

Ingrid, braver with each passing moment, allowed her arms to drop and stood up straight, wading out as far as me. The muck, however, was unpleasant to stand in, and after my initial bravado, I feared what creatures might be lurking in it. I made my way to the rock and sat down.

Ingrid, standing near me, shrieked. I clapped a hand over her mouth.

"Shhh! We must be close to Haggard House," I whispered, glancing round. "They'll hear you."

Seeing the width of Ingrid's eyes relax somewhat, I removed my hand.

"Your...your..."

"What is it?" I asked.

"Your," she whispered, "legs."

I looked down. There, clustered on both limbs were long, slimy, wormy creatures—leeches. I clapped a hand over my own mouth to keep from screaming.

"Help me get them off Ingrid."

She squeezed onto the rock next to me, both of us balancing to keep from falling from the narrow edges. Ingrid's legs were covered in mud-brown leeches too. I covered her mouth before she screamed again.

"It's all right," I said, though I felt far from it. "We'll pick them off."

I took hold of one of the fatter ones upon myself. It wriggled and tightened its suction. I pulled so hard that it broke in half, both ends still attached to my leg, my own blood oozing from its middle. I felt my face blanch, and I thought I would be sick. Then I had an idea.

"I've a pen knife in my skirt pocket on the shore," I said. "Go and get it."

I couldn't bear the thought of more leeches, and Ingrid was

braver at these sorts of things than I, though she didn't show it. She took a great breath and plunged away. She returned shortly with the knife, accompanied by more leeches. I took the tool from her and opened it. I would experiment on my own leg, and if it worked, I would let Ingrid remove hers first. It was only fair since she'd gotten the knife.

Starting on a whole leech, I slid the knife's edge just between my skin and its mouth.

Ingrid said, "Von't their teeth be stuck in our..." again the whisper, "legs? Then ve vill die?"

"You can't die from leeches," I said, faint at the sight of the wriggling creature. It took two attempts, but at last the knife point pried away one end. I hurriedly removed the other, flinging it into the water, and watched as little drops of blood dripped from where the leech had sucked. Now that I saw my idea had worked, some of my courage came back.

"Just think, Ingrid," I said, attempting to be humorous, "If the doctor called, we would have to pay for these." Neither of us found the comment as funny as I had meant it, and I used the knife to pick the leeches off Ingrid and myself in silence. At last, they were all gone, and we sat disconsolately. All the fun had been sucked away.

"Let's go back," Ingrid said.

I gasped. How had I been so foolish?

"We'll get covered again," I said. Ingrid looked as if she was about to cry. I scrambled round to face the opposite direction. "Look." I pointed deeper in the water. "There's sand just beyond this rock. If we jump, we can miss the muck and come out through that thin line of cattails."

Ingrid glanced at the blood oozing from her limbs. "Vat if there's leeches there too?"

"You remain here, and I'll try it." I balanced on the rock, judging the distance. Then I leapt. Finding my footing, I said, "It's perfectly sandy. No leeches." Feeling the warmth of the water and the sand scraping between my toes, my excitement returned. "We can swim after all, Ingrid. Come on!"

Ingrid sighed, but she stood and leapt, splashing as she landed. Her eyes lit up as she wiggled her toes in the sand.

"See?" I said, laughing.

The water was shallow, so we crouched, allowing it to rise to our necks. I closed my eyes, bright sun warming my ears.

"I wish we knew how to swim," I said. "We could go as deep as we liked."

Ingrid shook her head. "I don't vant to go deep."

"Well, we can go a little farther anyway. It's so shallow here, and I believe it's still sand farther out."

"You go," Ingrid said. "I not vant to move."

I took mincing steps under the water. I surmised that I might make it half-way to the center of the lake without needing to fully stand.

Suddenly, there was a commotion behind us.

"Stop!" a voice cried. "Don't go any farther!"

I turned and saw Adam on the shore, but as I did so, my foot, which had been poised for another step, instead of planting on the sandy bottom, sank. I tried to brace my hands against the water and kick myself backward, but instead I slipped deeper. I heard Adam shouting and briefly saw Ingrid waving her hands wildly for assistance. The water suddenly changed from warm to cold as I sunk beneath the surface.

I had not been under for more than a moment when a strong hand gripped mine and pulled me back to standing. I took a deep breath and found that I was standing opposite Adam, Ingrid just behind us, frozen in fright.

"You all right?" Ingrid asked.

"Yes," I said, water draining from my soaked hair.

Adam had stripped of his coat, vest, and shirt; only his trousers remained. I was very near him, so close I felt the heat from his body radiating onto my own cold one. Embarrassed, I turned my glance away from his bared skin and into his eyes. They were full of concern. I caught my breath when I saw myself reflected there: it was then I recalled that I was naked.

Adam looked away. I crossed my arms to cover myself.

"Thank you," I said. "I'd no idea it was deep there, or I..."

He was already stalking back to the shore.

Ingrid and I followed, but he had already disappeared into the woods. We picked off more leeches and dressed. The whole time, I kept glancing about, hoping to catch a glimpse of Adam. I was uncertain if he had gone or had merely stepped aside out of decency's sake. It seemed to take ages for Ingrid and me to help each other with our stays. I wished to see Adam, to speak to him. At last, the dressing was accomplished.

I called into the woods. "Adam? Are you still here?"

Ingrid turned to me. "Happy? You nearly die and scare me half to death. Ve go home now."

"I'm sorry, Ingrid," I said, gripping her hands. "You're right. But I must speak with Adam. You start home, and I'll follow as soon as I find him."

Ingrid shook her head but started off. No doubt she would be in a mood for days, but that was nothing to be anxious about. I'd apologize again, then all would be cleared away.

"Adam?" I called. "Adam!"

He reappeared from farther down the path, now fully dressed. I was elated, but that changed as I noted his dark expression.

"Thank you," I said. "I'm so grateful—"

"Did you go down this path?" Adam asked, pointing from whence he had come.

"No. We came through Farmer McNeil's woods, and we stopped here at the lake. As you saw."

Adam examined me. "Is that true?"

I nodded vehemently. "Certainly. Yes. Why would I lie? And in any case, would it matter if we had taken that path?"

"Yes," Adam said. He had drawn himself up and his eyes were

no longer soft and caring but cold and hard. "It would matter. Never come here again. Do you comprehend? Never come farther than Farmer McNeil's place."

"Well, we didn't go down that path," I said, eyes flashing. I pulled myself up to my full height, which was perhaps half an inch taller than Adam's. "I'm sorry you had to get wet, and undoubtedly you had to remove some leeches afterward, but I didn't know the lake dropped off." I crossed my arms emphatically.

Adam again searched my eyes. "I believe you," he said. "But you must believe me, Penny, it is because I...because I care for you...that I ask you not to come here." His tone became pleading. "Please stay away?"

His confession melted me instantly. "Very well," I said, maintaining a pretense of offense. "Since you ask instead of ordering, I will do as you say."

His shoulders visibly relaxed, and his eyes softened. He changed so quickly.

"Shall I bring you another apple pie?" I asked, eyes twinkling in fun. "As thanks?"

"You had better not." He meant it, but there was a gentleness to his tone that melted me again.

Adam gazed directly at me and, for the first time, I couldn't meet his eyes. I held out my hand. He took it, and we shook in an odd, formal manner. He held my hand for a trifle longer than necessary before releasing it. We turned away, suddenly bashful, and as we returned to our respective places of belonging, my heart leapt with joy.

Chapter 33

The Narrative of Penny Haworth

Time had improved Thomas' character. He no longer taunted me, or anyone else for that matter. There was a change in his external appearance too. His hair was no longer stringy but washed and cropped close, and he had grown tall. He became quite steady, and I often found his eyes wandering to mine.

One day, as I began my daily walk, I came upon him in the street. He was leaning against the wall of the saloon, deep in thought. I tilted my head downward and tried to hurry past, but Thomas, glancing up, strode to my side. I increased my speed, hoping to leave him behind.

"Wait," he said. "Please. May I join you for a moment? I have some news. I'd like to share it with you. If I may?"

I stopped, wary. "What is it?"

Excitement crept into his figure as he approached. "Perhaps I might walk with you a ways?"

I couldn't imagine what it was Thomas might wish to speak to me about, but my curiosity was sparked, and I said, "If you must." We walked on, and after a long silence, I asked, somewhat impatiently, "What is it you wished to tell me?"

With a touch of pride, he said, "Peter says I've been doing well

—better than he ever expected. He wants to take me on. Add my name to the shop in another two years."

"What about Adam?" I asked. I could scarcely believe that Peter had really asked such a thing when he had his own son.

Thomas shook his head. "Adam doesn't wish to take on the business."

I stopped short. "Then what does he intend to do?"

"Hearing his talk, I'd guess he wants to go off and find something new, though I don't know for certain."

"Go off where?" I tried to hide the quaver in my voice.

"I ought not speak of Adam," Thomas said. He put a hand on my shoulder. "Ask him yourself. I know nothing certain."

"He didn't say he was leaving then?"

"No...not those precise words."

"Well, I'm very happy for you," I said, forcing a smile.

Starting off again, I hoped Thomas would lag behind, but he still dogged my steps. Uncertain what else to say, I asked, "How is your brother?" It came out cutting, though I hadn't intended it that way.

"Oh," said he, "He's well enough. Living at the saloon with us again...when he's here, that is. I heard about what happened. The robbery. If I'd seen anything...found anything...well, you know I'd have made him return it."

"Would you?" I asked.

He glanced down at me, uncertain. "I hope...that is...I wish to apologize for how he...how *we* behaved in the past. I've changed, and...well, I know I've caused you pain, and I'm sorry for it."

For the first time, I really looked at him.

He seemed embarrassed, for he immediately dropped his eyes.

Never in my life would I have imagined that Thomas would apologize. No wonder he had wished to speak to me. He must have had this upon his chest and wanted to unburden himself. Again, I walked, thinking now for certain he would leave. He did not. He followed me until I was nearly home.

"Well, thank you for your news," I said.

"I...thank you for hearing it."

With that, Thomas hurried up the street toward Peter's shop. I stood for a few moments longer, then opened the gate. It was certainly out of character for Thomas to speak to me like that. What must he be thinking of?

Chapter 34

The Narrative of Adam Bolton

P a, standing at the bench, thudded his wooden mallet against a short piece of finished wood, driving the tenon into the mortise. He was nearly finished framing the first of many windows for the Somervilles, an overflowing family who had taken residence at the inn and were now in a position to afford a frame structure. Thomas and I worked side by side, planing planks for more frames and chiseling their mortises when, through the open wooden shutters, who but McDonnell should thrust his head inside. I was in awe to see the man, having heard varying reports of his death during the war.

"Peter?" he said.

A second head, a woman's, popped through the window.

"McDonnell!" Pa said, laying down the partially completed frame on the bench. "Come in. Come in."

"Alive then?" Pa asked, smiling broadly as McDonnell and the lady entered. He took his hand and shook it heartily.

"Alive and well and brought the missus," McDonnell said, gesturing to the woman.

The woman, dressed smartly in a blue poplin gown and small black cap, stepped forward. "Pleased to meet you," she said, shaking Pa's outstretched hand. Her face, and everything therein, was wide—wide nose, wide eyes, wide mouth.

McDonnell saw me and laughed. "That Adam?" he said. "The one as smacked his head on the ice when he let his first fish get the better of him? Last I saw you, you were knee-high to a bullfrog. Shake my hand."

There was something so jubilant about the hunter, that despite my embarrassment—and that before Thomas—I shook the man's hand heartily.

"Hope your fishing has improved since last I saw you."

My cheeks reddened. "A fair bit," said I.

"Well," McDonnell said, turning back to Pa, "I'll be needing something a bit better you know, home-like, for Mrs. McDonnell. I wondered if I might prevail upon you?"

"I've my hands full," Pa said. "But with my boys here, I'm certain we can."

It was childish, but to hear Thomas named with me as Pa's *boys*, was like a knife to my heart.

"Well, well," McDonnell said, rubbing his beard. "Nomaton's growing, sure. Soon enough, Whittemore's Prairie won't be prairie no more. I seen three new homes there already."

"Yes," Pa said. "Business is thriving. But we'll make time for yours, McDonnell. Can't keep the little lady waiting too long, can we?" Pa winked at Mrs. McDonnell, and she blushed.

"Kind of you," she said.

McDonnell tipped his bare head, tucked his new wife's hand into the crook of his arm, and left, calling out behind him, "Good man, Peter."

Once he had gone, we returned to work. I glanced up at Thomas, and my bitterness increased. He had grown into his height, head and shoulders taller than me. His features had evened out and were almost delicate but not unfavorably so. Whilst my plane hastened along as if there were not a moment to lose, Pa's wooden mallet and Thomas' smoothing plane thudded and scraped in the unhurried unison of a perfectly matched pair of oxen drawing a cart.

"Son?" Pa said. "That," he nodded to a tenon saw hanging from the wall, "needs filing."

"Yes, sir," said I.

"Oh," Pa said, coloring violently. "I meant it for Thomas."

"Yes, sir," Thomas said. He swiftly removed the saw and took it to the grindstone. Then came the creak of the treadle and scrape of wet stone against metal.

"I misspoke," Pa said without looking at me.

"It's nothing," said I.

I wished more vehemently than ever to leave Nomaton.

Chapter 35

The Narrative of Penny Haworth

wo years passed, and I was now seventeen. When I caught my reflection in the looking-glass above the mantle, I saw someone beautiful staring back. I was not proud of this. In fact, it seemed that this person was too beautiful to be me. I dressed well, not to emphasize my appearance, but simply because I could. About town, I heard my own observation confirmed. The whole village had noticed.

There was, however, a person who seemed to take an especial interest: Thomas. He was always discovering a means of placing himself in my path. After a day apprenticing in Peter's shop, Thomas would take the long way back to the saloon so he could walk past our home. If he happened upon me, he made certain to tell me how well his apprenticeship was coming, and how he would soon be adding his name to the establishment.

Having seen the change in him, Mother was now of the opinion that I should pursue his interest in me. She saw Thomas as an eminently suitable suitor, a much less dangerous match than the young personage from Haggard House; it had been well enough that Adam and I had had an affinity for each other as children, but now Mother saw it, subtle as it was, as something alarming. So, she began pressing me to invite Thomas to call and to acknowledge him as a suitor. I refused again and again. At last, Mother's entreaties became so strong and so insistent, I decided I must step out with Thomas if only to put an end to it all. However, before I had the opportunity, an event occurred that urged me still further to silence Mother upon this topic.

After the incident at the lake, Ingrid no longer accompanied me on my outings. I kept my promise to Adam, never venturing beyond Farmer McNeil's field. During these walks, I began to feel the strong sense of being watched, perhaps even followed. Strangely enough, I wasn't frightened: in point of fact, this sense somehow put me at ease. Why, I couldn't say.

My walks led me to the swamp, where blueberry bushes grew on a raised patch of ground, pale pink and white blooms just beginning to bud. It was a lovely spot. Rays of sun sifted through the trees and lightened the bramble-filled hollow. I would climb into the nook of a rotting red maple trunk and sit with one of Father's books or simply enjoy the sights and sounds about me.

One cool evening in early spring, I sat nestled in my place in the maple when I heard heavy, plodding footsteps. I couldn't move without making noise loud enough to reveal myself, so I turned into the tree's shadow as best I could and hoped whoever it was would move on. However, the footsteps continued to near, as if the person sought me out.

A thick figure entered the line of trees and looked in my direction. It was Minister Judd.

"Penny, my dear? Is that you?"

I kept silent. Minister Judd neared, skirting his way with uncertain steps through the swamp to the blueberry bushes. He came so close that I could see his thick neck rolls.

"Penny, dear?"

The way the words lingered on Minister Judd's tongue made me suddenly ill.

"It's me," I said, hurriedly slipping from the tree. To my right were thick brambles. Behind and to my left was the swamp. I was left the choice to either walk straight toward the minister or retreat farther into the woods.

"I'm sorry. I shouldn't be here."

Deciding upon the former, I walked rapidly in his direction, hoping to edge my way round and place myself safely on solid ground. He anticipated me and moved his hefty frame, blocking my way.

"Don't worry, my dear. You wish to be near a man of God. No apologies needed for that." The minister caught my waist.

"Let go!" As I struggled to free myself, I heard sharp cracking in the woods behind.

Minister Judd cried out as Adam's powerful grip caught his hand and wrenched it away. Adam then circled my shoulders and rushed me deftly along, deeper into the woods. His steps, unlike mine, were silent along the track. At last, we burst out at the far edge of Farmer McNeil's field. I paused to catch my breath, and Adam's arm instantly dropped from me.

"Thank you," I said.

His dark hair was tightly slicked under a round-crowned hat. His wool coat, trousers, and vest were ill-fitting, but despite this, he looked handsomer than I had ever seen him.

His eyes met mine for an instant, then darted away. I sensed inner turmoil as the lines of his jaw tightened. He did not speak as we continued to walk.

"You've been following me. Haven't you?" I asked.

More silence ensued, and I took this as confirmation. I reached down and plucked a stem of grass, rolling it between my fingers. Adam suddenly halted, putting his finger to his lips. A feeble mewling sound came from the field. He trod carefully between the low, green rows of winter wheat, then caught up a tiny creature and handed it to me. It was a fluffy orange kitten with white paws. The kitten mewled again and curled into a little ball, looking up at me.

"He's so tiny," I said.

"Must be the runt of the litter. Keep him." Adam pressed his hands over the kitten, fingers touching mine as he did so.

I gently slipped the purring kitten into my pocket, its tiny head poking out into the warm air. As we neared the end of the field, I stopped short. Looking up into his eyes, I wished I could wipe away the dark circles that ringed them and give him undisturbed rest. I couldn't think what to say, so I repeated my earlier words.

"Thank you, Adam."

All at once, he grasped my waist and pulled me to him. His hand caressed my cheek, then my hair. His face drew close to mine. I could scarcely breathe. That thrill I had felt, naked in the lake, coursed through me again. My body went slack in his arms.

He pulled away. It was so sudden, I nearly slumped to the ground.

"I must go." He turned and fled like a deer with hounds at its heels.

I could scarcely believe what had nearly occurred. It took time to collect my wits. The thrill that coursed me, slowly but surely died away. I calmed my breathing and returned home, tiny orange tabby purring in my pocket.

Chapter 36

The Narrative of Penny Haworth

The plank sidewalk *dud-dudded* under the heels of my brown boots. I stretched out my arm, allowing my hand to trail along the buildings leading towards Main Street. A moment later, I quickly withdrew it, wincing. A sliver had stuck through my glove and into my finger. The sliver, however, was a small pain in comparison to the thorn at my side, that thorn being Thomas. Thomas had called a quarter of an hour past, and now we walked side by side through town.

"I've been attending service in the next town over. In Wasaki," Thomas said. "I never much cared for Minister Judd's sermons, though it might be sacrilege to say it. He never seems to preach from anything other than the Old Testament and Revelations. I find it strange in a minister, especially a Baptist."

He glanced at me, giving me opportunity to air my opinion. No doubt he thought I would readily agree since I never attended, but I remained silent. My encounter with Minister Judd in the swamp had left me with a vague fear of the man, and I didn't wish to continue the subject.

Upon receiving no reply, Thomas continued. "Have you traveled there? To Wasaki, that is?"

"Yes, I've gone with Mother for supplies. It's a long way to go for service. It must take you the entire day."

"Well, I've nothing better to do with my time at present," he said, glancing at me.

I couldn't bear the insinuation, so I distracted myself by removing my glove and examining the sliver.

"What's happened?" he asked. His voice was tender enough to have melted any other girl's heart, but it had no effect other than to irritate me.

"Nothing. A sliver. That's all." I squeezed at the surrounding flesh, turning it bright red.

"Don't do that. Let me see," he said, taking my hand in his.

I stiffened, wishing I could shake off his touch but not wishing to offend. He gently pulled at the visible bit of the sliver.

I must put him off immediately. It wouldn't do to put him through more misery by making him believe there was any chance of winning me over. "Thomas..." I began.

As soon as the word was out of my mouth, Adam came into view, approaching quickly. His head, usually held high, was dropped low, and he appeared deep in thought. As habitual with him, his hands were tucked neatly behind his back.

Before I had time to withdraw my hand, Adam looked up. He saw Thomas and me. A cold, hard look flashed across his eyes.

"Hello, Adam," Thomas said, nodding as Adam neared us.

He hurried past as if he hadn't heard.

I yanked my hand away. I longed to run after him, but that was impossible. I had still the unpleasant task of informing Thomas that there would be nothing between us. Jumbled as my thoughts were, I did not let him down as gracefully as I intended.

"Thomas, I'm so sorry. I've only agreed to step out with you to tell you that there can be nothing between us."

When I had played this turn of events through my mind, I had been calm and detached. However, seeing the wounded look upon Thomas' usually composed and cheerful face struck me with pain.

"I'm so sorry," I repeated, meaning it now.

"Why?" he asked, searching my face.

"I...there's someone else." I immediately regretted my words.

Thomas' expression turned stony. "Who?"

"I cannot say. I'm so sorry."

No longer able to bear his wounded expression, I dashed away. I felt horrid, but I had to find Adam and set things to rights. I could easily imagine what he must be thinking. Breaking into a run, I raced down the sidewalk, mindless of the villagers' surprised glances as I bounded past. Though I followed the street to its conclusion, I did not see Adam. I retraced my steps, running between houses and shops, looking everywhere. He was nowhere to be found.

Crestfallen, I returned home. When I told Mother that Thomas was no longer a suitor, she guessed that I had put him off. I attempted to deny it, but she knew the truth. More than that, she knew why. We quarreled for the rest of the evening. All the while, my kitten, Boots, lay curled in one of the velvet chairs, content as could be.

Exhausted, I retired early. Boots, who had turned out to be quite an affectionate kitten, joined me. I fell asleep with a vague feeling of loss, and when morning dawned, I woke to find the feeling had persisted through the night.

Chapter 37

The Narrative of Adam Bolton

I stood in my somberest manner, hands tucked neatly behind my back, facing Mother and Pa. The room seemed to crowd in upon me, stifling and oppressive. Mother crossed her arms and bit her lip, for once at a loss for words; Pa ran a large hand through his thinning hair and looked at me quizzically.

"I'm sorry," said I. "My mind is made. It is God's will."

Mother fixed her eyes upon me, examining my features. If I were merely using God's will as a pretext to leave, she would surely see it. However, hours in secret prayer had convinced me that the urge I felt in my soul to leave came from Above.

It was true that I had longed to head west. However, seeing Penny with Thomas had given me an urgency that had not been there before. The sight had wounded and angered me, perhaps more than I cared to admit. And when I asked God if it was His will that I should leave, I felt an answer so profound it nearly knocked me over. Never, in all the times I had sensed the voice of the Lord in my mind, had I heard an answer so plainly: I was to go.

Mother looked away, disappointed.

"God's will?" Pa said. "I suppose I ought to be glad the war is well over, or you'd be traipsing off to death in the Lord's name too."

I waited for Mother's retaliation, but she appeared too deep in thought to have heeded.

"I'm happy for you, Adam," Pa continued. "I know one day every man must break with his ma and pa and seek his own life, but why must you do it so far away? And railroading at that? Work you know aught of."

Mother closed her eyes: she was deep in prayer.

"I do not know why the Lord has called me to go," said I. "Why was Jonah called to Nineveh? Why was Moses chosen to speak to Pharaoh? Why was Saul called on the road to Damascus? None can say, only the Lord. I go by His will, not my own."

Pa, emboldened by Mother's diverted attention, said, "If you truly feel you must go make something of yourself, to learn a new line of work—that I could bear. But thoughtlessly rushing west, doing such dangerous labor, all for the sake of the Lord? It's a fool's errand."

"How can you call the Lord's will foolish?" asked I, bristling. "Do you think I choose my own path? To serve my own carnal wishes and desires?"

Mother stirred; her prayer near its end.

"No. You are right," Pa said. He sighed deeply, resigned. "I see now that you cannot choose your own path." He clapped his arms round me and squeezed.

"You'll be gone when I return?"

"Yes, sir," said I.

He nodded, regarded me, and then left, closing the door behind as Mother's eyes fluttered open.

I felt a pang of remorse as he disappeared, recalling the day I had accepted his love freely for those few, precious moments. However, I was not the master of my own destiny, and though I was deeply desirous to leave, the Lord had placed that desire within me.

Now, I waited for Mother. It mattered little what she said; God had spoken, and I would go with or without her blessing. I had no doubt that she discerned my thoughts, for the next moment she said, "It is God's will. Come. I will assist you in your preparations."

Chapter 38

The Narrative of Penny Haworth

I pushed my breakfast from me, untouched, then tucked my knees to my chin. Mother, who usually scolded me for my childish poses, said nothing. Presently, she stood, came round the table, and sat next to me. She placed a hand on my shoulder and brushed my copper hair, not yet styled, away from my eyes. I was still wrapped in my dressing gown.

"I'm sorry we quarreled," she said. "I never should have pressed you to walk out with Thomas. Perhaps if I'd let you alone...But never mind now."

Her words did not move me. My loss felt just as fresh as it had been in the night. I didn't wish to speak to Mother. I didn't wish to speak to anyone. I pushed back my chair and stood from the table.

"It's all right," I said. "I'm not angry. I wish to be alone. I'm stepping out for a walk."

"I'll leave you to yourself if that's what you wish. But you're certain you're no longer angry?"

"No." Softening, I threw my arms round Mother. "I'm not."

I returned to my room and dressed for the day. As I did so, I resolved to go to Peter's shop to seek out Adam and explain what he had seen. Both Peter and Thomas would see me. They would know what I was about, but there was nothing for it. I could not go an instant longer with Adam mistakenly believing there was something between Thomas and me.

I saw my future with Adam laid out before me, everything perfect and in its place. Suddenly, I began to feel hopeful and bright again. I returned below and swung the front door open. It was as if time had been rolled back like a scroll, and I was again a child, staring at a horrifying sight.

In front of the door hung a deer's head. Blood was matted in the fur across the nose and round the neck. It was little more than a fawn. The sight disturbed and angered me. Thomas had doubt-less shared my refusal with Gunther, and this was Gunther's repay-ment. This time, Mother would not speak for me.

I marched off toward the shop, now in search of Thomas. When I knocked on the door, it was Peter who answered. His warm breath puffed in the cool morning air as he scraped his plane back and forth, slender shavings of wood curling up in its wake. A quick glance told me that Thomas was absent, as was Adam.

"Where is Thomas?" I asked.

"He's returned home for his coat."

"I see." I hesitated.

Peter lifted the wood and ran a roughened finger over it. "Thomas is a good man, Penny."

"That he is," I agreed, shifting uneasily in the doorway, uncer-tain what Thomas might have communicated.

He straightened and looked me full in the eyes. "I know you care for another, and while it's something I would have wished for once, I can't say as I do now."

I stood irresolute, face flushed. Was my affection for Adam so obvious that Peter had divined it? And why would he not wish for it? What was it that I lacked?

"Can the leopard change his spots? No," Peter said. "You see, though he's the one that reads it night and day, I know a bit of the

Bible too." He lay the wood back down on his workbench and thrust the plane across it again, more wood curling up and away from the sharp iron. "He's gone, you know."

"Thomas? Yes, I know. You've just told—"

"Adam."

"What?" I gave an involuntary start.

Peter again ran a finger across the wood. Satisfied, he set it down with three other similarly carved pieces. "Gone. Left this morning."

"Why? Where?"

"Went west to work on the railroad." Peter appeared very old, broad shoulders slumped and eyes bloodshot. He wiped a large hand over his perspiring forehead.

I attempted to keep my voice steady. "When does he return?"

He shrugged. "Couldn't say."

In utter dismay, I put my hand to the door. "I ought to be going. I'm sorry to have bothered you."

Hurrying through the streets, my thoughts flew with my feet. I had heard Mother speak of the railroad, slowly streaking across the continent. There was work to be had; hard, grueling work, but steady work with decent pay. Adam might be gone for months, but if he continued west, he might be gone for years. He might never come back.

I suddenly hated Thomas for walking out with me, and I hated Adam for seeing it and coming to a false conclusion. Yet, Adam hadn't even spoken to me. He had just left. He had not so much as asked why I was with Thomas. Furthermore, Peter, usually a plain-spoken man, had spoken in parable. What could he mean by saying Adam could not change his spots? Perhaps he was only angry and resentful at Adam's departure. Or perhaps he found fault with me. Perhaps I was the leopard in the parable. Perhaps Minister Judd had poisoned Adam's ears against me after the incident in the woods. However, the weight of Adam's absence drowned all else.

Adam was gone, and I knew not for how long.

Chapter 39

The Narrative of Silas Whittemore
1828

I mpressed upon my mind was the image of Eve sitting stubbornly on the stump before the missionary's cabin, refusing to enter. There was something in her eyes I could not shake the feeling of, though I suppose I was grateful, in a measure, that she had at least allowed the child inside.

I was long in returning to the missionary's. Once I had discovered Eve's trunks, I was obliged to walk past the harbor in the opposite direction of the cabin until I came back to town. The empty street had given the appearance that the place was dead, but inside, it was brimming with life. There were half a dozen taverns, all of which were filled to the brim with soldiers, Indians, and furriers with their wives who, like me, had come to the island to offload their twelvemonth's collections, to be packed and shipped off to merchants in the east and abroad. I continued straight for a time, then ducked down a narrow alley. A painted, wooden sign, swinging violently in the wind, announced the tavern.

The room seemed to sway with bits of its intoxicated occupants: red caps, brass buttons, thick skirts, buckskin breeches, and moccasins. There were French Canadians, Ojibwe, Odawa, Irish, Métis, and British. A fiddler stood in the corner of the room grating away, not terribly skillful, at a dancing tune. In the center of the room, a French-Canadian man and an Odawa woman danced, both with colorful ribbons attached to their persons.

"The new King and Queen," bellowed a woman from the edge of the room.

"Hurrah! Hurrah!" Tumblers raised and drinks sloshed.

Men were being engaged for the forthcoming season, and these little extravaganzas, I knew from my own foray into such, were simply a means of extracting the monetary advances given. The man now dubbed *King* had paid for this dance with his *Queen*.

I pressed through the throng to the bar. Mr. Gauthier, who had been ever so *kind* as to ferry my wife across the lake, was deep in a glass near at hand.

Looking up and recognizing me, he said, "Ansome wife you 'as."

Paying no heed to the man, I called the barmaid. She quickly appeared, face flushed with the heat of the room.

"Saw your wife here earlier. A little dainty, ain't she?" said she.

"I must beg to hire your horse and cart," said I.

"For ees wife's trunks," interjected Mr. Gauthier. "I dreenk your wife's ealth."

I glanced scornfully at the Frenchman and turned back to the barmaid.

"Very well," said she. "Must return it tonight, though. Landlord's got supplies arriving in the morning."

"Certainly," replied I.

"Bet she finds se accommodations you've got er fine as a castle. Staying wis sat old meeshionary?"

I again ignored Mr. Gauthier's remarks and pushed my way back into the open air. I discovered he had accompanied me.

"Why have you followed me?" asked I.

"Early to bed," replied Mr. Gauthier with a grin, then disappeared down the lane.

By the time I regained the cabin, it was so dark as to be necessary to light the cart's twin lanterns. The dim light showed that my wife was no longer outside. Relieved, I unloaded the trunks into a dilapidated shed at the rear of the cabin, returned the horse and cart, and finally came back through the gale on foot.

As I neared the place, I saw the missionary standing in the middle of the road with a lantern, my child at the open door.

"Mrs. Whittemore!" the missionary's booming voice rang into the night. "Mrs. Whittemooore!"

I quickened my gait and called out, "Has she left the cabin?"

"Left the cabin? She never entered it!"

"Never entered?" I quickly calculated. "Then she's been gone two hours, at least! Remain here with the child."

I turned and ran back in the direction from whence I came. Perhaps my wife had returned and sought hospitality from one of the taverns, perhaps the very one I had come from. By the time I returned, it was louder and more raucous. At each place, I pressed through the intoxicated mob and made my inquiry. None of the proprietors or barkeeps had seen her. I even returned to Mr. Douglas' house. He had not seen her. No one had seen or heard anything of my wife.

It was late when I gave up my search for the evening and returned to the cabin in the rain. I would continue by daylight. The missionary's snores and snorts rumbled from the crude bed as I lay down upon the floor to sleep. My child, after her arduous journey, lay rolled up in a tattered blanket upon the floor near me.

I slept fitfully, and when I woke, the missionary and my child sat silently at the table in the cool morning air, eating cold salt pork and hardtack soaked in a bit of water.

"We didn't wish to wake you," said the missionary, eyes crinkling at the corners.

"Any word of my wife?" asked I.

"No word," said he, stabbing his fork into his meat and masticating noisily.

I left the cabin and returned down the muddy lane to the

harbor to collect my thoughts. A light mist was all that remained of the heavy rain that had poured overnight. Gray light from the rising sun forced its way through the clouds.

My wife couldn't have gone far, certainly not removed from the island. A vague notion began to crowd my tired mind. I tried very hard to remember which direction Mr. Gauthier had walked the prior evening. Even if the man had left with my wife, I surely would have passed them. A vision of the pair watching me, hidden on the side of the lane, came to my mind. No action taken by my wife would surprise me, and no action taken by a Company man would surprise me.

I gazed across the water and noticed the faint outline of a bateaux. There was nothing unusual about this, as many birchbark canoes and bateaux landed upon the island each day. However, this boat was not arriving—it was departing. None of the furriers would have departed at this time, for any reason. Most had been away from civilization for twelvemonth, some longer. They would not relinquish their opportunity to drink and revel until the very last fur had been packed for shipment.

Perhaps I was mistaken, but I believed I saw the color of geranium betwixt the rowers' white shirts and red worsted caps. I hastened back to town and inquired again at the tavern. Here, I was met with the news that Mr. Gauthier had left an hour before, just as the rain slowed. When I inquired further, I found that two persons had seen the Frenchman with a woman matching my wife's description.

There was no need for further search. My fears were realized. My wife had abandoned me, alone in the wilderness with our child.

Chapter 40

The Narrative of Adam Bolton

A s I left Haggard House, my thoughts were many. I hoped to make sense of them, but for now, they were jumbled and tangled; there was no loosening the knot that they formed.

It was a journey of several weeks, first by foot, down the wagon track that led out of the village, from thence by steamboat down through the Green Bay and Winnebago Lake, farther south by rail, connecting to the Iowa Central line which took me all the way to the Missouri River, where I took yet another steamboat. I spent one night in Omaha. I was glad to be rid of the place. It was a filthy, overflowing city, full of vice and depravity. I took my final train, the one upon which I would work. The carriages were marked in tall, white letters—U.P.R.R.

It was early afternoon when I came upon the end of the line just beyond the town of Ogallala. There it was: track spanned out in the dirt, grading, a good two feet above ground-level, running beyond as far as the eye could see. As I made my way from the rail carriage in which I had ridden to the end of the track, I saw what appeared to be a veritable army: men, so many that they appeared as ants; horse-drawn wagons, full of iron rails; rail carriages full of supplies, pulled right up to the end of the track; and a large herd of bellowing cattle trailing in the distance. A man with a pointed beard carrying a bullwhip walked up and down the line, watching the insatiable activity with the keen, merciless eyes of a hawk. His supervision, however, appeared superfluous. Not a man among them was inactive. The sounds came regular and rhythmic, like a piece of music: the foreman's *"Up, Down!"*; the spiker's *clank, clank, clank*; the ballast men's *swoosh* of sand from their barrows.

Yet before I had time to take it all in, the roar of, *"Time!"* was heard from one of the foremen, and the hum of activity suddenly ceased. The herd of men lumbered, like the buffalo I had seen from the train, into one of the rail carriages. As they did so, a large man with a triple chin and a bowler cap noted my presence and made his way toward me.

"If werk is what yer lookin' fer, there's the foreman." Sweating profusely, he tipped his hat toward another man who made his way toward the rail car.

"Baxter!" the man called, presumably to the foreman. "Got a fresh 'un!" With that, he stampeded past me and into the dining car.

"Thank you," called I.

I waited as the foreman, a slender man wearing a yellowed shirt with an even yellower collar, reluctantly neared.

"Here for work?" He eyed me sharply.

"Yes."

"Any experience railroading?"

"No."

"Any skills?"

I considered for a moment. Certainly, I might say carpentry. I had seen the carpenter's rail carriage upon the tracks, yet something kept me silent. I had not come all this way to take up Pa's old trade. I had come to forge my own path.

"Any skills?" the foreman half-shouted.

"I'm strong," said I. "I can lift a deal of weight."

The foreman shot a ball of spittle from his lips as he sized up my small, compact form, chuckling as he did so. "Strong, eh? How old?"

"Nineteen."

"Don't look above sixteen." The foreman gazed upward, squinting in the sun, and fumbled with his fingers as if counting. "Okay. See that man there?" He shot a hand in front of me and pointed to the man in the bowler cap standing outside the dining car, waiting his turn to enter.

"Yes."

"That's Big Joe. He lays track. Say you're strong?"

"Yes, sir."

The foreman chuckled again, as if it was all a joke. "Big Joe likes your work, you're in. Pay's two dollars and a half—a day. If you can do the work, that is."

"Yes, sir."

He gave me a sly smile. It was clear he thought I could not, but I had only to wait for the completion of the meal to prove him otherwise.

"You eaten?"

"No, sir."

"C'mon. Room for one more I dare say."

I followed the foreman to the dining car. When we reached the wide-open door, I was nearly knocked over by the stench. The close car was pungent with foul sweat, one hundred and more men seated on both sides of a long, narrow table loaded with hot coffee, mounds of beef, and steaming potatoes. There was the splash of tin cups dipping into the coffee, the clank of forks, and grunts and chewing; but there was no speech, the men too hungry and exhausted to talk.

The foreman pointed to the bench closest to the door where there was hardly enough room. I sat, half of me spilling uncomfortably over the edge. Big Joe was seated somewhere in the middle of the table. He forked a thick slice of roast beef into his mouth. The man next to me, particularly reeking, reached across me to a plate piled with bread and, with grime covered fingers, stuffed the lot into his mouth. A boy, perhaps no more than fourteen, clattered a plate, utensil, and tin cup before me. I gripped the fork, stabbed it into the wobbling stack of meat, and ate. Though my stomach churned in excitement—and fear—of my new work, I forced the food down, eating as much as I could contain. I knew I would need it for the labor ahead.

Before I had half finished, Big Joe, apparently done, lifted his plate, stepped onto the table and, dodging plates, cups, platters, and hands, deftly walked down the length of the car until he passed me.

"Big Joe," the foreman said, mouth full of beans. "Got a new track layer. I want you to show 'im how it's done."

"Track layer, eh?" Big Joe looked from me to the foreman and back, letting out a full-bellied laugh. "I was fixin' to take a nap, but I s'pose that's off now?" The foreman didn't reply. Big Joe rubbed his belly. "All right then, come 'long with me."

The diners were dispersing now, climbing onto the table and walking along it to the door, nearly knocking me over in the process. Big Joe waved for me to follow as a new line of men filtered into the dining car.

"Yeh stick jest behind me," Big Joe said. He took a dudeen from his pocket, lit it, and puffed slowly, savoring the tobacco. He sauntered along, in no particular hurry. "Lucky you come along when you did and not earlier," he said. "Trouble up the line only two days apart. Surveyors one day and graders the other. Sioux kilt upwards of ten men, scalped a few too. 'Course, those weren't our crews, but you'd better keep your wits about you out here. See the stacks of rifles in the dining car?"

I nodded. They were hard to miss, covering an entire wall.

"Trouble comes, you make for them. That's the first thing you should know."

He took me to the head of the line where there was a horse-drawn flatcar full of rails and spikes. "This is yeh an me," he said.

"After the ties get laid, we got five of us to a rail. Today'll be six with yeh. Yeh'll be up front with me. We lay the left side of the rails, and another team, the right. Yeh take those," he pointed to a pile of tongs lying in the dirt, "and clamp onto a rail. We lift and drop. Got to drop it right in place, else we lose time. Then the gauger comes behind. Makes certain we got the right width 'tween the rails. Then 'nother team comes 'long and spikes them down. Then the ballast men. Got that?"

"Yes, sir." Having already seen the work in action, I knew just what the man was saying. He was looking at me now, sizing me up as the foreman had.

"The rails er more'n seven hundred pounds apiece, yeh understand?"

Again, I nodded. He didn't believe me strong enough.

The locomotive behind us suddenly gave a sharp, shrill blast, and the lazy landscape sprung to life. The men from the dining car and the men who had been reclining in the shade of the rail carriages filed past a man dressed in a neat, clean suit. He marked each laborer in a ledger. Big Joe waved at the man and pointed to me.

"If yeh wanta be paid, gotta get counted. Three times a day paymaster marks us."

Four other men appeared near, all a good head taller than me. There was no time for introductions. Big Joe jabbed a finger toward me and shouted something, and then I found myself racing with them to the wagon loaded with rails. I kept tight to Big Joe and, following his lead, grasped a pair of tongs, opened it, and clamped a rail. Almost simultaneously, we lifted and pulled. As soon as the rail was far enough forward, the other three men clamped and lifted the back. We raced toward the newly graded path stretching into the distance.

"*Down*," came from somewhere up the line.

"Lay er easy," Big Joe grunted, releasing the rail from his tongs.

I followed his lead, leaving the rail perfectly aligned with the one behind it. We raced past the gauger back to the wagons.

"Keep up," Big Joe called to me. "This is Jim." Big Joe gestured behind me to a lanky man with a perfectly twisted mustache.

Jim regarded me and grunted. "Foreman got you on trial?" he asked, squinting.

"Yes, sir."

As we clamped another rail, Big Joe's eyes widened at the ease with which I lifted.

"One of 'em small but tough ones, eh?"

I merely tipped my head in assent, not wishing to be prideful.

Big Joe laughed. "Not much of a talker, eh? Suits me fine. I ken do the talkin' fer both of us."

Under the weight of our burden, we rushed to the front of the line and released on, "*Down.*" Throughout the course of the day, we laid more rails than I would have believed possible, more than two miles. Big Joe's mouth never closed through the many hours. In grunts, while running back to the wagon, he told me about the different men who worked the railroad, where they came from, and why they came. He spun yarns about the different places they had been through, mixing truth with lore. He pointed to the many rail men, still wearing blue coats from the war. Hard men, they were, he said, with hard lives and not to be fooled with. He told me how the railroad worked and who did what.

When the sun finally began to fade in the west, the foreman called quits. I fell to my supper with more vigor than I ever had. Yet even after eating, there was still work to be done. Alongside Big Joe and Jim, I erected a large tent. Where there had previously been nothing but open prairie, there was now a small village of canvas.

Big Joe fished inside his pocket and produced a harmonica. He then proceeded to play a melancholy tune I had never heard before, and as I collected brushwood with Jim, it set me to thinking about Penny. When we had finished and sat on our coats or bits of wood round a warm, roaring fire, Big Joe started the tune again, and Jim sung the words here and there when he could remember them. "'A hundred months have passed, Lorena; Since last I held that hand in mine.'" There was a long silence between lyrics and then, "'The hopes that could not last, Lorena; They lived, but only lived to cheat,'" and finally, "'Our heads will soon lie low, Lorena; Life's tide is ebbing out so fast.'"

The haunting words and melody struck me to the core, and I could not listen further. I stood and neared the tent in preparation to enter. The harmonica stopped.

"Where yeh going?" Big Joe asked.

"I'm tired," said I. "I mean to sleep."

"Not in there yeh don't," Big Joe said. "Your place is in the swayback." He nodded to a long, sagging rail carriage. "Got to earn yer place in the tent."

Unoffended, I moved in the direction Big Joe had pointed. There were customs to this place, just as there were customs at home. It was too dark to read, but I found a lit kerosene lamp, hanging upon the door. I went inside, the stench of working men powerful. I hurriedly took a blanket from atop one of the tightly packed bunks, wrapped it round me, and sat near the door with my Bible. At first, it was difficult to concentrate—men passing me to enter, snores coming from within, and conversation, much of it so foul it made me blush. Mismatched tunes and bits of song came from the white canvas tents, along with the swears and curses of gamblers as they lost their day's wages and more. However, after some time, I found I could disregard the sounds.

When I finished my reading, the whole place, excepting the snores, was silent. I was stiff from my cramped sitting position. I turned out the kerosene lamp. There were patches of light from the dying fires before the tents. I didn't think I could tolerate the stench inside the swayback, so I followed the example of some men I had seen earlier, mounting the carriage itself. Once atop it, I stretched out on the roof, tucking my blanket round me as best I could, and closed my eyes.

Tired as I was, my mind was still wide awake. Though I was yet angry—seeing her with him—I allowed myself to take the key and open the door to the room full of her memories. It was like stepping into a beautiful, delicately scented garden. I felt an instant sense of peace and calm. My face, which had been drawn and tight, relaxed. Her copper hair was wild and flowing, and I bathed my face in it. It smelt sweet, like Queen Anne's lace.

Chapter 41

The Narrative of Penny Haworth

For the first week that Adam was gone, I held onto an unreasonable hope that he would change his mind or perhaps come upon insurmountable difficulties and return. During my walks, I would pause near the schoolhouse and scan the lane through Whittemore's Prairie, hoping against hope to see him, with his quick, sure stride, following the path toward his pa's shop. However, at the conclusion of the week, I had neither seen nor heard any sign of him. I went through alternate periods of despair and then hope, hope and then despair. Always, at night, I felt the pain of his absence most. Even so, I did not give up faith in his return.

During the day, I was kept busy with the running of the household and the tending of the kitchen, garden, and animals. One afternoon, finished with my work earlier than usual, I crossed the street and knocked. After some moments, the door opened to reveal Ingrid's mother, Mrs. Nilsson, hands encased in tattered gardening gloves. Behind her, the table appeared to have been recently vacated, for there were still two dirty plates left upon the table.

"Is Ingrid in?" I asked.

"Yah. Pleass," she said, showing me inside.

The little frame structure was so unlike our brick home. The larger front portion served as dining room, sitting room, and bedroom; the smaller back portion housed the kitchen. Every surface was covered: a cat, curled in the corner of the room, nursed five pint-sized kittens; the rough-hewn beds were piled in laundry to be washed; tables were cluttered with baskets, bits of fabric, and yarn; and chairs were tumbled over, serving as toys for the smallest three children. Even the few shelves on the walls were piled with odds and ends, anything that might be useful at some time or another.

Just then, Ingrid appeared from the back, face and hands red, fingers dripping. She appeared tired and irritable. "I was just washing the dishes," she said, collecting the remaining plates from the table. "I'll only be a moment."

"Sorry, I cannot stay," her mother said, shrugging apologetically. "I have vork in garden."

As she disappeared through the back, I took a seat on one of the high-backed wooden chairs surrounding the table. Ernst, all of two, the last of the family, looked up from his game of scooting over and under the overturned chair, and seeing it was only me, went back to his play. Ingrid reappeared shortly, wiping her reddened hands on her apron.

"I wasn't expecting you," she said. Her words were slow and clipped, only a trace of her accent remaining now.

"No," I said. "I didn't expect to come myself, only, I finished my work a little early and thought you might like some help with your darning."

"Thank Heavens," Ingrid said, a little of the irritation draining away. "It seems I've hundreds of them to do." She lifted a basket from the floor and put it upon the kitchen table between us. I removed one of the stockings and fitted the heel with the wooden darning egg, Ingrid doing the same. Before either of us had taken half a dozen running stitches, she jumped up, dropping her stocking and darning egg on the table with a thud. "There he is!" she said, hurrying to the side of the window facing the street.

"Who?" I asked, whirling round in my seat.

Ingrid remained behind the scant window dressings. I joined her, hidden from view. Ernst dragged the chair he had been playing with to the window center, climbed upon it, and stared out.

"Who is it?" I whispered.

"Who it?" Ernst repeated loudly.

Ingrid simply pointed. It was a tall man, neatly dressed, handsome in a plain sort of way. He stopped for a moment before my gate, looked up at the house, and then proceeded on his way.

"Thomas," I said. "Is that all?" I moved from my hidden position directly before the window with Ernst.

"He'll see you!" Ingrid said, eyes wide.

At that moment, Thomas turned and glanced directly at me. He looked away, embarrassed. Then, he paused, acknowledged me with a tip of his hat, and hurried on. Ernst, finding the object of interest had disappeared, dragged his chair back to his corner of the room to play.

"He comes every day," Ingrid said. "It is out of his way, you know."

A little pang of guilt wrenched me. I ignored it and resumed my seat at the table, Ingrid joining.

"I see him from my window," she continued. "You ought to have accepted him. He good—is—a good man."

My running stitches flew, becoming farther apart and crooked. "Well, I didn't. And I don't intend to. I don't care how good he is."

"Don't be angry," Ingrid said, glancing up from her work. "I'm only thinking of you. You might become lonely here."

"I might *be* lonely here," I corrected. "I'm not, though. I have Mother, and I have you."

"No," Ingrid said. "*Become*." She put her stocking aside and returned to the window. "I am leaving soon."

"What?" I said, looking up in amazement. "Leaving where?"

"I vill get married," Ingrid said, losing her proper English in her excitement. "You have met the new Mrs. McDonnell? She has a brother back in New York looking for a vife. She wrote to him and tell him about me. He vants—wants—to marry me."

My mouth dropped in astonishment. "How is it possible? You've never met the man."

Ingrid shrugged. "I think he is likely better than men here. Not many left after war. Besides, then I will see New York."

"But you won't like it," I said. "It's nothing like Nomaton. There's no green, and the streets are foul. Why would you do such a thing?"

"I would like to try it," Ingrid said. "Perhaps Nomaton is better for you, but perhaps New York is better for me."

"You're not accustomed to city dwelling though, Ingrid. You've lived in the country all your life. And what if this man turns out to be disagreeable—or violent?"

"I spoke much with McDonnell's wife. He is not like that. He very agreeable man."

"*Is* he?" I asked. "And when do you leave? You're only just telling me?"

"Within the week," Ingrid said.

I pushed aside my work and stared at my friend, incredulous.

"Johanna," Ingrid continued, referring to her younger sister, "will be here to help Mother. You see now why I wish you have someone to care for you? I do not wish you to become lonely."

"Everyone is leaving," I said.

"You may come visit me in New York."

A lump formed in my throat as I took up my work again. Ingrid was leaving, and I was staying. Ingrid was to marry, and I was not. I wished that I could be happy for my friend, but instead,

I felt a bitter pang of jealousy. Ingrid was getting along in the world, and I would be left behind.

"I'm very happy for you. Congratulations," I said without looking up.

"Thank you," Ingrid said.

We continued darning, but a heaviness had settled upon the room.

Chapter 42

The Narrative of Adam Bolton

For the next week, the railroad moved slowly but steadily, farther and farther west. The air became unseasonably warm. There was little variation in the days for me. I enjoyed the heavy work, and I even enjoyed Big Joe's constant ramblings. It took my mind off Penny, Mother, the Word of God, and Haggard House—in that order. Any rest from my constant thoughts was welcome.

At the conclusion of the week, Big Joe told the foreman that I was a hard worker and had taken to the trade quickly. I believe he was surprised I had not dropped out the first day. Again, he sized me up, only this time without that hint of mockery. And so, I was welcome to travel and work with the crew as long as there was work to be had.

Shortly after my trial week was up, I began to see the vice and depravity that attended the railroad. It was not only the men, carrying their "pocket pistols"—what I discovered were not pistols at all but flasks of whisky, but it was also the vile transitory towns —composed largely of canvas tents and shanties—that sprung up at the end of the line. Workdays were quietest, the only vices being those within the camp. However, the evening before the Sabbath, the holiest of days, was the most defiled. It was then that the men let loose, drinking to oblivion, dancing and gambling away the very last cent of their earnings.

Upon only my second occasion witnessing these vices, something occurred which changed my status within the crew. As I observed to be usual occurrence, hastily constructed buildings, along with large canvas tents, appeared almost instantaneously at the end of the track. I could not understand how the shanties went up so quickly. However, I learned from Big Joe that the structures were numbered so they could be swiftly assembled, then disassembled.

That evening, I steered clear of the hastily constructed village, instead, sitting at the door of the empty swayback, reading my Bible in preparation for the Sabbath. For an hour I read, but my mind scarcely took in the lines, for the sounds of the band in the Big Tent were spilling across the plains, and I found that when I finished a page, I had comprehended nothing.

Darkness had fallen, but even from the distance I was at, the glare of the kerosene lamps scattered flecks of light across the brush and clumps of grass. At last, I gave up my reading for the night and clambered between the rail carriages in order to get a view of the web that had caught so many men.

The light was more dazzling than I had ever seen it. Men, even a woman, straggled across the dirt path from one grog shop to another. Yet, the Big Tent was the main attraction. It was, by far, the largest tent I had seen in my life, as long as the towering white pines surrounding Haggard House were tall. Clusters of men stood round the front, smoking pipes and speaking—shouting, rather—to be heard above the sound of the band inside. The interior, partly seen through the open flaps, dazzled the eyes— somehow glittering, as if of jewels. Big Joe had invited me to join them, but I had, in no uncertain terms, declined this and all such future invitations. Now, I was ill at ease. I had not joined in the vice, but something within warned me of danger. I watched the tent for a few moments, but there was nothing untoward to be seen. I clambered atop the swayback and, after entering that calming room in my mind—the one filled with Penny—fell into a light sleep.

Harsh, angry shouts brought me to again, and I bolted upright. By my best guess, it was perhaps one or two o'clock in the morning, and the Big Tent showed no signs of abatement. It was, in fact, louder than ever. The shouts came from a sharply dressed, burly man with a thick beard and flashing eyes, and were directed at none other than Big Joe.

"Say it again, why don't you!" the burly man shouted, placing his large hands onto Big Joe's chest and shoving.

Big Joe stumbled slightly, then caught himself. "I'll say it all night long, if yeh like. Yeh're a liar and a cheat. I seen what yeh did."

Something about the burly man's face changed, and I knew there was not a moment to waste. I hastened down from my perch and into the carriage. There were rifles in the swayback as well as the dining car. I snatched the closest one and rushed round the carriage to where the men were standing. I was not a moment too soon—the burly man reached for the revolver in the holster on his hip.

"You murdering dog!" Big Joe shouted.

"Stop!" cried I. My rifle was poised and fully cocked.

The burly man looked from me to Big Joe and back. I had never seen such an expression. He was ready to kill, to murder; I saw it in his eyes. He slowly removed his hand, spat upon the ground, and returned inside the tent. Big Joe looked on, as if he could not understand what had just happened.

My heart, which had been hammering so fast I thought it might burst, gradually slowed. I lowered the rifle and, more alert than I had ever been in my life, made my way to where Big Joe stood.

"That lying, cheating, murdering son of a bitch!" Big Joe shouted, stumbling toward the tent.

I caught him before he neared the door.

"Stop. He means to kill you," said I, gripping him by the shoulders. On any other occasion, I would not have been able to hold him, but his resistance was somewhat hampered by his intoxication.

"Give me that rifle and we'll see who means to kill who," Big Joe shouted at the tent.

"Shh," hissed I, slinging the rifle over my shoulder and bodily turning him round toward the train.

It was fortunate he didn't persist, for I couldn't have held him. He paused for a moment, then did as I said. I had to take him all the way round the train at the front, for he never would have been able to step between the carriages in his state. I got him a tin cup of water from the barrel, which he downed immediately. He suddenly appeared very tired, almost as if he'd forgotten what had just transpired. I helped him to the canvas tent, where he slumped and fell immediately into sleep. I took one of the wool blankets and covered him with it, his boots poking out the end. Then I returned atop the swayback, rifle cradled in my arms.

I didn't sleep for the rest of the night, ears alert to every sound, expecting at any moment for the burly man to return and finish what he had started. It was in the early hours of the morning that I found I had drifted off to sleep. I was awakened by a shot. Again, I bolted to a sitting position. There was a man down before the Big Tent, only it wasn't Big Joe. One of the men who worked alongside us, stringing up the telegraph lines, stood over the very man who had threatened Big Joe. The burly man was stone dead, shot clear through the head.

The sound seemed not to have disturbed anyone else, for the band inside the tent still played, and no one came to see why the shot was fired. The telegraph man looked up at me and shrugged his shoulders.

"He cheated," was all he said.

Chapter 43

The Narrative of Adam Bolton

There was no mention of Saturday night's events nor the murder upon Sabbath morning. The only remaining evidence was a mound of dirt behind where the Big Tent had been staked. Big Joe kept to himself, sleeping away most of the day and then avoiding me—apparent by his quick departure upon any occasion of coming within my sight. Perhaps he was embarrassed, or perhaps he simply did not recall what had occurred. However, when Monday came round, and we toiled together in the hot sun, Big Joe was quieter than usual. In matter of fact, he hardly spoke. When time was called for the day, I retired to the swayback to do my nightly reading. About an hour afterwards, Big Joe returned and beckoned me.

"C'mon."

Believing that he at last wished to discuss the events of the previous night, I carefully closed my Bible, tucked it under my arm, and followed. A good fire burned, clear and hot, before the tent. Half a dozen familiar faces, including my fellow rail setters, sat round the fire, talking, laughing, and singing. Jim sat a little apart, using his blue coat as a seat and smoking his clay pipe.

"Bit young, aren't yeh?" Big Joe said.

"Nineteen," said I.

Big Joe ignored my declaration and continued. "Young like a baby goat. A kid." He scratched his head thoughtfully. "Kid," he said in an undertone, then laughed. "Heh, Jim, what do yeh think? Kid?" Big Joe gestured at me and waited for approval.

Jim stared for a moment, puffing at his pipe, and smiled. "Yep."

"Kid it is," Big Joe said. "Kid, listen. I ever tell yeh about the time Will Cody killed a buffalo for my personal supper..."

Big Joe rattled on. I was not overly fond of the new title, but I understood this meant that I had been accepted. I was no longer an outsider. For what seemed an interminable while, Big Joe carried on with his stories. At last, it was time to turn in for the night, and I stood, making for the swayback.

"Hey, Kid. Where yeh going? Yeh don't sleep there anymore. Yeh're in the tent with us."

I looked from Big Joe to Jim and back. It wasn't a joke: he meant it. It seemed he remembered after all, though he had said not a word about the matter.

Shortly after my full acceptance into the crew, the railroad extended its way to a small town. Though there was nothing but empty, open prairieland, dotted here and there with the occasional frame house; Main Street was oddly clustered with businesses, squeezed against each other as if there were no room.

When the day's work was finished, it was a relief to find lodgings in the large, though dingy hotel, tucked between a saddler's shop and bakery. It was an enormous, plain structure composed of horizontal slats of wood, with the second story covered in a long row of matching, rectangular windows. The hotel being full to the brim, Big Joe and I were situated together in a single room with a single bed. He dropped back on the bed, kicked up his feet across the metal bars, and closed his eyes.

"This makes it all werth it. Don't it? Snug bed. Prettiest damned girls downstairs. Heh. This is the life."

Laying my bundle down, I opened it and retrieved my Bible, pulling up a bare wooden chair to sit in. Big Joe squinted at the book.

"Coulden help but notice. Yeh read that Bible ev'ry night." He chuckled.

I did not reply, opening to the day's reading.

"D'yeh mind if I ask...What fer?"

My heart quavered. This was the purpose for which I had come. Perhaps if Big Joe saw Christ's light, then others would follow. Instead of answering directly, I flipped through the worn pages and read aloud, "'And these words, which I command thee this day, shall be in thine heart: And thou shalt teach them diligently unto thy children, and shalt talk of them when thou sittest in thine house, and when thou walkest by the way, and when thou liest down, and when thou risest up. And thou shalt bind them for a sign upon thine hand, and they shall be as frontlets between thine eyes.'" I looked at Big Joe composedly, waiting so see what effect the Word had upon him.

A hint of grin flickered round Big Joe's thick lips. "Why ern't they dangling tween yer eyes then?"

My mouth straightened, and my jaw tightened. Big Joe merely made a jest of the Word. "That's not the meaning."

"Well, that's what er says."

"It simply means that we must always keep the Word of God before us. We must constantly read it and keep it in our hearts and minds."

"But that's not what er says."

My face turned stony. Perhaps Big Joe was like the swine one should not cast one's pearls before. "You don't understand."

Sensing my seriousness, the slight smile disappeared from his face. "Pr'aps not." He glanced round the plain room, half whistled a tune, then rose from the bed and disappeared to the bar-room below.

I was glad of the quiet and solitude in which to read. Unbidden, Big Joe's words returned to my mind. *But that's not what er says.* I attempted to read but couldn't focus on the words. I pressed the book closed. *But that's not what er says.*

As evening wore on, noise ascended from the bar. There were hoots, followed by raucous voices singing, accompanied by a banjo and fiddle. "'Ooh in eighteen hundred and forty-one; My corduroy britches I put on; My corduroy britches I put on; To work upon the railway, the railway...'" After an hour or so of attempting to sleep, I shoved my head under the pillow, hoping to stifle the sound. It was rife with the stench of previous travelers, and sound still seeped through. A moment later, Big Joe burst through the door, reeking of spirits. His body seemed to fill the whole room as he swayed from side to side.

"Kid," he said in a loud whisper thickened by whisky. "Yeh awake?"

I remained still, hoping he would give up and return below. Instead, the pillow was yanked from my head.

"Too early te sleep. Come on. I've a drink wi yer name on it."

Next, I was dragged from the bed.

"Down te stairs."

As Big Joe pulled me along, I realized I was only in my nightshirt. "I'm not dressed. Let me go."

The heavy grip on me didn't release, and a moment later, I found myself at the bottom of the stairs in the glowing light of the bar-room. I expected to be met with a chorus of laughter, but either the occupants of the hotel were too drunk or didn't care. Big Joe dragged me right up to the bar.

"A drink for Kid here," Big Joe called.

"At last! He's come," Jim said, slapping my back heartily—if not a little painfully.

The room was stuffed to the brim with at least fifty or so of my railroad companions, men from the town, and half a dozen bright-cheeked and red-lipped women in low-cut, riotously colored décolleté gowns.

"No drink, Big Joe," said I, bracing my hands against the bar to push myself away. "I won't drink it. It'll be a waste of your wages."

Big Joe shook his head and raised his voice. "Ev'ry man here will be offended if yeh don't have one, Kid. Bible or no Bible. Just one." His booming voice commanded the attention of the room, and suddenly, it seemed the whole swirling mob stopped and looked upon me.

My cheeks burned.

"It's fer savin' my life, Kid," Big Joe whispered.

"Just one then," said I, intending to toss the drink upon the floor whenever Big Joe turned away.

"Heh! Heh! Proud of yeh, Kid. Cheers to that. Yer a real railroad man now!"

Big Joe raised his glass of whisky, and Jim and the rest followed.

"To the railroad men!" a woman in a dazzling, plunging red gown cried.

"To the railroad men!" the hotel echoed back.

I would have to feign to drink. However, as soon as the glass was upon my lips, I found that I couldn't return it. Big Joe's thick hand held the glass and tipped upward, leaving me the choice of being drenched in whisky or allowing the spirit to slide down my throat. Instinctively, I chose the latter. The liquid burned, and I coughed and sputtered.

"There yeh go, Kid!" he hooted.

As I recovered, I noticed Big Joe disappear to a corner of the room and whisper to a woman close to my own age. She was beautiful by lamplight, not as beautiful as Penny, but certainly the most attractive woman in the room. Her hair and eyes were dark, and she was head and shoulders shorter than me. Both her lips and cheeks were covered in paint. Despite my sheltered life, I understood what that meant. I turned away, but, despite my best efforts, my eyes roved back. An intense fascination with this woman of sin sprung within me.

Big Joe returned. "Another. Another, Kid."

My lips tightened. "I certainly cannot have another, sir."

"I don't know much about the Bible, but I know one verse." Big Joe scrunched up his face as if thinking the hardest he had ever thought in his life. "'Giv whisky ter the man who's sad.' Heh! Heh!"

Although Big Joe's Scripture was not remotely accurate, I was aware of what he had attempted to quote. The effects of the drink I had just consumed were already beginning to work upon me; a sort of freedom from care, which I had never before felt, crept through my blood. For a moment, I even inwardly congratulated him on his ingenious use of Scripture.

"Very well," said I, reluctantly accepting the glass that appeared before me. "This is the last."

"Hee-ya, Kid. There yeh go!"

Two drinks turned into three, and three very shortly turned into four. Pleasantly, by the fifth drink, all thoughts of Mother, the Word of God, and Haggard House left my mind. Yet in direct proportion to their fading, my thoughts amplified upon Penny.

The woman I had seen Big Joe speaking to earlier approached with a timorous smile. It was too loud for much speech, so she touched my arm and indicated that I should follow. I did so willingly, believing I could do her some good, and she led me outside. The comparative silence of the street was welcome. The night was cool, but I was too far removed by drink to feel it.

"Your friend told me you might need some company," she said softly.

I thought how kind it was of Big Joe to think of me. Then, realizing in embarrassment what the woman meant, I backed away. "No. No. Nothing of that sort."

The woman laughed. "Don't worry. A little conversation, perhaps?"

I paused reluctantly.

She smiled. "You're not afraid of me, are you? A grown man such as yourself? You may choose what you do or do not do with me."

I suddenly felt that this was a test. The woman was right. Only I had power over what was or was not done. Surely, a little conversation could not go astray. Indeed, it might do her some good. My limbs, which had stiffened like planks, relaxed.

"What manner of conversation?"

"Perhaps about your woman back home?"

Her words made me start; I searched her face. How was it possible she should know such a thing? I had not spoken of Penny, even to Big Joe.

She laughed and smoothed her salmon-colored décolleté gown. "I am correct then? What's her name?"

Unbidden, the word suddenly poured from my lips. "Penny." It was a relief to say it.

The woman smiled and closed some of the distance I had put between us. "Tell me about her."

More words came tumbling out, all wrong. "Beautiful. She's beautiful. She comprehends me. And...when I'm with her, I forget my troubles."

"Troubles? What troubles can you have? Such a young man?" she said.

My gaze dropped. These were things of which I could not speak. With quickening heart, I noted the rounded flesh bulging from the deep neckline of her gown. "More than you could imagine," replied I, forcing my eyes away.

"Why aren't you with her, your Penny?"

"I cannot be. She is a heathen." In my mind's eye, I still saw the woman's exposed flesh.

"I see." The woman was directly before me now. She placed a hand on my arm. "Perhaps your mind needs a rest from all that. All your...troubles."

I glanced up and stared blankly at her. It was as if she had read my mind. "Yes."

"Then come. Another?"

She took my arm again, and I followed her back inside. There, she presented me with a drink.

"To resting our minds," she said, holding the glass and touching it to mine.

Chapter 44

The Narrative of Penny Haworth

"Goodbye, Ingrid." I embraced my friend and stood back, holding her at arm's length.

"Goodbye, dear girl," Mother said, taking her turn. "Keep your wits about you."

Ingrid, dressed in her traveling costume, a gift from me—a gray poplin dress covered with a thin, black paletot—hurriedly kissed me. I couldn't help it; a tear ran down my cheek. Ingrid too looked as if she would cry, but instead, she kissed her gloved hand toward us and half ran to the docked steamboat. A crowd had gathered, and piles of goods and traveling trunks, both unloaded and yet to be loaded, stood off to one side.

I clambered back into the buggy with Mother and waved at Ingrid as she boarded, double smoke-stacks towering in the air and flags whipping in the wind. We waited until the twin clouds of black billowed behind, boat moving from shore across the glistening water. Ingrid would cover some of the same ground as Adam, yet she would diverge and travel east instead of west.

The Morgan was champing at the bit, and Mother guided the buggy over the bit of corduroy road leading to Nomaton. The extra jolting from the uneven logs, combined with the heat and humidity, made me feel ill. To distract myself, I reached down and opened the mail sack on the floor. There were only a handful of letters and one telegram inside. I rifled through them again, hoping against hope that I had missed one. None came from the name I longed to see. Disconsolate, I shoved the mail back in the sack and crossed my arms. We traveled in silence until the clatter of the road quieted as the track became dirt.

"Thomas is getting along well," Mother said.

"Yes, I'm happy for him," I said.

"It's a pity you wouldn't have him." I offered no reply, and Mother continued. "Would you have done? Had it not been for... Adam?"

I slouched in my seat. The air was stifling, and now, so too was Mother. "No...Perhaps...But it's of no use to think of such things." I paused for a moment, then continued. "I've something to tell you."

"What is it?" There was apprehension in her voice.

"I've decided something."

Mother sat tall and alert.

"Everyone has left me now." Glancing over I quickly added, "Everyone but you, of course. And I must make something of myself...must *do* something." I thought I saw Mother heave a sigh of relief. "I've spoken with Mr. Tenney. I've offered to put up bread and pies for sale at his shop, and he's agreed. With so many settlers coming into Nomaton, he says there's great demand. I hate to drain our savings, for who knows what might happen? It will supplement what we have." I waited for a response. "Well?"

"It's a wonderful idea Penny..."

"Yet...?"

"Yet, I'm afraid you've a rash inclination to rush headlong into undertakings that you're not equipped to carry out."

My ears grew hot. "I'm not a child, and this isn't a sampler."

"No. You're right. Only, are you certain you can carry on with such an endeavor? It will be a load of work, and you've already so much to do."

"I'm certain," I said. "And I'm to start this very afternoon."

"Well, then that's settled." Mother said it in such a way that I felt it was not settled.

"It's not my sampler," I repeated.

"No. You're right there. Your sampler is in the chest, half finished, along with half a dozen others."

Her words stung, but I did not reply. Words were not needed —actions were. I would show her that I could carry out what I intended. By the time Adam returned, he would find me celebrated throughout the village. I would be known and accepted by all. I would do what I could not with my words: I would show them.

Chapter 45

The Narrative of Adam Bolton

Upon waking, I experienced a profound sense of shame. At first, I could not place it. I remembered nothing from the previous night. No, I did remember something—drinking, heavily. I was parched, and my head felt thick. As I sat, I realized my hands were shaking, and my vision was blurred.

Big Joe suddenly leapt from the far side of the bed. No matter if he slept one hour or twelve, his body always awoke him in time for work. He poured the entirety of the scant supply of water from the pitcher and washed his hands and face in the basin.

"Yeh surprised me, Kid," Big Joe said, drying his face on the dingy towel. "Always the quiet ones that er the wildest, eh?" He grinned.

I stood and stared at the water in the basin, longing to relieve my parched throat. "It was wrong," answered I. "It will not happen again."

"Here," Big Joe stepped away from the wash basin. "Splash yer face. It ull help."

My lip curled at the sight of the gray water, but I did as I was told. Big Joe was correct in his observation: the cold water helped clear my mind considerably.

"This'll help too." Big Joe cracked open the plate glass window overlooking the stable at the back of the hotel.

As fresh air filled my lungs, I suddenly realized how foul the atmosphere was inside. The stench of spirits and sweat seeped through our skin and permeated the room, but there was another odor I couldn't place.

"What is that?" said I, sniffing.

Big Joe slapped his knee. "Heh, heh, heh. Yer pullin' my leg."

"No. What is it?"

Big Joe appeared as if he didn't quite believe me. When he realized I was in earnest, his face reddened, as if it were one thing to hint, but quite another to say. My heart, already unsteady from the ravages of liquor, faltered yet again. I was afraid of what Big Joe might say and suddenly wished I could take the question back. The sense of guilt that filled me told me there was more to be ashamed of than just the drink.

"Got to get ter werk. Ef the memory don't come back, I'll tell yeh."

Though it was only temporary respite, I was glad of Big Joe's silence.

Like desperately trying to recall the beginning of a story one cannot remember, my mind returned over and over to the barroom, the many drinks, and my talk with the woman of the night. There was nothing after that. My next memory, only moments before the present, was of waking. As I worked, I replayed those pieces again and again, both hoping and hoping *not* to remember the rest. My lethargy and the rich stench coming from my body were constant reminders of my sin. I felt as foul as I smelled. I wished to cleanse both mind and body. Even Big Joe, usually so full of talk, remained silent and kept his head down to his work.

By mid-afternoon, I struggled to keep up. As the foreman disappeared farther up the line, Big Joe stopped and wiped his forehead. He eyed me and said I looked, "Sicker 'n a dog."

"Go on to the river," Big Joe continued. "Foreman won't be

back down the line for an hour or two yet. Take a breather and get cleaned up."

We dropped the rail, and I stepped aside. "And you?"

"Don't werry about me. I'll cover fer yeh if the foreman gets back quicker."

I wandered across the plain towards the scrub and trees that descended down the bank. A quarter of an hour later, I felt pure relief as I slipped into the cool water, clothes on shore. Keen remembrance of nearly drowning as a child kept me near the bank and in the shallows. The water revived me somewhat as I scrubbed myself as best I could with my hands.

Afterward, I dressed and settled upon a large boulder to dry. A beaver on the opposite bank scurried back and forth, building its dam. Knowing my rocky bed would not allow me to sleep for long, I closed my eyes and allowed myself to be lulled by the sound of the river and the birds. My sleep was intensely full of dreams, but as anticipated, I woke within a quarter hour. I felt refreshed in body and cleaner than I had felt all day.

As I rose from my resting place, a memory from the previous night flashed before me. I remembered stumbling up the winding stairs to my room. Someone was present, helping to support me, but I couldn't think who. And that was all. I attempted to remember what came next, but there was nothing.

Returning to work was difficult. Although I felt somewhat refreshed, a good half day's hard labor still lay before us. Big Joe, having much more experience in recovery from heavy drinking, had resumed his cheerful, chattering self. He continuously dropped hints of our *grand night* and our being *real men*. I began to think I would never recall the evening at the hotel and that, even if Big Joe told me, it would be difficult to discern what was real and what was yarn.

My hand slipped the tongs mid-way between the wagon and the graded path.

Another memory returned.

"Oiiii! Watch out there!" Jim cried.

In a daze, I followed the men to collect the next rail. My mind attempted to refuse the images it presented, pressing them toward some other room in my mind, but it was not to be.

"Heh. Heh. Coming back to yeh Kid, ain't it?" Big Joe chuckled, looking infinitely pleased.

I felt anything but. I wished I could erase the restored memory. More than that, I wished I could undo the events themselves. I felt more ill now than I had upon waking in the morning. I stumbled a ways from the railroad and retched.

"Take a minute, Kid," Big Joe called, laughing. "Probably feel better soon with that outa yeh."

It wasn't the drink that caused my insides to heave but the memory itself; not only images, but scents, sounds, and most of all, sensations coursed through my body. My nose filled again with the scent of cheap cologne. My ears filled with Big Joe's booming laughter and grunts. My body felt again a new, but profound pleasure.

Aroused and inebriated beyond all reckoning, when the woman had tugged at my shirt, I followed her up to my room. Big Joe and a buxom lady were on the stairs before us, laughing and tripping over the steps. Despite everything in my mind reminding me that it was wrong, or perhaps *because* everything in my mind reminded me it was wrong, I had allowed myself to be led into our room.

In the cramped quarters, Big Joe and the buxom lady had peeled the clothes from each other first. I kept my eyes on my own woman as she stroked me. Grunts and laughter erupted from the single bed, and exposed flesh bounced up and down over Big Joe's belly.

Unlike Big Joe, I had taken my time over my clothing. I had taken time over the woman's clothing. I had taken my time placing her in the bed next to Big Joe's woman. I had taken time easing myself into her. And I had taken time waiting for the right moment to solicit my final relief, all the while catching glimpses of Big Joe and the buxom lady rising and falling next to me.

As I relived the previous night, I realized with horror that the third scent in the room—was the scent of woman.

Chapter 46

The Narrative of Adam Bolton

"'M̲ember when we switched partners, Kid?" Big Joe asked me, nudging my arm with his elbow that evening as we lay in the tent. "What a night, eh?"

I couldn't remember doing such a thing, but I couldn't be certain it hadn't happened, either. Rather than responding, I rolled over on the ground. Big Joe grunted and rolled over too.

This was the first night I had failed to read my Bible. I did not even attempt it. Fragmented memories of the previous night haunted me. Wracked as I was with guilt, a part of me whispered that I had enjoyed it. A part of me whispered that the person who took the beautiful woman upstairs, next to Big Joe, and knew her —was the real Adam. Perhaps I had even known two women in one night. The part of me whispering enjoyment crept back. Then the Holy Scripture filled my mind, railing on what I had done.

I couldn't sleep, so I wandered to the fire before our tent. After stoking it with more dried brush, I sat on my coat in the grass, took up a bit of wood, and began to carve it mindlessly with my pocket-knife, just as Pa had shown me as a child. As I whittled, a shape became apparent.

Big Joe stirred, then emerged from the canvas and rubbed his eyes. He took the piece from my hand. "Not bad. Seems yeh know something o' wood. That's something, that is."

I took the miniature horse-head back and continued carving in silence.

"Yeh don't have te feel bad, Kid...'bout what happened," he said, squatting. "Most nat'ral thing in te world."

I whittled faster.

"Are yeh angry with me?" Big Joe asked.

My lips tightened, but still, I did not reply. He stood and sighed.

The workday brought no improvement in my mood. I, as Big Joe put it, *sulked*. My face took on a new expression, more tense, stony. During noon break, instead of eating with the men, I disappeared into the neighboring woods. I didn't return until work had already begun again.

"Where were yeh?" I had not seen Big Joe angry, but here he was, ears and face red with it. "I covered for yeh with the foreman. Told him yeh were takin a piss. And what's that 'pon your shirtsleeve?" He grasped my arm and yanked it upward, revealing a red stain.

"You oughtn't have lied," said I, disregarding his question.

Big Joe grasped a pickaxe and flung it. I jumped out of the way just in time: the tool stuck in the dirt just beside me. Big Joe snorted and stalked down the line.

Jim cast me a sympathetic glance. "Not often his temper gets riled, but when it does. Whew-eee!"

I saw Big Joe speak to the crew laying rails opposite, and a moment later, one of their men crossed to our side to replace him. For the remainder of the day, Big Joe worked opposite us. The foreman appeared surprised when he saw the change, but he merely spat and made no comment. The work was being done.

It was Big Joe who attempted to make amends as we set up camp that evening.

"Didn't mean to hurt yeh with that pickaxe. Just blowin' off some steam. Yeh know?" He managed a laugh, but it was forced and soon died away.

Without a word, I unrolled my blanket in the tent we had just finished erecting.

"Must miss yer family an all. Yer still a kid, heh?"

I neither looked at nor spoke to Big Joe; I simply rolled away from him on the blanket. I took out my Bible and read as if my very life depended on it.

"Well, I am sorry, Kid," he repeated.

For the next week, tension built. I refused to say a word to Big Joe unless it related to laying track, and he stalked about looking dejected. At the end of the week, Big Joe permanently switched teams. Apart from a few words necessary to work, I never spoke to him again. I had gained and lost my first friend.

Chapter 47

The Narrative of Peter Bolton

About a year after Adam left for the railroad, a change took place in Haggard House. It begun when I spent a night in the shack where I had lived as a bachelor. The first time it happened, I expected Sarai to be furious. I feared I would receive a notch in my other ear. The air were so heavy and oppressive in that dark, lonely place, I could no longer bear it. So, for the first time, I spent a night away.

When I returned home the following evening after a day in the shop, I stopped short at the sight. Haggard House, haggard as it had always been, seemed to have shrunk and withered in upon itself twice over. Something else were different too. It were darker and more silent. Though it were still bright outside, the windows showed no light nor life within. I forced myself to enter. Sarai slapped a cold dinner upon the table before me and said nothing.

I begun to spend the odd day away. Still, nothing happened. Each night absent gave me a feeling of blessed relief. I had not realized how heavily the place had weighed upon my spirit. The evenings I returned, my heart sank lower and lower as I neared the shrunken house that waited to swallow me.

Since our marriage, we had spoken very little. I were always a man of few words, and Sarai had only spoken when she had reason to chastise me. But now, a profound and unbreakable silence reigned. When I entered after an absence, I found that either I couldn't speak or didn't wish to. In either case, I found myself using gestures to communicate, and those only when it were absolutely necessary—a tilt of my cap at the door to announce my exit —a pat on my belly to show the animals were fed. Sarai too kept from breaking the silence. She appeared calm for the first time. It were unsettling. I waited for her to shout or hit me. I preferred that to the unabated stillness settling into the house.

The shouting, the hitting—they never begun. My nights away from home increased. One night a week turned into two, which turned into three. Only once did Sarai speak of my absences. One night, when I come down for my nightly ladleful of water, a habit I were unable to break since Adam's childhood, Sarai stopped pacing to fix her cold, dark eyes upon me. I could not stand the intensity of her gaze, so I dropped my eyes to the shrunken wooden boards beneath my feet. I wished to say something to break the hold I felt Sarai exerting but could say aught. Unable to move or utter one word, I waited and waited. It were then I made the fatal mistake of looking up. She caught my gaze, and for what seemed an hour, Sarai's eyes gripped mine. Standing so long thus made my muscles to quiver. I thought I might collapse at any moment when she finally spoke.

"A man belongs at home. 'He that troubleth his own house shall inherit the wind.'"

For a moment, I were nearly relieved when Sarai held back her arm, ready to strike. The sparkle of youth were gone from her eye; something else had replaced it, something bad. There were another gleam there, not pleasant. Her arm went limp of a sudden. Unable to speak, I stumbled up the steps. I turned briefly at the top and once again found Sarai's eyes latched onto me.

After this incident, I stayed a whole week in my shack. Once the week had expired, I found I were incapable of ever returning to Haggard House.

Chapter 48

The Narrative of Peter Bolton

The tongues of the villagers begun to wag about my absence. No doubt what they said reached Sarai's ears through the minister. She surely knew now that I were gone for good.

For the first time, I were not certain what to expect of life. I had left Haggard House and, though day-to-day brought a lightness I had not known for nigh on twenty-one years, the evenings were still oppressive. I could not comprehend why. By all rights, I ought to feel happy at my release. I were even able to know myself now that I were alone. But I found after only one experiment that I could not complete the act. When I attempted, a searing pain entered my notched ear. It were as though Sarai were there, punishing me. I were both free from and chained to her.

After a fortnight away, I begun to experience an irrational fear of the dark. I stayed awake for as long as possible. I burnt through an inordinate amount of lamp oil. I read and reread *The Pilgrim's Progress*, which I had smuggled from Haggard House. I even considered returning while Sarai were out to snatch Foxe's *Book of Martyrs*, but the stories in it were too gruesome. It only would have made matters worse. Too, while Sarai never touched *The Pilgrim's Progress*, she read Foxe daily.

It were no surprise when Minister Judd come for a little visit. I had suspected he would come round sooner or later. He come in the middle of business. It were just like him to pull some stunt like that. It were fortunate I'd no customers about the shop and that Thomas were out.

"Sarai tells me you've not been home, Peter," he said. His voice suddenly rose to a thunder, like he used upon the pulpit. "'Therefore take heed to your spirit, and let none deal treacherously against the wife of his youth.'"

"There's been naught treacherous," I said. "Everything I earn, excepting the bare necessities for myself, whether it be fowl, eggs, milk, or money, it all goes straight to Sarai. You can ask her herself."

"It's not filthy lucre of which I speak. A man belongs at home —with his wife. Imagine the gossip, the rumors that are spreading about her."

"Well," I said, "Any God-fearing person ought not to gossip, as I believe I've heard you say upon the pulpit many a time."

Minister Judd looked at me, aghast. I don't believe he ever thought I'd have had it in me to speak so to him. Yet without the threat of Sarai to hold me, I were suddenly finding my courage.

I continued.

"Sarai may come to town and contradict the rumors if she likes." It were all I could do to keep myself from grinning.

"I see it's true, what Sarai told me," he said. "You are reprobate, past all conscience or saving."

"Perhaps," I said. It weren't useful, arguing with the man. Even so, his words angered me. I thought onto something that'd been festering. It were a new idea, something that'd occurred only once I'd left Haggard House. In truth, it were one of the things that kept me awake at night. "That may be true," I continued. "Yet, I believe there are worser sins. Ones with worser punishments." I then quoted to him Proverbs 6:29.

Watching the man's face were like watching a wildfire in

reverse—huge flames licking trees and scrub, then falling back and disappearing to the mere spark they began with. So were his face, full of life and righteous indignation, suddenly draining and becoming pale as a corpse.

"You do not know of what you speak." Despite his weakened expression, he still held that righteousness in his voice.

"Now, there might be something that would interest the village tongues," I said.

"It's not true, and you know it." The words hissed through his teeth like he were a snake. "You wouldn't dare spread such a rumor."

I smiled. It were so long since I'd had any power, and now that I had it, I couldn't help but use it to its full extent.

"Perhaps not." His expression were always well guarded, yet I saw that flicker of relief. But before it had fully crossed his face, I added, "Yet, a reprobate past all conscience and saving might."

The many years with Sarai at Haggard House had rendered me like a rabbit, caught and batted at by a wolf cub, always fearful, always hoping for escape. Yet, here I were, well escaped, and now I were the hunter, a man, and it weren't the cub I were dealing with but a full-growed wolf; I couldn't help but enjoy watching the beast in the snare after it had robbed me.

"You want something," he said. "What is it?"

"I wish to be left in peace," I said.

"And then you will not tell this—lie—this tale?"

"I promise nothing," I said. "Now git." I lunged at him.

He turned and fled. I followed as far as the door and spat so loudly he could hear it as he retreated.

As I returned to work, my anger drained. It were true, then. Strange, for though I'd felt that I'd lost Sarai many years since, I still felt a sense of sadness.

A week passed, and as were my new custom, I rested in the worn armchair of my bachelor days and read. It were cold, and a sharp wind rasped against the edges of the shack. The lamp were burning low, nearly out of oil, and I begun drifting to sleep. Just when I were comfortably between alertness and slumber, I heard what I thought were footfall outside my shack. I waked fully. There were no windows, so I stood and listened intently. The sound, whatever it were, ceased. For some time, I stood and listened. But finally, satisfied that nothing were outside, I filled the lamp and read until I drifted off.

In my sleep, I dreamt that Sarai were young and beautiful again, without that pinched look upon her face. Adam were two, perhaps three years old, and the three of us walked the woods behind Haggard House, which, strangely enough, were not Haggard House at all, but a lovely, bright home. Sarai smiled and laughed. Adam, instead of being dark-haired and dark-eyed like Sarai; were a miniature of me, big-boned and soft-eyed. It were warm and scented of damp leaves. I were completely at peace.

Just as soon as I had begun to feel secure in my new surroundings, Sarai and Adam were gone. I rushed through the woods to find them, stumbling again and again on undergrowth and brush. As I looked wildly about me, I realized that, while I ran and fell and scrambled, I weren't moving forward.

And then I saw it: nailed to a tree ahead of me were the carcass of a goat, eyes slashed in the shape of a cross. Then the tree weren't a tree anymore, but Sarai's cross. And beside the cross stood Minister Judd, laughing. Next to Minister Judd, a pinched-faced, old hag stood laughing. And finally, next to the hag, stood little Adam, face mirroring hers. But Adam didn't laugh; he were frozen to the spot, just like me.

A wave of consciousness crossed, and I woke enough to realize that I were shouting. The sound were muffled, though, and I could scarce breathe. A hand covered my mouth. My body were petrified. My mind were awake, but my body were not. Sunken features I thought were like the ones in my dream glared down. Cold, dark eyes peered into mine. A hand with a knife poised above my throat. Horrified, I recognized the face.

Chapter 49

The Narrative of Penny Haworth

Peter's grave was set near the back of the churchyard, and Mother and I had to walk past all the other graves in order to reach it. The other villagers, including Sarai, were already gathered round the vacant hole in the ground. Sarai wore her usual bonnet, her severe black dress, and her usual severe expression. Peter's wooden coffin, fashioned by Thomas, rested to one side. Peter had become like a father to Thomas, and he had been the unfortunate one to find the body. I felt for him.

The villagers had concluded that Peter had been robbed in the night. All of Peter's money was missing. The robber had either murdered Peter and taken the money after, or having been confronted in the act, killed him then. Shortly after the news of the murder, Gunther Fowler disappeared. The marshal, along with Mr. Riblet and Mr. Tenney, having no other suspects, went in search of him. However, as he had with his previous thefts, Gunther had left no evidence behind; it mattered little in any case, for he was never found. When Sarai received the news, she took it stoically. But this was to be expected, the villagers agreed, knowing her as they did.

"'For dust thou art, and unto dust shalt thou return.'" Age had drawn the skin round Minister Judd's eyes downward, exposing damp, pink flesh.

A chilly, easterly wind blew, kicking up freshly turned dirt and coating the women's dresses and the gentlemen's suits in a fine, thin layer of it. Sarai stood at the head of the grave, the other villagers giving her a wide berth. Mother and I, last to arrive, stood back a distance. As Minister Judd droned on, a head before me moved, exposing the grave and Sarai's solemn form. For a moment, Sarai's gaze met mine. There was something in her flat expression that turned me cold. I could not say why. The head in front of me moved back, and Sarai vanished with it.

Once the service was complete, Thomas, along with three other of the village's young men, lowered the coffin into the grave. They took up spades and methodically dropped earth into the hole. As they did so, the villagers reluctantly made their way toward Sarai. Mother and I were the last to give our sympathies. No one had dared hug Sarai or offer her a hand, but Mother embraced her. Sarai's spine stiffened, and a slight motion made it appear that she would push her away.

"I too know what it is to lose a husband," Mother said to Sarai.

Mother retreated, leaving me alone to give my regards. I felt not a shred of sympathy for the woman before me.

"Truly sorry for your loss," I said. As I turned to go, a claw-like hand gripped my arm.

"Wait."

I resisted the urge to tear away from her grasp. "What is it?"

The wind turned into a gale, blasting Sarai's black dress against her spindly limbs and loosening graying wisps from her tightly drawn hair.

"What news have you had from Adam? Where is he?"

I sensed a hint of desperation in her voice. "I don't know. I haven't received news of him."

Sarai's eyes narrowed. "I know everything. I found the trunk. I've discovered what Adam has been hiding."

I yanked my arm from her grasp and hurried away.

"Again, I ask where my son is!"

Whirling about, I said, "I told you truth when I said I do not know."

Sarai, hair like ruffled feathers, strode toward me. "You will not have him. When he returns. You will not have him. He belongs to the Lord and to the Lord only."

"Adam is his own," I said. "He belongs to no one."

Another step brought Sarai very near. She put her lips to my ear and said, "You are the whore of Babylon. You will not destroy my son."

"How dare you!" I half ran from the horrid woman toward Mother, who had been waiting at some distance.

"What did Sarai say to you?" Mother asked.

"Nothing," I said, keeping my eyes averted.

When I gave a final glance at the scene behind me, I saw Minister Judd and Sarai walking arm in arm together toward the parsonage.

Chapter 50

The Narrative of Adam Bolton

For another year, I followed the railroad. Then it was finished —as was I. It wasn't that I couldn't get more work; on the contrary, there was work in any direction I chose to travel. However, when we laid the final rail at Promontory Point, I felt a sense of completion, and nothing could have persuaded me to find more labor in that line. During my two years on the road, I had saved a goodly amount. Unlike the others, I didn't drink, gamble, and whore my wages away at each make-shift town that assembled as we passed through.

Two years away from Haggard House had caused a growing sense of discontent toward the people connected to it, especially Mother. I had seen a little of the world. More than that, I had experienced a little of it. Having done so, it was impossible not to perceive the difference between the life I had been accustomed to and the lives lived by others. Yet, however much I might wish to stray from my religious training, I was incapable of it. I was still racked with guilt for my evening of sin and debauchery. The memory of Mother, stern face and drawn lips, was always enough to evoke righteous anger and shame at my own sin and heretical ideas of straying. So, after that last rail had been laid, I found myself pulled by an invisible string back toward Haggard House.

Knowing the dangers of the open road, I took some trouble to secure my savings. First, I converted my heavy gold into greenbacks. I then removed the lining of my goatskin coat, sewed all but the money I would require for my travels into pouches throughout, and resewed the lining. Mother's teaching served me well in this endeavor, and I thanked her inwardly.

I took return passage on the train whose tracks I had helped lay. Yet, as I retraced my path up the Missouri by steamer and across the western plains by rail, I began to dread my arrival in Nomaton. After crossing the Mississippi at Dubuque, I found myself standing at the rail station, waiting to purchase a ticket. I was yet nearly three hundred miles across country from my destination. The spring air was sharp, reminiscent of recent winter. I pulled my coat closer about me. A handful of Dubuque's younger residents had gathered at some distance, and they stared at those of us in line, wondering who we were and where we were traveling.

Bowing my head to keep the spring cold from my neck, I closed my eyes. Immediately appeared the house within my mind. I saw the locked room in which I was certain to find Penny, and across from it, the room which contained Pa. I did not wish to see these things, so I descended to the first floor of my mind-house. The front door opened and, unbidden, Mother entered.

Leave! I shouted. The voice within my mind was so loud, my very skull vibrated with its force. *Leave this place at once! You don't belong here.*

She would not go. She glanced up the stairs. Somehow, she knew. Despite all the distance which I had placed between us— Mother knew about Penny. A tremendous noise swept my mind-house. Every joint strained, and the boards began to draw inward. Panic struck. I grasped Mother by the shoulders and forced her out. Then I rushed back inside, bolting the door behind. She knocked violently, but then left off. The mind-house became still again.

I forced my eyes open and saw the passengers ahead of me, all of whom were turned and staring. Had I called with my real voice? Had they heard my shouting?

Trembling, throat dry, I hurried from the line, Dubuque children and passengers following me with their eyes. I moved rapidly until my exertion stopped the trembling. My mind was daily becoming more tumultuous. I needed time and space in which to set things to rights. I had formed no plan as to what I would do once I arrived, and the thought of being stifled by the train's close, smoky atmosphere and jolted along the hard tracks, all while hurtling towards my destination, was too much to bear. I could travel no farther by train. Therefore, I resolved to travel by foot until I reached the next town, from whence I would procure a horse and go on my way alone.

I had not traveled above three days on my northeastern journey when I made the acquaintance of a traveling reverend. I had been covering ground quickly when I heard a deep, resonant voice leading others in the hymn "O for a Thousand Tongues." I followed the sound over a ridge and discovered a man leading a congregation in song under the open sky.

The reverend, upon looking up and noting my presence, called loudly, "Come join us, friend!"

I descended the hill and did as he suggested, standing at the back of the tightly-packed group. We sang two more hymns before the reverend closed in prayer. I waited patiently at a distance while he greeted his congregation. He was five years my senior—I later discovered—wore a black, wide-brimmed hat, and had a broad face and open manner.

Once everyone but myself had dispersed, the reverend addressed me warmly.

"Hello, friend."

I drew a hand from behind my back and shook his. "Sir, I'm

sorry to say I missed your sermon and arrived only in time for the hymns."

"Please, don't call me *sir*. My name is Samuel Lemming. Call me Samuel. Come. Walk with me. I dine with the Beryls tonight. And what is your name, friend?"

"Adam Bolton."

Samuel had a quick, sure step, much like mine, and I found this to my liking. The reverend collected his horse, and we walked briskly to the road from which I had wandered. The sun had just begun its descent behind us.

The journey to the Beryls' residence was spent discussing my work of the past two years, my birthplace, and my present destination. Reverend Lemming had been traveling and extending his circuit west above three years. He had only just begun his return east, where he planned to settle, marry, and retain a congregation of his own. His open face and manner led me to believe that he was an honest soul, and so I spoke more freely than I otherwise would have. Samuel appeared to find my company just as agreeable. It seemed only a moment had passed before we arrived at the Beryls' homestead. Reluctant to bid my company goodbye, I stayed myself at the door.

"I fear we must part here," said I.

"Friend Adam, stay and dine with us. The Beryls are infinitely obliging, and I am certain they would be happy to have a guest as agreeable as yourself."

The scent of fried pork and cornbread coming from the cabin would have been enough to tempt any man. With my scantly rationed meals of pemmican upon the road, I found myself famished and accepted Samuel's offer. After stabling his horse, he introduced me to the Beryls. As he had intimated, they were infinitely obliging. Mrs. Beryl, a short, stout woman, was as warm and friendly as Mother was rigid and stern, and I couldn't help but make comparison. A place was prepared at the large table for me, and soon the whole family was seated round it. There were ten children by my count, the youngest still a babe.

Conversation was lively. Reverend Lemming kept us entertained with tales of different villages and towns he had visited. He was not averse to describing, in detail, some of the most vivid characters from each place. To my great relief, I was not called upon to make much speech. I had little in common with this animated, good-natured bunch, and to speak would only prove it. Once the evening had worn late, the children said goodnight and lined up for a kiss from each parent. I couldn't have said why, but a pang struck through my chest as I saw this. When they had gone, Samuel turned the conversation upon his hosts.

"It must be difficult to keep so many fed."

"We have sufficient means, and the Lord has been good enough to bless us with abundance," Mrs. Beryl said.

"Is there a bank nearby where your funds may be kept?" he inquired.

"No bank," Mr. Beryl said. "But our home is far out of the way. We seldom get visitors. It's quite safe."

"You don't mean to tell me you keep your earnings here?" the reverend said in shock.

"We do," Mr. Beryl replied. "It's quite safe, I assure you."

Reverend Lemming shook his head. "I've been across this wide country. Please believe me when I say that no place is safe." He gestured toward me. "He's seen as much of the dangers of the west as I. Adam, oughtn't they find a bank for their wages?"

"Yes," agreed I. "And lose no time in doing so. Murder is done for less."

"Well, we will make inquiries on where to place it," Mrs. Beryl said. "For now, though, we must retire. It's late."

Samuel and I were settled comfortably in the loft of a large barn behind the cabin.

"It's been a happy day, friend Adam," he said, settling into the hay.

"It has," said I.

"It would greatly please me if we were to travel together eastward. Would you be my companion on the journey, friend? I'm certain I don't need to remind you that, 'Two are better than one. For if they fall, the one will lift up his fellow: but woe to him that is alone when he falleth; for he hath not another to help him up.' It will doubtless be a longer journey for you, what with my sermons, but perhaps you are not disagreeable to such a notion?"

The recitation of Scripture further warmed my heart toward him. As to making the journey longer, this was precisely what I desired. Feeling lighter than I had in many months, I readily agreed, and it was settled.

As I slept, I was troubled with dreams of Penny. She flowed, like water over a dam, through the cracks round the door and in the walls I had built in my mind, rushing across the floor to my corncob mattress. There, she teased and bothered me in shameful ways—ways I could not speak of.

It was still dark when I suddenly woke. I turned to see if Samuel had stirred, but he was no longer by my side. A moment later, he appeared.

"Have you wakened? Our friend nature called, but I've returned. Go back to sleep."

I settled back into the sweet hay. When I woke in the morning, I was happy to have once again found a friend.

Chapter 51

The Narrative of Adam Bolton

The first order of business before continuing our eastward journey was for me to procure a horse. So, the next morning, Samuel accompanied me to a horse trader to see if there might be anything suitable. Only one stood out—a bay that reminded me of McDonnell's mare. The trader named his price of two hundred dollars. It was a substantial sum, but it was far better than the prices I had seen in Omaha. I was about to accept when Reverend Lemming pulled me aside.

"Friend, it is too much," he whispered. "The man wishes to take advantage of your youth and inexperience. I know that you are no simpleton, though. Counter with one hundred and fifty."

Not wishing to appear the fool, I countered with the reverend's price. The horse trader countered again with one hundred and ninety and, after a subtle shake of the head from my friend, I made my price one hundred and sixty. When all was said and done, we agreed upon a price of one hundred and sixty-five dollars. This done, Samuel suggested I test my new mare's speed, and I readily agreed. Our quickened pace rapidly put distance between ourselves and the town. As we finally slowed to a walk, I spoke.

"I owe you a debt, Samuel. Your assistance has preserved some of my fortune."

"Think nothing of it," the reverend said, tipping his hat.

Traveling with Samuel made my journey pleasant. The reverend stopped within or near small towns and gave sermons to whomever would gather. Sometimes the sermon was given in an open field, sometimes in a barn, sometimes in a home, sometimes in a meeting house, and, more rarely, in a church. Invariably, a family who had heard the reverend speak would ask us to dinner and, as often as not, offer us a place to lodge. I could not have found a more edifying means of travel, spreading the Word of the Lord and meeting people of His flock.

The only fault I found with Reverend Lemming was that he did not rain fire and brimstone on his congregations frequently enough. He spoke too much of Heaven and not enough of Hell, and forgiveness was mentioned more than refraining from sin. Regardless of my entreaties, Samuel continued to give gentle sermons, and the passages he chose relied heavily on the New Testament. I had, of course, read the New Testament, but my study had always been devoted to the Old Testament and Revelations, the books Mother most heavily relied on. There was something contradictory about Samuel's beliefs, and Mother's and Minister Judd's. I doubted very much whether Mother or Minister Judd would consider Reverend Lemming's sermons profitable. In the evenings, we discussed passages of Scripture, and a mental sparring of sorts sprung up between us.

One such evening, still far from the next settlement, we were forced to camp in a field with no roof over our heads but the stars. The air, providentially, was dry, and no rain threatened to dampen us. I took it upon myself to provide dinner. Using Reverend Lemming's rifle, I disappeared into the woods and returned shortly with two rabbits. I made short work of cleaning and skinning the meat, and Samuel praised my skill.

As we roasted them on a make-shift spit, we whiled the evening away in discussion.

"You read the Scriptures too literally, friend Adam. Did not our Savior speak to His disciples in parables? Why, then, would you think Him to do differently in the Old Testament?"

"Was He indirect in His words to Moses?" asked I. "Are the Commandments then parables?"

Reverend Lemming laughed. "Your Sword is sharp, friend Adam. Certainly, there were times when our Lord spoke plainly, but oft as not, His words were in parable. It's your taking all of God's Word as if it were meant to be law, this is what I take caution to."

My jaw tightened, and I turned the spit—a slender bit of green branch. Drops of blood sizzled in the fire below.

Samuel laughed again. "Is it possible that you see the error of your ways?"

"You don't understand." This, I spoke, because I could think of nothing better to say.

Though I maintained my views, I had begun to wonder if the reverend might be correct, at least partly. The passion with which I debated him was beginning to wane. When I pointed out the need to sacrifice for sin, Samuel quickly offered the sacrifice of Jesus. When I recounted the prophets guiding the way to the Promised Land, the reverend countered with Jesus guiding the way to Heaven. To acknowledge that I may not understand Scripture as well as Reverend Lemming was too great a wound for my pride. Yet, inwardly, conceptions I had maintained without question began to come under assault, and seeds of doubt formed.

Even so, certain personal habits of Reverend Lemming caused me to question the man's doctrines. Samuel went so far as to accept strong drink from our hosts if it was offered and, once, I even observed him to gamble. However unsettling these things were, I liked my friend too much to be put off.

I thought of Penny too during this time, but thoughts of her were painful. Surely, she would be wed to Thomas by now. Despite this, I suddenly found myself desirous to return to the village of my youth more speedily. My new friend was quite willing to accommodate, and it was decided that the reverend would stop in Nomaton with me before continuing east. Samuel joked that he might even find a wife of his own.

After the first day of quickened pace, we calculated that we were roughly a fortnight away from Nomaton. With excellent hosts along the way, we had a pleasant journey. We traveled so rapidly that we arrived in the village neighboring mine, three days before anticipated. The reverend persuaded me to get lodgings at the tavern, and I reluctantly agreed. Once we had settled our horses and ourselves, Reverend Lemming suggested we sup and drink a tankard of cider. After my evening of debauchery, I had sworn to myself never to drink again, but the reverend was a moderate man. Sharing one drink with him could not be a sin.

The place was small and out of the way and, having arrived early, we were the only persons who occupied it. The tavern had once been a house; it was clean and orderly, nothing like the hotel in which I had sinned so greatly. Reverend Lemming had a few words with the proprietor, a slender individual with gleaming hair drenched in Macassar oil, before joining me at the table. Along with a dinner consisting chiefly of johnnycake and salt pork, we each drank a tankard of cider. Lemming proposed one more in honor of my new life, and I, finding the cider refreshing, agreed. The second drink tasted quite strong, but the reverend appeared not to notice. We became engaged in a lively debate, and the mood was light and cheerful. I enjoyed myself so heartily that when Samuel proposed a third and final tankard to toast my excellent company and friendship, I again agreed.

Not long after that third drink, my head began to swim, and I felt violently ill. I announced that I would retire to the bedroom, and Samuel agreed and said he would join me presently. I stumbled up the steps and upon reaching the room, removed my coat and fell upon the bed. Almost as soon as I lay down, I sunk into oblivion.

The crowing of a rooster was the first sound that greeted me when I awoke. I found a cup of water on the table near me and gratefully drank it. The reverend must have already wakened, because he was not in the room. Something else seemed to be missing, but I was too bleary to note, if anything, what it was. I went below.

"Has Reverend Lemming breakfasted?" asked I of the proprietor.

"He has, sir," the man said without meeting my eyes.

"Do you know where he has gone?"

"I do not, sir," he said, keeping his gaze upon the glasses he was drying.

Fear clutched my heart. I hurried to the stable where our horses were lodged. I saw my own horse there, crunching on hay, but Samuel's horse was gone. I tore to my room in the tavern, the fear that clutched me tightening. I burst inside, nearly knocking the door from its hinges. Something besides Reverend Lemming was missing. I flung the covers of the bedclothes aside in search of my coat.

There was no coat to be found.

Chapter 52

The Narrative of Adam Bolton

Trembling with anger, I collected the rest of my things and stormed below.

"Where has he gone?" demanded I of the proprietor.

His heavily oiled head would not rise to mine, "Sir, I've told you already. I do not know where your companion is."

Only then did I understand that this man was part of the plot. I leapt over the bar, sending an avalanche of clean glass smashing to the floor, and grasped his neck with my hands, the force of my motion propelling us both to the ground.

"I say that you do, sir," roared I.

He gripped my arms but was powerless to move them. At last, he threw his hands upward in a sort of surrender. His breaths were fast and labored when I released him and stood. After some preliminary coughing and sputtering, he said, "The reverend left about an hour after you returned to your room."

"Which way?" asked I, placing my foot upon his neck in case he was inclined to lie.

"West. Sir, I don't know more. I swear. He rode west."

I removed my foot in disgust. The man was then so good as to name a neighboring village which he believed the reverend might've been traveling toward.

"I hope for your sake that you've told the truth," said I.

As soon as I could bridle and saddle my horse, I thundered over the westward road. Reverend Lemming had had the advantage of a full night's ride. At the village the proprietor had mentioned, I made inquiries. Hearing nothing to suggest that he was there, I stopped for a fresh horse at the livery stable, using the little money I had kept on my person for my travels, and thundered farther west. On and on I rode, halting only to speak to people on the road or in adjacent towns. No one had heard of a Reverend Lemming or had seen anyone who looked like him. At last, I began to believe I had overshot the mark and had either passed him or was traveling in the wrong direction.

Exhausted from the day's riding, I came across a shallow stream. Dismounting, I led the horse to drink, then gulped water myself. I sat upon a rock at the edge of the stream to think and fingered the thin supply of money in my trouser pocket: no more than five dollars was left to my name. Two years' wages disappeared in one night. Two years' wages lost to a foul preacher full of lies.

Without money, there was nothing left for me to do. I might search for Reverend Lemming forever and never find him. I released a deep cry of anger, and it echoed eerily from the forest across the stream. If ever I were to find the man, I would exact righteous judgement. But here and now, I felt keenly the loss of two years' heavy labor.

I mounted my hired horse and rode back in the direction from whence I had come.

Chapter 53

The Narrative of Adam Bolton

The hired horse knew its way well. Finding itself without a guiding hand, it returned to the livery stable from whence it came, and consequently, me along with it. I gradually formed a purpose: I would return to Nomaton, as I had planned. It would not be the triumphant return which I had imagined, but there was nothing for it.

I retrieved my own horse and rode all night until I reached the village of my birth. It was the dark, early hours of morning when I arrived. As I drew near Haggard House, I saw the familiar lamp burning in the familiar window of the familiarly shriveled house. Mother was up betimes, doubtlessly reading or praying, perhaps for my safe return.

The closer I drew, the more agitated my horse became. The bay shrieked and reared on her haunches, nearly throwing me. Inside the house, the lamp suddenly extinguished.

"Easy, girl."

She laid her ears back, and rolled her eyes, revealing their whites. Though I coaxed her to move forward, she would not budge. I dismounted and attempted to lead her. Still, she would not move. At last, I blinded her with my pocket handkerchief and led her to the barn. Pa's old gelded Belgian, with his sagging back and gray, wispy whiskers, shoved his nose across the aisle and nickered at the bay. I stroked his forehead and foddered the mare. I had planned to go immediately to the house, but a sudden urge overwhelmed me.

A familiar earthy scent filled my nostrils as I entered the northern portion of the barn. The domed travel trunk was just where it had always been. For many moments I stood, undecided. To open it was to give in to temptation. I had only just returned: how could I be capable of such a thing? And yet—I did open it, my whole being tingling with anticipation at once again seeing my treasure, the few precious articles once belonging to Penny.

The items were moved, pushed to one side of the trunk, and the sprig of pine Penny had given me was crumpled, half-empty of needles.

Mother had been through my things; there was no doubt. I returned to the house, a foul mood blistering under my surface. She had no right. They were mine and mine alone.

I knocked at the rear door. Footsteps scuffled inside, but no one answered. I knocked louder.

"Mother, it's Adam," called I.

Once again, the dim glow of the betty lamp flickered inside, and footsteps neared. The door opened a crack, then fully. All of my building rage dissipated in that moment. The face that met me should have been familiar—it was anything but. I took an involuntary step back. At first, I thought it could not be Mother. It was.

Her face and form had shrunken. She appeared as she did in winter, deadly pale. Most appalling were her eyes. Something sinister was there—something that had not been there before. Her lips smiled, but it was hideous to behold, stretching and contorting her face in a way I had only previously seen on Minister Judd.

"Adam. You've returned. Come inside."

Despite my initial shock, I could not turn away from the woman who had raised me. I stepped into the house. As I did so, a fog seemed to cloud my mind. Even the wick in the lamp sputtered, as if the air sought to choke it out. The interior was as shriveled as the outside. It was smaller and darker than I remembered, and it smelt musty and fetid.

Mother's piercing eyes read my features.

"Have you kept to God's path?"

I changed the subject, glancing up the attic steps. "Is Pa asleep?"

Mother averted her gaze and settled herself at the table, motioning for me to do the same.

It was not like Mother to look away. I was suddenly alarmed that something had happened to Pa. My whole frame constricted, every muscle tightening.

"Where is he?"

"You've had a long journey," said she, suddenly standing from her chair. "You must be famished."

She removed a shriveled loaf from the shelf. A weevil scurried from underneath. She plunged the knife into the bread, sawing back and forth, and then offered the slice to me.

"Eat." The command in Mother's voice left no room for argument, and I gnawed at the putrid bread.

"Better." Mother's lips twisted upward, rippling wrinkle after wrinkle across her face. Still she did not look at me.

"What has Pa done?"

She sighed as if bored. "Don't worry, my son."

I felt curiously cold, so I changed the subject. "What changes in the village?"

"Another bite. You must be famished."

I choked down another mouthful. The first piece was already twisting my stomach into knots. Mother's bread had been well enough at one time, but now I was used to something better.

"I've been forced to hunt in order to feed myself."

"What?" said I. "But what of Pa's wages? What of your

savings?" I knew Mother kept silver hidden somewhere in the house, only I wasn't certain where.

"The savings are meant for you," said she.

This line of discourse did nothing to alleviate my worry, so I changed it yet again.

"What of the twins? Gunther...and Thomas?"

"I know not."

"Surely, you must know something of Thomas?" said I.

"Enough questions," said Mother, rising. "You must be tired. Come to bed."

Seeing that I would get no answers, I dutifully followed her to the attic. When I saw that Pa was not there, I started back.

"Peter is not here," said Mother.

I considered. Business had no doubt increased since I had been away. Perhaps Pa had an order that could not wait. It was not unheard of for him to leave for the shop at this early hour, even before I had left. Exhausted, I put the subject to rest. There would be plenty of time to sort things out.

Chapter 54

The Narrative of Adam Bolton

I woke only a few hours later. To my surprise, Mother had not yet wakened. I rose quickly and decided to take a walk in the cold morning air. I fed my horse and Pa's Belgian and attended to the other animals about the farm, just as I had done two years prior. The late spring air was clear of clouds as I made my way down the familiar path through the woods and out to Whittemore's Prairie. Once I had crossed halfway, I stopped for a moment at the crest of a hill, stunned at what I saw. The portion of prairie nearest the village was no longer prairie. A dozen new homes spread out across it on either side of what had once been merely Pa's cart path. It was familiar and yet unfamiliar, like Mother. I disliked the feeling this change produced, so I hastened on my way.

My first order of business was to check the shop, so I followed the street to the opposite edge of the village. If Pa was not there, then Thomas might be early and could perhaps inform me of his whereabouts. However, here too was evidence of the village's expansion. The carpentry shop, once on the southern border of the village, was now only one of several new businesses lining the street, opposite which were more homes.

There was no sign of life. The windows were shut up, and the door was locked. I rattled it and listened. No sound came from within. The shack behind was similarly bolted. Neither Thomas nor Pa were there.

Disappointed, I made my way toward Bard's Tavern. I took the long way round, past the Haworth's house. It was still dark and quiet within. As I neared the tavern, I saw a familiar figure hurrying in my direction. His collarless, checkered flannel was rolled up at the sleeves, and he wore a low-brimmed hat over short, cropped hair. Lines creased under Thomas' gray eyes as he suddenly recognized me.

"The prodigal has returned," Thomas said, approaching.

I tucked my hands behind my back and said, "And if I'm the prodigal, who are you? The elder son?"

He frowned. "I meant it only in jest. I am happy to see you're come back, Adam. Good day."

"This is the long way round for you, Mr. Fowler," called I to Thomas' retreating form.

"It is." Again, he attempted to depart.

Realizing I ought not to have begun in animosity, especially as my errand was of such great import, I called for Thomas to wait.

"Pa wasn't home last night," said I. "Have you seen him yet this morning?"

Thomas' face contorted, and he stared at me as if I had lost my wits. "You've not heard?"

"Heard what?" asked I, the cold feeling returning.

There was pain and reluctance in Thomas' features, and he opened his mouth only to shut it again.

"What is it?" asked I.

"Perhaps you ought to ask your mother," he replied.

The muscles in my neck and jaw drew taut. Whatever there was to know, I must have out with it, though it came from Thomas. "Please, tell me."

He dropped his head and bit his lip. Then he met my eyes. "I'm sorry to inform you. Your pa...your pa was killed."

I swallowed hard but otherwise betrayed no emotion. "Killed?"

"It was a year ago now," he continued. "It was believed to be a robbery. The culprit, whoever he was, was never apprehended." He waited for some response from me, then said, "I'm sorry to be the one—well I'm sorry for the loss of your pa. He was a good man."

It was all I could do to keep myself composed. I wished to be alone—away from Thomas, away from the village, and away from Haggard House.

"I...thank you for informing me," said I, eyes to the ground to hide the growing moisture there. "I must be going."

I hurried from the streets and disappeared into the woods past Farmer McNeil's field. I followed the old path past the lake and allowed my grief to find, grip, and pass through me in heavy sobs. Pa had always been kind and loving. Though I had been too frightened to enter it of late, I opened the room within my mind, full of his memories. Remorse filled me, both for my coldness to him and my absence these past years. When my tears subsided, an aching, empty feeling filled my chest. I longed for something to keep me occupied and take my thoughts from Pa; I returned to Haggard House.

It had been too dark to see the prior evening, but the morning light revealed that a corner of the roof had crumbled. I was relieved to find something to put my energies into. I collected Pa's tool chest and entered the attic. Mother was there, kneeling in front of the chest of drawers, holding her cross in her hands. The dark circles under her eyes were sunken so deep that they appeared wide and ghostlike.

"I know about Pa," said I. Then, unable to bear looking at Mother for fear of weeping, I turned away. "I'll repair the roof."

"I'll leave you to your work," said she, struggling to her feet. "You've not gone to see—?"

I knew she was thinking of Penny.

"No."

"That is well. Do not do so."

Again, I felt the change that the passage of two years away had worked. Mother's command irked me, and a rebellious spirit arose. I wanted nothing more than to revile her for taking Penny's things from the trunk, but my fresh loss, and the remembrance that the trunk did not belong to me in the first place, cooled my anger and rebellion. I did not respond, and she left the attic, leaving me to work in peace. I opened the familiar mahogany tool chest. Some of Pa's warmth seemed to creep into my hand as I ran it across the tools. It was then that I decided upon my future. Suddenly, it was simple: I would take up Pa's trade.

I spent the remainder of the day attempting to repair the roof, but however much I tried, nothing quite worked. As evening approached, I patched the corner as best I could and let it be.

Haggard House could not be repaired.

Chapter 55

The Narrative of Adam Bolton

I wandered listlessly through the village, deeply troubled by Pa's death; though I didn't show it outwardly, sorrow, such as I had never known, filled my heart. I slowed my gait further as I reached Bard's Tavern. Up the street, a stray dog barked. The rough shouts and laughter of lumbermen tumbled into the evening air.

A familiar voice from inside the tavern arrested my movement. I listened, catching only fragments. The man I heard had, for many years, seen Pa here nightly. However, to speak to him would be to break Mother's express command. A moment's hesitation gave way, and I turned in the direction of the churchyard. As I retreated, I heard the tavern door open, shouts and laughter doubling in volume. It closed once more, and footsteps sounded behind me. Instead of looking round, I hurried on.

As I entered the churchyard, I saw several unfamiliar gravestones. None were Pa's. I skirted the edge until I reached the back. There, I finally found it. As I read the inscription, I thought the stonemason must have made a mistake. It read: "Here I lay my burden down." I had seen this epitaph before, but there had always been a second line: "Here I lay my burden down; Change the cross into the crown." Without the second line, it felt strange and foreboding.

"Sad loss," a voice behind me said.

I turned to see the old drunkard. He swayed lightly, steadied himself, then closed the space between us.

"It is," replied I. Two years prior, I would have hurried away from the man, obeying Mother's command. Now, I stayed. He was perhaps the only person with whom I could speak of my Pa.

"Great loss," he said. "He was a good man." He exhibited no outward change in the intervening years. He wore the same faded shirt and worn, old-fashioned knee breeches. His nose was as red as usual. Red worsted hat in hand, he reached up, smoothed his iron-colored hair back, and straightened a little. "I know she's filled your head brim full of poison about me."

I sniffed, tucking my hands behind my back. "You've been a sound drunk all your life. No one had to tell me that."

"No. No. I only started drinking steady when Sarai was a young woman. Of course, I did indulge on occasion before that, but never steady." He paused, then went on. "Adam, I know perhaps now is not the proper time, but I never see you, you see? And now you've returned, I have something I wish to speak to you about. Something important. Something about your mother—"

"Regardless of when you began," interjected I. "It's clear you're not to be trusted."

The old man fingered his hat. "Is that what you think? A drunkard must be a liar?"

"One sin leads to another, does it not?"

"Then it matters naught what I say. Does it? You won't believe a word I speak."

"Did you ever speak with Pa?" asked I. "At Bard's?"

He neared the grave and rested a hand on the cold stone. "I spoke to your pa but twice. The first night he ever came to Bard's and the night before he died."

"At the tavern?" Though I gave no credence to the old man's words, I found I must know. "What did he say?"

"Peter—your pa, told me of his life with Sarai. The things he spoke to me of—the things she believes. I ought to have warned him. I did try—about the house, at any rate. He repulsed my efforts even then, though. Already poisoned against me by his wife's words. There are things she hasn't told you—things she's lied about."

"Stop!" said I, holding up my hand. "I've heard enough. Unless you've words of consolation pertaining to Pa, we've nothing left to speak of."

"You ought to listen, Adam," the old man continued.

"No. I'll not listen," said I.

I turned and hurried away, the old man's words following in my wake.

"Adam! Adam! Listen to me. I'm not a liar, Adam. I'm—"

I stopped my ears.

Chapter 56

The Narrative of Adam Bolton

I bestirred myself and settled on a course of action. I sold my horse, and Mother gifted me the money she had hoarded from the sale of Pa's shop to Thomas, with which I used to set up my own shop in town. It was then that I discovered where she kept the money, though she thought I did not see.

Although I had never applied myself to it as a youth, I had sufficient knowledge of the carpentry trade to get on in the beginning. As time passed, I garnered enough business to support myself. Then, as soon as I had amassed the funds, I plunged every cent into a planing machine. Now, I was able to do in one day what might take Thomas a week. Added to this, Thomas, though he had worked tirelessly through the years, lacked the talent I naturally possessed. And so, betwixt man and machine, I quickly surpassed my rival. As I became more and more celebrated for my work, Thomas began to see fewer and fewer patrons.

I rose betimes daily. I rarely saw Thomas, and as I avoided the street on which she lived, and only came to and fro for my work, I never saw Penny. Mother said nothing of either, and I did not make myself agreeable to gossip. So, a month passed in which I was wholly unaware that the pair had neither courted nor married. It might have continued thus for many months more, had it not been for a visit I received at my new shop.

Deeply engrossed in work, I had my back to the door when I heard it open behind me. I wiped the sawdust coating from my hands onto my leather apron, tucked them behind my back, and turned to greet my customer. What I saw took my breath away.

The vertical black and white stripes of the woman's dress made her appear tall and commanding. A stiff, white collar stood out smartly from the black bow and broach at her neck. Copper curls flowed freely under a small black hat. The passage of two years had somehow polished Penny. High spirits still glimmered in her eyes, but no longer on her face. Her spirit was sobered but not quenched. The sight of her, eyes searching mine, intoxicated me; for a moment, I was unable to speak.

"I've an undertaking for you," she said. Her voice too had changed. It was more confident and commanding, like her dress. "Our dining table has cracked and is in need of repair."

Collecting my wits, I said, "Surely, your husband can repair it."

"I have no husband," Penny said, lips parting in surprise.

My clasped hands loosened, and my arms dropped to my sides. Her gaze was unwavering. My pulse quickened, and I found it difficult to breathe. I wished to speak, to say something, but I could find neither the words nor the breath.

"Your mother must be pleased that you've returned," Penny said.

I forced myself to inhale. "She is."

"When will you come to repair the table?"

"Two weeks hence."

"Two weeks?" Her voice rose.

"I have much work." I broke our gaze and returned to my bench, back to her. "If you're unsatisfied with the wait, you may ask Thomas."

"No." Her voice was firm. "Thank you. I'll wait." I heard her footsteps retreating. "Until then."

It took some time to return to my work. Though I stood at my bench, I could not make my hands move, and when I regained the ability, they trembled. Penny had not married Thomas. In two weeks' time, I would see her again. I'd spoken truthfully when I said I had weeks of work, but I had a secondary motive; I needed to think.

When the workday ended, I returned to Haggard House. My habits had returned to what they had been before I left, but my heart was no longer in them. This evening, as always, I paced and read with Mother late into the night, but the practice exhausted me. I took no joy in it, and something within me realized that I had never done so. Other habits were similarly undertaken with no pleasure.

The fortnight expired, and I made the Haworth residence my first call of the day. There were deliveries to be made in the afternoon, so I hitched the Belgian to the cart. When I reached the Haworth home, the memory of my evening spent there returned. It was one of the fondest in my recollection, and it warmed me both to the place and to Penny. I secured my horse and made my way to the entrance, carrying the mahogany tool chest with me.

Penny swung the door open before I could knock. Once again, my pulse thickened as she ushered me into the dining room. It was warm and clean and just as I remembered it. An orange tabby, which I recognized as the one I had given Penny, streaked away towards the kitchen.

"I'm glad you've come," Penny said. "You see the crack." She pointed at the corner of the table where the sheets of wood had begun to separate.

It would be an easy repair, but my thoughts were far from this fact. "Your mother is home?"

"No. She's traveled to Wasaki for supplies."

I started. All my assumed calm fled. "You shouldn't have allowed me in," said I.

As I turned to go, Penny placed a hand on my arm. "Please. Stay."

Looking into her eyes, I could not force myself to the door. I felt myself trembling. I was as Joseph with Potiphar's wife, and I knew it was better that I should flee and leave my coat behind than to stay. "You ought to have asked Thomas to do the repair. You are, or perhaps were, courting, were you not?" I allowed my anger to replace temptation.

"No." Penny shook her head vehemently. "There has never been anything between us. That day you saw us together, I was only putting him off."

I was unable to speak, shocked as I was by this confession.

"I've never cared for Thomas," she continued.

"I see," said I, collecting my scattered wits. "I'm sorry to have presumed."

"As am I," Penny said.

I thought I detected a note of bitterness in her tone, but her features remained pleasant, whatever her feelings. I drew a deep breath. She took a seat at one of the dining chairs opposite and leaned back carelessly. I could not bring myself to look at her. Though it was cool within doors, sweat poured down my back. I set the chest down and went to work, separating the peeling section of wood, replacing the pegs, gluing and clamping them back together. Penny watched as I worked. We did not speak, but I was always aware of her presence, and she, mine.

I stood, work complete. "I'll return for the clamps tomorrow."

Penny leapt from her chair, startled. "You've finished already?"

"Yes," said I. "It was not a difficult repair."

I was at the far end of the table, and I ran my hand across its long surface as I made ready to take leave. Penny too touched her fingers to the table, and as we moved down the length of it, her hand drew nearer and nearer to mine until they were but an inch apart. Almost before I knew what I was doing, I thrust my hand across that fraction of a chasm separating us and took her hand. I could no longer contain myself.

My hand slipped from hers, and I lifted her from across the table and brought her atop it. She knelt upon her knees there, looking down upon me. It was then that I had the wickedest thought I had ever conceived, far wickeder, even, than my night of shame with the woman of the night. In her knelt position, I wished for Penny to worship me as I worshipped God. I yearned for her entire devotion.

I entwined my fingers behind her head and brought her face close to mine. When our lips touched, it was unlike anything I had ever known—even my bits of recollection from that bedeviled night. This kiss was gentle, uncertain. She had never shared her lips with another. Once the initial introduction had been overcome, our mouths seemed to meld into one. The ecstasy that coursed through my veins was more powerful, more intoxicating than even the most frenzied religious fervor I had ever felt. Hair wrapped in my fingers, I drew my face back, reveling in my sense of power. She desired but could not have me. I grasped her shoulders and pushed her back till she lay down. I climbed atop the table and atop her. Her breathing was frayed, first deep long breaths, then quick shallow ones. Her head lifted, lips searching mine. She must have me, and I would not deny her.

I hoisted up her skirts. She unlaced the stiff wire crinoline, which had all this time kept me from her. I wrenched it unceremoniously from her waist, cloth ripping in its wake. Next, she unlaced her drawers and, unable to bear waiting for her to complete the task, I ripped these too from her body. I unbuttoned and unlaced my own trousers and drawers. Incapable of delaying a moment longer, I entered her body.

She winced, seeming to be in some discomfort. I held my place, not wishing to hurt her. I gazed into those most beautiful of eyes, and she into mine, until I saw the discomfort flee. She pulled my face to hers, and we began to move, like the coupling rods of a locomotive, gently up and down, up and down, always bringing the destination closer. No longer did mind control body. Body controlled body, and we moved in unison instinctively, thinking nothing, only feeling. Sounds and sensations merged until they were indistinguishable. Penny cried out in ecstasy beneath me, and at nearly the same moment, came my own cry. I rested atop her for a moment longer, kissing her damp, tumbled hair, the corners of her eyes, her neck. She heaved a great, contented sigh.

As I had so many years ago, I felt as the moon, glowing with Penny's warmth, only this time with the warmth of her body. I rolled next to her on the table, gently caressing her skirts back over her limbs to cover her. We lay there, breathing coupled. She took my hand in hers. There was no need of words. My body was supremely sated. Never had my frame and muscles been so completely loosed. As to my mind, it was utterly free; not one thought crossed it. Penny squeezed my hand, and I closed my eyes.

I meant only to enjoy the nearness of my love, but I suddenly found myself starting awake. I jerked upward.

"How long have I slumbered?" asked I.

Penny remained on the table next to me, smiling. "Only a moment or two." She sat up and placed her hands on either side of my face. "Lie with me again."

Almost the very words Potiphar's wife spoke in her attempted seduction of Joseph! The room in my mind, full of Penny's memories, came flying open, and I was confronted with the enormity of my wicked act.

"Only for a few more moments," she said.

My mind was so torn betwixt Penny and what I knew to be right, that I felt it should rend in two. I longed to stay with her, to sup upon her body again; yet, I longed to run away, to cleanse myself of this abomination, to beg atonement for this sin.

I extricated her hands. "I'm sorry. I'm sorry," said I. "Forgive me." I slid from the table and hoisted up my drawers and trousers.

Penny watched. "What are you doing?"

"We've done wrong," said I, loathing myself for the wounded look in her eye.

"Have we?" Her voice had sharpened.

She would not—could not—understand. I pressed my hands over hers. "I beg your forgiveness, Penny." I gathered my chest of tools, forcing myself to walk composedly rather than run as I wished to do.

"I don't understand," she said, following me into the hall. "We've done nothing wrong."

Again, I gazed into her eyes. I had wounded her. "I'm sorry," said I. "I must go."

Unable to bear another glance, I paused at the door to make certain my clothing was in order.

"Adam!" Penny said, dress limp and dragging without its crinoline.

"I must go," repeated I, rushing from the house.

All the rebellion that had filled me during those two years from home slipped away in this one act with Penny. As I crossed the threshold of Haggard House, I fell upon my knees.

"I'm sorry," said I, choking in tears.

Stumbling forward, I grasped Mother round the waist, burying my head there. A stale odor, like death, clung to her skirts, and I felt suffocated. She clutched at me and would not allow me to move. Already she knew, as she always did.

"The temple of God has been desecrated?" asked she.

"It has." I wept. "I'm sorry, Mother." The very house seemed to shudder with my confession, boards creaking and groaning.

Instead of sharp words as I expected, she only sighed. "You must be wed. There is nothing else for it."

Still unable to extricate myself from her powerful clutch, my voice rose meekly from her skirts.

"Yes, Mother."

Chapter 57

The Narrative of Penny Haworth

I had made a go of the baking business. It was not as successful and glowing as I had imagined. Though I hated to admit it, it was just as Mother had said. It was hot, tiresome work, and before long, I missed an order or two, then three or four, and Mr. Tenney told me he would rather not have pies and bread at all than never know when they were coming. So, I gave it up altogether.

Adam's appearance had been a shock. The years had drawn so long that I had begun to doubt if he would ever return. His sudden warmth, and the sudden way in which we had come to know each other, had been as shocking as his return. His manner at our parting troubled me, but I was certain he would come round. Instead of pining, I kept my thoughts aglow with those precious moments together atop the table.

Stepping out onto the warm veranda, I was suddenly chilled.

There was a goat's head, milky blue eyeballs staring at me. The work was fresh, for a pool of blood had formed where the stump hung over the veranda floor.

It was too much—first Adam's coldness, now this. I clambered onto the veranda rail, leaning out, reaching, and undoing the knot securing the rope. As I did so, my waist brushed against the head, soaking my dress in blood. I slipped down from the railing and marched behind the house. Lifting the head, I hurled it with all my might into the woods. Let the wolves have it.

I returned shortly with a basin of water and a brush. It couldn't have been Gunther. Could it? There was a rumor that he had returned, though I was not certain why. No one had seen him. Perhaps he was lurking, camping somewhere in the woods, sneaking into the village at night and stealing what he needed. I doubted it.

As I continued to scrub, a chill of sudden revelation crept through me. Perhaps it was Adam's mother. No, that was foolish, for Sarai was much too frail for a task of this kind. And yet, it seemed the woman had more strength than she let on. Sarai somehow knew everything her son did, and perhaps had discovered our union yesterday. The more I thought of it, the more certain I became. Gunther seemed to have become Nomaton myth, a scapegoat for all wrongdoing. No doubt he had taken his part in meanness and cruelty. Yet Sarai, I was now confident, was responsible for the hideous heads at my door. Despite scrubbing, the blood left a dark brown stain in the wood that nothing would eradicate. I did my best to put the occurrence out of my mind.

All day I waited. Boots, sensing my anxiety, lurked close, swishing his tail back and forth against me and getting underfoot. I hoped that Adam, despite his words, might come. He did not. Nor did he come the day following, and I began to fear that he never would.

On the third day, he did appear, looking exceedingly tired, as if he had not slept since our last meeting. He came inside briefly, and Mother thanked him for repairing the table. He removed the clamps, then asked if he might accompany me on a short walk. Mother hesitated; I was afraid she might say no. However, permission was granted, and we walked down the dirt lane, past the edge of town and away from the village. The spring greens were brilliant about us, and birds swooped and soared and sang above, so very at odds with my feelings.

"I've done wrong by you," Adam said after many minutes of silence.

"You've done me no wrong." I looked up. "I don't regret it. I think of it constantly."

"It was wrong regardless. It was a sin against God and against our own bodies." Adam halted. He would not look at me. "Do you not see?"

"No," I said. "I do not. If it was a sin, we would never have goats or cows to milk, or foals to raise to pull our carriages, or geese to pluck for our beds."

Adam's hands clenched so tightly behind his back that the color drained from them.

"We are not beasts, Penny. We are separate. It is not the same."

"Is it not?"

"No. There is a proper order for things."

Not wishing to contradict him, we walked on in silence. Suddenly, he stopped. He took my hand, but there was no warmth in the motion.

"Penny, will you consent to be my wife?"

The hollowness, the formalness of his tone wounded me. For two years past, I had wished and hoped for this, but now, it seemed that Adam only asked to ease the guilt he bore. I searched his dark eyes for some sign contrary.

"Why?"

"Mother has—"

"Stop." I held up my hand. "No more. I won't—I can't hear it."

"It's not only her..." he said, fumbling. "I wish it for myself."

"For yourself? And what of me?"

"I wish it for you too."

"Why?"

"Because it is my duty to set things to rights."

"Duty?" I shook my head in disbelief. "Two years I've waited for your return—even prayed for it. Yet, for you it is only duty that binds us." I drew myself up, for doing so brought me half an inch higher than him. I knew he would dislike this. "Have you nothing else to say?"

Adam closed his eyes and rubbed them. He appeared more tired than ever. "I..."

I waited with bated breath for his words, but they never came.

"Please don't seek me again unless you have something of more interest to say," I said.

With that, I whirled round and parted from Adam, hurriedly increasing the distance between us. When I reached town, I saw Thomas. He called out a friendly, "Hello," but I rushed by without acknowledgment.

Chapter 58

The Narrative of Penny Haworth

A month passed quietly. The time would have been spent far more anxiously, had not the previous two years of uncertainty prepared me for it. Yet, I did not regret my actions. Adam must come to me of his own accord and in his own time. I would not have him any other way. During the intervening time, I only saw him once, and that was at a distance.

It was good of Mr. Tenney that he never again mentioned or reproached me for my baking episode. All the same, I felt the shame of it every time I entered his store. On this day, I had a long list of items to purchase, and had just placed it on the counter before him when I beheld Adam rumbling down the street, hauling lumber in his wagon. My heart leapt at the thought of a chance encounter with him, and I searched for some excuse to hasten from the store.

As I stared out, Mr. Tenney said, "Strange man, Adam. Though he's turned out to be quite a craftsman, greater even than his pa. Least, so I'm told." He leaned across the counter and lowered his voice. "They say he's building something in the woods. Got to be a house with all that lumber."

I moved a little closer to the window, hoping in vain that he would turn and see me. Mr. Tenney began to collect my items in his slow, methodical way.

"Could you hurry?" I said.

He glanced up, surprised. Then he looked out at Adam. His expression reminded me of Jakob's face when he had finally understood how to get the answer to his first sum in arithmetic. My face burned as Mr. Tenney quickly collected my things and gave them to me with that knowing look.

Basket of goods tucked under one arm, I rushed outside. Adam's cart was already a long way down the track leading from town. My heart leapt as he chanced to glance back. I was certain he saw me, for our eyes locked. Yet, he didn't stop. He turned round without so much as a friendly nod. A wave of sickly grief coursed through me.

For many weeks, hope had been my constant companion, but now hope gave way to despair. I couldn't stand in the street. I ran. Once home, breathless, I ripped off my hat, dropped upon my bed, and wept like a lost little girl. I had been so certain that once he had time to consider, Adam would return. But here he was, carrying on business as usual, not caring one jot about the woman he had offered his hand in marriage.

The bedroom door creaked open.

"Penny?" Mother moved to my four-post bed and wrapped me in her arms. "What is it?"

It was then that I unburdened myself of all that had happened. Mother accepted the news quietly, with little sign of her thoughts. She sat with me, smoothing my hair back from my face. At last, she spoke.

"Should Adam return and make you another offer, you will not accept it."

I abruptly separated from her, cheeks hot. I attempted to keep my voice steady.

"Why? Do you too still believe the schoolyard tales?"

"I don't wish to upset you further." Mother sighed. "I don't believe the rumors, per se. I do not believe anything monstrous or supernatural, but I have observed that family for a long time now. People are material, and the people connected with that place have come to no good."

My assumed calm vanished. "What of Adam?" My voice rose. "You say he has come to no good? He has done nothing wrong. He has, in fact, come to my aid more than once. He has spent two years in hard labor upon the railroad. He set himself up in business and, in only months' time, has come to be respected. What can be your objection to him?"

"Penny, it is for love of you that I say this. Adam has professed that he, like his mother, is deeply religious. Even now he attends every service and prayer meeting with her. Yet, the boy has committed this act with you, against his religion. That says something of his character."

"He is a *man*," I corrected. "And he is free to choose religion or not as he likes."

"Certainly." Her tone became pleading. "But he has chosen it, and yet does not live by it. And there are rumors—"

"See!" I interjected, rising from the bed. "Your words and command stem from frightened children's tales. I can hear no more." I began to leave but checked myself at the door. I turned to face Mother. "If Adam returns and asks me for my hand, I *will* accept."

I rushed from the room and out of the house, but Mother's words stung like a bee, small yet acute. What if Adam had strayed somewhat from his religion? What was that to me?

When I was finally out of hearing, in the woods behind our home, I again burst into tears. I would not allow her words to erode my love. Adam loved me, of that I was certain. And I loved Adam. No obstacle could interfere. I wiped my eyes.

Today was a day of tears, but I was certain that tomorrow would bring hope.

Chapter 59

The Narrative of Penny Haworth

Another week passed and still no word from Adam. I carried out my daily tasks as usual, but such a heaviness descended upon me that, at times, I would burst into tears in the midst of whatever I was doing. I never allowed this to happen when Mother was near. I avoided town as much as possible. To see him, even from a distance, only wounded me more.

The heat of summer waned, and the warm fall rains brought mushrooms which I collected in the woods behind my home. One day, as I collected the fungi clinging to rotting oak stumps and hiding among the crumbling brown leaves of the forest floor, I felt a sudden compulsion. I stopped what I was doing and, leaving my basket, made my way to the miniature house that Adam had built when we were children. I listened: there was nothing but the rustle of leaves in the breeze. Neither word nor sound disrupted the air. I scanned the woods, but there was nothing to be seen.

I examined the little house. Adam had been right those many years ago. The nails had indeed rusted. Not only that, but I now clearly saw that they were too short to hold well. One wall was sagging away from the roof. Looking at it now, I regretted not having listened to him.

Like an apparition, Adam suddenly appeared before me. I screamed.

He put a hand to my mouth and held his finger to his lips. "You'll be heard. Someone will think something's wrong and come after you."

I calmed and pulled his hand away.

"What do you want?" I asked.

"I want to show you something. Come." Adam turned and began to tread an invisible path through the woods.

I attempted to recall the anger and disappointment I had suffered all these months, yet new hope and excitement overwhelmed them. Adam was almost out of sight.

"Hurry," he said, waving me toward him as if nothing had ever happened.

Curiosity piqued, I followed his quick, silent tread. I again tried to conjure up my anger, yet already, I was inwardly offering him forgiveness. Then I became indignant with myself for allowing the insult of his proposal and many months of silence to be wiped away so easily. Even so, by the time Adam halted in the woods, I had all but forgotten the past and eagerly awaited whatever was in store.

"I must cover your eyes," he said.

As Adam neared, his presence nearly stopped my breath. He took his pocket handkerchief and bound it about my head. I felt the warmth of his hand against my back as he guided me through the trees. It was not long before we halted once more. I trembled as Adam removed the blindfold.

Before me was a charming little house set into a clearing in the woods.

"It's for you. For us." Adam grasped first one hand, then the other, facing me fully. "Please forgive me my past mistakes. I—I was overcome by all that had occurred. I was overcome by you, and I blundered my words. I spoke of Mother—I never meant to. It is *I* who wish to marry you. I have thought of it and dreamed of it and prayed for it many, many years."

He lowered his gaze. "I do not wish to misspeak again. So, you see, I have prepared for you. For us." He lifted his eyes and spoke, suddenly vehement. "Marry me, Penny. Please."

I could scarcely believe what was happening. My mouth knew my mind better than I did, for I suddenly heard myself say, almost in a whisper, "Yes." I flung my arms round him and shouted, "Yes! Yes, I will!"

Adam lifted me and spun in a circle.

When he put me down, he whispered into my ear, "I love you." His words were so bashful and gentle, it was as if this was the first time he had ever uttered them in his life.

"I love you," I repeated.

I too became bashful and dropped my head. He lifted my chin, face drawing very near mine. I could scarcely breathe. Then he swept me close. Our lips sought each other. The intensity of his kisses was like that of a man dying of thirst in the desert suddenly coming upon water and draining it all. His lips needed mine, and he drank and drank and drank until he had drunk all he could.

After, Adam stepped back a pace. We looked at each other and laughed. He sprinted toward the house, catching me round the waist and pulling me along.

The inside, though small, was beautifully crafted. The wainscot encasing the first-floor rooms glistened with polish. There was a small parlor, a dining room, and a kitchen with a scullery. There was even a tiny door set into the back kitchen door for my cat, Boots, to come and go as he pleased. The table, shelves, and chairs, all crafted by Adam, shined with smoothness. Large glass windows flooded the place with light.

He led me upstairs. There were two chambers, the larger of which we would share. An adjoining room contained a sitting room for my personal use and would serve as a nursery when children came. Even the home of my youth had never felt so snug and so full of belonging.

"It's wonderful," I said.

The house, the moment, and Adam's words so moved me, that I hoped and longed for a repetition of the occurrence upon my family table. However, he hurried me away from the chambers and back down the steps. Through the window, I caught a glimpse of the well, not far from the kitchen.

"Come," Adam said.

"What now?" I laughed.

He was leading me back out of doors and down a well-worn track through the trees when I took a sudden, involuntary step back. At the termination of the path was Haggard House.

Chapter 60

The Narrative of Adam Bolton

The churchyard was poorly kept, for Minister Judd was too old to perform the work required to maintain it. It was early morning, and already cold crept into this part of the world. I stood gazing upon Pa's gravestone when I heard a familiar voice call from the parsonage.

"Happy to see that you've come, my boy." The minister stood on his veranda.

Leaving the unhappy stone, without haste, I made my way to the house. Once I neared, he slapped me heartily on the back. I recoiled under his touch, but seeing as I had business, I thought it best to do it as civilly as possible.

The parsonage was cold and white. Even the chairs Minister Judd and I settled into were white. There were plenty of windows, filling the place with light; despite this, I felt ill at ease. He, like Mother, seemed impervious to the cold, for there were only half-live coals upon the hearth.

"At last, I welcome Adam to my humble home." The minister waved an imperious hand over the whitewashed room. His eyes rolled, revealing their yellowed whites. "I've heard some fine accounts of your workmanship, Adam. I wonder if I might commission you to build a wardrobe? I've one already, to be sure, but it's sadly worn and there's a family in the parish who will put it to better use."

"You might find Mr. Fowler more capable, sir, as I've just begun my trade," replied I.

"Nonsense. Your reputation precedes you, my boy. I think you are just the right man for the job. It would have to be whitewashed, of course."

"I could whitewash it, but over time the veneer would chip away."

The pupils of Minister Judd's eyes snapped to attention. "Well then, perhaps there is a wood you could use that's whiter than the rest. Then there would be no need for whitewash."

"I'm afraid that, to match your house, sir, there is need of whitewash."

"Well, that's settled then," the minister said. He wiped his face with his kerchief. "Now, my boy." He smiled. "You've piqued my curiosity. To the matter at hand. Yourself."

I stood, indignant at the minister's continued use of *my boy*, and paced the room. "Sir, I've come here of my own purpose."

His eyebrows lifted. "Is that so?"

"I've come to request that you marry Miss Haworth and myself."

"You surprise me, my boy. Does your mother know of this plan? I was at your home only yesterday, and she spoke nothing of this to me."

My ire increased. I briefly considered traveling to Wasaki to engage the minister there, but thinking of Mother's anger, quickly abandoned the thought. I faced Minister Judd and replied, "Mother is aware of our plans, and she gives her blessing. Will you do the service or no?"

"No need to snap so, my boy. If your mother indeed gives her blessing, then I shall perform the marriage."

Relieved that my loathsome task was nearly complete, I held

out my hand to seal the agreement. Minister Judd's clammy flesh met mine.

"I'll bring the wardrobe in a fortnight's time, if that's acceptable."

Without waiting for the affirmative, I retreated through the door, clapped it shut behind me, and hurried past the churchyard containing Pa's bones.

Having succeeded with the minister, now free from the oppressive chill of his house, my mood rose. Somehow, the impossible had occurred. Not only was I to wed the woman I loved, but I had Mother's blessing of the union. To be sure, the circumstances leading to my betrothal and her blessing were far from ideal. In truth, I looked upon my actions with Penny with shame and regret. However, my sins were done, and I had repented of them.

I meant to start upon a new life—a new life with Penny— where none of the darkness of my past could follow me into the bright home I had created for us, for my wife. *Wife!* I could hardly believe the word, yet it was to be.

Chapter 61

The Narrative of Penny Haworth

Our marriage day dawned. Apart from Thomas Fowler, the whole village gathered, and I heard the villagers comment amongst themselves how much this day was like that of Peter and Sarai's wedding. My joy would have been perfectly complete were it not for my wedding raiment. Sarai had offered up the lavender silk dress she had wed in. I had attempted to refuse, but Sarai was insistent. Not wishing to give offense, I reluctantly accepted. Mother spent a fortnight industriously removing many years' worth of stains and altering the garment to my size. Despite the material, the dress somehow weighed heavily upon me. However, I would not allow such a trivial matter to cast shadow upon my joy.

Minister Judd accomplished the ceremony with fewer drowsy nods than usual, after which I found myself atop Adam's lumber wagon, waving at the villagers and Mother, who had tried her best to reconcile herself to the match. Sarai rode with us, for our homes lay near.

The seating board could comfortably accommodate two, but we were forced to seat three. Sarai, discontent sitting on the outer edge, squeezed between Adam and me. I was vexed by her presence but attempted to maintain my joyous mood—a difficulty, with her cold, bony body pressed against my side.

There was no barn for our new home, and as no road had been built to it yet, Adam directed the wagon to Haggard House. The place loomed before us, and I felt fortunate that I would never reside there.

After Adam handed me and his mother down, Sarai wordlessly disappeared into the house. He unhitched the wagon and stabled the horse. We followed the short footpath through the woods, arm in arm, to our new home. I fancied that I saw a weight lifted from Adam as we approached. His eyes suddenly danced, full of fun, and he caught me up and carried me across the threshold. I laughed, pretending to struggle free from his arms.

Somehow, even the sun seemed stronger on this side of the clearing, and the house was flooded with light. He gently lowered me back upon my feet, and Boots, whom Adam had brought that morning, trotted up from his perimeter prowls and rubbed his head against my dress, rumbling with purrs.

A large, leathery bundle with bits of fur protruding from the edges was situated just before the fireplace.

"What is it?" I asked.

Adam unknotted the cord wrapped around it, grasped the edge, and flicked his wrist, unfurling the parcel all at once—a large bear skin, black fur glistening in the light.

"Who do you think left it?" I asked.

"McDonnell, I'm certain." Adam stood. "I've a gift for you." He led me to the kitchen table.

A square of burlap covered something with jagged peaks. I lifted the material, then laughed. It was a wooden chess set.

"I carved it on my travels," Adam said. "I've never forgotten you, you see."

I threw my arms round him. "It's wonderful. Everything is wonderful," I said, looking about the house. Lifting me again, he carried me up the stairs to the four-poster bed. Once there, I gave myself over to my husband, and he knew me, tenderly.

The evening was spent alternately playing games of chess—which I won as frequently as Adam—and repairing to the bearskin rug or the bed in the upper story. Though the night was not chill enough for a fire, one was lit regardless. Adam claimed the chimney need be tested, and I, always a lover of comfort and warmth, made no objection. When we grew too tired to remain awake, we lay on the bearskin before the fire. Adam wrapped his fingers in my hair, his face so close to mine that I could feel his breath upon my cheek. There, weariness at last took us over, and we spent our first night as man and wife.

Chapter 62

The Narrative of Penny Haworth

I woke late in the morning to an extinguished fire and an empty bearskin. I searched the house, looking for my husband, but he was not to be found. Nor did I see him in the yard. Was it possible he'd gone to the shop? I had thought he would at least take the day to spend with me. The evening had been so extraordinary and pleasurable that it was difficult to think of resuming an ordinary routine so quickly. However, I was now responsible for a home of my own, and though taking care of it would not fill me with the same pleasure as Adam's company, I would find some measure of fulfillment in it.

Laden with two wooden pails, I went outside to fetch water from the well. With deep dismay, I saw Sarai hurrying down the passage between the houses. We met simultaneously.

"Give me to drink," Sarai said, thrusting her own pails forward.

I nearly laughed at her stiff movement and peculiar words, but seeing that she was indeed serious, I lowered the rope, the weighted well-sweep lifting high in its wake. I did not allow the bucket to fully submerge, only sinking it half-way before allowing the well-sweep's weight to lift it again. As I did so, Sarai stood silently, glancing darkly at the little water.

"Are you not accustomed to drawing water for your household?" she asked.

"I didn't wish to make them too heavy for you."

"Fill them up, girl. God has given me strong arms."

She meant to insult me, but I would not be insulted. Again, I lowered the bucket, this time filling it, and then its twin, to brimming. Without another word, Sarai gripped the pails with her claw-like hands and marched back toward Haggard House. I drew a breath as she disappeared.

Though there was yet no garden, Adam had constructed a fence west of the house where one might be made. Here I spent much of the day, removing rocks and overgrowth. To my relief, I did not see Sarai again. When the afternoon began to wane, I withdrew to the house to prepare the evening meal. As I stepped inside, I was surprised to find a putrid odor and a loaf of bread upon the table. Upon closer examination, I found that the odor and the bread were one and the same. Sarai must have brought it in while I was working in the garden. I shuddered, pushing the loaf into a bowl, and dumped it in the woods just beyond the house. Then I washed, and prepared Adam's meal with the provisions my own mother had kindly stocked the kitchen with over the past week. There was a lovely corn stew, cold meat and vegetables, and freshly baked bread, also compliments of Mother.

I was thoroughly rewarded for my efforts when I saw Adam's pleasure as we dined. He eagerly filled his bowl and plate with seconds. Seeing how happy he was, I was loath to mention the bread Sarai had left, but I decided that the communication must be got over sooner rather than later.

"Adam," I said. "I believe your mother may have brought in bread whilst I was out. I found a loaf upon the table when I returned." Adam's jaw slowed as he chewed. "I don't wish to speak poorly of her baking, but I'm afraid the loaf smelt so badly that I had to dispose of it in the woods."

"Did Mother see you do so?" he asked.

"No. She was not here when I returned," I said.

For a long time, Adam said nothing, and I began to fear he would leave the matter. However, at last he said, "I will speak with her. Now that you're my wife, it is your responsibility, not hers. She will understand."

I was ill at ease. Adam did not seem to comprehend the full import of the incident. It was not simply that Sarai had made bread for him, but also her manner of coming into the house unannounced to deliver it. And there was the offensiveness of the bread itself. However, Adam seemed not to heed any of these points but saw only responsibility. Yet still, if he spoke with her, then the occasion was not likely to be repeated, and that was the main thing.

"Thank you," I said.

Adam's jaw relaxed, and he resumed chewing at his usual speed.

That evening, I could scarcely believe Adam's tenderness. Each moment seemed better than the last. If these first nights were any indication, ours was to be a happy and full marriage. It was more than repayment for my patience, more than repayment even for Adam's coldness after our first knowing.

I awoke earlier than usual. It would be difficult to conform to Adam's daily schedule, being so much earlier than my own. Yet, I wished to repay him with the happiness I felt, and I could not leave him to shift for his own breakfast. So, I made porridge, perfectly tender and not overly thick. Again, I was rewarded for my efforts by his delighted face.

"I've never tasted such wonderful porridge," he said.

I blushed with pleasure.

Adam's jaw suddenly slowed, and my breath caught; even from

such short experience, I knew this meant he was thinking of some uncomfortable topic.

"I've not thought of it before now, but..." He paused, clearly hesitant to speak his mind.

"What is it?" I asked, taking his hand. "You can tell your wife."

He looked up and smiled. "Well, it's simply that I must ask you to do all of your cooking and cleaning for tomorrow—today."

"Why must I—" Suddenly, I understood. "Ah, I see. I can manage." I forced a smile, though I was more than vexed by the unexpected double workload.

"I'm sorry to ask," Adam said, squeezing my hand. "Only— Well, you understand?"

"Yes. Certainly. It shall be done!" I said, rallying my spirits.

The thought of stale food all of Sunday—and all the following Sundays—was not enticing. However, it was a small sacrifice for gaining the man I loved.

The next morning, my dreams were disturbed by my body being shaken. For a moment, in the confusion of waking, I forgot where I was and did not recognize the face looking down upon me. I bolted upright, frightened half out of my wits by the intense gaze coming from a set of dark eyes.

"It's only me." A smile flickered across Adam's face as he sat beside me on the bed.

I stared until memory slowly dawned. These were my husband's eyes. I shook off my fright and laughed at myself.

"You've slept a long time," he said. "You appeared so peaceful. I didn't wish to wake you, but it's nearly time to leave for service."

I peered out the window into the dark morning. Again, I deeply regretted the disturbance to our domestic bliss, but there was nothing for it. Making my voice as gentle as possible, I said, "But, Adam, you know I never attend church."

The kind look on Adam's face disappeared, and his lips set in a hard, thin line.

"I know. But I'd hoped—"

"Of course," I interrupted. "I won't stop you from going. *You* must do what *you* think is right."

"I see," Adam said, expression taut.

As much as I wished to appease him and wipe away the disappointment I saw so clearly, I could not in good conscience feign beliefs I did not hold. Too, the thought of sitting in the cold church for upward of two hours listening to the minister's rambling sermon, would have made a less resolute woman than I take a stand.

"I'm sorry," I said.

After a long pause he said, "Very well. I will meet you after."

"Yes." In hope of lightening the mood, I added, "You've a delightful lunch waiting."

"I've something for you too," he said. "A gift. It's in your sitting room."

"Truly?" I asked, nearly leaping from the bed.

"Wait until I leave to find it," he said, restraining me with his strong hand and smiling at my impetuosity. He retreated and called up, "Until the afternoon then."

I jumped out of bed and rushed down the stairs, intending to kiss him. Adam anticipated my movement though, and grasping my arms gently, held me apart from him. "Not upon the Sabbath," he said.

Surprised by his reception, I froze on the spot and could say nothing.

Seeing my pain, Adam pulled me forward and kissed my forehead. "This afternoon...love." He smiled sheepishly and was off before I knew what had happened.

Looking round the room, it felt sadly vacant. Then, suddenly remembering, I hurried into the sitting room. There, upon my desk, was my gift, wrapped in a bit of muslin. I took a seat and ran a hand across it. I was touched. It was easy to see that it was a book, and I thought how kind it was of Adam to purchase it for me so I might have something to do of a Sunday. I hoped it was something thrilling.

Turning it over, I unfolded the bit of fabric. It was a thick volume, but I could not tell from the back what it was. A metal clasp held it shut. The front did not reveal the title, either. I could read it on the binding but decided to open the book and read the inscription first. It simply stated that the gift was from Adam and presented to me. I had hoped for something more, but I turned the first few pages to find the title.

It was *The Holy Bible*.

I ought to have guessed. What other book would Adam give? I recalled the night he was stuck in our home during the blizzard. At the end of the evening, he had read a long passage of the Bible, and I had worked hard to keep an expression of interest throughout, though I nearly fell asleep. I pushed the book from me almost angrily. Then, with a pang of guilt, I pulled it back. He had taken the time and expense to surprise me, and that was all that mattered.

Opening the Bible again, I began in Genesis. I read only a chapter before my head began to nod. Pushing the book closed, I left the house and visited with Mother until Adam returned for the afternoon. He was in fine spirits, and his glances, whenever he looked at me, melted my very heart. Even so, he spoke little and disappeared upstairs for upward of an hour, alone in prayer.

As we lay in bed that night, I found that the day had been easier than I had imagined; if tithing to Adam's God one day of every week was the cost of being with the man I loved, then so be it. I was willing and happy to do so.

Chapter 63

The Narrative of Penny Haworth

One Sabbath, about a month into my marriage, I arrived at my childhood home and was surprised to find an empty kitchen. I took the stairs to Mother's chamber. There, she lay in bed upon her side; despite the warm fall day, she was heavily wrapped in blankets.

I hurried to her.

"What's wrong? What is it?"

As Mother opened her eyes, they glittered unnaturally. "Could you find more blankets? I'm dreadfully cold." Her hand suddenly went to her side and held it tight.

I rushed about, tearing blankets from the linen cupboard and laying them upon Mother. "How long have you been in this state?"

"Perhaps a quarter of an hour." Her breaths were labored and heavy.

Anxiety flooded me. Uncertain how to help, I retrieved a cup of water from the kitchen and placed it to Mother's lips.

"Drink this, and I'll fetch the doctor."

She drank the proffered liquid, and as soon as it was drained, I rushed from the house.

The doctor was a church-going man, and as it was still early, service had not yet begun. When the spire came into view, I found the doctor shaking hands with Minister Judd at the door.

"Doctor Brigham!" I shouted, running to within arms-breadth of him. "You must come with me," I said breathlessly. "Mother is ill." Consternation crossed Minister Judd's face as I stepped between them and grasped the doctor's hand. "You must come now."

"Ride with me," Doctor Brigham said, moving toward his buggy.

Suddenly, Adam appeared at the church door, Sarai close behind.

"Your mother is ill?" he asked.

"Yes." I did not stop. My thoughts were only upon Mother, and I hurried after the doctor.

"Wait," Adam called.

Pausing, I turned back. Sarai cast a dark glance and whispered in Adam's ear. He faltered.

"I must go," I said, looking desperately after the buggy.

Sarai took Adam by the arm, but his face suddenly hardened.

"I will accompany you," Adam called, pulling away.

Together, Adam and I quickly gained the distance between ourselves and Doctor Brigham, and as a trio, we made haste to Mother's residence. As I looked back from the buggy, I saw Sarai's eyes smolder as we disappeared.

When we arrived, the doctor, requesting us to wait outside, entered the bedroom. From inside came short, rasping coughs. I paced the upper hall as Adam, hands tucked behind his back, gravely looked on.

"She has pneumonia," Doctor Brigham said, closing the bedroom door behind him.

"What should we do?" I asked.

"Plenty of water. She'll need a light diet—soup, broth, milk—things of that nature." He produced a corked glass bottle from his bag. "I've some Dover's powder you can use to make her more comfortable for now. She'll need constant supervision. I'll stop by periodically to check on her progress."

I stood, watching, as Doctor Brigham collected his coat from the cloak stand. It was difficult to believe. Mother had always been healthy and strong. Throughout my entire existence, I could only remember half a dozen occasions upon which she had been ill.

The doctor offered his hand.

"Thank you," I said, trembling as I took it.

He tipped his hat gravely and left.

"I will remain with you," Adam said. "We will watch in turns."

The weight of it suddenly descended, and I began to cry. Adam caught me up in his arms.

"All will be well," he murmured into my hair.

All was not well. The disease took a course painful to watch. Her fever burned, her pulse quickened, and her dry cough became bloody. She wasted away over the course of eight days. Adam was as gentle and tender a nurse as any woman I had ever observed. Doctor Brigham monitored her illness and administered all possible treatments, but at the termination of only a week and a day, Mother's life expired. I, Adam, and Doctor Brigham were witnesses to the end, and I held her hand at the last labored breath.

I buried my grief in the duties attendant with death. I saw to the funeral and burial. Mother's body was laid to rest in the churchyard beside Father's. I saw to Mother's house. First, I considered occupying it, as it was larger than ours and in town. Yet, Adam had built such a lovely little home just for me, and I couldn't bear the thought of someone else inhabiting it. So, my childhood home was sold to a new doctor and his wife who had been lodging at the inn until they could find a place to purchase. I took Mother's silver candlesticks and most everything from the kitchen. The furniture and movables we sold.

As I wished a final, tearful goodbye to the house, the couple drew up in their carriage. After the transfer of property had been signed, Adam and I turned toward our own home. As we did so, I looked back and saw the new occupants carrying their possessions into what had once been my home.

I nestled my head against Adam's arm. Adam had been nothing but kind throughout Mother's illness. He had left my side only to sleep or to fetch supplies. He had even refrained from attending church, very much against his mother's wishes. We had forged a bond stronger than anything I could have imagined. Mother's death was a heavy weight, but less so, than had I carried the burden alone. I now had only Adam left in the world.

Our return was made in silence. The ground was still wet with rain from the previous night, and the wind blew in the direction of our travel. As we neared, the wind subsided, and a soft gray flake, almost like snow, landed on my shoulder. I brushed it away absently. Several more flakes landed, and I suddenly caught the unmistakable scent of smoke. It was billowing upward from somewhere between the trees.

I looked at Adam in horror, and we broke into a run. Haggard House loomed ahead, desolate as ever. The smoke came from the other side of the short footpath. As one, we rushed into our own clearing and stopped, horrified. Before us, blazing up into the sky, was our home. Aghast, coughing and sputtering, I looked round the clearing.

There was Sarai. She locked eyes with me.

"It was that cat," she said. "Shouldn't have been allowed in the house. Knocked down a candle. Once it got going, I couldn't stop it."

Chapter 64

The Narrative of Penny Haworth

By the time the fire subsided, cinders and smoking rubble were all that remained. Adam had tried to pull me from the doomed place, but I had stubbornly stayed put through the night. I had sat on the ground, arms wrapped round my knees, handkerchief over my nose, eyes fixed upon the mesmerizing flames.

Two great losses in such a short time.

Sarai too had stayed, pacing back and forth, muttering to herself I knew not what. Nor did I care.

Now, without encouragement, Sarai said, "No one had been to the place in weeks to clean. I took it upon myself." She left off as if no other explanation was needed.

"It is—was—a bright day," I said bitterly. "Candles were unnecessary. I'd no idea you were so fond of light."

Sarai turned to Adam. "I'm truly sorry."

As the sun staggered above the tree-line, the gravity of the situation set in.

"We need a place to stay," I said, thinking of the inn.

"You may stay with me," Sarai said, voice full of godly resignation.

I nearly laughed at the absurdity of the offer, but when I turned to Adam, he was anything but amused.

"Yes," he said. "We've not much choice now. We're sorry to impose on you, Mother."

"It's no trouble," she said.

"Adam, may I speak with you a moment?" I said, half under my breath.

"I see I'm not wanted," Sarai said and hastened down the footpath.

"We can board in town," I said. "We've money from the sale of my mother's home."

Adam shook his head. "I won't use it on something so wasteful as lodgings. I'm behind in my work already. I won't have time to build another house until spring, so until then, we will remain with Mother."

His countenance was strained, and I was too engulfed in anguish to argue. I allowed him to take my arm and lead me toward Haggard House. I would persuade him to take up lodgings elsewhere at a later time. As we walked, Adam muttered under his breath. I only caught a handful of words. "Punishment...straying..." Yet, I was too worn to question him.

As Adam entered Haggard House, I halted at the threshold.

"Come." He held his hand out. I stood, fixed, unmoving.

"What are you waiting for?"

"I have a strange feeling," I said.

"What is it?"

"Let's stay at the inn. I know it will cost, but we have enough, surely, until we find something more permanent."

Adam's expression became almost stern. "I will need that money if you ever wish us to have a new house. Come."

He retreated deeper inside. There was no room left for discussion. Reluctantly, I stepped across the threshold. Though it was now broad morning, I felt as if I had suddenly stepped into night. There was a distinct scent of rot in the air. At the far end of the room, the floorboards were stained a dappled, unnatural color; it recalled to mind the blood stain upon the veranda of my old home.

Was I really to live with the very woman who had left a severed deer's head at my door? I longed to run back into the fresh air and light. However, I consoled myself with the thought that it would be but one night. Tomorrow, I would persuade Adam to leave this place.

As my eyes grew accustomed to the darkened room, I saw Adam and his mother conversing in hushed tones.

"Mother says we're to have the attic," he said, turning to me. "We'll make up a bed for her here in the kitchen."

"Thank you," I said, mustering all the gratefulness I could manage. "It's very kind."

The remainder of the morning was spent moving Sarai's few items into the far corner of the lower hall. Sarai positioned her rocking chair in the center of the room and calmly watched the proceedings, interjecting instructions as she saw fit. I assisted in bringing Adam's old corncob mattress down for Sarai, then we ascended to collect the chest of drawers. Adam reached the attic first. Just before I cleared the landing, I heard Sarai's voice, low enough that only I could hear.

"Careful on the stairs, or you'll break your neck."

I whirled round and gave her a withering glance. She gazed out across the room as if she had not spoken.

Once we were settled, I suddenly thought of Boots. I had been so distraught by the loss of our house that I had forgotten him. Rushing outside, I called his name. There was neither sight nor sound of him. I neared the woods and called again. A familiar mewling met my ear: just beyond the line of trees, I saw the arch of Boots' back. I heaved a sigh of relief, hurried forward, and gathered him up in my arms. The end of his tail was singed, but he was otherwise all right.

Kissing his fur, I walked back toward the house. The nearer we drew, the more distraught Boots became. A gurgling, growling sound emerged from deep in his throat. At the threshold, he drew his claws, ripping my dress sleeve and leaving three bloody scratches on my arm. I immediately dropped him, and he streaked across the room, jumped upon Sarai's mattress, and stuffed his head under the Job's Trouble quilt, violently whipping tail still visible.

I began to laugh. I pictured how I must look, wearing black mourning apparel, laughing hysterically at my cat. It was unseemly, with all that had happened, but I couldn't help it; and the more I thought of how unseemly it was, the louder I laughed.

Sarai bolted up from her rocker. "Animals live out of doors. Take it outside."

I stopped laughing as suddenly as I had started.

"He's accustomed to being indoors," I said, smile still half upon my face. "I'll let him out in the morning. He won't soil your house."

"You'll take him out. Now."

My smile disappeared. I turned to Adam, who had just returned downstairs.

Shifting uncomfortably, he said, "The cat has lived indoors before. Perhaps we can—"

"Adam!" Sarai said. "It's we who have dominion over the beasts of the field! Not they over us! The cat stays outside."

"He can't stay outside, Adam," I said. "You yourself said that he is accustomed to living indoors!"

"Perhaps you're both right," Adam said, gathering up Boots from the mattress. "I'll make up a place for him in the barn."

"I don't want him in the barn," I said, stamping my foot, though I knew it was childish.

Adam's voice became entreating. "I'll make him a bed with rags."

I felt Sarai's cold eyes upon us.

"He'll stay in the attic," I said to Adam. Then, turning to Sarai, "He won't bother you. You don't have to be so—"

Completely unmoved, Sarai kept her gaze fixed on me, and for many moments we glared at each other. Seeing that I would not win, I reluctantly signaled Adam to take Boots outside. Adam quickly disappeared.

My head throbbed, thoughts muddled from the smoke and the sleepless night. I nearly collapsed upon one of the hard wooden chairs. My chin quivered, and I tried stilling it to keep the tears back.

"Really," Sarai sighed, shaking her head. "It's only a cat."

A sudden, violent thought gripped me. I imagined myself rushing toward the hag-like woman, gripping her by the throat, and choke, choke, choking until the smug look in her beady eyes died out.

As I thought this, Sarai's cold voice said, "God can hear your thoughts, my dear."

Chapter 65

The Narrative of Penny Haworth

When I woke, Adam had already left for the shop. During the night, I had a troubling dream in which Sarai was watching me from a crack in the attic door. I examined it to see if there was such a crack, and strangely enough, there was. It was only a slit, but large enough to see through if one put one's eye directly upon it.

Glancing out the attic window, I found that it was still early morning. I decided to go downstairs and make breakfast. Across the room, Sarai slept on her side, facing me. I could scarcely believe how sunken and skeleton-like she appeared. Though I could see the woman's eyes were closed, the disturbing notion came over me that Sarai was watching.

Moving silently, I searched for quite some time to find ingredients for breakfast. Nothing was where it should be. When at last I found the flour barrel and removed the lid, I leapt back in disgust. Weevils had found their way in, and the flour crawled with them. I glanced at Sarai, but the sudden movement had not woken her. Dragging the wooden barrel outside and across the yard, I dumped the spoiled flour on the grass just past the line of trees. It was impossible to make food in this place. I returned, and replaced the empty container under the shelf.

As I turned, I nearly screamed. Sarai stood directly behind me.

"I was just leaving," I said.

Her beady eyes followed my every motion as I hurriedly collected my shawl.

I half ran down the path, feeling every breath grow freer as I left Haggard House behind. I determined to go directly to Adam. Expense or no expense, I could not spend another night in that wretched place.

He was in his shop, filing saws. I watched him at the door for a moment. He was so absorbed in work that he did not look up. The rings under his eyes were as deep as ever, but he was still remarkably handsome. His dark hair glistened with sweat, and the intensity of his focus shone in his eyes. I was loath to interrupt him, but my shoe struck a rock in the dirt floor and caught his attention. He smiled when he saw me, but it was a troubled, forced smile.

"I'm sorry to disturb you," I said.

"It's nothing." Adam stood upright from his work.

He appeared so tired. I felt for him. I was not the only one to suffer loss. Adam had too, and the weight must be a tremendous burden upon his shoulders. He now had a wife to care for and no house in which to do so. He had been proud, even in childhood, and his nature would not—could not—allow us to live in any place he did not feel belonged to him.

"Is anything wrong?" he asked.

"No..." I replied, resolve giving way. "I only wished to see you."

Suddenly, like a wolf pouncing upon its prey, he grasped me, swung the door closed, and laid me upon his worktable. There, he knew me with a ferocity that both frightened and pleased me.

When it was over, he became pensive. "I should return to my work."

I dressed, watching his methodical movement as he buttoned his shirt. It was strange, how he could change so quickly; intense and ferocious at first but stiff and wooden afterward, almost as if we had not been so close. However, before I left, he gave me a warm kiss goodbye. Whatever troubles there were, I was certain that Adam loved me. This certainty was enough to cast a fog over my thoughts concerning Haggard House. I could—and would—endure. I was not of such timid stuff as to be put off by a few troubling occurrences.

The remainder of the day I spent away from Haggard House, combing over the blackened skeleton of my home. I was relieved to find the silver candlesticks and cutlery from Mother's house. Amidst the rubble, I also found my tortoise-shell comb, but it was badly burned. Everything else had either succumbed to the fire or been damaged by the crumbling house. When, at last, it grew dark, I was forced to make my way back to the dreaded place. In my arms, I carried the few items I had managed to save. Adam, returning from the shop, met me in the clearing, and we entered together to find Sarai waiting for us, arms crossed.

"Adam, your wife has been out all day and left me to do the chores on my own."

"Is that true?" he asked.

"I was searching for anything we might salvage," I said, laying the silver and damaged comb upon the kitchen table, as if the soot covering my mourning dress and hands were not enough proof.

"It's no excuse," Sarai said. "That ought only to have taken half an afternoon at most." She glanced contemptuously at the comb. "Vanity," she mumbled. Then, louder, "'Vanity of vanities saith the preacher. All is vanity.'" There was a pause. "And do you know that she's discarded my flour?"

Adam's searching gaze turned upon me.

"It was spoiled," I said. "It was crawling with vermin."

"Vermin? Nothing but more to fill your belly," Sarai said.

I bit my tongue and said, "I'm sorry I emptied your flour. I ought to have asked first."

A scathing glance came from Sarai. "Yes. You ought."

Though I believed myself, in usual cases, to have remarkable control over my temper, I felt boiling-hot anger.

"Then again, I say I'm sorry," I said. I didn't sound it. "Now if you'll excuse me, my clothes are soiled. I'll change before dinner."

I mounted the stairs, but entering the sleeping attic afforded little relief when I realized I no longer had other clothes. The creak of feet climbing the attic steps startled me from my reverie. It was Adam.

"I'm sorry Mother was so...harsh. She only wishes the best for you," he said, taking my hand.

Nearly snorting, I bit my lip.

"I know you were only trying to be of help." Adam's tone was so tender that I would have forgiven almost anything. Despite my filth, I wrapped my arms about him and held him to me.

As I slept that evening, wearing Sarai's odorous night-gown, I heard the grandfather clock through my dreams, chiming midnight. I awoke and found myself alone, Adam's warmth absent from the bed. Listening intently, I made out the sound of footsteps creaking across the floorboards, back and forth, back and forth; shortly thereafter, I heard the muffled hum of two voices in unison. Using the crack in the attic door as a peephole, I peered below and caught a glimpse of Sarai and Adam, both with Bibles in hand, pacing and reading. Sarai led, and Adam, with ghostlike visage, almost imperceptibly, followed. Of the troubling things I had seen and felt over the last day and night in Haggard House, this was the most disquieting. Frightened that Sarai might observe me, I hurried back to bed. I wished for Boots: I would have pulled the orange tabby into bed, possibly restoring my ability to slumber. As it was, hearing those monotonous voices below, there was little chance I would fall back asleep.

Chapter 66

The Narrative of Adam Bolton

None could imagine the intensity of the pressure building within. Upon my return to Haggard House, and to Mother, it was nearly impossible not to fall into prior thoughts, beliefs, and habits. Newer ideas that had begun to formulate, seemed now foolish, and lacking depth. Mother was as she had always been; not a jot had changed. Mother knew the Truth. Her assuredness in this gave me assurance.

As for Penny, though Mother never breathed a word of her in her presence, she often chose such Scriptures for our reading as: "Her feet go down to death; her steps take hold on hell,"—and— "Such is the way of an adulterous woman; she eateth, and wipeth her mouth, and saith, I have done no wickedness." Further—"Be ye not unequally yoked together with unbelievers: for what fellowship hath righteousness with unrighteousness?" And though I did what I might to keep these words from influencing me, I found them as a continual dripping in my thoughts.

Fears that I had nearly forgotten—fears for Penny's very soul— fear for mine—returned, and along with this fear came tortuous uncertainty. How could I press forward with such opposing ideas?

Little need to hide Penny's memories, which had now all been exposed, within my mind-house. Instead, as I had done with Pa's those many years ago, I placed in this room my love for her. Only on rare occasions would I open this room; even at these times, the intensity was such that it frightened me; and I found it a great struggle to push that love back into its place.

At this time too began great headaches—aches so terrible, that at times I thought my head might split in two. Though I attempted to hide it, I was irritable and cross.

Never had I found the verse in Matthew truer: "No man can serve two masters: for either he will hate the one, and love the other; or else he will hold to the one, and despise the other."

Chapter 67

The Narrative of Penny Haworth

Boots, who had been an affectionate kitten and cat, became increasingly wild as the sojourn at Haggard House continued. Once removed from the dwelling, he never came nearer than the shed. He strayed far and sometimes did not return at night.

My spirit drooped lower and lower, my only pleasure being the short overnight journey to Wasaki to procure a new wardrobe. Adam knew me at night, but he lacked the passion from the beginning of our marriage. He was not unkind, but neither was he tender; he seemed to be fulfilling yet another obligation.

In order to stay away from the house as much as possible, I spent my days in Sarai's garden. Weeds had choked out the meager array of vegetables, and the turnips and potatoes had not yet been turned up. Laundry too, I took upon myself, for Sarai rarely did it. I took the washtub outside, though it was extra labor to bring out the hot water. I preferred it to the still and doom of Haggard House. In the evenings, I would follow Adam indoors and eat a revolting dinner, consisting chiefly of vermin-infested bread and watery soup. Our passionless knowing would take place, then we would sleep. At midnight, I would secretly watch as Adam slipped down the stairs to join his mother. My sleep was always uneasy and filled with nightmares. In the morning, I would wake to do it all over again. Time became an endless void of monotony, and I wondered how long I had been here and whether we would ever escape.

Though I had never attended church service before, I was compelled to do so upon my first Sabbath there. Sarai, in her usual stern manner, had told me I must attend. Adam had stood behind his mother with an entreating gaze. I might have put up more of a fight, were it not for my desire to be anywhere other than Haggard House.

One Sunday, at second service, Sarai wedged herself between Adam and me in the pew, as she sometimes did. Midway through the service, the church door opened, and I was surprised to see Thomas Fowler.

A sudden, razor-like sensation nearly made me cry out, bringing my attention forward. Sarai had dug her claw-like nails into my arm and pinched. My eyes were watery with pain, and I turned sharply to her. She only stared straight ahead. Without thinking what I was doing, I dug *my* nails into Sarai's arm and held them there. She did not flinch; she only turned her cold, beady eyes to mine. I stared back defiantly. Though Adam did not glance our way, I felt his attention drawn. Minister Judd's droning voice kept Sarai from holding her gaze, but before turning back, she smiled at me contemptuously.

When the meeting was complete, Sarai went to speak to the minister, and Thomas stepped from the back of the church to greet us.

"Penny. Adam. Wonderful to see you."

Adam thrust his arm through mine and tightened it to his side. "Thomas," he said with a nod.

"Penny, you are well?" Thomas asked.

"Yes, of course," I said, forcing a smile.

"Are you certain? You look ill. Has she been poorly, Adam?"

"My wife is perfectly well," Adam said, further tightening his grip.

There was no looking-glass at Haggard House, but I guessed what Thomas must see. I was in the same condition as one of Mr. Fowler's fighting dogs after its usefulness had faded. My frame was wasting away, and even my gloves fit loosely.

"As Adam says, I'm perfectly well," I said, forcing my smile broader.

Just then, Mr. Riblet beckoned Adam. "I'll be back presently. My love," Adam said, looking at Thomas as he spoke.

Thomas lowered his voice and spoke hurriedly. "Penny, if ever you're in trouble, I hope you know that you have a friend in me. You're not alone."

The look of concern, mingled with kindness in Thomas' eyes as he said this, nearly made me burst into tears.

Sarai suddenly appeared.

"I'm sorry, Thomas," she said, "but Penny must be going."

Again, my arm was clutched, though this time by Sarai, and I was hurried outside the church. Adam joined us shortly.

Thomas' expression haunted me. What must he think? Undoubtedly, he believed Adam was to blame for my appearance, but nothing that had happened had been Adam's doing. Indeed, I held out hope that as soon as winter passed and our new house was built, all would be well and happy again.

All the journey home, Sarai walked with a smug posture and did not look back. As we moved along, black clouds came into view, and a breeze picked up, whirling dead leaves in little circles.

"We ought to hurry. A storm is coming," Adam said.

Before we had completed half of the return journey, rain came. At first, it was a light sprinkle, but it soon changed to a pelting, driving torrent. My clothes were soaked through in mere seconds. The drops were so thick that I could hardly see before me. Sarai became a black blur, then disappeared altogether. Adam began to run, holding my arm. The ground was quickly softening beneath our feet. My Sunday shoes were no match for the mud, and I repeatedly slipped. Never did I think I would welcome the sight of Haggard House, but when I glimpsed it through the downpour, I was grateful. The inside, though cold, provided welcome relief from the storm.

"Where is Mother? Is she here?" Adam asked, looking round the room.

"Perhaps she went upstairs," I said, water dripping from my dress and pooling on the floor.

He disappeared to the attic. My skin was numb from the cold and wet. As sheets of rain slapped against the window, a dark form appeared against it. I leapt back, and for a horrible moment, I envisioned Sarai's hag-like face looming there. Another second revealed that it was merely a tree branch buffeted by the wind.

Adam returned with a thick oilskin coat. "She's not above. She must have gotten lost in the rain. Her eyesight is not what it was." He pulled on the oilskin. "I must search for her."

Panic seized me. I got the horrible feeling this was all a trick, and that Sarai had disappeared on purpose to draw Adam to her.

"Don't go," I pleaded.

For the first time, Adam looked at me coldly. "She is my mother. I must find her." With that, he disappeared. A gush of rain slapped inside the house before the door closed behind him.

Heaviness settled into my limbs, and I could hardly move. I knew I must not stay in my cold, wet clothes, yet I was reluctant to change. Instead, I went to the fireplace. The embers had died out, so I attempted to light a fire with the tinderbox. No matter how many times I lit the kindling or attempted to coax the flicker into a flame, the fire refused to burn. My efforts in vain, I looked up at the window and realized it was dark outside, not only due to the storm. It was already late.

I remembered Boots, out in the elements. I hurried into the torrent to see if he was safe in the barn. It wouldn't have been strange if he was absent, skittish as he was of late. However, there he was. Out of sheer defiance, I picked him up, nestled him inside my cloak, and brought him back to the house. He screeched at the rain and clawed me horribly at the door, but I managed to get him inside. Once there, he streaked up the stairs, and I followed. Though the heaviness I felt earlier still weighed on me, I found the strength to change into dry clothes and, exhausted, lay down next to Boots, who had settled himself on the bed. Despite my anxiety over Adam—I cared not a jot about Sarai—I fell asleep.

Chapter 68

The Narrative of Penny Haworth

I woke the following morning to find Boots sitting in the windowsill facing the woods. He gave me a reproachful look, as if he blamed me for bringing him here. As the previous day's events recalled to mind, I bolted upright. Where was Adam? In my half-wakened state, I stumbled down the stairs to see if he might be there. Neither Sarai nor my husband was present. I hurriedly dressed and made my way to the front door. As soon as I opened it, I let out a scream.

A red fox head hung before me, red-brown eyes frozen in terror. Boots streaked past and leapt, swinging as he clung to the head and licked the blood from the severed neck.

"Boots!" I shouted.

He ignored me and tore flesh with his sharp teeth. All the while, the fox's eyes seemed to plead for help. Again, I shouted but to no avail. Even as I cut down the head, Boots would not let go. If I neared him, he hissed and spat. He refused to drag the head away, instead remaining by the door where he ripped his prize apart.

It was then I discovered that I was very ill. The chill had not left me, and my head felt thick. I hurried from the house and the gruesome fox head as quickly as I could. The fresh air and sunshine helped my head feel a little clearer, or perhaps simply moving away from Haggard House did so. Felled branches and debris from the storm were scattered about the ground. Hurrying on, I made quick time to Adam's shop. I was somehow surprised to find him there—and he seemed surprised, yet happy, to see me. He wore only his undershirt, and despite his change since our removal to Haggard House—the cold words, the passionless knowing, the refusal to rebuild—I felt again his powerful draw.

"Are you unwell?" he asked, halting his work.

"Yes, a little. You were gone for so long." I shivered in my mantle.

"It was as I thought. Mother was lost in the storm. I found her, though." Adam examined me. "You truly look unwell. Allow me to take you home."

I shuddered. It was the first time I had ever heard him call Haggard House *home*.

He donned his vest and, tender as could be, wrapped me in his coat. Putting his arm about me, he led me back towards Haggard House. The sky was clear, but the air was sharp with late-autumn chill.

"Adam, there is something I've been reluctant to speak to you of." The arm holding me stiffened.

"What is it?" he asked.

"Four times in my life now, I've found heads at my doorstep. Animal heads. At first, I thought it was Gunther. Perhaps pranks or meanness. But I found one today, and it couldn't have been placed there by Gunther. He hasn't been seen in years."

"Have you any idea who it might be?"

Here, I realized I had stumbled into a very delicate matter. If I told Adam that I believed his mother responsible—and this while living under Sarai's roof—well, nothing good would come of it. If, however, I told him nothing, things were likely to continue as they had.

"No. I can think of no one." I felt a pang of guilt. It was the first time I had been dishonest with him.

"Can you think of any reason for these...heads...being left for you?" he asked.

"No," I said, again wincing inwardly.

"Perhaps there is a reason you haven't thought of?"

"You believe I deserve it?" I asked.

"No. No. Certainly not. Only, perhaps whoever is doing this believes they have a reason."

"Possibly. Though, I can't begin to think what it might be," I said.

Adam offered no further explanation, and I was left utterly confused. I was reminded of Peter once speaking to me in parable, about a leopard not changing his spots. However, I was too tired and ill to press the subject, nor could I think clearly of it myself.

"I've a request for you," I said.

"What is it?"

"I tried to light a fire with the tinderbox last night, but it was no good. Would you stop by Tenney's and purchase some lucifers? I'm surprised your mother hasn't any."

There was a pause.

"I'm sorry, but I can't," Adam replied. "Mother won't have them in the house."

I glanced up in surprise. "Why not? We had them in our own home."

Adam appeared flustered. "It's the name."

"The name?" I thought for a moment before the realization dawned on me. "No. It can't be. She really...? It's only a name. They're called that for light, not for the Devil."

"Nevertheless," he said.

I thought I saw a tinge of crimson flood across my husband's cheeks. Indeed, I hoped that I did. He ought to be embarrassed. How could Sarai object to matches only on account of their name?

Matches themselves couldn't be the Devil. It was one of the silliest things I had ever heard.

"You don't believe as your mother does, do you?" I asked.

"In that regard, no."

Of that, I was relieved. It was an annoyance, though—while Adam would not buy the lucifers, that did not mean I could not. I would buy some the first chance I got. There was, of course, the scent to contend with; perhaps if I aired the rooms after lighting one, the sulfurous smell would dissipate, and Sarai would be none the wiser.

When we arrived, the fox head had disappeared, as had Boots. Even the streaks of blood had been washed away. Adam glanced at the void, then at me, but said nothing. When we entered Haggard House, his manner became markedly changed. Though not unkind, the tenderness left him, and he appeared eager to leave as soon as he'd tucked me into bed.

"Adam, will you make certain Boots is all right too?" I asked. "He acted so wildly today."

"Certainly." His expression was blank, unreadable. He kissed my cheek perfunctorily and closed the door.

I was left alone in the dark attic.

Chapter 69

The Narrative of Penny Haworth

Things might have continued unbearably, had it not been for Adam's large purchase of lumber. I surmised that it must be for our own new home. I knew the lateness of the season would make it impossible to complete a house before snow set in, but the purchase gave me hope that Adam would at least make a start.

Our brief life together away from Haggard House had taught me that my husband was a different man outside of this place.

As I had no person left to cling to, I attached myself to Boots. The cat would not re-enter the house. Though I had tried once while Sarai was out, growls and scratches were all the thanks I got. However, he would wander along the outskirts of the property, and when I came near him, he warmed almost like the kitten I had first taken in. Like a faithful dog, he followed me wherever I went.

Meanwhile, I tended to the animals morning and evening and prepared the garden plot for spring planting. Often, I would simply devour a turnip from the garden at lunchtime. When I had whiled away all the time I could, I took to the paths in the woods, always avoiding the one leading farther past the lake, for I still remembered my promise to Adam. Most days, the weather was not too cold, and walks were a pleasant diversion.

Early one evening, I worked at the edge of the garden near the parsnips, upending the roots and piling them in baskets to store in the cellar below the barn. Beyond the fence, withered wildflowers bent in the sharp breeze. A dry stalk brushed my face under my broad-brimmed straw hat. I looked up and saw Adam trudging down the path. Standing, I straightened and waved. Instead of entering the house, he came round back and stopped just outside the garden fence where I was.

"You're tired," I said, looking at his dark-rimmed eyes.

In one of his increasingly rare moments of warmth, Adam reached across the fence, wrapped his arms round me, and held me tight. We stood this way for some time. At last, he gently released me. As he was in a softened state, though I hated to do so, I decided I must make the most of it.

"Adam, perhaps we could hire out the work for our house."

"You've done beautifully with the garden," he said.

"Thank you...love." He made no sort of response to my endearment. "But it would be all the better if it was our own garden near our own home." Again, Adam did not reply. "Perhaps we could ask Thomas? I'm certain he would give us a discounted rate. Please let me speak with him."

Adam's features grew taut. "Even Thomas would not come here to work."

"He would if I asked him."

Adam's arms immediately dropped from round me, and he stood back, scrutinizing.

"Why?"

Seeing his mood altering so quickly, I assumed a new line of attack. "Perhaps you could join forces and work together. Set up one shop. Then your work would be lighter."

Adam snorted. "And have my name compromised by one who does inferior work?"

I was growing desperate. The past month had been nearly unbearable, forced as I was to live with a woman I hated, in a house

I hated still more. Worse than that, being with his mother at Haggard House had changed Adam. I wondered, for the first time, if he didn't intend to build our new home at all.

"I haven't time to do the work," he continued, "and I won't hire or work with Thomas."

"Why did you buy the lumber then? If you don't intend to build?"

"The lumber—You believed that was for our home?"

"Yes, what else?"

Adam shook his head. "The lumber is for McDonnell. His wife wants a barn to house their stock. The foundation is already set, and with McDonnell and the help I've hired, it will go up quickly."

My ears grow hot. How quickly my fears were coming to fruition.

"You must turn down some work. You must build our house before the ground freezes. McDonnell would help you—and so would Thomas—if you'd only let go of your stubborn pride. I won't last the winter here. I can't!" I stamped my foot.

Any lingering softness in Adam's face disappeared. "Mother is aging quickly. You saw what happened in the storm. She needs someone about the house."

I stalked along the fence, stormed out the gate, and stood before Adam. "And I suppose you expect me to do it?"

"You're my wife."

"Yes, your wife. Not your mother's keeper. Tell me straight, Adam. Will you build us a home, or do you intend for us to live with your mother forever?"

"I cannot leave her now that she is old."

I ripped the straw hat from my head and flung it to the ground. "So, you intend for us to stay here?"

"I do."

This was to be my life. There would be no respite. Even Adam's rare moments of warmth were not enough return for a lifetime of darkness in this wretched house with the wretched woman that he called Mother. A sense of absolute despair flooded me and, for the first time, I wished I had not bound myself in marriage to Adam.

The front door of the house suddenly slammed shut: Sarai had been listening. No longer did I attempt to rein in my feelings. I screamed at the top of my lungs, and the sound echoed eerily through the clearing and about the house.

"I won't, Adam! I won't! You must build me a place away from that hag and this horrible house!"

Adam, unmoved, stared with stony eyes. "How dare you call Mother by that word."

His words were flat and passionless, but they frightened me. Without a backward glance, he stalked into the house, slamming the door.

Despite the coming darkness, I took to the woods and wandered through them disconsolately until it grew dark enough to fear an encounter with wolves, and I was forced to return to the horrible place of my existence. As I crossed Haggard House's slight veranda, I tripped on something in the dark. I lifted it and immediately knew it was some kind of dead bird. When I opened the door, the dim light inside revealed a headless chicken. Blood from its neck covered my dress and hands. Furious rather than frightened, I charged at Sarai, who sat in her rocker, reading.

"It's you!"

Adam, who had been in the attic, quickly descended the stairs.

Proffering the animal corpse, I said, "Your mother overheard us this evening, and she placed this on the veranda to frighten me. It's not the first time, either."

"You impudent—" Sarai said.

"It was certainly not Mother," Adam said, hardly glancing at the headless chicken. "You've no proof. It might have been anyone. There's two dozen and more children who might wish to play a prank on this place."

"You said yourself that no one dares step into this clearing!" I shouted.

Adam held his hand out. "Give it to me. I'll take care of it. Go clean up. You're hysterical over nothing."

I had been clutching the body of the chicken to my chest like an infant, but now I reluctantly released it into Adam's hands. Nothing could be clearer: Sarai was the culprit.

As soon as Adam was gone from the house, I pointed straight at Sarai, who sat smugly in her chair. "I know it was you."

Chapter 70

The Narrative of Penny Haworth

I t was late morning when I woke to the sound of a scraping knife. My heart was heavy, but I compelled myself to dress, and hurried below. Sarai was there, slashing a meager amount of meat into cubes and tossing them into the iron spider, full of boiling water for stew. The motion of her knife halted as I appeared.

"Where is Adam?" I asked.

"My son is at his shop, seeing as it is mid-day. Don't worry. I've completed your chores."

I forced my expression to remain calm.

"You've caused my son much distress with your sin, you know," Sarai continued.

What sin could she be speaking of? The woman well-nigh believed anything and everything to be sin.

The knife scraped across the board again, and Sarai tumbled more meat into the pot. It must be the chicken from the prior evening.

"I will take the liberty of saying that you look very ill, my dear," Sarai said. She waited a moment before saying, "I will excuse your forgetfulness of manners and tell you that I, myself, am very well.

It must be the illness which makes you forget to ask after my health."

Indeed, I constantly felt ill during my sojourn at Haggard House, but sometimes it was difficult to ascertain whether the illness was real or imagined. A moment later, I knew it was not imagined, for a growing pressure was building behind my nose. I turned my head, but when I opened my eyes, I saw my sneeze had splattered Sarai's cross. Horrified, I gently lifted and wiped it with my handkerchief. I recalled the old line, *"Sneeze on a Friday, you sneeze for sorrow."* It certainly appeared true in my case.

The cross was suddenly snatched from my hand.

"How dare you desecrate my things!"

I began to apologize, but Sarai's shouts only increased. Instead of staying for a berating, I hurried from the house as quickly as I could. Huge black turkey buzzards with their red heads cawed and circled above a spot in the field. Something had died, and the buzzards were making a meal of it. I felt as if I might retch—I was truly ill. Returning to the house, I rushed upstairs. A sudden fear made me, with some difficulty, barricade the door with the chest of drawers. This accomplished, I felt calmer, albeit sleepy, and I dozed uncomfortably for most of the day.

The clatter of bowls woke me. I removed the drawers from before the door. No doubt Sarai heard. I descended the stairs to find that it was dinnertime. Sarai ladled a wondrously scented stew into three bowls. Adam had returned from the shop and sat at his place at the table. He must have washed outside, for he didn't appear to have any knowledge of my having blocked the door. Sarai motioned for me to join them. I sat reticently and looked from the stew to Adam to Sarai.

"As you're unwell," Sarai said, "I've made you a special dinner. Taste."

"That was kind of you, Mother," Adam said. "Thank you."

"Yes...thank you," I said.

My head had grown thicker after sleeping. It felt as if I was viewing myself from afar, seated at the table with Adam and Sarai. Again, I looked round, from Sarai's unnatural smile to Adam's dead calm.

"Eat," Sarai said with a little laugh.

Lowering the tarnished pewter spoon into my bowl, I lifted it to my mouth. It was neither too watery nor too thick. The only fault I could find with it was that the meat was very small and scant. I had not seen any food as wholesome upon Sarai's table. Sarai watched expectantly as I swallowed. The stew was delicious. Another spoonful woke my appetite, and I ate the remainder ravenously. Sarai clapped gleefully, and Adam appeared supremely satisfied. I suddenly reproached myself for my unkind thoughts and actions toward Adam's mother. Sarai was now so attentive that I could hardly remember my former grievances.

"Thank you," I repeated, only this time truly grateful. "As Adam said, it was very kind." I paused. "Adam, have you seen Boots? I've been too ill to look for him today."

"To bed," he said. "You need more rest."

Back to bed I went, but this time I had difficulty sleeping. Though the warm stew had temporarily assuaged my pain, I felt thickness returning to my head. Adam came up and lay next to me for a while. He seemed penitent, but I felt no comfort from his presence. When midnight struck and he went below to pace and read with Sarai, I felt the oppressiveness of the house grow stronger. Thinking fresh air might help clear my head, I opened the window facing the woods. It was a struggle, for the wood was stuck, and I almost thought the glass would shatter as I pulled. Finally, it lifted, and an icy blast met me. I quickly shut the window, but the room was already colder. Shivering, I returned to the rusted iron bed and pulled the threadbare quilt over me. I closed my eyes and willed myself to sleep, yet sleep refused to come, and now, I was bitterly cold.

As my eyes opened in defeat, panic seized me. The room had shrunk, and the very walls began closing in. Whether this was real or conjured by my illness, I did not wait to find out. Hurrying to the door, I listened for a moment, and satisfied that all was quiet, I left the attic and slipped quietly down the stairs. Sarai was there, sleeping, or at least so I thought. Adam was not below. Troubled and frightened, I grasped my mantle from its hook near the door. I could not rid myself of the notion that there had been something strange about the flavor of my dinner, and a sickening idea had been growing in my mind.

Frost spread along the grass and dirt, making the ground solid but slippery. It was bitterly cold, but the moon brought enough light to see. Following the path away from Haggard House, I found the place where I had seen the buzzards circling. Tall, brittle milkweed and Queen Anne's lace stalks snapped as I progressed toward the spot. A small carcass lay frosted to the ground. Loath to see, and yet incapable of leaving without doing so, I stooped until I was close.

I recognized the creature. Horribly ill, I retched upon the ground. Boots had been skinned, and the only bits left were his coat, tail, and head. His eyes had been dug out by the buzzards. He looked nothing like the sweet kitten that Adam had found among the wheat stalks and presented me with, nor the affectionate cat I turned to during Adam's two years of absence. Dead and distorted as he was, his corpse looked wild and evil.

Shaking, I stood and stumbled from the field, weeds snapping left and right as I did so. My mind was unable to comprehend the horrible thing—the horrible deed—that had been committed. I recalled Sarai's sudden kindness and the wonderful stew.

The stew. I retched again.

Chapter 71

The Narrative of Penny Haworth

I refused to believe the grotesque thought, yet I could not rid myself of it. Half crazed, I began to run, stumbling into the house. A gloomy, dark mist seemed to spill from inside. Sarai was gone from her bed. I gathered her cross and the two Bibles.

Stalking back outside, I settled myself in the frosted grass before the house. First, I attempted to smash the cross. When, after trampling on it and wrenching it with my hands, and finding that nothing I did would break it, I threw it down. I ripped page after page from the Bibles and flung them upon the cross. Returning again to Haggard House, I brought the tin match-safe full of lucifers which I had secretly purchased, and then sat, facing the fluttering pile.

A haggard face appeared with a candle in the attic. Faster than I would have believed possible for such an old woman, Sarai bounded down the attic steps and out the door. I lit the lucifer and dropped it just as she reached me. The wafer-thin pages, once lit, burst into blaze. I watched in supreme satisfaction as her wild eyes stared at the cross in the center of the fire.

Instead of lunging at me, as it appeared she might do, she lunged instead at the fire and reached her hand in, grasping her cross. A hideous shriek poured from her mouth as she lifted it upward, still flaming, in her hand. Then she brought it down and pressed it to her chest; the flame went out. The scene seared itself in my mind, but still made less of an impression upon me than my feeling at the moment of Sarai's anguished cry. I felt not pity, but joy. I was in ecstasy over her pain.

A far-off voice and the sound of running feet approached. Words, rapidly drawing closer, became clear.

"What have you done?"

A moment later, Adam knelt at his mother's feet, examining her burned hand. "What have you done?" Adam repeated, looking at me in horror.

"Come. See your mother's work!" I said, dashing from the charred papers, across the field to Boots' corpse.

It took some time before Adam followed, for he went back inside with his mother, apparently helping her bandage her hand. I waited, shivering. Already, from the look in his eye, I feared he would not comprehend the reason for my actions, Boots or no Boots. At last, he returned out of doors and neared. There was no expression on his countenance, either good or bad. He glanced down at the frosted remains, and though his eyes remained there, they seemed not to see.

"And this is the reason for destroying the Word of God?" Adam finally said. "This is the reason for burning away the names of my ancestors in our family Bible. For harming Mother? A cat?"

It was strange, how I had felt so justified in my actions but a moment before, yet now was filled with sudden, unreasonable guilt.

"Sarai did this," I said, voice faltering along with my conviction. "She killed Boots. And I didn't harm her. She put her own hand in the fire."

Adam, turning from the scene upon the ground and looking directly at me said, "You will apologize to Mother."

I considered what I might do. Was I in the wrong after all?

Perhaps it had not even been Sarai: I had no absolute proof. Perhaps I ought to apologize. The sky before us was brightening with early morning light. My glance again caught hold of Boots' butchered body.

"No," I said. "I will not apologize."

Chapter 72

The Narrative of Penny Haworth

I got up, followed the boards that didn't creak, and crept to the window. There, I placed the quilt upon the floor and knelt. The grandfather clock below struck two in the morning. Then it struck four. My eyes ached from staring into the dark woods.

The remainder of yesterday had been wretched. Adam had refused to speak to me. Sarai had wandered round the house, hand bound in white, looking like an innocent, wounded creature. I hated her. When Adam returned from the shop, he was just as cold. He would neither speak to, touch, nor look at me.

When finally, I had attempted sleep, Sarai and Adam had remained below. I had waited at the crack in the door for some time to see what they would do with no Bibles to read. They simply paced and recited Scripture from memory.

There was one thing of which I was certain, one thing which held me in the house: a head would be swinging in front of the door by morning. I would catch Sarai in the act. Surely, if Adam had proof of his mother's cruelty, he would wish to take me as far away as he could from her.

I was nearly asleep at the window when a creak upon the stairs brought me back to wakefulness. My body stiffened as I readied to sprint back to bed should the ascent continue. The step creaked once more, only this time in retreat. Then the front door opened and closed, and all was silent. Willing my eyes to see through the black night, I caught a dark, hunched figure hurrying into the woods, cloak billowing behind. I leapt up and bounded down the stairs. My footsteps lost their hold half-way down, and I tumbled forward. At the bottom, I leapt back up, recalling Sarai's words, *"Careful, or you'll break your neck."* My wrists, which had broken the fall, hurt horribly. It was as if Sarai had placed a spell upon me.

In the confusion of the tumble, I fancied I saw a lump in the bed where Sarai's body might be, but that was impossible. The house was playing tricks again. I grasped my own cloak and hurried into the woods. Far ahead, I caught a glimpse of the haggard figure. I picked up my pace and sped forward, silent as I could. The figure appeared utterly unaware of my presence. On and on we went, lit by a full moon.

My breath came in quiet gasps. Sarai moved quicker than anticipated, but I had seen this once before, when she had hurried down from the attic for her burning cross. I raced on, keeping the figure in sight, maintaining a safe enough distance not to be discovered. The figure followed the lake, then continued north. It was the very path that Adam had appeared from, that day in the woods with Ingrid all those years ago, the path forbidden to me. Never had I been so far into the forest in this direction.

The figure disappeared behind a boulder. I slowed and crept to the edge of the rock until I was close enough to see. Beyond, the trees led directly to a ledge that plunged downward. My heart quickened as I discovered that I had been running along the precipice for some time. A few errant steps and I could easily have gone over. No wonder Adam had warned me off.

Betwixt the boulder and the ledge, a square structure constructed of rock glittered strangely in the moonlight. At each of its four corners was a horn, facing outward and upward. A goat was tied to a stake in the ground close at hand. In the moment it took for me to see these things, the figure slit the goat's throat and lifted it upon the structure. As blood poured from the gash, the goat bleated faintly, struggled, then went still. The figure dipped its fingers in the blood and sprinkled it round.

I waited, half holding my breath for fear of being discovered. The figure's back was to me, and in the moment the personage passed my location, the light was too dim to see clearly. The figure turned the goat, now dead, upon its back and slit the skin across its belly, from neck to hind legs. After removing the entrails, the figure carefully separated the fatty parts from the meat and placed these, along with the kidneys, on the structure.

As I crouched behind the rock, the figure lit the kindling beneath the carnage. The flames gradually increased and licked the flesh. As they did so, the night air choked with the scent of burning fat. Despite the gruesome scene, I was spellbound, mesmerized. I could neither move nor speak. The figure added more and more fuel, and the flames shot up, ascending so high they seemed to reach Heaven.

Suddenly, for no discernable reason, I no longer wished to catch the culprit in the act. I wished to be away from this person and this place in the woods. I took a cautious step backward.

The figure turned, aware of my presence. It was not the hag-like face which I had been expecting. The fire shot up higher. A desire to retch, weep, and beat the figure, all mingled into one. Rushing forward, I collapsed on the ground before him.

"Adam?" I said, scarcely audible, tears fighting to burst forth. "Adam? Why? Why?"

My husband stood, looking down upon me. When I looked up, I saw the same vacant, stony look I had seen upon him at the discovery of Boots' carcass. It was as if this was someone else, another being, not Adam.

"I did it for love of you," he said, voice emotionless.

"What? For love?" I said. The tears had forced their way

through and streamed down my face. "What is this?" I waved my hand wildly at the structure and burning flesh.

"'Many are called, but few are chosen.'"

"I don't understand," I repeated.

He knelt before me and laid his bloodied hand upon my shoulder; not as my husband, but as I had seen Minister Judd do with a sinful congregant.

"'How few they are.'"

"Stop speaking that way," I said, pulling away. "Speak to me as Adam, as my husband."

He stood abruptly. "I speak to you as Adam, as a child of God."

"A child of God?"

"I have been chosen. The secret knowledge has been revealed, from God to Minister Judd, from Minister Judd to Mother, and from thence to me. The sacrifices of the Old Testament were never meant to be done away with. They are yet necessary. As atonement for sin and salvation from Hell.

"But now, I see. Mother was wrong. I understand that you too are chosen." He neared again, knelt, wrapped blood-soaked arms round my waist, and buried his head in my night-gown. "I can share this secret knowledge with you. You too can be saved. No longer must I sacrifice to atone for your sins. You may sacrifice and be saved of your own accord. You will not die only to burn in Hell as Pa—" Adam's voice broke. He collected himself and continued. "This is the secret knowledge, the secret truth, that has been revealed only to us—to the elect. Yet now, I see. God has spoken: you too are chosen. I am certain Mother will accept this. She will accept that you are one of the elect of the Lord.

"Penny," he said, looking up at me, "You know not how many years I've sacrificed for you. How many years I have hoped and prayed you would be saved."

"Oh, Adam!" Anguish burned in my voice, and I attempted to push him away. He held me tight.

"I built a place within my mind. I tried to keep you separate, but you always slipped out. I could not keep you locked away. And now—now I see that it was all for the good. That you too have been chosen. No longer must I keep your love locked up."

The earnestness of his look pierced me.

"I don't understand," I said. I pushed at his arms, but my hands slipped on blood.

"It is to save you from Hell!" he said. "To save you from eternal damnation. Where there will be weeping and gnashing of teeth. Where there will not be a single drop of water for your burning tongue."

I stared into his dark-ringed eyes. He meant every word he spoke. He truly believed that his sacrifices were saving my soul.

"And Boots?" The image of the cat frozen to the soil was indelibly marked upon my mind. "What did he do?"

"You care too much for earthly things," Adam said, pushing me away.

I shook my head, unable to believe what was before me. "No. No. No." My words faltered with tears held back. "It can't be you. It's Sarai. It's your mother."

"I did it for your good," he said. "For the saving of your soul."

"You cannot believe that," I said.

He no longer shook with emotion. He was calm again, certain of himself, certain of his belief. I stumbled to my feet. Tearing forward, I pounded my fists into his chest. He did not resist. When my arms tired, I dropped them to my sides and stared at the man before me. Exhausted and ill in mind, I collapsed. He caught me, but held me coldly.

"You must pledge yourself to Him," Adam said. "You must do it now before temptation draws you back to the Devil."

Who was this man? It was not Adam, not the Adam that I had known and loved. Tears again threatened loose, but I would not allow them, not here. I pulled away and looked him in the eye.

"I don't want your hateful God or His hateful atonement," I said, voice shaking.

Adam grasped my arms tightly, and for a moment, I feared he would do me violence.

"Please, Adam," I said.

He looked at me for a long while. It was a look that I would never forget—haunting—far darker and more frightening than anything I had ever seen of Sarai. It was as if I were peering straight into the Hell of which he was so frightened. Yet, the Hell was within him.

Suddenly, he let me go. I took a step back, then another, and another. When my foot struck a root, I turned and fled. On and on I ran, aimlessly through the trees.

Dawn broke but still, I ran.

Chapter 73

The Narrative of Penny Haworth

I girded up my courage, and my dress, and pressed forward. Besides that I was heading roughly west, I hadn't the faintest idea where I was or where I was going; I only knew I had to get away. My legs tired, so I exchanged my run with a quick trot, then a brisk walk. Again and again, I saw the image: Adam slitting the goat's throat. I could scarcely comprehend what had just occurred. It was like a dream.

The initial shock and anger of my discovery had pushed deeper sentiments aside, but now all my limbs trembled as they came flooding to the surface. I was betrayed. My life with Adam, even the beautiful moments at the start of our marriage, had all been a lie. Perhaps he had never loved me. Perhaps that too had been a lie. Perhaps he had never even desired my companionship, only to save me. He sought to redeem me for his God. I had been blinded by love. He was not the man I had believed him to be.

I sank to the ground and wept. There was no part of my being that was not in pain, and I momentarily wondered if the agony I felt was like the Hell that Adam so much feared. Presently, my sobs subsided, and the warmth of the growing sun on my bare neck caused me to stir from my position on the ground.

By late afternoon, the trees thinned and opened onto a wide meadow with a swift river rimming its western edge. At the northern edge were two dilapidated, abandoned cabins. At the center, a lone wigwam stood. I was about to turn back for fear of encountering the occupants, when a woman, hidden until now, but a dozen paces from me in the heathery grasses, stood, uprooting a vine with dozens of potato-like growths. Her dark hair was braided with bright ribbons. She wore a plain calico waist and a black broadcloth skirt trimmed at the edges with embroidered silk.

The woman appeared surprised to see a stranger, but then she smiled. She spoke something I could not understand, what I guessed to be in Menominee, and motioned for me to follow. Too tired to think or care what might happen, I did as instructed and advanced with the woman toward the dome-shaped dwelling. As we neared, she motioned me to wait. She disappeared into the cedar-covered wigwam and returned a few moments later with a man whom I recognized as an old patron of my father's at the saloon, the village drunkard. His attendance there had been short-lived, for he had been unable to regularly pay his bill, and Father did not keep such men about. Afterward, he had returned to his usual haunt, Bard's Tavern, and came and went as he was able to pay.

The old man did not recognize me, but this was no surprise. His time in Nomaton was largely spent late at night and indoors, in a place I had no business to be.

The woman said something to him in Menominee. He eyed me for a moment, then spoke.

"My good woman seems to think you are in trouble, miss." He was sober, at least for the moment.

I shook my head. I had no wish to relate my heavy burden to this man. "I'm not in any trouble." The old man surveyed my appearance—night-gown peeping out beneath my mantle, tear-stained face, and uncovered, wild copper hair. What must he think? "I've...I couldn't sleep," I said, forging an explanation. "I've been on a long walk and just happened upon this place."

He was less disposed to friendliness than the woman, for he threw up his hands, said something to her, and turned back to the wigwam. However, the woman must've reprimanded him, for he sulkily returned. He scrutinized me again before speaking, as if something stirred in the back of his mind.

"Is there anything we can help you with, miss?"

I was weak and exhausted and wished for a place to pause and think. I thought it best not to reveal my identity, for then he might not be willing to help.

"Yes, I...need to rest before returning home. Perhaps I might trouble you to allow me to sleep in your lodgings?"

"I want no trouble," he said.

"There will be no trouble."

He sighed and scratched his head. He turned to the woman and spoke under his breath. She waved a welcoming hand toward the wigwam, and I gratefully followed them. Inside, a raised bench ringed the inner edge of the abode, and colorful mats covered the walls. The old man pointed me to a place on the bench, but the woman glanced at him sternly and motioned me to a seat opposite the door.

He chuckled. "She gives you the seat of honor."

"Thank you," I murmured.

Skirting round the fire and kettle in the center of the wigwam, I settled myself on a thick bear hide. The woman, apparently called Agnes, produced a wooden bowl containing a mash with bits of dried meat for me. The mash was sweet and tasted of corn and maple. The dark of the wigwam and the hearty food had a soothing effect. I finished the mash and put the bowl away from me.

"Now that you've been fed at my expense, I believe you will be wanting rest?" said the old man, preparing his pipe with tobacco.

I was overcome with exhaustion, and while my recent exertions had made me forget my illness, my head now began to swim. I closed my eyes and nearly lost my balance on the seat.

"Agnes believes you ought to lie down," he said.

"Yes. Might I sleep here? Just for a few moments?" I asked.

They spoke for several moments in Menominee, the old drunkard's voice growing louder, then subsiding at the woman's soothing tones. Finally, clearly having been bested, the old man said, "You may rest here, but you must leave before nightfall. I want no trouble."

I nodded gratefully at Agnes. "I only need a little rest."

From the slant of the sun, I figured it must be one or two o'clock in the afternoon.

He left the abode, and the woman placed a blanket over me and tucked me into it like a child. Then she too left the wigwam. In mere moments, I fell into a long and dreamless slumber.

Chapter 74

The Narrative of Adam Bolton

I did not go after Penny, not at first.

When I discovered that she had been watching me, I had been almost glad. No longer must I hide myself. No longer must I hide the Truth—the secret revealed to me. Upon the instant I saw her, I knew that the Lord had ordained for her to take part in those mysteries that had been first revealed to Minister Judd. Though Mother had often said that only the three of us had been chosen— a perfect trinity—I felt God's guidance in this. It was His word that it should be so. For once in my life, I felt that God directed his Truth, not through Minister Judd and not through Mother, but through me.

Why then had Penny been so frightened? Why then had she looked at me as if I were some monster from whom she must run? She had been a heathen since childhood, but I had been so certain that the weekly sermons, the readings from the Word, my secret prayers—had softened her heart. I was certain that God had spoken to her, as he had to me.

As for the cat, Boots, I could see that what happened had hurt Penny. Yet did she not see that it was necessary? That my love for her was greater than any earthly love imaginable? Did she not see all that I had done to save her very soul? Had not my own Mother done the same for me those many years ago? Removing too great an earthly love, also in the form of an earthly creature—a mere dog —so that I could draw closer to my Savior? Even so, I recalled my own revolt at that time—my own clinging to that which was to fade in eternity. How much harder must it be for one such as Penny, who had grown in expectation of worldly comforts? She did not understand. She did not see that her clinging to this world was drawing her towards the very thing which I intended to save her from—Hell.

I was confounded. I knew not what to do. I felt lost and without hope. Yet then I recalled that it had been Mother who had brought me back to the fold, again and again. With great patience, time and again, she had led me back from the edge of the quag. If I went to her now and told her all—how it had been revealed to me that Penny was one of the elect—I knew she would help. Mother would help me persuade Penny to come to the Lord—to enter in at the narrow gate—to make atonement for her sins.

Something like hope filled my soul, and I went in search of Mother to help me set things to rights.

Upon my return, I found her sitting upon the bed in the sleeping attic.

"Your wife is not here," said Mother. She gave me a meaning glance. "I came at sunrise, and she was not here."

I fell on my knees before her and confessed all that had happened in the night.

She looked at me for a long time before she spoke. Her voice was gentle, but her words grated.

"Do you not think it strange that I have not had this vision of Penny as one of the elect?" she said. "That it has not been revealed either to myself or to Minister Judd?"

"Has not the Lord, from time to time, chosen to reveal his Truth to his weakest vessels?" said I.

"The Devil," said Mother, "may disguise himself as the Light, and put into our ears words that seem to come from the Lord."

"If that be the case," I said, "then how might we ever know which words are the Lord's and which are not?"

"By seeking out the counsel of our elders. We will go to Minister Judd."

"And how do we know the Devil has not disguised himself as the Light and poured his words into Minister Judd's ear?" I asked.

"How could you speak such a thing?" said Mother.

"You do not know all that Minister Judd does—has done."

Mother stood from the bed, straight and stiff as a board. "What mean you?"

Though I had hidden it away, the memory had not escaped me all these years—Minister Judd's hand caught round Penny's waist.

"I mean that I have sensed—that, after seeing the world, I now *know*—that his intentions have not always been pure."

"How dare you entertain such a thought of the Minister," said Mother. "He has walked side by side with the Lord since before you or I were born. Think you that you know the ways of the Lord better than he? Think you that you care for the Lord more than he? Whatever you think you might have sensed—Whatever you think you *know*," here she gave me a withering glance, "you are mistaken. Minister Judd does, and has always done, only what was right in the sight of the Lord. And where he has not, he has made atonement for his sins—as have you. 'He who is without sin cast the first stone.' Are you, my son, so blameless as to cast one at the Minister?"

I could not answer yes.

"Are you so pure? Well?"

Mother was not cold. She was boiling. Where I knelt at her feet, I felt the heat, radiating from her presence. There was aught I could say. Had I not spent a night of the most deplorable debauchery with a woman of the night? Had I not done the same with a heathen? Had I not then married that heathen—knowing full well she would never be saved—that we would always be unequally yoked? Never had I felt more profound shame.

"Nay," said I.

"And would God impart his special Truth to one so full of sin?"

"But I have sacrificed," said I. "I have atoned—"

"And the Lord has forgiven you. But do not be so foolish as to believe He would impart this secret knowledge after all you have done. Believe not that."

There was nothing more I could say. Mother had made her case, and I knew it to be true: the Lord was not with me. I could not trust the revelation I had so fervently believed and put my trust in only hours before.

"Fall on the Rock," said Mother, "and be broken. Better than to be crushed by Him."

She need not have quoted the Scripture thus. Already, I felt crushed. Whatever had risen inside me was defeated.

"Now," said Mother, sitting down upon the bed again and placing her hand on my shoulder. "Let us go and find your wife—before she brings shame upon this household."

Chapter 75

The Narrative of Penny Haworth

I was wakened by the sound of loud voices. I sat up. The light sifting through the hole in the wigwam roof had shifted, showing that it was now late afternoon.

"We only wish to know if you've seen her."

My body stiffened: it was Adam's voice.

"Why do you wish to know?" the old drunkard asked. "Not many people travel this way."

I sat absolutely still, not daring to move in case a sound should give my presence away.

"It's none of your concern." This was Sarai's voice. I could scarcely breathe. "We've lost her, and we simply wish to find her."

"Lost her, eh? Seems to me some people leave other people. I'm not certain that's what you might call lost."

Even through the wigwam, I could feel Sarai's freezing glance.

There was a silence.

"You know me," Sarai said, voice lowered. "You know that I intend nothing ill when I say we are searching for my son's wife."

"Yes, I know you," the old man said. There was another pause, and I trembled, awaiting his decision. At last, he said, "I've seen nothing and no one. I am sorry I cannot help you, Sarai."

There was another pause: she was weighing the truth of the man's words.

"Very well," she said. "We will be on our way."

As the footsteps retreated from the wigwam, I caught my breath. Several minutes passed before the old man and Agnes entered. When he did return, he puffed excitedly at his pipe, eyes keen and irritable. Agnes sat next to me and put an arm about my trembling shoulders until the shaking lessened.

"I was certain you would bring trouble. I was certain." The old man puffed at his pipe violently. "Women. My trouble has always begun and ended with women." He removed the pipe from his mouth and sighed. Suddenly, he began to chuckle. "It's funny, almost. Do you know what I've learned after all these years?"

I shook my head.

"I've spent some time thinking of it. It's this: All human relationships dangle by a thread, swinging ever closer to the edge of an ever poised and ever present blade." He stopped and looked at me keenly. "I know you. Don't I?"

"Yes, sir," I said.

"Haworth's daughter?"

"Yes, sir," I repeated.

"Hmph. Ought to have known. Adam's wife." Again, he examined me. "What do you know of his mother? Sarai. Of her history?"

"Very little," I said. "Only that she was an orphan, taken in by Minister Judd at a young age and brought here."

The old man, whose name I now recalled as Mr. Whittemore, glanced at me sharply. His posture sagged, and he lowered himself onto the bench opposite, heaved a sigh, and puffed ever so slowly at his pipe. After a long silence, I believed he was finished with the topic.

"Thank you, again, for sheltering me," I said.

He glanced up, but not as if he had heard my words. "It's nonsense," he said. "Invented by Sarai herself."

"Invented?" I asked. "You must know Sarai very little. She is," I searched for the right word, "...she is a religious fanatic. She would never lie. It's against everything she believes in."

Mr. Whittemore laughed and shook his head. He gave Agnes a meaningful glance and spent many moments translating what had been spoken into Menominee. I heard my name once, and Agnes glanced up in surprise. I shifted uncomfortably. At last, it appeared he was asking her some question. She waited a long time, then nodded her assent. He settled more comfortably upon the bench.

"You do not know it, but you are married to my daughter's son. I suppose that makes you my daughter-in-law."

I looked at the old man with new eyes.

"Perhaps you know my name from the prairie at the edge of your village. Named after me. Silas Whittemore. As for Sarai, she grew up in the cabins you saw close to this wigwam. With me, her father, but mostly with...well, he was then known as Missionary Judd."

I turned to Agnes in disbelief, but she only nodded, confirming the man's words.

Mr. Whittemore took a great inhale of smoke and said, "I'd like to tell you the story, if I may. I've bottled it up, excepting her," he said, nodding to Agnes. "And I can tell you, it's poisoned my insides. I don't know what your troubles may be with her son, but I am certain that knowing his mother's history may help you. If you've no objection, I will tell it."

I paused, uncertain if I wished to know any more of Sarai than I already did. I believed it could only make my hatred and aversion stronger. However, I assented, buying myself time to decide upon what course to take. Agnes again put her arm round me, and it gave me great comfort, reminding me of my mother. I tilted my tired head onto her shoulder and listened to Mr. Whittemore's story.

Chapter 76

The Narrative of Silas Whittemore
1828

W hy my wife had traveled so far into the wilderness, only to abandon me and our child, was a mystery. To me, it pointed to some kind of mental defect. Indeed, this was not the only occasion that had planted such a thought in my mind. However that might be, I was now in a plight. I had a daughter of three; I had the full fur season ahead; I had no family connections in this new country. I could send my daughter, Sarai, back to England, but—and here I admit to being slightly mercenary in thought—I would lose not only a season of my trade, but also my men, doubtless to the American Fur Company. It was equally impossible to take the child with me, subsisting on a diet of lyed corn and tallow and carrying whatever she was able at every portage. Other furriers did such. They did it with wives and children and dogs. I would not.

My better motive was that I wished for her to get what education she might—in a place as wild and rugged as this. My lesser motive was that I did not wish to be impeded in business—especially as I was just at its beginnings.

I had but one alternative, Missionary Judd. Though I confess that I disliked the man, I did not think him dangerous. Far better to place the child with him and be within safe distance of her, than to take her back to England to live wholly apart from me. When I approached him on the subject, I found the missionary not only agreeable to raising the child, but to take some measure of joy in the thought. Doubtless, in his lone position in a strange place, Missionary Judd welcomed a child to care for and, in some measure, call his own. It was decided that the missionary would care for her until the winter seasons, when I would return to my cabin and care for her myself.

Once my time on Michillimackinac was at an end, furs packed and ready for shipment to merchants out east, the lot of us—myself, the missionary, my men, and the child—embarked for the mainland, making our way into the mouth of the Menominee River and rowing north to my winter quarters. As it was not winter, but late summer when I must be out plying my trade, I left Missionary Judd in possession of my cabin, along with the child.

When winter arrived, and I with it, I was pleased to discover that the missionary had already made great progress with the girl's education. Now four years of age, she read to me a short selection from the Bible and recited one or two other selections by heart.

"Very well done," said I.

I believe Missionary Judd beamed more at my compliment than my child.

Three unexceptional years passed, and on this winter return, the girl, now being seven, could read very long passages at a stretch. While I was pleased with her learning, I began to see that she, even at that tender age, was becoming something of a religious zealot. Of a Sunday, she refused to do anything other than read her Bible and eat and pray. When I attempted to convince her otherwise, she gave me a wounded look and said, "Do you wish me to profane the Lord's Day?"

Of course, I could not say yes. And while I was loath to inter-fere with Missionary Judd's methods—as he was now more Father to her than I—I decided I must speak to him on the subject. He had now a cabin of his own, very near mine, and once Sarai had gone to bed for the night, I knocked on his door.

He poured me a glass of whisky—whisky which he did not drink himself but kept on hand for my enjoyment. We first spoke on some topics relating to the region; the farmers trickling into the area east of where we resided and the decline in the demand for fur. Finally, lips loosened by drink, I broached the subject I had really come for.

"Missionary Judd, I wish to thank you for all you have done for my daughter. Her writing and arithmetic are always perfectly executed, and she reads her Bible with hardly any help from me. In point of fact, at times she knows the meaning of words that *I* do not."

The missionary nodded, pleased.

"There is one small matter that I wished to consult you on, however," said I.

"Yes, of course," said he, leaning forward as far as his belly allowed, sparkle in his eye on being asked. "I am happy to give advice whenever it might be of use."

"I notice that Sarai is becoming...somewhat severe in her religious beliefs."

"How do you mean?"

"Only yesterday she chided me for trading for fur, simply because it was the Sabbath." Missionary Judd opened his mouth to interrupt, but I spoke first. "Certainly, I wish her to have religious training. I would not expect any less. However, given the nature of my business, and the rough place in which we live, do you not think some of her ideas might be somewhat...excessive?"

Missionary Judd drew himself back, crossed his arms across his belly, and regarded me.

"Is it excessive, I wonder, to wish a child, or any person for that matter, to reach Heaven? Is it excessive, I wonder, to teach the laws of God so that the girl's soul may escape Hell?"

I gave a lighthearted laugh. "What must you think of me then?"

The missionary ignored my question and plied ahead. "I hope that you will not interfere in matters of the child's soul," said he. "In all other matters, I will, of course, defer to you. But when it comes to eternity, there is no such concept as *excessive*. I will do all in my power to save her from everlasting suffering in Hell."

The room was oppressive with the repeated word.

Yet, I had no alternative on where to place the girl. Even had I, she was fond of the missionary, and it seemed cruel to part them. A little religious zealotry was a small price to pay for a superior education and a parental figure.

"Well," said I, "of course, you know more than I in matters of religion. You must do as you see fit." The mortal dread of Hell still hung heavy in the air, so I added, "I hope I have not upset you. Certainly, I trust your judgement."

He relaxed visibly and smiled. "Yes, yes. Don't worry yourself." He refilled my glass. "You mean the best despite your misguided beliefs."

His words irked me, but I did not wish to anger him.

I took another swig.

Time progressed, the only thing marking it being the wane of my trade and the closure of the American Fur Company, which while it increased the demand for my own goods for a time, I already saw as the mark of my eventual ruin. Engrossed in my business as I was, I hardly noted that my girl had become a young woman of fourteen.

It was then that something happened—the worst that could happen. A group of former Company men, who had grown wild and wanton without work, knew of my daughter living alone with the missionary. Through one means or another, they discovered that Missionary Judd, unbeknownst to me, planned to travel south with an interpreter for two days, visiting with and preaching to some of the natives of that place, leaving my daughter behind.

The furriers came while he was away and took her to an old, abandoned house in the forest near the newly forming village, and did such things—

At the time she was afflicted with the woman's curse, and when they had finished their vile work, the floor was covered in red.

Missionary Judd returned after the two days. He searched and found her, drenched in her own blood and praying upon her knees on the wooden floor.

I hunted down every last one of those men who defiled my girl. Killed them. I knew a hundred and one places no one would ever search. And none did. When it was finally noted that they had gone missing, it was supposed that their canoe had overturned in one of the rapids. The truth was never known, except by Missionary Judd and myself.

It was then that I began to drink heavily.

After these events, I abandoned my trade for upward of a month and kept my daughter with me. She began to have great difficulty sleeping. Always, she woke at the stroke of midnight and remained awake for much of the night reading her Bible, one of the few possessions left behind in her mother's traveling trunk. The girl was mostly silent, but one day at supper, she suddenly spoke. She told me, in a low voice, that when she had been alone in that house, she had had a vision, that God himself had spoken to her. He had told her that her salvation must be worked out, and that Missionary Judd would show her the way.

I told her not to think of such things—that she must try to forget the past and only look forward. When I returned her to Missionary Judd, I warned him of what she had told me. He agreed with me that he too would discourage such notions.

A full year passed before I discovered the man's deceit, and by that time, it was too late. I discovered a strange structure in the woods, an altar, behind the abandoned house where those terrible things had occurred. When I questioned my daughter at length, I discovered that Missionary Judd had not only reminded my daughter of her vision but claimed he'd had the same. He taught her certain rituals, sacrifices, claiming that they were only revealed to God's children, the chosen elect. He had done the opposite of what he had promised.

I tried to put a stop to it—attempted to take her away, but she would not leave him.

Sarai began to claim that I was not her father, even convincing herself of this. At this time there was an influx of new settlers, adding to the growing village, which had by then been named Nomaton. The fur trade was all but dead, and anyone who knew the truth of my daughter's parentage had disappeared. The villagers only knew that she lived with Missionary Judd, and that he was her guardian.

As to that place, that house, I tried to warn Peter before he purchased the land deed. Though no one knew the truth, there were rumors even then about the place being cursed. I suppose something like that has a way of seeping into people's minds. But Peter wouldn't listen. He had been commanded by my daughter not to speak to me. She had claimed I was a liar who called myself her pa but really wasn't. And why ought he to have believed me?

Chapter 77

The Narrative of Silas Whittemore

There in the wigwam, utterly exhausted, copper-haired woman sitting across from me, I ended my narrative.

Penny, despite her own troubles, leaned forward and took my hand, squeezing it gently. Her kindness surprised me, for she had only known me as a degenerate, a drunk without family.

"Stay the night," said I. "You need rest."

My head throbbed.

Agnes was busy about Penny, finding blankets and making her comfortable as I left my abode. I turned my face towards the village and struck out. I badly needed a drink.

Chapter 78

The Narrative of Penny Haworth

I knocked on the door of the shack, but there was no answer. My legs ached from the long return from the wigwam, and my mind still reeled with Silas' story. I could not but believe it was true, and I felt for Sarai, for the girl she had been. Even so, I could not forget the Sarai that now was, the woman that had, with the help of Minister Judd, driven Adam and I apart.

It was late, and the air smelled of imminent snow. I walked round the building, but it was useless, as it was windowless. It was for the best; I would be hidden from the villagers' prying eyes if I was allowed in. A tall silhouette appeared from the neighboring building and approached. I dropped my head, suddenly ashamed. The weight of everything that had befallen me had seemed somehow suspended, but Thomas' familiar face brought it all crashing down. Tears formed, and powerless to stop them, I began to shake with sobs. Thomas rushed forward and caught me in his arms.

He fumbled with the shack door and helped me into the solitary armchair. There, I buried my face in my hands. For a long time I wept, and Thomas, who knelt on the floor at my feet, whispered over and over, "It's all right now."

As my sobs slowly died away, I felt as if a gaping hole had opened in my bosom. I pressed my palms there, as if I could fill the emptiness with my hands. Standing from the chair, I wiped my tears, attempting to compose myself.

"I'm sorry," I said.

Thomas remained kneeling. There was sorrow in his eyes, sorrow for me. He asked nothing, only waited. I could scarcely bear it.

"I'm sorry," I repeated.

"You've nothing to apologize for," he said.

His kindness made tears suddenly flow again, and I turned away. I understood full well the position I was placing myself in and what I would be asking of Thomas. I understood what the consequences of this decision must be. Yet, I had no money and no place to live. I had no one to help me when—I would not think of that now. Choking back my tears, I turned to him.

"I'm sorry to impose upon you. And I understand the effect it may have upon your reputation. But I've nowhere else to turn. Is it possible...Could I stay here...with you?" I hurriedly added, "It would only be until I decide what to do."

Thomas stood and paced to the door. For many moments he said nothing, and I began to fear that he would say no. At last, he spoke.

"I care nothing for my reputation, but do you understand what this will do to yours?" He stopped and looked me in the eyes.

"I do," I said.

"Do you also understand that...You know Adam will never welcome you back...if you stay here? He is too proud. It would be against his nature."

"Yes," I said slowly. "I know this too."

He waited a very long time, as if to make sure that I was truly certain. Then he said, "If that is the case, you are welcome to stay as long as need be."

A sense of relief flooded me.

Already, he was examining the small room. "You'll have the bed, of course. I will sleep in the chair."

Upon any other occasion, I would have insisted that I take the chair, but my exhaustion was too complete to argue. "Thank you," was all I could say.

As Thomas hurried about the small room making arrangements as best he could, I sunk deeper into the chair in a fatigued stupor. My night in the wigwam had afforded me little sleep. All night I had seen, again and again, Adam's face at the altar, blood gushing from the slit in the goat's neck. How many times had Adam been constrained by the wild beliefs he had been taught, to make these sacrifices? Did he truly believe the path to Heaven was paved with the corpses of innocent creatures? I recalled Boots' butchered body bonded to the frozen earth, and I shuddered.

"You're tired," Thomas said. "Perhaps you ought to sleep."

I climbed into the narrow bed, and Thomas pulled the thin blanket over me.

It was midnight, or so I fancied, when I woke. For a moment, I forgot where I was, believing I was in the sleeping attic of Haggard House. Panic flooded me until my true environment gradually became evident. Thomas snored heavily in his chair. His head had toppled over the arm and dangled uncomfortably there. Sour sweat pervaded the close quarters.

There was a sound near the wall next to me, and my breath stopped. It sounded like a hand trailing the edge of the shack. Then I thought I could discern faint footsteps. The sounds disappeared, and I realized I had been holding my breath.

Thomas still slept soundly.

Chapter 79

The Narrative of Adam Bolton

After our visit to the old drunkard, we had gone to visit Minister Judd. That visit was the worst of my life. Minister Judd addressed himself only to Mother. From time to time, he glanced over her shoulder, speaking in the low voice he used when addressing sinners, calling me a lost and confused lamb and saying that the Lord had not revealed any new member of the elect— saying, in short, that nothing had been revealed to me—that I was a liar and that it was the Devil who had convinced me Penny should join the flock.

I did not challenge him. I knew of old that once he and Mother had joined in a resolution, there was no stopping it. To argue my case, to insist that it was indeed God who had spoken to me, would only set her opinion stronger. Not only that, but the extraordinary strength of their conviction was taking a toll on my own. I began to question whether God had truly spoken.

That same night, I went to seek Penny. I did not know what I would do if I found her—only that I must see her. I went to the village and tried my luck there. I would not ask if anyone had seen her, but I walked up and down every street, many more now since childhood. I saw nothing, nor expected to see aught. I wandered farther than the village, into the damp night.

It was then I thought of Thomas. I knew that Penny considered him a friend. I went to his shop, but of course it was bolted. I went to Pa's old shack, where Thomas now resided. As I walked past the place, I suddenly had the fancy that if I touched the wall, I might discern whether or not Penny was inside. I did so, but discerned nothing and so returned home.

The following day, I left my work in the shop and wandered the streets of Nomaton again, straying once again to Thomas' shack. The door opened, and I hastily stepped back into the shadow of a side street. My heart told me not to look at whomever might come out the door, but I could not look away.

Oh Penny!

I did not have time to grieve. Two, dark-haired boys, playing some game, went barreling past, shouting and halloaing down the next alley. Fearful of Penny's discovering me, I set my face towards home, leaving all my day's work behind.

How could she have gone to Thomas of all people? In my mind's eye, I saw a thousand and one things they did in that shack, alone together. The horror of those images was more than one could imagine. They spun round and round and tainted every good memory and association. I was betrayed.

I returned in a jealous rage. Instead of going to the house, I made my way to the northern portion of the barn and stormed inside, fully intending to tear to shreds the old traveling trunk holding the few things I had left of her.

What surprise to see that Mother was already there, doing the very thing I had intended.

When she looked up, I knew immediately that our thoughts were the same.

"You will relinquish this heathen?" said she. "You understand that it is not to be? That your carnal love for her will sink you both to the fiery Pit?"

My mind! How it raged.

"Yes. I see. I know now that it was never His will."

"And you will do what I instruct?"

"I will."

"Then you must annul your marriage. You must loose yourself from this Jezebel."

Even with all that had happened, that word struck me as horrible, but my anger overcame it, and I said, "I will do as you instruct." Then it struck me that it would be impossible to annul the marriage, as there was no cause. "But how can it be done?" said I.

"We must report that the marriage was never consummated," said Mother.

"But," I said, "that is false."

Mother shook her head. "In God's eyes, it was never consummated, for 'what communion hath light with darkness?'"

I was astonished at Mother's proposal. "Would it not be better to try for a divorce?" asked I.

"Do you not remember?" said she. "God has said he 'hateth putting away.' It must not be done."

"But if there is to be an annulment, I must make some claim as to why it was not consummated, and what might I say? I must fabricate some lie."

"Have you forgotten Rahab the harlot?" said Mother. "She was justified by her works when she hid the spies and told the king of Jericho that she knew not where they had gone? So shall we be justified in all that we do in these righteous proceedings."

Never had my mind been more fraught.

Mother stepped aside from the trunk, motioning me towards it.

I lifted it high in the air and hurtled it against the barn wall. The wood splintered into a hundred pieces.

Chapter 80

The Narrative of Penny Haworth

B efore I knew it, a month had expired. I could not have said how I passed the days, for it seemed that the days passed me. I ate; I slept; I woke in the middle of the night, and could sleep no more. Strangely enough, Adam had not sought me again. It became known about Nomaton that I was residing with Thomas. And yet, he never came.

Thomas, true to his kind nature, returned to Haggard House to collect my things. Fortunately, no one had been present at the house to deny him, and so he was able to return my clothing and Mother's dining set and candlesticks. He never questioned me. He continued his work as usual, excepting that his days, which had already shortened due to Adam's success, became shorter still as he gained notoriety for living with me.

I too fell under the village's contempt. On the occasions when I found it necessary to visit Tenney's for supplies, I was met with hushed tones, whispered words, and sideways glances. The usually talkative Mr. Tenney was silent with me, and I began to think that, soon, he might refuse to fill my orders at all.

As I returned to Thomas' shack after one of these trying experiences, I found a note tucked under the door. My breath caught, and I opened it with shaking fingers.

It was in Sarai's handwriting. It said simply:

Adam is willing to dissolve your marriage. He will seek an annulment. This can be easily done, as the marriage has never been consummated. I will attest to the fact.

There was no signature, no apology. No regret was expressed. The note was cold and business-like.

All this time, I had simultaneously anticipated nothing and something. Yet to hear word of this nature, and not from Adam but from Sarai, stung more than words could express. The wound made by my discovery of Adam's sacrifices wrenched open even further; my heart hardened against him. Yet, even now, I knew that if only he attempted to make things right, perhaps there might still be hope for us.

I sat in the armchair holding the letter when Thomas returned in the afternoon. I looked up and was surprised to see that he too held a note.

"You've received one as well?" I asked.

Thomas looked confused. "As well? I've received a response to my inquiry."

"What inquiry?"

"I've been seeking work elsewhere. This is word of a position along the coast. A position as a light-keeper."

Thomas intended to leave. What would I do then? Where would I go?

"I see," was all I could say.

"I'm sorry I haven't spoken to you of it," Thomas said, voice quickening. "I didn't wish to upset you."

"I'm happy for you," I said, pushing away the tightness forming in my throat.

Thomas' eyes glistened, and he took my hand in his. "Come with me. We'll both start over."

"I'm married still, Thomas," I said.

"I don't care," he said.

"Truly?"

"Truly. Come with me."

My hands trembled again. I was frightened of Adam, frightened of Thomas, and even frightened of myself. My mind reached for something to hold onto. There was something, and I clung to this thing for dear life. I handed Thomas Adam's note, studying his expression as his eyes scanned the page.

"Accept this offer, Penny. Marry me. We'll leave for the coast as soon as it's settled."

"I still don't love you, Thomas."

His face hardened for a moment, but then relaxed. "It matters not. For, I love you," he said, looking deep into my eyes. "Perhaps, one day, you will feel the same."

I could only nod my assent as tears welled.

There was, however, an impediment to be got over. I had one final piece of news. Happily, this did not affect his request any more than the first. It was agreed that I would accept Adam's offer of annulment and that we would be married quietly after.

It seemed that Sarai had no aversion to telling falsehoods when those falsehoods worked for her benefit. She testified that Adam regularly knew himself, the solitary sin, and as such was unable to perform his husbandly duties. Within the month, the annulment was complete.

Chapter 81

The Narrative of Penny Haworth

The church in Wasaki was brick and towered with a soaring spire. The skin under my eyes was dark, and my sober, gray silk was tight over my plumping frame. With the exception of a new hat, only Thomas' twinkling eyes gave away his joy on this occasion. His arm linked with mine as we made our way to the arched double doors.

The overcast, late winter day reflected my feelings. How different they were at this second marriage! Hardly had there been time to ease the pain of the life that had been torn from me. This marriage with Thomas was not of love but necessity. There would be no going back.

I paused upon the church steps.

Adam's cold face throughout the annulment returned to me. Sarai had looked me in the eye many a time, but not once had Adam. He had studied the floor or the wall or gazed vacantly across the bare room.

Thomas trembled, and he released my arm. He seemed to sense my misgivings. "I...I'll not coerce you," he said, looking down upon me. "We must leave now if you've any...any doubts."

I did have doubts, yet I battled them violently. *Adam! If only you'd asked for forgiveness. If only you could have poured out your wrongdoings and abandoned your wild beliefs, I could have forgiven all! But not once did you attempt it. Not once did you look at me or speak to me. You clung to your mother's apron strings like a child.*

Why, Adam? Why?

The clergyman, in black robe and white clerical collar, appeared at the door. "Everything is in order. Your witnesses are present and waiting. Please, step inside."

The struggle was over: I gave way. I took Thomas' arm with a smile, but my heart ached as the minister led the way down the aisle. I hardly saw the pair of witnesses and curious townspeople who had collected in the pews. The sunlight streamed blue and red upon us through stained glass. The clergyman's voice repeated the familiar words, but I scarcely heard them.

"If either of you know any impediment, why ye may not be lawfully joined together in Matrimony, ye do now confess it."

I looked round the church, half hoping to see Adam. He was not there. The remainder of the ceremony was completed.

It was finished.

With a heavy heart, I climbed into the cart containing our few belongings and looked back in the direction of Nomaton, the village that I had called home. We traveled light and soon arrived upon the remote peninsula on Lake Michigan that held our new home and the lighthouse Thomas would man.

The residence was small, but comfortable. Thomas, reliable and hardworking, was suited excellently to his new line of work. Our position was isolated, but after the horrors of Haggard House, I welcomed the solitude. It kept me away from the prying eyes of the villagers, who soon would have noticed the swelling of my belly, and no sooner noticed, but counted upon their fingers and discovered that the child could not be Thomas'. There, we continued comfortably, weathering spring and arriving, if not happily, at least contentedly, to summer.

Chapter 82

The Narrative of Adam Bolton

Life, alone with Mother in Haggard House, grew stagnant and wearisome. My days were spent in the shop, and my nights were spent endlessly reading and pacing. I grew thin and gaunt. Though she never chided, I found Mother's presence more and more irksome. I would not wander, like Pa, to the tavern, but I did wander to Pa. Nightly, I left my shop and walked to the churchyard near the parsonage. I would stand, troubled, near his grave.

Minister Judd must have observed me from the house, for one night in early spring, he ambled through the dark and appeared at my side. Sensing the man's presence, my flesh crawled. I stepped away a pace, eyes fixed on the stone.

"My son," Minister Judd said, "you must let this man go."

"Sir, I will not ask you again. Do not call me that. I am no son of yours."

There was a long silence. Seldom was Minister Judd at a loss for words. I turned to see his face.

"You're wrong, Adam. You are my son. Not only in God's eyes, but in man's too."

The aversion which I had carried for Minister Judd my whole life could hardly have strengthened further, yet it did.

"How dare you imply—"

"I imply nothing. I only speak truth. The man you called your pa was a weak man without God. That is why your mother chose me, so that her son could be a son of God twice over."

"You lie."

"Ask your mother, if you will not believe me. She has a token from me—a small wooden cross. She keeps it now by her bedside."

Whirling round, I gripped Minister Judd by the neck and squeezed. The thick rolls of flesh about the man's neck were like putty in my fingers. Yet, the minister was not at all concerned about the lack of breath. His face relaxed, and a smile even crossed it. Disgusted, I released him.

The minister rubbed his neck and said, "Ask your mother, my son."

Tormented in spirit, I turned and hastened down the path back toward Haggard House. The rooms I had built within my mind stretched and pulled from each other at every joint. I tried to stop them, closing my eyes and forcing them back together. Pegs flew out of the walls, and every time I raced to mend one, another stretched and heaved behind me. I could not keep the rooms separate. Penny rushed out, wildly calling my name. Pa too came, calling, "My son, my son." I couldn't stop them. They raced down the stairs to the first floor. With relief, I realized I had locked Mother outside on my last visit. Yet, there was someone there, banging and battering on the front door until it burst open. Mother was the first to enter, followed closely by Minister Judd. It was he who had broken open the door. My mind felt as if it would break into pieces.

No longer able to bear it, I forced my eyes open—returning to the present—and hurried on. I crashed through the door of Haggard House. It flew off its hinges. I cared not. Mother sat in her rocker reading her new Bible, ignoring my violent entry.

"You're past your usual time," said she. I could tell from her carefully measured tone that her calm was assumed. She was really frightened.

"I've just exchanged words with Minister Judd," I said, crossing the room with a few long strides.

Mother closed the Word. "Yes. You've been there every evening, I've heard."

I loomed over her. "He told me that he is my father."

She looked up with a cold, startled expression. "Why has he said this?"

"You must tell me, Mother. Is it true?"

Her assumed calm vanished. She stood and slammed the Bible into the rocker. Never had I seen her so careless with the Word.

"Why has he said this?" repeated she.

"Is it true?"

Ducking round me, she hurried to the kitchen, opened the flour barrel, and dumped scoop after scoop into the earthenware bowl containing her putrid leavening. "Help me make our bread."

I bounded across the room, taking the bowl from her hands and flinging it into the fireplace. It crashed and clattered into pieces over the ashes, dough dripping onto the backlogs. I grasped Mother by the shoulders.

"You're hurting me, Adam!" shrieked she.

"Tell me!"

She turned, but I grasped her chin and forced her to face me. As I did so, she released another shriek and called, "Help! Help!"

"No one will come to help you. You've made certain of that. Now, tell me." I felt no remorse, no pity. It was as if Satan himself stood before me.

Trapped, Mother waited, mute.

"Tell me!" My voice shook the very house.

Icy eyes locked with mine. "It's true."

Immediately, I released her. I could scarcely believe it. The falsehoods upon falsehoods that had been piling upon each other

—both those I had been privy to—and now those that I had not. I could no longer reconcile, by any verse of the Bible, by any pretense or trick of the mind, what even the most shameless heathen would not attempt to justify. I, for the first time, saw clearly. All I had been taught—all I had been led to believe—all was lies. And oh, how it had cost me!

Bounding up the attic steps, I returned several minutes later, carrying my trunk.

Mother's voice cracked with terror. "What are you doing?"

"Leaving this wretched place."

Claw-like hands gripped my arm. "Don't go. You don't understand."

"I understand enough," I replied. "All has been a lie. You've cost me everything, and now it will cost you."

Wrenching myself from her grip, I exited through the empty doorframe.

Mother shrieked like an animal crushed in a trap. "No!"

She hurried after me and wrapped her arms round my waist. I did not halt, plowing ahead. Mother, unable to get a firm grasp, stumbled and fell, clutching at my ankles. I did not relinquish my quick stride, dragging her on the ground behind as she maintained her vice-like grip. With one hard kick, I was rid of her. She lay, face-down in the dirt at the edge of the clearing of Haggard House.

As her voice faded, the images in my mind returned full force. The pressure was immense. I put my hands to my head, feeling as if it might explode. There they all were: Pa, Mother, Minister Judd, and Penny. The planks shuddered. At any moment, the structure would implode, killing us all. Each of them called my name, screaming for me to save them.

"I cannot save you all!" I cried.

For one moment, everything became quiet, and I heard one voice and one voice only. It was Pa's, my real father, no matter whose blood I carried.

"Save yourself, son. Save yourself," he said.

With that, I turned and ran from my mind-house. The instant I made it outside, every board sucked inward, crushing all life within. I heard their screams, their agony. It sounded as the fiery pain of Hell. Through their cries, a real voice, calling my name, brought me back to the present. It was Mother.

"Come back, Adam! Come back!"

I knew what I must do.

I shut my ears and continued down the lane, Mother's shrieks continuing ineffectually behind me.

Chapter 83

The Narrative of Adam Bolton

M y feet led me in the direction which Mother had taken the day Penny left—the old drunkard's place. It was late when I reached it, but the hundred and one dangers that lay in wait in the dark did not frighten me.

I paused at the blanket serving as a door. Too much had already happened. I would speak with the old man, and yet, I suddenly felt I could not face him tonight. I recalled that I had seen abandoned cabins on my last visit, and I decided to rest in one of these until morning. I neared the closer—and humbler—of the two. The windows were covered in deer-hide, pulling away in places, enough to offer some visibility from the moonlight. As I opened the door, I sensed the cabin was occupied—no doubt a possum or a skunk. I peered through the dark. It was no possum, however; it was the old man, Silas. The place reeked of spirits, and he lay snoring against the wall on a wobbly old wooden bedframe.

He suddenly darted upright, snatching a pistol from beneath his pillow and aiming it at me.

"Who are you, and what do you want?"

I could hear his heavy breathing in the dark. I threw up my hands so that he would know I was no threat.

"It is Adam. Sarai's son."

He slowly lowered the gun and bade me enter.

"Light a candle so I can see your face," he said.

I did so, and seeing nowhere to sit, remained standing, looking down at the old man. He leaned back against the wall, wearing his worsted red hat as a night-cap.

"What are you doing here?" asked I. "Why aren't you in the wigwam?"

"Oh. That. The good woman kicked me out for the night. She won't tolerate my drinking in her lodge. I've spent many a night here."

"Do you recognize me, sir?" I asked.

"I do indeed. And you came to me not so long ago in seeking your wife." He scratched at his beard. "Funny—funny that my grandson should come to me in his distress—even without knowing who I am."

"Grandson?" I frowned. I didn't have patience for drunken folly, though he looked somewhat sober now.

"I suppose you'll not believe it," he said.

Suddenly, I laughed. "Certainly. You're as likely to be my grandfather as Minister Judd was to be my father. I know not what the truth is anymore. So yes, you may be my grandfather."

He looked at me keenly. "As likely as Minister Judd...What do you mean?"

"Only what I say. I've discovered—this very night, that Pa was not my pa. And Mother has confirmed it."

Silas leapt out of bed, pistol raised. "I'll kill the old bastard." He went running out of the cabin before I could stop him, calling out into the night air, "Should've killed him long ago. That son of a bitch. I'll kill him at last." He halted and turned to me. "It's true, isn't it? It's true?"

"It's true," I said.

Suddenly, his shoulders began to shake. He fell to his knees in the frosted grass and sobbed like a child. "I couldn't protect her. I *didn't* protect her," he said through his tears.

It was true then—what he said—Silas Whittemore was my grandfather.

"Come," I said, putting my hands under his arms and lifting him to his feet. "Come."

Reluctantly, he followed me back into the cabin, turning his head back and forth, back and forth, as if following a trail, attempting to reach some long-forgotten destination he had never quite made it to.

"What is it?" I asked, seeing he was calmer.

I saw he had found it, whatever it was. He shook his head, as if he himself could not believe it.

"It was Minister Judd that killed your pa."

"What? How do you know?"

"I...I saw him enter Peter's shanty, the night he was killed. I was half asleep in the alley. I woke for a moment and saw him. I...I thought it was just a dream...or a vision...you know...from the drink. But now...now, I see it was real."

I could have snatched the pistol from Silas and hunted the man down—killed him that second. Yet, something stopped me. Before, perhaps I would have called it the voice of God—but no longer.

"You'll swear you saw him?" I said.

"Yes. Yes. I would swear it on my daughter's life!"

"Come," I said. "We have a visit to make to the marshal."

Chapter 84

The Narrative of Sarai Bolton

Adam came back to me, as I knew he would. It was a promise: "Train up a child in the way he should go: and when he is old, he will not depart from it." However, I realized that just because God had promised it, did not mean the Devil could not interfere. And he had. I soon saw that the visit was not for my sake. Adam came through the blanket I had strung up where he had knocked the door off its hinges. At first, I believed him to be penitent. Certainly, we must sacrifice for his sin in leaving me, yet what was that to an eternity in Hell? I cared only for his immortal soul.

"Mother," said he.

I noticed immediately that he did not speak the word with the same respect he had nearly always shown me.

"You've returned," said I, moving toward the kitchen, my back to him, so that he knew where he stood with God and with me.

"I've come for a purpose," said he.

"I know," said I, turning to him. "And I am ready, able, and willing to forgive. God too, will forgive. You know the way."

Then, with his face broadening in that sinful, heathen way, he said, "I've not come for that. I've brought someone to speak with you."

The next moment, the old drunkard, the one always claiming to be my father, entered. His head was bare, and it was clear he was sober, for the moment, at least. Adam knew better than to bring sinners of that ilk across my threshold.

"I won't speak to him," said I. "How dare you bring him here. He's a liar and a drunk, as I've told you a thousand times."

Silas had that false, pretending look, as if he cared for me and was sorry to see me in such a state. But I knew the worldly and their many tricks.

"Sarai," said he. "I'm so sorry. I'm sorry for entrusting you to that man, for leaving you alone, for allowing—"

"Silence," said I.

He continued anyway.

"There's no need to pretend, Sarai. Adam knows the truth. We have come here, together, in hope that you will see the error of your ways."

My eyes darted to Adam, who had made a warning gesture. They were in collusion! They had been appointed by the Devil to tell me lies, to try to force me from the straight and narrow!

"You, Adam? You, of all people, come to try and ensnare me?"

"Mother," said he. Oh, the trickster! He softened his voice, honeying his words, but I knew what he was about and who was behind it—that serpent in the garden. "We offer to take you from this place. Look," he pointed to the doorway. "You cannot stay here. It's not safe."

"Oh? And what of the error of my ways? Isn't that the true reason you've come?"

"We've only come to take you to a safe place," said he. "We know of Minister Judd. We know what he's done. It would be best for you to leave. There's no telling what he might do when the truth comes out."

"Minister Judd," said I. "What has he had to do with this?"

Adam looked at me for a long time. Why, that snake! He was turning everything he had learnt of me, upon me!

"I see that you know," said he.

"*You,* my dear, know nothing!" said I. "You do not know what you speak."

"I do," said he. That grave voice. Those simpering words. Oh! How had I raised such a son? "I do," continued he. "I know all. You must relinquish pretense. You have admitted once already to your lies. That you lied about Pa. I've discovered many more. But you needn't hide any longer. We've not come here to judge you. We've come here to help. If you'll allow it."

"Judge me?" said I. "Who but God can judge me? None! I will not hear any more of this blasphemy. I've spoken no lies in this house nor anywhere else. I've never claimed that Peter was your pa, have I?"

Adam appeared surprised. How dare he call me a liar when I had never once said Peter was his father.

"Please, come," said Adam. "Minister Judd will be exposed, and whether he is sentenced or no, he will feel the censure of the village. It will be hard for you alone here, being connected to him as you are. Please, please come with us."

Just as the snake spoke to Eve! The wickedness of my son knew no bounds.

"Leave," said I. "Leave this house at once. I will not have the presence of the wicked adulterate this house of God."

Both Adam and Silas exchanged more pretending glances, looks that said, *Poor Sarai. Poor, lost Sarai.* What they did not know, was that they were the lost ones. They were the ones tumbling with their burdens into the slough.

"I will not come."

The boy—I could no longer bear to call him my son—understood my seriousness. It was then he took an action I did not expect.

"It must be done," said he. "Come, Grandfather."

He and Silas went to my rocker and overturned it.

"No!" cried I.

It was too late. Silas and Adam were already wrenching up the floorboards, pulling out the bags of money. Filthy lucre that I had hidden so Adam might keep his mind on God.

"Stop!"

I ran and scratched at Adam's face. I tried to grasp a bag, but he held it back.

"We will not take all of it," said he. "We leave enough in your care to last you two lifetimes. Though, I know it's useless, for you will only hoard it and gift it to Minister Judd, who will pocket it in his turn."

After his robbery, Adam, still restraining me, spoke.

"Please. Please, Mother. Do not allow what those men did to you all those many years ago, to destroy the rest of your life. You have an opportunity, now, to leave the past. To step away and forge a new path. Please, come."

I looked into his eyes. He was in earnest. He truly thought there was a way out. Perhaps he was right. Perhaps I could go with him. Perhaps this place—

I saw a bit of something sticking out from Silas' pocket, something red—a furrier's cap. Furriers...

I pushed Adam away with all my force. How could I have allowed myself, even for a moment, to consider what he said? Oh, the Devil was sly! He dressed himself in the wool of a lamb.

"Leave this house this instant, and never, never come back."

There was some pretended torture on their faces. The old man bowed his head and left, but the boy glanced at me once more and said, "I am sorry it ends this way, Mother. I wish, for your sake, you would have come with us."

He disappeared through the blanket.

I went to my rocker and righted it. I took my Bible from the shelf and began to read. Tightness came into my neck and shoulders. It felt as if the Devil himself were squeezing. The tightness spread, working its way to my head. I closed my eyes at the pain of it.

Then, there it was. I had not gone to that place in many, many years. There was the house, locked and bolted. I knew the key was within my pocket, but I would not touch it. Something suddenly swept under my feet, forcing me to the window. I tried to look away, but I could not. There it was. There was the memory I had locked in that house. The memory that sometimes slipped out but was always put back. There was that girl. There were those furriers.

I opened my eyes. No. It did not exist. It was an old dream. That was all.

Standing, I left the house and entered the woods, taking the trail to the place where Minister Judd's altar stood. Once there, I sat with my back against the rock, feet over the ledge.

Adam. My son. Suddenly, all my being ached. It was sinful to care so much for an earthly being, yet I could not stop. There was such an ache for the loss of Adam, for the loss of his immortal soul, the only thing that I had any power to save. He would burn forever in Hell. I had failed in my one and only purpose. How many years had I tried? How many years had I lovingly disciplined him in the ways of the Lord, sacrificed for him? Now, all was lost.

As long as Adam had been at Haggard House, I kept up my strength, not allowing him to see the weakness within me. Yet now, I no longer had power over myself. A tear swept down my face. First one, and then another.

How was it that God had put within us the nature to care for our children, only to call upon us to separate, should they leave His path?

Chapter 85

The Narrative of Penny Haworth

I gave birth to a fine son, strong, with dark hair and dark eyes like his father. Thomas devoted himself to the boy, and though I did not love Thomas with the passion I'd had for Adam, I began to feel a certain warmth toward him. I did my best to treat him as kindly as he treated me. Thomas was consistent, and I never worried, from one day to the next, whether he would be warm or cold toward me and my child.

One morning, when the babe had reached his second month, I was sewing near the fire when I heard a sound from the front veranda. A dense fog had settled, as it often did, around the house. From my rocking-chair, a gift from Thomas, I could see nothing but little droplets of water streaking down the windowpane, and the gray beyond.

Reluctant to leave the cheerful fire and the sweet sight of my son sleeping in his cradle beside me, I turned back to my work. The veranda boards creaked, this time without a doubt. The nearest neighbor was miles away, and I could think of no one who might call upon us. I stood, avoiding the window, and put my stitching into the wicker basket at my side. From the window's edge, I stared into the fog, knowing full well I would not be able to see a thing.

Perhaps I only fancied it, but for a moment, I thought I saw a man's figure retreating, hands tucked neatly behind his back.

I opened the front door a crack and peered out. All I saw was thick fog. I pushed the door a little farther, and a breeze kicked up, displacing some of the mist.

I nearly cried out for Thomas. Something shaped like a head swung from the veranda roof. Before I called out, I glanced once more from the corner of my eye. Then I noticed that it was not a head at all. Turning back, I neared and saw the thing was nothing more than a round, leathern pouch. A pang of sorrow went through me as I removed it from the cord. It was exceedingly heavy, and I had to place it on the veranda floor. When I opened the pouch, I saw two things. One was a vast, glittering pile of silver coin. The other was a bit of paper, folded and refolded several times into a square: it was a note.

Penny,

Please do not be alarmed by the delivery of this note. I will not trouble you any further after this date. I only write to ask forgiveness for the pain that I've caused you. Though not an excuse for my actions, I will put forth here, a history of what led me to them.

My mother held strange doctrines. She chose Scripture as it suited her; and Minister Judd, I believe, helped her along, having as he did, a motive of his own. She became so entrenched in these beliefs that she thought herself to be God, or as near Him as any human creature can become.

The sacrifices upon your doorstep were mine. I left them in hope that you might be redeemed. Yet, when I saw you with Thomas, I believed all to be at an end; and I ran from the village. During my time working upon the railroad, I sinned greatly. Despite sacrificing for myself, I could not ease my guilt.

When I returned, I found Mother greatly changed. She seemed almost to be diseased of mind, but after our marriage and the immediate calamities that followed, I was convinced that they befell us because of our sin.

And so, after our return to Haggard House I found myself ensnared again in her beliefs, which were harsher than they ever had been. It was then that I continued to make atonement for you by way of sacrifice. What I did to Boots was inexcusable. I can only say that, at the time, I believed it to be for the best. I never would have fed the meat to you. Only afterward did I discover that Mother had taken the poor creature's remains and used it in the stew.

When I returned to find you burning our Scriptures and discovered Mother's hand wounded, my heart hardened, and afraid of hellfire and damnation, I found that I could not relinquish her doctrine's hold upon me. Yet, when you left, her words were like poison in my ear. But the house and her influence, running the length and breadth of my lifetime, overcame me, and I resigned myself to it.

It was not until I discovered that Mother was as much a liar and fraud as a foul preacher I had met upon the road, that I was able to finally shake loose the doctrines and beliefs that had chained me. At the same time, I shook loose the woman that conjured them. I cannot believe that what I have been taught is true, any more than I can believe the woman who created them is true.

In the pouch is the money from the sale of your mother's house, along with a little something more. It is only right and fitting that you should have it. It is the only amends in my power to make. I beg your forgiveness, on behalf of the two people who have so wounded you. Forgive me if this frightened you.

As for myself, I am without belief of any kind now. I find I cannot so much as enter a church.

Please forgive me, Penny.

Adam

There had still been a place in my heart for Adam, somehow, even after everything; even after my marriage to Thomas. Yet now, with his note in my hand, I felt a powerful sense of finality. Adam must find his own way, and I must find mine. There was a bittersweetness in that. Perhaps if we had met in another time, in another place, in another life—but there was no point thinking that way. What was, was.

Peter cooed in his crib, stirring me from my reverie. I took up my sewing again but could not concentrate. I lifted the note, which I had placed on the side table and read it once again. Peter fussed, and I picked him up, caressing his strands of dark hair and swaying him gently. With my free hand, I tossed Adam's letter into the open fire.

"Goodbye, Adam."

Just then, I heard the clatter of Thomas' feet as he entered the house. He came to me immediately, and I smiled up at him, such a smile as I had never given him before. A look of joy crossed his face, and he wrapped his arms round me and his child.

There we stood, before the fire, a family newly forged.

Chapter 86

The Narrative of Adam Bolton

There was insufficient evidence to charge the minister. The night after this discovery, both Silas and Minister Judd went missing. It was no secret to me what had occurred, and inwardly, I thanked my grandfather for it. Had he not done so, I would have— and what would I have become after that? Grandfather had said it a long time ago, back when I believed him to be nothing more than a drunk and a poacher.

"When you've lived and seen the things I have, you'll see. You won't judge me then."

Now, I understand.

I did not linger in the village. Like many men before me, I traveled west. It was not gold I was in search of; I knew better than that. I set myself up in carpentry and made a living—a good one too. I became a prominent tradesman. No longer bound to keep myself separate, I soon found myself promoted as one of the village leaders. I accepted this role with great gravity, understanding as I did, that the same flaws and vices and mis-judgements that afflict other men, afflict me too.

There are days when I look back upon the past. I do not do this often, for it is full of pain and regret. The villagers in

Nomaton had always been frightened of Haggard House, and in the end, even I became frightened of the place, cursed as it seemed. Yet now, I see that the true Haggard House was the one I had built, room by room, within my mind. That was the Hell which I ought to have feared—the Hell within myself.

However, some days, I recall the beautiful moments: Penny's bright smile, her copper hair falling across my face, her form close to mine; and on those days, I begin to have hope. Hope that I could love again—only this time—freely.

THE END

Author's Afterword

In the last year of my teens, and the first of my twenties, I worked as a summer lifeguard at the historic Grand Hotel on Mackinac Island, Michigan. While *Haggard House* was not so much as an inkling in my mind at that time, I knew even then that Mackinac was a special place. Cars are banned (except for a handful of emergency vehicles), so all movement and transport is done by foot, bicycle, or carriage—with several horse stables being on the island. Those were magical times in many ways for me. Islands and the idea of islands have since dominated many of my stories. While Mackinac—called Michillimackinac in this novel, as it had been before being shortened—plays only a small part in *Haggard House*, I owe it much in the way of inspiration, and I am so grateful I had the opportunity to spend so much time there.

As for Nomaton and Wasaki, they do not exist. They are fictionalized, based loosely on real towns in Michigan, approximately in the same area as described in the novel. However, all other towns or cities named are real.

While this novel is a work of fiction, I have done my best to be historically accurate to the time period. My bookshelf is practically sagging with the weight of my research books. One thing I discovered while researching: the trouble with being historically accurate does not come in the questions you know to ask—What did they eat? What did they wear? Where did they sleep?—but in the questions you don't know to ask. For example, in the scene in which Mrs. Haworth and Penny go to the saloon to confront Mr. Fowler about the rabbit head, I originally had the pair of them entering through the front. However, I later learned, quite by accident, that saloons had a special entrance on the side "For Ladies Only." This is something that never would have occurred to me. And so, I can only say, any historical inaccuracies remaining are mine and mine alone.

Acknowledgements

There is a saying: "It takes a village to raise a child." While I have never liked the comparison of a book to a child, I can certainly say it takes a village to write a novel.

Thank you to the experts who were kind enough to answer my research questions: Clark Kidder, author of *Orphan Trains and Their Precious Cargo*, as well as multiple volumes on rural schools in Wisconsin, for answering my questions on one-room schools; Noreen M. Johnson, President of the West Shore Fishing Museum in Menominee, Michigan, for answering my questions about historic ice-fishing; Brian S. Jaeschke, Curator of Collections for Mackinac State Historic Parks, for answering my questions related to the fur trade, as well as providing me a copy of the Map of the Island of Michilimackinac by Lieutenant William Sanford Eveleth of the U.S. Army Corps of Engineers, November 1817, and helping me find a copy of Michilimackinac I, Shewing the Surveys of Private Claims by John Mullett, November 1828; Patricia LaBounty, Curator of the Union Pacific Museum in Council Bluffs, Iowa, for answering my questions about railroading recruitment and employment; Sharon Salinger, Professor of History at the University of California, Irvine, for answering my *barmaids* question and for writing the excellent book, *Taverns and Drinking in Early America*; and to my brother, Jeremiah Rhoads, for lending me his logistics expertise by poring over maps of the Iowa Central Rail Road and helping me plot Adam's path west to work on the Union Pacific Rail Road and east on his return to Haggard House.

The research books I consulted are too numerous to list, but these, I found especially helpful: Stephen E. Ambrose, *Nothing Like It In the World: The Men Who Built the Transcontinental Railroad 1863-1869*, Simon & Schuster, 2001; David Haward Bain, *Empire Express: Building the First Transcontinental Railroad*, Penguin Books, 2000; Ruth Goodman, *How To Be A Victorian*, Viking, 2013; Ida Amanda Johnson, *The Michigan Fur Trade*, Lansing Michigan Historical Commission, 1919; many books by Eric Sloane, including *A Museum of Early American Tools*, Ballantine Books, 1973; and *Historical Collections*, Michigan State Historical Society, Michigan Historical Commission, 1874-1929.

I would also like to thank my editor, Amanda Doering, for helping me get to a new draft when I was stuck and didn't know how to continue; my editor, Katie Schwab, whose crystal-clean line edits helped the writing shine and who inspired me to write an additional three chapters, without which the novel would have felt so incomplete; and my wonderful proofreader, Sutherland Lovell. Also, a big thank you to Allison Michele Horwath, my cover designer, for somehow creating the perfect cover for *Haggard House*.

Thank you to the writers who encouraged me along the way: Nami Mun, who gave me the idea to be a writer in the first place; Jennifer Dornbush, who taught my first (and only) writing class— screenwriting, which was invaluable in teaching me about dialogue and story structure; Richard Bausch, whose generosity and kindness to new writers is unparalleled, and whose encouragement helped give me the push I needed to make *Haggard House* a published book; and to my fellows in Richard's Community Writing Workshop—Theresa Keegan, Margaret Elysia Garcia, Davis Powers, and Jenilee Lopez—each incredible writers in their own right, for being so encouraging.

I would like to thank my *village* of early readers, including: my wonderful husband, Ken Cunningham, who not only read just about every draft I wrote and gave me invaluable feedback, but also had to hear about *Haggard House* for the four years I wrote, researched, and edited it, as well as the additional year and a half it took me to publish; Stephanie Jackson, who unfortunately had to read my very earliest novels, and still somehow signed up to read this one; Jeremiah Rhoads, who, in addition to helping me plot Adam's path, read multiple drafts of the novel and offered feedback; Hilda Smits, who gave me the idea for the multiple points-of-view and was instrumental in helping me envision the final version; Michael Smith, for not only reading and giving feedback, but connecting me with my first editor; and Tracy Neis, for reading one of the final versions and offering helpful suggestions on improvement.

Before concluding, I would also like to thank some very important people in my life, who have supported me before and throughout the writing of this novel: the late John Ostman, for being the best boss I could ask for, and for believing in me; Beth Hopp, for coaching me out of a very dark period and helping me move toward the kind of life I truly wanted to live; Dave, Roberta, and Brian Sprague, for being such kind, supportive, and generous friends and for helping me even when they did not realize they were; Ritika, Amit, and Gauri Agrawal, for always wanting the best for me and being supportive of my dreams; Saeko Croft for so patiently tutoring me in Japanese for the past five years and listening to my non-stop chatter about this novel; and Kayoko Hirabayashi, my mother-in-law, for being a better mother than I could ever ask for, and for being my biggest fan—even before I had any. Thank you.

About the Author

Elisabeth Rhoads is the author of *Haggard House* and numerous short stories. She holds a Bachelor of Arts in Theatre and is the Vice-President of the California Writers Club, Orange County branch. Since 2021, she has been a volunteer juror for the Scholastic Writing Awards. Originally from Michigan, she now lives in California with her husband, and enjoys learning Japanese, fermenting foods of all types—although mainly kombucha—and pretends to enjoy exercise-related activities, such as kayaking and running.